VIRAGO
MODERN CLASSICS
720

D0130724

Nancy Spain was a novelist, broadcaster and journalist. Born in Newcastle-upon-Tyne in 1917, she was the great-niece of the legendary Mrs Beeton. As a columnist for the *Daily Express* and *She* magazine, frequent guest on radio's *Woman's Hour* and panellist on the television programmes *What's My Line?* and *Juke Box Jury*, she was one of the most recognisable (and controversial) media personalities of her era. During the Second World War she worked as a driver, and her comic memoir of her time in the WRNS became an immediate bestseller. After the war she began publishing her acclaimed series of detective novels, and would go on to write over twenty books. Spain and her longtime partner, Joan Werner Laurie, were killed when the light aircraft carrying them to the Grand National in 1964 crashed close to the racecourse. Her friend Noël Coward wrote, 'It is cruel that all that gaiety, intelligence and vitality should be snuffed out when so many bores and horrors are left living.'

CINDERELLA GOES TO THE MORGUE

Nancy Spain

Introduced by Sandi Toksvig

VIRAGO

This paperback edition published in 2021 by Virago Press
First published in Great Britain in 1950 by Hutchinson

1 3 5 7 9 10 8 6 4 2

A CIP catalogue record for this book
is available from the British Library.

ISBN 978-0-349-01400-5

Typeset in Goudy by M Rules
Printed and bound in Great Britain by
Clays Ltd, Elcograf S.p.A.

Papers used by Virago are from well-managed forests
and other responsible sources.

Virago Press
An imprint of
Little, Brown Book Group
Carmelite House
50 Victoria Embankment
London EC4Y 0DZ

An Hachette UK Company
www.hachette.co.uk

www.virago.co.uk

Contents

Introduction

*'The world of books: romantic, idle, shiftless world so
beautiful, so cheap compared with living.'*

NANCY SPAIN

I never met Nancy Spain, and I've been worrying that we might
not have got on. It bothers me because I'm a fan. That's probably
an odd start for someone writing an introduction to her work, but
I think it's a sign of how much I like her writing that I ponder
whether we would have clicked in person. The thing is, Spain
loved celebrity. In 1955 she wrote, 'I love a big name ... I like to
go where they go ... I always hope (don't you?) that some of their
lustre will rub off against me ...'

I don't hope that. I loathe celebrity and run from gatherings of
the famous, so I can't say I would have wanted to hang out with
her, but I should have liked to have met. I would have told her what
a brilliant writer she was, how hilarious, and I'd have said thank
you, because I also know that I might not have had my career
without her. I've been lucky enough to earn a crust by both writing
and broadcasting, and I do so because Nancy Spain was there first.

During the height of her fame in the 1950s and early 60s she did something remarkable – she became a multimedia celebrity at a time when no one even knew that was a desirable thing. She was a TV and radio personality, a novelist, a journalist and columnist for British tabloids. She did all this while wearing what was known as 'mannish clothing'. Although her lesbianism was not openly discussed, she became a role model for many, with the closeted dyke feeling better just knowing Spain was in the public eye being clever and funny.

I am too young to have seen her on TV, but the strange thing about the internet is that people never really disappear. Check Nancy Spain out on the web and you can still see and hear her performing in a 1960s BBC broadcast on the panel of *Juke Box Jury*. She has the clipped tones of a well-bred Englishwoman of the time, who sounds as though she is fitting in a broadcast before dashing to the Ritz for tea. It is a carefully contrived public persona that suited Spain as a way to present herself to the world but, like so much of her life, it skirted around the truth. She was selling the world a product, a concept which she would have understood only too well.

In 1948 Spain wrote a biography of her great-aunt, Isabella Beeton, author of the famous *Mrs Beeton's Book of Household Management*. Although it was an encyclopedic presentation of all you needed to know about running the home, Isabella Beeton was hardly the bossy matron in the kitchen that the book suggested; in fact she wrote it aged just twenty-one, when she can hardly have had the necessary experience. Isabella probably knew more about horses, having been a racing correspondent for *Sporting Life*. The truth is that she and her husband Sam saw a gap in the book market. So, rather than being the distillation of years of experience, Mrs Beeton's book was a shrewd marketing ploy. I wonder how many people know that Isabella never did become that wise old woman of the household because she died aged just twenty-eight of puerperal fever following the birth of her fourth child? There are parallels here too, for Spain's background was also not what it seemed and she, like Isabella, lost her life too early.

Far from being a posh Londoner, Nancy Spain hailed from Newcastle. Her father was a writer and occasional broadcaster, and she followed in his footsteps quite aware that she was the son he never had. Her determination to come to the fore appeared early on. As a child she liked to play St George and the Dragon in which her father took the part of the dragon, Nancy marched about as St George while, as she described it, her sister Liz 'was lashed to the bottom of the stairs with skipping ropes and scarves'. No dragon was going to stop Spain from being the hero of the piece.

From 1931 to 1935 Spain was sent, like her mother before her, to finish her education at the famous girls' public school Roedean, high on the chalky cliffs near Brighton. It was here that her Geordie accent was subdued and polished into something else. She didn't like it there and would spend time getting her own back in her later writing. Her fellow classmates seem to have varied in their attitude towards her. Some saw her as exotic and clever, while others found her over the top. It says something about the attitude to women's careers at the time when you learn that in his 1933 Prize-Giving Day speech to the school the then Lord Chancellor, Lord Sankey, congratulated Roedean on playing 'a remarkable part in the great movement for the higher education of women', but added, 'In spite of the many attractive avenues which were now open to girls', he hoped 'the majority of them would not desert the path of simple duties and home life'.

Deserting that path was Spain's destiny from the beginning. It was while at school that Spain began writing a diary of her private thoughts. In this early writing the conflict between her inner lesbian feelings and society's demand that she keep them quiet first stirred. She began to express herself in poetry. Some of her verse-making was public and she won a Guinea prize for one of her works in her final year. This, she said, led her to the foolish notion that poems could make money.

Her mother harboured ambitions for Spain to become a games or domestic science teacher, but it was clear neither was going to happen. Her father, who sounds a jolly sort, said she could stay home and have fifty pounds a year to spend as she pleased. She joined a women's lacrosse and hockey club in Sunderland because it looked like fun, but instead she found a fledgling career and her first love. She became utterly smitten with a fellow team member, twenty-three-year-old Winifred Emily Sargeant ('Bin' to her friends) a blonde, blue-eyed woman who could run fast on the field and rather glamorously seemed fast off it by drinking gin and tonic.

The Newcastle Journal decided to publish some reports about women's sport and almost by chance Nancy got her first job in journalism. Touring with the team meant she could both write and spend time with Bin. When she discovered her feelings for Winifred were reciprocated, she was over the moon.

> *Dearest – your laughter stirred my heart*
> *for everything I loved was there –*
> *Oh set its gaiety apart*
> *that I may feel it everywhere!*

She bought herself a second-hand car for twenty pounds and began making some local radio broadcasts, getting her first taste of fame when she played the part of Northumberland heroine Grace Darling in a local radio play. Meanwhile she and Winifred found time to escape. It was the 1930s and they were both supposed to be growing into 'respectable' women. The pressure must have been unbearable as there was no one with whom they could share the excitement of their feelings for each other. They went off for several weeks to France on a touring holiday, which Spain described as idyllic. It was to be a one-off, for they returned to find Britain declaring war with Germany. They both joined up, with Spain enlisting in the Women's Royal Naval Service, the Wrens.

She would later describe her time in the service as the place where she found emancipation. She became a driver, scooting across the base and fixing the vehicles when they faltered. Based in North Shields, where many large naval vessels came in for repairs, it was often cold and there was no money for uniforms. Some trawlermen gave her a fisherman's jersey, and she got a white balaclava helmet that she was told was made by Princess Mary. She also got permission to wear jodhpurs on duty. It was the beginning of her feeling comfortable in men's clothes.

At the end of 1939 news reached Spain that Winifred, aged twenty-seven, had died of a viral infection. Unable to bear the grief, she didn't go to the funeral, but instead wrote poetry about the efficacy of drink to drown sorrows. The Wrens decided she was officer material and moved her to Arbroath in Scotland to do administrative duties. It was here that she began to shape the rest of her life. She became central to the base's many entertainments. She took part in broadcasts. She wrote. She was always busy. She did not talk about her life with Winifred. Years later, when she wrote about their dreamy French holiday, she wrote as if she had gone alone. Her only travelling companions apparently were 'a huge hunk of French bread and a slopping bottle of warm wine'. The descriptions of the trip are splendid, but they mask the painful truth.

After the war, Spain was set to be a writer. An outstanding review by A. A. Milne of her first book, *Thank you – Nelson*, about her experiences in the Wrens, gave her a first push to success. She sought out the famous, she lived as 'out' as she could in an unaccepting world. I don't like how the tabloids sold her to the public.

The *Daily Express* declared about its journalist, as if it were a selling point: 'They call her vulgar ... they call her unscrupulous ... they call her the worst dressed woman in Britain ...'

She called herself a 'trouser-wearing character', with her very clothing choices setting her apart as odd or bohemian. I suspect she was just trying to find a way to be both acceptable to the general public, and to be herself. It is a tricky combination, and was much harder then. She may not have known or intended the impact she had in helping to secretly signal to other lesbians and gay men that they were not alone. She lived with the founder and editor of *She* magazine, Joan 'Jonny' Werner Laurie, and is said to have slept with many other women, including Marlene Dietrich. Fame indeed.

I am so thrilled to see her work come back into print. Her detective novels are hilarious. They are high camp and less about detecting than delighting, with absurd farce and a wonderful turn of phrase. Who doesn't want to read about a sleuth who when heading out to do some detective work hangs a notice on her front door reading 'OUT – GONE TO CRIME'? Her detective, Miriam Birdseye, was based on Spain's friend the actress Hermione Gingold whose own eccentricities made her seem like a character from a novel. Miriam's glorious theatricality is complemented by her indolent sidekick, the (allegedly) Russian ballerina Natasha Nevkorina, who has to overcome a natural disinclination to do anything in order to do most of the actual detecting. They work incredibly well together as in this exchange:

'And she is telling you that you are going mad, I suppose?' said Natasha.

'Yes,' said Miss Lipscoomb, and sank into a chair. She put her head in her hands. 'I think it is true,' she said. 'But how did you *know*?'

'*That's* an old one,' said Miriam briskly. 'I always used to tell my first husband he was going mad,' she said. 'In the end he *did*,' she added triumphantly.

There is something quintessentially British about these detective novels, as if every girl graduating from Roedean might end up solving a murder. The books contain jokes that work on two levels – some for everyone; some just for those in the know. Giving a fictitious school the name Radcliff Hall is a good queer gag, while anyone might enjoy the names of the 'intimate revues' in which Miriam Birdseye had appeared in the past, including '*Absolutely the End*', '*Positively the Last*' and '*Take Me Off*'.

Seen through the prism of modern thinking, there are aspects of Spain's writing that are uncomfortable, but I am sad if they overshadow her work so thoroughly as to condemn it to obscurity. P. G. Wodehouse has, after all, survived far worse accusations. Thomas Hardy is still recalled for his writing about 'man's inhumanity to man', even though by all accounts he wasn't nice to his wife. Should we stop reading Virginia Woolf because she was a self-confessed snob? I am not a big fan of the modern 'cancel culture', and hope we can be all grown-up enough to read things in the context of their time. Of one thing I am certain – Spain was not trying to hurt anyone. She had had too tough a time of her own trying to be allowed just to survive the endless difficulties of being other. My political consciousness is as raised as anyone's, and I see the flaws, but maybe it's okay just to relax in her company and succumb to being entertained.

Nancy Spain died aged forty-seven. She was in a light aircraft on her way to cover the 1964 Grand National when the plane crashed near the racecourse. Her partner Jonny was with her and they were cremated together. Her friend Noël Coward wrote, 'It is cruel that all that gaiety, intelligence and vitality should be snuffed out, when so many bores and horrors are left living.' She was bold, she was brave, she was funny, she was feisty. I owe her a great deal in leading the way and I like her books a lot. They make me laugh, but also here I get to meet her alone, away from the public gaze, and just soak up the chat. Enjoy.

Sandi Toksvig

To find out more about Nancy Spain, you might like to read her memoirs, *Thank you – Nelson, Why I'm Not a Millionaire* and *A Funny Thing Happened on the Way*. Also the authorised biography, *A Trouser-Wearing Character: The Life and Times of Nancy Spain* by Rose Collis.

HAMPTON COURT

presents

A GRAND CHRISTMAS PANTOMIME

THEATRE ROYAL, NEWCHESTER

CINDERELLA

Characters in the Pantomime:

Prince Charming	*Vivienne Gresham*
Dandini, his valet	*Marylyn Franklyn*
Bad Baron de Broke of Hardup Hall	*Fred Cunningham*
Phobia ⎱ His two elder daughters ⎰	*Banjo DeFreeze*
Mania	*Harry DeFreeze*
Cinderella (his youngest daughter)	*Betty Byng*
The Fairy Queen of Starry Nights	*Esmeralda Greenaway*
Broker's Men	*Mic and Mac*
Buttons (the Baron's servant)	*HAMPTON COURT*
The Fairy of the Powder Puff	*Valenka*
The Mount Charles Male Voice Quartet	
The Royalettes	
The Twenty-four Tottenham Tots	*By courtesy of Mme Cariocola*
Specialty Number	*Banjo and Harry DeFreeze*
Stage Manager, Press Representative	*Tony Gresham*
Wardrobe	*Estelle Furbinger*

*Costumes and scenery designed by Tony Gresham
and executed by Atkins and Marshall, Newchester, Ltd.*

Other Characters in the Story:

Natasha	*A White Russian ballet dancer of the original Diaghilev Company*
Miriam Birdseye	*A genius*
Timothy Shelly	*Of County Cork, Eire*
Thomas Atkins	*Of Bayleyside in the County of Northshire, Lord Mayor of the City of Newchester*
Kidder	*His wife*
Sary O'Driscoll	*Personal maidservant to Hampton Court*
Peters	*Dresser to the DeFreeze Brothers*
Doris	*His daughter*
Detective-Sergeant Robinson	*Of the Newchester Police*
Police-Constable Bowes Police-Constable Truscott	*His colleagues*

Chorus of Haberdashers' Assistants, Shoppers, Theatre audience, etc

BOOK ONE

EXIT PRINCE
CHARMING

I

It was one of those surprising fine late afternoons in December that often follow upon many sad days of wind and rain and fog in Newchester. The winter sun had shone all day and had failed to warm anyone. There was frost in the air, and excitement. Christmas was only a week away. The red sun slanted below the mist and lengthened the shadows in 'Atkins Street'. A pleasant street that had curved graciously down towards the River Tame since it was built in 1815. Its present title was a sop to the Lord Mayor of Newchester: a great philanthropist.

There was a theatre in Atkins Street, the Theatre Royal, with a colonnaded portico and bright hoardings that announced the Christmas Pantomime, *Cinderella*. There were several fine bay-fronted houses in Atkins Street. There were solicitors' offices with brass plates, typewriting agencies, multiple chain stores, oddly housed in fine buildings that had once been high-class city residences. And there was a cab-rank, composed of smart black Austin motor-cars and a solitary growler.

The evening mist, lurking down back lanes in gutters, seemed to rise and hang shimmering in front of the shop windows. As the daylight failed the electric light in these shops became important. Oranges and lemons, crackers and bowls of *glacé* cherries, brilliantly jacketed children's books and festoons of Christmas cards proclaimed the season of the year. Scarlet was a predominant colour. The oranges glowed like the sun. The *glacé* cherries glittered like precious stones in their cave. The Christmas cards were, perhaps, more intellectually exciting.

Natasha DuVivien and her friend Miriam Birdseye paused on the pavement to consider a bookshop. Their arms were full of parcels, their faces were flushed with cold and generosity and childish apprehension about Christmas.

'This,' said Natasha, in her slow, elegant Russian voice, 'is the part that I am loving most about Christmas.'

Natasha's voice was not so obviously Russian that it might be described phonetically by the syllables 'Boo, boo, boo'. It was, nevertheless, a little odd.

'You mean the weeks beforehand, dear?' said Miriam Birdseye absently. She disengaged an unpleasant street child from her shopping-bag. 'Not today, thank you,' she said to it severely. 'I will not give you a penny for singing a carol. Christmas Eve is the time for carols.'

She turned to Natasha and agreed with her.

'Yes,' said Miriam. 'The weeks before Christmas are fun. But I am not so certain, myself, about Christmas itself.'

These two ladies stared at their reflections in the winking plate-glass window of the high-class firm of Nutson, Mawd and Pander, Stationers and Booksellers, Newchester.

'I *hate* book tokens,' said Miriam suddenly. 'They spoil everything.'

II

At the same time Johnny DuVivien, Natasha's ex-husband, sat gloomily in the front row of a non-stop variety theatre in London. His decree absolute had come through that morning. He was deeply depressed. Even faced by the undeniable fact that Natasha had run away from him he had believed, until the very last moment, that Natasha would contrive *something* – send him some sign to show that she didn't want to be divorced. Natasha was a White Russian and an ex-ballet dancer. This had made her a little unstable and difficult.

But God knows Johnny didn't want a divorce. He adored Natasha. He had only agreed to it to please her. He had no idea how hopelessly lonely it would make him. Oh dear. He wished he was dead. And as for the Theatre (Natasha's beloved drama), he *hated* it. It bored him stiff.

He looked vaguely up at the stage.

Capering women and monkey-faced men. All as unnatural as hell. The show dragged on and on and on. Once Johnny had been uncompromisingly intolerant of the Theatre. Now he was trying, pathetically, to recapture some of Natasha's love of drama. Even this tawdry non-stop revue had something in it for *her*. It said nothing to him, blast it.

And when Natasha could not get enough of this elusive commodity she ran up dramas in her own life. Not to be wondered, really. She was always getting innocently involved in quite appalling muddles ... Even murders and things. It was all extremely dangerous. Perhaps she *liked* danger. She was an extremely naughty girl. Oh God, he *missed* her so ...

Johnny moved restlessly in his seat. He had paid no

5

attention to the show for at least half an hour. Suddenly he could bear it no longer. Life without Natasha was intolerable. He *must* know what she was doing. He sat up straight. He must make one more effort to get her back. On the stage a young lady began to sing 'People will say we're in love' in a sweet, painful soprano. The effect on Johnny was electric. He covered his eyes with his hand. That tune. The last time he remembered hearing *that* had been at the first night of *Oklahoma* ... with Natasha.

He rushed for the exit, tripping over feet as he went. People looked at him strangely. Let them, damn them.

Five minutes later, back in his hotel with the telephone directory spread in front of him, and a list of Natasha's friends and acquaintances at his elbow, he began to dial. He began by dialling Miriam Birdseye's London number.

III

As it so happened Natasha was still reflected in the window of Nutson, Mawd and Pander. She was agreeably decorative, by any standards. She wore conventional tweeds and a pale-blue blouse. A phantom beaver coat swathed them. Her ash brown hair hung to her shoulders. Miriam Birdseye was taller than Natasha and there was a general effect of mink that seemed a little theatrical for the provinces. She had been a revue artist of genius. She was not good-looking. Behind them both the traffic lights flickered from red to green and back over again. In the dusk (thought Natasha) they looked like brightly lit boiled sweets.

Natasha and Miriam stared in at an idle display of books.

They both sighed. They were agreed that, once again, it would have to be book tokens.

'And,' pointed out Natasha, 'this is meaning that we will be having to spend half a crown more. It is always so with book tokens. I have noticed it.'

Suddenly Miriam gave a little cry.

'I thought I saw someone,' she said slowly, 'reflected in the glass . . . Someone I knew . . . '

Natasha transferred a heavy shopping-bag to her other hand and gazed up and down Atkins Street. There were a great many people, pushing and hurrying and calling out to one another, buying newspapers and even (in extreme cases) carrying turkeys. But there was no one whom Natasha knew. She said so.

'Not you – me,' said Miriam in a muddled way. 'And not walking in the street. In a motor-car. A Rolls Bentley.'

'Oh,' said Natasha vaguely, 'that is quite different. Who have you thought you are seeing?'

'That bloody man Hampton Court,' said Miriam slowly and viciously. 'That horrible ape. I expect I was mistaken.'

Natasha was vague. Her wide, hazel eyes were untroubled. Miriam's face had twisted with rage, like an expensive jade figure.

'What is Hampton Court?' said Natasha.

'It is a man,' said Miriam. 'A bitch of a man. The music-hall artist. You know, dear. The comedian. The man who wrote that filthy autobiography and no one dared to sue him. He said he was warped because his mother dropped him at birth. *That* man. He was involved in that swindle about a share transfer . . . He's supposed to have gone into pantomime production this year, like the Littlers. I hate him,' she ended vehemently. 'But he is the best Buttons in the business.'

'Buttons?' said Natasha, surprised. 'Business?'

'Buttons, dear, in *Cinderella*, dear,' said Miriam, by now in a furious rage and hissing like a queen cobra. 'Perhaps it's one of his pantomimes here. Let's go and see.'

IV

There were three theatres in Newchester-on-the-Tame. There was the Universe, cunningly concealed in a side street, devoted to first-class variety in all its glory. There was the Pallindrome, in one of the main streets, also devoted to variety and fallen from grace. There were turns with performing dogs here, and sometimes, in the summer, shamingly, circuses. And then there was the Theatre Royal, Atkins Street, concerning itself purely with all that the profession considers most legitimate: with companies touring prior to London production, with revivals of Ibsen and new and difficult productions by J. B. Priestley. Mrs Siddons once played here. Sarah Bernhardt suffered from pains in her leg here. Irving complained of it. Mrs Patrick Campbell was sick in it. A leading lady, who shall be nameless, was divorced as a result of 'goings-on' in its dressing-rooms. In short, the Theatre Royal was a fine old provincial theatre with over a hundred years of tradition crawling up and down its red velveteen curtains, blinking in its houselights, reflected from its white walls and in its gilt looking-glasses and ancient cloakroom attendants.

For the five winter months of the year the Theatre Royal (in common with the Universe and the Pallindrome) devoted itself to Pantomime. But whereas at the Universe and the Pallindrome there were, habitually, white-tongued Scots comedians playing in travesties of pantomimes like *Mother Goose* or *Goody Two Shoes* or even, one year, *Little Cock Riding Boots*, at the Theatre Royal the pantomime was always a classic like *Cinderella* or *Dick Whittington* or *Jack and the Beanstalk*.

Newchester expected this of 'the Royal'. Newchester at Christmas time went to the Universe and the Pallindrome for 'a good laff'. It went to the Royal for Beauty. This covered equally the gracious curves of Prince Charming, the Ballet of the Bells (Turn again Whittington) and the white lace or green beanstalk transformation scene, where everything went miraculously 'up' and turned itself into the ballroom scene or the outside of the Castle of Giant Despair. The Theatre Royal was, as we know, in Atkins Street, and it happened to be less than a hundred yards from Nutson, Mawd and Pander.

It was the usual stage door, tunnelled in the side of the Theatre Royal, crested with a globe-shaped light, date 1830. There was a stage-door keeper too, in shirt-sleeves with expanding elastic grips, who habitually wore a cloth cap and drank tea from a chipped cup. His name was George and everyone was fond of him. He never spoke.

By the time that Miriam and Natasha arrived beside George they had read the flaring hoardings. They were in full possession of the news that this was 'Hampton Court's production of *Cinderella*' (in association with Atkins, Setter and Byrne), with Hampton Court as Buttons, with book and lyrics by Hampton Court. Natasha who, as a White Russian, should have been uneducated about pantomime, suddenly became knowledgeable about *Cinderella*.

'I thought,' she said slowly, 'there was no actual *book*. I thought oll that picnic and oll those hunting scenes were made up by the comedians. The Ugly Sisters. With only the dances and so on constantly the same.'

'I wonder who are the Ugly Sisters,' murmured Miriam. One year, at the height of her fame in intimate revue, she had been approached by a pantomime king and offered the part of the taller Ugly Sister in Sheffield. Miriam had refused sulkily. She had never stopped regretting it.

'As you know,' she whispered to Natasha, 'I am mad to play Prince Charming.'

Natasha was kind.

'Perhaps their Prince Charming is not feeling very well,' said Natasha comfortingly.

They went on down the dimly lit whitewashed underground passage that connected the dressing-rooms to the stage door and the outside world. Small electric light bulbs flickered like glow-worms. George had disappeared. They pressed forward down ankle-breaking stairs towards the dressing-rooms. As they paused at the foot of the stairs outside Number One Dressing-Room, the temporary property of the leading lady, they heard (or thought they heard) the sound of someone crying in one of the dressing-rooms.

Yes, they were not mistaken. Someone *was* sobbing bitterly.

V

'*Poor* little thing,' said Miriam impulsively. She pushed forward towards the lighted doorway. 'It sounds like a girl . . . '

It was not a girl. It was a good-looking young man with fair hair in flannel trousers and a lemon-coloured slip-over whose face was already glazed and shiny with weeping. His blue eyes were bloodshot and swollen. He was obviously deeply upset.

'What's the matter?' called out Miriam. 'Can we help?' There was a pause and then she gave a little cry of recognition. 'Why, it's Tony. Tony Gresham.' She spun between him and Natasha with a vague gesture of introduction. 'What are you crying about, Tony? Not like you to cry. Tony and I,' she went on gaily, turning to Natasha, 'were in *Absolutely the End* together. Tony makes lovely cakes. He's lovely to be in a show with. He was our Press Agent.'

Tony Gresham laughed hysterically. Miriam's muddled kindliness slowly restored a normal foundation. He searched his pockets for a handkerchief.

'*That* little thing will not be being any good,' said Natasha. 'What you will be wanting will be a good blow. You must blow on one of these men's handkerchiefs which I am just buying in Newchester for my Christmas presents.'

Natasha gravely undid a small flat green cardboard box that contained six men's handkerchiefs. They had been intended for an acquaintance of hers, but Natasha had then discovered that those who gave handkerchiefs to their love would one day wave them goodbye. She was, therefore, glad of an opportunity to dispose of them.

'And now,' said Miriam brutally, 'will you kindly tell us what you're crying about?'

Tony Gresham, sniffing, began to explain.

'It's that devil Hampton Court . . . ' he began.

Natasha and Miriam exchanged a glance.

'He's been absolutely vile,' he went on slowly, his blue eyes losing their parboiled appearance. 'I'm doing the press and publicity for this pantomime, mostly on account of *mother*. *You* know, Vivienne Gresham. She's principal boy. Shakespeare is really *far* more in my line. I only did it to oblige.'

'My God!' said Miriam, before anyone could stop her. '*That* old trout. She may *easily* drop dead. I shall *certainly* stick around.'

Miriam put her large shopping-bag on the floor and sat in the only chair in the room. In the looking-glass, the solitary, naked electric bulb reflected strange shadows. They were many feet below street level, in a kind of whitewashed cavern.

Natasha glanced uneasily over her right shoulder.

'What's the matter?' said Tony Gresham sharply. 'There's no one in the theatre but us and George—'

'It is nothing,' said Natasha slowly. 'I am only feeling a shiver when Miriam says Vivienne Gresham may be dropping dead . . . It is nothing, nothing at oll . . .'

VI

Tony Gresham went on. Hampton Court, as anyone might see from the hoardings outside the theatre, was the self-considered star of the pantomime. He was also (and he had pointed this out many times), 'a terrific draw with the kiddies'. Also, it was *his* production in that he was putting up a third of the money for its presentation. At this point the Newchester papers demanded a detailed 'story' of 'their old favourite, Vivienne Gresham'. Tony had provided this for them. He could hardly do anything else. The *Newchester Journal* had published a two-column photograph of Vivienne and half a column about her personal life beneath it.

Hampton Court, who had been fobbed off with a tiny paragraph in 'Newchester Notes', was furious.

'He said,' said Tony Gresham, breaking down again, 'that I was no good as a Press agent and I'd never have got the job if Viv hadn't been my mother. And he said I had a mother fixation,' he wailed. The whole narrative was punctuated by sobs and sniffs. Natasha and Miriam again exchanged glances.

'Didn't I tell you,' remarked Miriam, in clear bell-like tones, 'that Hampton Court was an absolute bitch?'

There was a pause while Tony Gresham got himself under control. A voice interrupted them. It was a cold voice that penetrated nerves and made them snap, like violin strings cut by a bread-knife.

'Who,' said this voice quietly, 'is talking about me?'

2

No doubt Hampton Court was a genius by some standards. He certainly had an infinite capacity for taking pains. He was occasionally able to inspire others with his own fine opinion of himself. He was temperamental and tricky. Hampton Court was certainly convinced he was a genius.

He was a financial genius. He drank like a fish and drove a large motor-car furiously and to the danger of the public. Nobody liked him. Quite a lot of people were afraid of him.

They were afraid of his temper. They were afraid of his money. Most of all they feared his personal appearance, which was embarrassing.

Hampton Court was square and hairy and in the distance he looked like an angry baboon. Looking at him, one might ask oneself, puzzled, why that monkey was smoking (and, indeed, chewing) a large Corona-Corona cigar. It was only as one approached him that one saw his face clearly and realized that this was not an ape smoking cigars while its keeper's back was turned, but a cross gentleman of sixty. A number of people failed to survive this first shock and never spoke to him again. Hampton Court had grounds, therefore, for his savage inferiority complex. He was alone in the world, with a fat, personal confidential maid with glittering eyes like boot buttons, called Sary O'Driscoll.

He compensated for the inadequacy of his appearance by acquiring power. He bought factories, theatres, and newspapers and, at the age of forty, discerning that his effect on people in the mass was less unpleasant than upon individuals he became a 'trouper'. His success surprised everyone, particularly Sary O'Driscoll. In spite of his histrionic talent, he was not a genuine artist or showman. His work had a kind of amateur roughness that irritated other members of the theatrical profession. But overnight he *was* taken seriously.

His clothes, flamboyant before this date, now appeared subdued and better cut. He came out in morning coats and neat black homburg hats and carried a dispatch-case. He never found out (and no one dared to tell him) that he should wear cloth-topped boots instead of spats. Consistently, he presented the appearance of an ape, dressed as a pin-striped financier.

II

He stood in the doorway now, leaning his head against the door jamb. He whimsically wrinkled his mouth into a wildly unbecoming moue. He had a cigar in one hand, already much chewed about the butt.

'Ah,' he said. 'Tony crying. I expected that.'

He gazed round the dressing-room with cold light eyes like a fish, and gave an overplayed start of surprise. 'But ... *Miriam Birdseye*? Well. This is a surprise. How nice, darling.'

He advanced mincingly on Miriam, who stood her ground.

Physical cowardice was not one of her faults. They delicately clashed jawbones.

'Natasha and I came to wish you a happy Boxing Day,' said Miriam.

Hampton Court stepped back an inch or two. He put his cigar in his mouth. He stuck his fists in his trouser pockets and giggled.

'Curtain shall not rise that night,' he said gaily.

Tony Gresham gasped. Miriam raised an eyebrow. Darling Natasha broke the silence.

'This is seeming such a pity,' she said in her slow, charming voice. 'Why shall it not rise?'

Hampton Court turned his fish's eyes upon her. He evidently liked what he saw, although he did not ask to be introduced.

'The Dun Cow is the reason,' he said grudgingly. 'And Madame Valenka, the *première danseuse*. And the Vauxhall Venuses. They find themselves an' the Dun Cow an irresistible combination.'

'And what,' said Miriam, 'might I ask, is the Dun Cow?'

'It is a pub, dear,' said Tony Gresham hurriedly. 'Outside the stage door.'

'Oh?' said Natasha. There was a light of interest in her lovely hazel eyes. '*What* is seeming to be wrong with your *première danseuse*?'

'Stinking,' said Hampton Court shortly. He exhaled a tremendous cloud of gin in all directions. 'She an' the Vauxhall Venuses were plastered at every rehearsal, that's all. Just now ...' He began to tell the story to Natasha with elaborate gestures. 'We're rehearsing the Ballet of "My Lady's Boudoir", and these two girls are supposed to come on dressed as lipsticks.

16

They wear kind of gold head-dresses, see, on the night? The Fairy Godmother has *changed* them into lipsticks, with a wave of her wand,' he concluded wearily, chewing at his cigar. Miriam, who was more than familiar with all the lunacies of British Pantomime, nodded enthusiastically and said she quite saw.

'And these two lipsticks do a little dance,' said Hampton Court gloomily; 'to show themselves off. It's just before the ballroom Transformation Scene and quite important.'

Hampton Court talked and gestured, and as he did so his fine manner fell from him. He seemed to stand in a gutter in a London ghetto, the epitome of all clever Cockney baboons, who are presently going to take advantage of the soft-hearted British Public. He used some shocking words to describe the unfortunate chorus girls. Natasha thought it was quite bad enough for them to be billed as the 'Vauxhall Venuses'.

'And they fell over, see?' went on Hampton Court, getting angrier and angrier, and throwing cigar ash in all directions. 'They came hiccupping across the stage, both of them, and finally fell into the footlights.'

Natasha and Miriam began to laugh.

'What's funny in that?' said Hampton Court suspiciously. 'Cost me a lot of money, I can tell you.'

'Why?' said Tony Gresham excitedly.

'I sacked 'em both, that's why,' said Hampton Court, and blew out his cheeks.

'Oh, my God!' said Tony Gresham. 'You *are* mad. Four nights to opening night and two short in the chorus.'

'If you don't watch out,' said Hampton Court, 'we'll be short a Press representative too.'

III

'Well then,' said Hampton Court, sneering unpleasantly into the silence that surrounded them after his other unpleasant remark, 'perhaps the high and mighty Miriam *Birdseye* would condescend to look in on one of my rehearsals?'

Miriam grinned like a crocodile. She might perhaps be better described as sweet and low, rather than high and mighty.

'Don't be a fool, Hampton Court,' she said. 'You'd better not go too far with Tony either, or he won't give you any cake when he bakes one. Lead on, you old Pantomime impresario, you.'

And she gave Hampton Court a friendly push in the back. Scowling, and biting on his cigar, he led the way up the stairs towards the stage.

This appeared in the distance. It was vast and slightly sloping, partially covered with coiled wires, coconut matting and open trapdoors. Two hands, in cloth caps and shirt-sleeves, stood in the middle of the stage, arguing with someone beyond the rows of cold, empty footlights. In the wings hung loops and strands of rope, like jungle vegetation. Beyond them, echoing, empty and cold, was the vast, shadowy, dust-sheeted auditorium. Someone was complaining fretfully in the front row of the stalls.

'I think it's a silly trick,' this person was saying fretfully, over and over again. 'I think it's a silly trick.'

Natasha wrinkled her eyebrows and lifted one of them at Tony Gresham, who made a face back at her. It was difficult to see in the half-dark.

'My mother,' said Tony, whispering. 'Prince Charming herself.'

Hampton Court stood as usual with his hands in his pockets. He glared down truculently at Vivienne Gresham. She lolled in an orchestra stall. She wore a black felt hat, drawn closely down over her ears, with a brooch of some regiment in front of it. Her bright brass-coloured hair peeped out round her forehead and also round her plump old chin. Large quantities of lace frothed and bubbled at her throat. She wore a dressy black suit. Her large, shapely legs were crossed well above the knee and she was making a remarkably indecent exposure.

'You keep a civil tongue in your head, *Miss* Gresham,' said Hampton Court smoothly. 'Two distinguished artists have come to watch you rehearse. Miss Birdseye—'

'Hiyah, toots,' said Mrs Gresham warmly. 'Haven't seen you since Bournemouth, 1918. You *have* got on, haven't you? But why aren't you playing Ibsen like you said you would?'

Miriam, who did not like to be reminded of the year 1918 at all, and who would have preferred that people should consider her of a more recent generation than Vivienne Gresham, frowned slightly. She opened her mouth to reply. But her speech of retaliation was drowned by Hampton Court, who was now introducing Natasha with a flourish of conversational trumpets.

'The famous *ballerina*,' he was saying. 'The one and only Natasha Nevkorina . . . I saw her dance in Cannes . . . for the great Diaghilev . . .'

This also was an unfortunate choice of gambit. Natasha, equally, preferred not to think of the past in accurate detail. She had never achieved the status of *prima ballerina*, and the last time she appeared for Diaghilev, there had been a history-making brou-ha-ha because of her refusal to wear a dark wig in *Les Sylphides*. And so Natasha frowned.

Somewhere beneath her feet they thought they heard a rude and hiccupping laugh.

'Come down into the stalls,' called Hampton Court suddenly, imperviously. He bounded through the pass-door like an india-rubber ball, throwing away the butt of his cigar as he went. 'Come along down into the stalls and watch "My Lady's Boudoir".'

IV

It was a partial dress rehearsal. It was almost impossible among all the coils of wire and loops of rope and dirty canvases, stacked about the stage, for the uninitiated to imagine how 'My Lady's Boudoir' would look on the night. Hampton Court attempted to sketch in a background. He indicated those parts of white imitation Honiton lace which would presently go 'up', revealing other pieces of white imitation Honiton lace also going 'up'.

'The music here,' he said, 'is the "Dance of the Hours".' He struck the ground in front of the orchestra pit with his little foot and called out, 'Mr Jenkins!'

'It always *is* the "Dance of the Hours",' said Vivienne Gresham. She intercepted a ferocious scowl from Mr Jenkins, the Theatre Royal conductor, who appeared suddenly in a mauvish lounge suit and waved a baton. He was in the orchestra pit, and so, apparently, were the orchestra, for there was a sudden squealing of flutes and wind instruments and brass. A little man, evidently the dance director, appeared from nowhere and screamed, 'Now then, Tots, peppy this time!'

'It is quite right, to be olways using the "Dance of the

20

Hours"', said Natasha, smiling smoothingly at Mr Jenkins. 'The orchestra by now will be so *used* to it.'

And so, a little spasmodically, the Theatre Royal orchestra and Mr Jenkins began that series of plucks, twitters and shakes that is universally known as the 'Dance of the Hours'. And on the stage, and not for the first or last time, was enacted that airy piece of pantomime persiflage, 'My Lady's Boudoir'.

First entered, in flimsy muslin *tu-tus*, with filthy dirty knees, the Twenty-four Tottenham Tots, who represented the 'Fairies of the Boudoir' (some of them). They staggered across the stage with Milady's Hand Mirror, or wrestled manfully with Milady's comb. They tottered wearily about with Milady's Giant Scent Spray, with collapsible rubber bulb, or did *pas seuls*, *pas de deux* and *pas de quatres* to indicate passionate devotion to Milady's Toilet Table generally. Two Tiny Tottenham Tots performed the Vauxhall Venuses' lipstick dance and then bent themselves to the more menial task of towing Milady's Rouge Pot round the stage on a small gilt waggon. There were approximately four Tiny Tots to each Toilet Implement.

'They're all reproductions of Marie Antoinette's toilet-set at Versailles,' said Vivienne Gresham in Natasha's ear, with a groan.

'To scale?' asked Natasha, gripping the arms of her stall.

'To *scale*,' said Hampton Court proudly. 'And now we have the climax. Now we have the dance of Milady's Powder-Puff. Madame Valenka,' he explained, under his breath to Natasha, 'is Milady's Powder-Puff.'

The music slid into Tchaikowsky's 'Dance of the Flutes'. And slowly, through one of the stage traps, there rose an enormous cardboard powder-box, painted gilt. The Tottenham Tots advanced upon it in lines, grimly gesturing with the right leg extended from the hip. Other Tiny Tots knelt in attitudes of supplication, pointing towards Milady's powder-box. They had abandoned the other instruments of Milady's Toilet. They raised the lid.

Inside the box was a great frothing of cotton wool. Among it was curled a small neat pink figure. The music changed again, to the 'Dance of the Fée Dragée'. The pink figure raised its head, crowned with the plastic knob of Milady's Powder-Puff. The figure hiccupped and fell forward out of the box. The figure was Madame Valenka. She was hopelessly intoxicated.

Of the remainder of the rehearsal: of Hampton Court's snowy-white and furious face, and his mouth with little beads of foam upon it, and his assault on Madame Valenka, Natasha and Miriam preferred not to remember too much. Her subsequent expulsion from the pantomime was more memorable, for when madame had been stripped of her rose satin corsage and white mock swansdown skirts, and had passed, shaking, through the stage door of the Theatre Royal for ever, Natasha, to her consternation, was offered the part of Milady's Powder-Puff.

'Only for the one dance, Miss Nevkorina, *please*, I can arrange for the Twenty-four Tottenham Tots and the chorus to cover *all* the others. The dance of the Powder-Puff *needs* a star. Oh, please say "yes". You needn't even represent a Clan in the March Past of the Clans,' said Hampton Court. 'Unless, of course,' he added, cunningly, 'unless you want to.'

There was a short silence, punctuated by Natasha who said 'Clans' dreamily, and then 'Clans' again.

Hampton Court nodded. He screwed a new cigar into his

mouth and lit it. The battle was over and he knew it. Natasha was silent. She was working out an exciting finale dress consisting of ballet skirts and tartan ribbon plaid thrown across one shoulder, with cairngorm.

'I should be being entitled to be wearing the McNulty tartan,' she said, eventually aloud. 'My grandmother on my father's side was being a Royal McNulty.'

After this strange statement everything disintegrated a little.

Vivienne Gresham, smoothing down her black, ribbon-bound revers, said Natasha was a silly fool to take on a job in an awful pantomime like this one. Hampton Court said Vivienne Gresham was a rose-red cutie, half as old as time, and told her to shut up. After this pretty speech he cried out that the occasion demanded champagne, and then rather meanly produced a bottle of gin and some baby bottles of tonic water. By this time they were in the manager's office, surrounded by photographs of Sarah Bernhardt, Mrs Patrick Campbell, Ellen Terry and Sir Henry Irving. Miriam was jealous of anyone having a job in a pantomime, and refused to speak.

The Twenty-four Tottenham Tots, who were standing about, waiting to see if they had to do Milady's Boudoir all over again, became extremely restive. Two of them (called on the programme Dawn O'Day and Dreme Child, but known to each other as Ginger and Nobby) burst in at the door, striking each other in the face, kicking and swearing. Their mothers had to be found. They had to be cuffed and told not to use horrid words and then all the Twenty-four Tiny Tottenham Tots were told to report tomorrow morning at ten sharp for another rehearsal. In the pandemonium that followed upon this incident Natasha and Miriam found themselves walking briskly across the road towards the Saracen's Head with Vivienne Gresham.

'Oh,' she said as she swung her big hips along, tit-tupping on the kerb in her high heels, 'oh, so you're stopping at the old "Saracen", too, are you? Good. So'm I.'

There was a pause. Natasha regretted her foolishness at becoming Milady's Powder-Puff at eight pounds a week. She must have been hypnotized. She felt very tired and incapable of dancing one step. She emerged from her swoon and heard Vivienne Gresham saying, 'My husband's been stopping at the County.'

'How curious,' said Miriam absently. 'Why not the Saracen's Head?'

'Not bloody likely,' said Vivienne Gresham, with a chuckle. 'I keep myself *to* myself.'

And she parted from them in the entrance hall of the Saracen's Head, amongst the brass and the revolving doors and the hall porters. She waved a white-gloved hand and disappeared upstairs. Miriam and Natasha, moving towards the reception-desk, to make arrangements to keep their rooms a little longer, exchanged meaning glances.

'What a strange way to treat a husband,' said Natasha. 'Whatever sort of a husband has she *got* that she is treating him like this?'

'Oh,' said Miriam vaguely, 'I think she married Harry DeFreeze of DeFreeze and DeFreeze, Eccentric Dancers, and there was that divorce because she went away with Banjo DeFreeze, the younger brother of the two. Harry DeFreeze and Banjo DeFreeze are still partners, but Banjo keeps her. At least, I think so ... Harry *may* be the husband still.'

'Goodness,' said Natasha. 'This is being *too* complicated. Are they in the Pantomime too?'

'Oh yes, I think so,' said Miriam, opposite the vast mahogany reception-desk and the plump little woman in black who guarded it. 'Of *course* they are. They are the Ugly Sisters.'

3

Natasha woke in the unfamiliar hotel bed, stirred, and kicked out her legs among sheets that she easily persuaded herself were damp. Her room was on the top floor. Miriam and herself were unable to stay one night longer in the Saracen's Head. There was a Conservative Congress in Newchester that week, and it had only been the non-arrival of the two candidates from Saffron Walden and Much Hadham that had permitted them to remain in the Saracen's Head for even *one* night. It was not surprising that Natasha felt apprehensive and home-less. There was no *need* for her to have said 'yes' to Hampton Court. She must have gone *mad*. Hampton Court *must* have hypnotized her. Natasha was by now utterly convinced the sheets were damp. She sat up and swung her feet over the edge of the bed. Various shawls and vests in which she had wrapped her feet fell to the ground in soft and muffling swathes.

Natasha put on her bedroom slippers and crossed to the window. She looked down into Atkins Street and at the front of the Theatre Royal. She scowled resentfully, like a Siamese kitten.

It was early morning still and it was raining. Atkins Street was dismal. The gutters ran, the pavements shone, and a street cleaner with a little hand-cart shovelled about in the middle of the road. He wore a glistening waterproof and he carried a long, hard brush over one shoulder. To Natasha he suddenly epitomized the whole soaking wet set-up of Newchester and Hampton Court and Milady's Powder-Puff.

'I am being hopeless,' she said crossly to herself. She held back the curtain. 'Getting myself into this pantomime. The trouble is being free to *do* it. I have now been too long free, from anyone, even Johnny . . .'

Johnny was her husband, from whom she had recently obtained a decree absolute.

'Johnny was not nice, but I knew him,' she said vaguely. 'What I am wanting is not a job in a pantomime, but another gentleman.'

She sat on a chair in front of the looking-glass and cleaned her face. She resolved that she would appear at the rehearsal at 10 a.m. and tell Hampton Court that *as* there was no suitable hotel accommodation for her in Newchester and that as she refused to live in theatrical lodgings, she was therefore unable to stay, and would give up her job as Milady's Powder-Puff.

She then very carefully combed her hair and went in search of a deep hot bath.

II

Miriam, also turning over in bed two floors below, was equally convinced that the sheets were damp. Through the sad hotel window she could, without moving, see the façade of the Theatre Royal: 'after the style of the Delphic Temple at Athens'. Gloomily she recollected the appearance of the hoardings below, blazing scarlet and white. They would presently carry Natasha's name and not Miriam Birdseye's. Angrily she thought about the framed photographs, lashed to the Delphic pillars with bits of string. Where Vivienne Gresham already hung, as Prince Charming, in black velvet with silver facings. Vivienne Gresham, indeed.

Miriam became very restless and decided she could not stay in bed.

As she dressed, and as she regarded her face angrily in the hotel looking-glass, she, too, remembered that the Saracen's Head would be unable to keep them both for another night. She became savage and caught her thumbnail in her stocking. She broke the looking-glass in her face-compact and cried a little from sheer nerves. Both darling Miriam and darling Natasha went down to breakfast in the coffee-room in filthy tempers.

III

But things got even worse at the Theatre Royal at ten o'clock. Miriam had admitted her jealousy and had said that she didn't think she would bother to come to rehearsal. She would do some more Christmas shopping, she thought. At nine-fifty-five, however, she was unable to bear it a moment longer. She followed Natasha into the front foyer in an absolute turmoil. She said out loud from time to time that her friend must be *firm* with Hampton Court.

'Not,' said Miriam, in a loud clear voice like an electric bell, 'that anybody has ever managed to be firm with Hampton – *yet*, you understand, but you might be the exception. Oh, I *beg* your pardon ... '

For Miriam had neatly avoided the back view of the theatre charlady, crouched on all fours, with a bucket and prayer-mat, scrubbing the floor of the foyer, which presented a splendid vista in black and white chessboard squares, to collide sharply with a heavily built stranger in grey tweed.

'I am so sorry,' she said. 'I didn't see you.'

The grey-tweed stranger now saw Miriam and smiled slightly. He raised his slate-blue felt hat. Then he saw Natasha. His hat remained poised in the air for an appreciable length of time.

'Not at all,' he said slowly; and then again, 'not at all. I was just – um – buying the panto seats, you know. Er – yes. We always buy panto seats for Boxing Day ... '

Miriam nodded and stepped briskly round the charlady. She was perfectly used to the effect that Natasha had on unsuitable gentlemen in thick overcoats, and it bored her. Natasha was now galloping up the red velvet stairs towards the auditorium as fast as her beautiful legs would carry her. The heavily built stranger watched her go.

'Well, excuse me, I must go now,' said Miriam.

'Your tickets, Mister Atkins,' said the lady booking-clerk through the brass grill at his elbow.

'Thank you,' said Mr Atkins absently. 'Thank you.'

He took the little envelope printed with its warning about 'No Money Returned'. He moved slowly, preoccupied, with his head bowed under his becoming hat. As he reached the street he suddenly halted. He turned and came back to the booking-office.

'Who was that I was just speaking to?' he said anxiously.

The lady booking-clerk did not look up.

'How do I know?' she said rudely. Then she looked up. 'Oh, I'm sorry, Mr Atkins,' she said in a great rush. 'Didn't see it was you. I am sorry, I'm sure. Those were two friends of Mr Court's, I think. Yes, that's right. Two friends of Mr Hampton Court's . . .'

Mr Atkins smiled.

'Any friend of Mr Court's,' he said gaily, 'is a friend of mine.'

This bright remark upset the lady booking-clerk. Mr Atkins turned away and began to mount the stairs towards the auditorium. His was a solid, prosperous figure.

IV

Inside the theatre things had gone from worse to impossible. There was a subversive character called 'Sid'. He sat at an upright piano and beat out numbers for Vivienne Gresham. Vivienne Gresham, in a fur coat, leant over the back of his chair and said at intervals, 'And then I come in there, see, Sid?'

One or two young ladies were being taught the pantomime strut by Hampton Court. A shapeless young woman in navy-blue slacks and a bulbous navy-blue blouse was hammering the floor rather too near Hampton Court. He had flown into several small rages about this hammering and had threatened to sack a local girl called Gladys. Natasha's clear and charming voice rang happily through the theatre and across the footlights.

'Mr Court!' called Natasha. 'I really cannot be being in your pantomime one moment longer. You see—'

Here Miriam cut in helpfully.

'There is nowhere for her to live.'

'There is nowhere for me to live,' agreed Natasha, and she drooped her lovely head.

The Twenty-four Tottenham Tots grouped themselves about the stage in repellent attitudes. One of them chewed at some gum. One had a bad cold in its head and snuffled. Another did not feel well and said so monotonously in a whining tone of voice. Ginger and Nobby quietly kicked each other on the shins. Mabel and Gladys giggled.

'What?' said Hampton Court. 'Nowhere to live?'

He advanced towards them up-stage. His mind was obviously working furiously. He was wondering if Natasha might best be intimidated or ingratiated. As usual, he did the thing that no one expected of him. His face lit up and he shouted over the footlights:

'My friend Mr Thomas Atkins will have you both to stay, won't you, Tom?'

Ami Mr Atkins remarked again that any friend of Hampton Court's was a friend of his. He stood at the brass bar of the orchestra pit with his monstrous overcoat open. He gazed round him vaguely. He obviously wondered which of the cast he was going to have to stay. Vivienne Gresham, on the stage, leant forward over Sid's shoulder, picked out a bar or two of 'Love walked right in' with one hand. He leered at Mr Atkins. Mr Atkins blew his nose.

'Is Mrs Gresham going to stay with me?' he said mildly.

'Hampton is *hell*,' said Vivienne Gresham. 'He has more cheek to the square inch than any other man I know. Honestly.'

Hampton Court did not seem angry. He stood with one hand on his hip. He stared up into Mr Atkins' face, which was flat like a tom cat's. Suddenly he jerked his head to the side and called, 'Come here, Mrs DuVivien, and you too, Miss Birdseye!'

'Very pleased to meet you ladies, I'm sure,' said Thomas Atkins, standing his ground. 'Very pleased, I'm sure.'

Natasha and Miriam were too shaken by the speed at which events were happening. They were perturbed at the thought that they would presently be very, very rude to poor Mr Atkins. They stood their ground and bowed. Mr Atkins said again he was pleased to meet them.

V

'I live outside the city,' explained Mr Atkins. He held his face very close to Natasha. Again she was reminded of a large friendly tom cat. 'When we made our little pile we bought our little place, Kidder and me, and we've been there ever since. Bayleyside. Out up the valley ...' He waved a square white hand. 'Kidder finds it lonesome. You'll be company for her.'

'Who is Kidder?' asked Natasha.

Vivienne Gresham idled up to the little group.

'*Kidder* is his wife,' she said. 'Isn't she, Tom?'

Tom Atkins smiled at Vivienne Gresham, dead pan.

'They'll like Kidder,' said Vivienne Gresham again. 'Won't they?' And this time she added, with a little curtsey and a side-long bob of the head, with a tinkling of her brassy curls and a shrug of her fat old shoulders, '*City Councillor* Atkins.'

'Matter of fact, I'm Lord Mayor this year,' said Tom Atkins, still dead pan.

'Well,' said Vivienne Gresham, 'imagine Kidder as Lady Mayoress.'

'Expect the City took that into account when I was chosen,' said Tom Atkins firmly.

'I expect they did,' said Vivienne Gresham, not altogether pleasantly. She nodded back at him.

'Will no one stop all this messing about?' screamed Hampton Court. 'Can't we get on with the rehearsal. Damn all the blasted pack of you. Get up there on the *stage* . . .'

There was a pause while Natasha tried to say something soothing.

'You, too, thanks very much,' said Hampton Court.

And he disappeared through the pass-door and was presently heard shouting elaborate blasphemies at the Tottenham Tots. Mr Atkins stepped away backwards into the stalls.

'See you about six,' he said gently, replacing his hat on his square mouse-coloured head. 'Pick you up at the entrance of the Saracen's Head, if that suits?'

At this same moment, in the darkness alongside him, appeared two fawn, twisty-faced little men. They smacked him on the back and made him choke. They called out, 'Hullo, Tom!' and 'If it isn't old *Tom?*' and 'How *are* you, boy?' and, 'Well, if old Viv won't be pleased about this . . .'

'And what in Heaven's name are these?' said Natasha to Miriam.

'Banjo and Harry DeFreeze,' said Miriam under her breath. 'The Ugly Sisters. Vivienne Gresham's husband . . . and – er – *co-respondent.*'

'For God's *sake!*' shrieked Hampton Court. 'Get up here on the stage, the two of ya. Just an hour and a half late, that's all . . .'

'Sorry, Hampton, ol' boy,' said one of the two brothers idly. ''Bye, Tom, ol' man.'

And the DeFreeze Brothers arrived lightly over the footlights amongst the Tottenham Tots, who scattered, whispering and cooing like a lot of dirty little pigeons.

'But which, in God's name, is which?' cried Natasha.

VI

Once Natasha had learnt them it was easy for her to tell Banjo and Harry DeFreeze apart. Harry and Banjo were brothers. Their real name was not DeFreeze, it was Pilkington.

Harry Pilkington DeFreeze was the older of the two. It was he who had married Vivienne Gresham. He had thin short hair that was rather badly cut round the neck and a fondness for gadgets (particularly cigarette lighters) of which he had an inordinate number. He was nervous in his movements, and if he could not move restlessly anywhere else, he moved to the local public-house and ordered a pint of bitter. He usually left this unfinished. He had nice eyes and an apologetic manner. Vivienne Gresham had *trompé-ed* him the very moment they were married and he had said that he did not mind. Of *course* Vivienne must have her fun. He had moved round the hotel bedroom talking the whole thing out, thrusting his hands into his pockets, inefficiently clicking at a cigarette with a lighter. But when Vivienne *trompé-ed* him with his own brother, Banjo, he was upset. There was no excuse for this, Harry thought. And so he divorced her.

Banjo DeFreeze was very different from his brother. Although he was the same size, and had the same sort of mobile, putty-coloured face, he was not nervous. He had fine thick curling hair which grew low on his forehead, and large dry hands which were capable and far from nervous. Unlike his brother he could sit quite still for hours on end if necessary. Women were delighted by Banjo, but he never married them. He had no intention of marrying Vivienne Gresham.

The three-sided drama between these three people was now old. No one but poor Harry Pilkington DeFreeze took it seriously. When the drama had first happened, when they had been playing Prince Charming and the Two Ugly Sisters in Sheffield, there had been a good deal of tension, a great many meetings (in solicitors' offices and elsewhere), and it had been agreed that The Show Must Go On, in spite of the divorce. Since then the three-sided drama had gone on monotonously, year in year out, sometimes in Sheffield, sometimes in Halifax, sometimes in Newcastle-under-Lyme, but always (let us face it) in *Cinderella*.

Unkind critics often wondered what Vivienne Gresham did in the summer months, when she was not able to appear in scarlet and white ('Hooray, hooray, the Prince will hunt today'), or rose pink ('This is the night of the Ball, and *that* little lady is most-beautiful-of-all'). Even the unkindest critics could not wonder about Harry and Banjo. DeFreeze Brothers were bill-toppers in every music-hall in Great Britain. They had a line of patter and an educated elegance that was unique in England. They closely resembled Fred Astaire. But the impact of their act was doubled because there were two of them. As the Ugly Sisters, they merely did a modified version of their music-hall turn, with a lot of silly topical lines thrown in about the residential districts of the particular city they were 'playing'. Nevertheless Harry and Banjo adored pantomime and infinitely preferred it to Music-Hall and Vaudeville. And as for the last forty-five Boxing Nights they had been driven on to the stage in wheelbarrows, with their elastic-sided boots waving high above their red sateen hunting-habits, it was superfluous for Hampton Court to complain that they were late for one rehearsal. The only person in the Theatre Royal who needed a rehearsal was Hampton Court.

In the middle of all this appeared Tony Gresham, picking his way through the extraordinary collection of props (The Baron's Kitchen) that the DeFreeze Brothers had thrown upon the stage. He stopped by Natasha and suggested in a friendly way she would like to relax. Natasha said she could not have agreed more.

'It's really most amazingly good of you, dear, to help us out. Do you want billing?' He opened his eyes very wide and they were very blue and appealing and innocent. He gently propelled her through the wings backstage. 'I'm afraid it's a little late to have the whole thing done over, dear. You see, the bills have already arrived from the printers. So I ordered your name on *stickers*. That is, I hope you don't mind being the same size that Madame Valenka was?'

He wrinkled his forehead and raised his eyebrows until Natasha thought he was going to burst into tears again. She found herself swept quietly away, out of danger of Hampton Court, downstairs towards the dressing-rooms.

4

Half-way downstairs they came face to face with Dandini, Miss Marylyn Franklyn. She was in a blinding rage. She had a copy of her contract in her hand and she started in immediately to tell Tony Gresham where he got off.

'As usual,' she shouted, waving the paper round her head like a flag. 'As usual. Siding with your mother. You wait till I show the *Newchester Journal* a copy of this contract, that's all. I wish you were *dead*. You and your mother.'

'They wouldn't understand a word of it, dear,' said Tony Gresham. 'I wouldn't do *that*, if I were you. Waste of time.'

Miss Franklyn glared.

'You ... you,' she said and gulped. 'You don't even know who yer own *father* is.'

She was a good-looking, thinnish, thirty-year-old woman with good legs and bright unnatural-looking eyes. She had the sort of temperament that goes with a bright blonde face. Her real name was Maggie Franks. Suddenly she noticed Natasha and her tone changed.

'Sorry, Tone,' she said. 'But it *isn't* a very nice way to speak to a person that's only got the show at heart. I'm doing everything I can to help you and all you can say is—'

'Don't show your contract to the Press, Miss Franklyn,' said Tony Gresham in a quick sing-song, after Mr Coward. 'They might not understand.' He looked at her through lowered eyelashes.

'Oh, *you*,' said Miss Franklyn. 'Everyone *knows* you've got a thing about your mother. But it's not very nice when it takes the bread out of the mouths of hard-working girls who only want to sing Chatinooga-Choo-Choo, instead of spraining their ankles over that dreary old White Christmas dance routine—'

'Yes, but, Maggie dear, you're such a good dancer, dear, and with such lovely legs, if I may say so.'

'You certainly may,' said Miss Franklyn.

'And you quite, quite often go out of tu ... I *mean*,' Tony Gresham pulled himself up apologetically, 'I mean you dance so awfully well.'

'I like singing,' said Miss Franklyn. 'And don't you Maggie me. Miss Franklyn to you, thanks very much.'

'But, Miss Franklyn,' wailed Tony Gresham, 'Dandini's a dancing part.' He wrung his hands helplessly. '*Do* be co-operative. After all, you are *under*studying my mother.'

'If Miss Franklyn is such an offully good dancer,' said Natasha suddenly, 'and with such offully good legs, too, she can be Milady's Powder-Puff.'

'Who're you, dear?' Miss Franklyn peered at her. 'Oh yes! The Russian that Hampton hired this morning. I *say*, what *about* firing old Valenka, dear?' She turned to Tony Gresham in quite a friendly way. 'What about that? I like Russians,' she

38

added suddenly, inconsequently. 'They're nice. Come and talk to me, dear. I'm bored.'

Tony Gresham melted away. Miss Franklyn shouted after him.

'And if you see that old Hampton Court you can tell him I want to see him. I *will* 'ave my rights . . . ' She turned flatteringly to Natasha. 'Don't you think I ought to 'ave my rights, dear? Well, this is nice. You came with old Mum Birdseye, didn't you? I knew a boy once who knew Mum Birdseye. He said she was nice.'

Natasha looked wildly round her for a way of escape, but she was being pressed, inexorably, into Miss Franklyn's dressing-room. And, also, she was fascinated. She said yes, Miss Birdseye was very nice.

'Where you stayin', dear?' asked Miss Franklyn, briskly. She flung her contract on to the dressing-table in front of her large, scratched looking-glass. She proceeded to forget all about it. 'I'm stayin' with old Ma Hitch . . . Mind . . . ' she went on, peering at herself in the glass. She patted two butter-coloured curls into place and spat on a forefinger before smoothing her eyebrows, 'Ma is nice. But she *is* homely. You know, you can be too homely. Wouldn't you say?'

Natasha, quite stunned, spoke slowly and distinctly. She wished to remind herself that she was still alive.

'I am living – or at least I have been asked to stay – with Councillor, or Lord Mayor, Atkins.'

Miss Franklyn spun on the spot and her eyes flashed jealously. She gave a short, sharp laugh. She leant back on her two hands and looked dangerously at Natasha.

'You're *what*?' she said. 'You're doing what? I say. That is a good one. On'y been in the company two minutes and you're already staying with Lord Mayors . . . ' She mimicked Natasha's charming broken accent. 'Lord Mayor *Atkins*. What next, I must say? I say, what about *this*?'

'Why?' said Natasha slowly. And she ever so slightly mimicked Miss Franklyn. 'What is the matter? Isn't Lord Mayor Atkins *nice*?'

II

Natasha was used to lunatics, and theatrical lunatics at that, but confined in the close quarters of Marylyn Franklyn's dressing-room, she began to feel claustrophobic. Miss Franklyn was not a pleasant lunatic. Natasha became tired of edging the conversation away from all the things that upset Miss Franklyn. Hampton Court upset her. So did the song, 'Chatinooga Choo-Choo'. And finally Miss Franklyn really alarmed Natasha very much indeed. Natasha inadvertently mentioned Vivienne Gresham. Immediately Miss Franklyn's features contorted. Her thin lips quivered.

'That *bitch*!' she cried.

Natasha stepped backwards. Miss Franklyn pursued her, breathing hard through her nose, staring up at her. She was about five inches shorter than Natasha.

'That bitch,' said Miss Franklyn again, in a low furious voice. 'I'm sick of the sound of her name, that's all. Now tell me, once for all, are you a friend of hers or mine? You'd better say which, that's all, and quick, or *get out of my dressing-room* . . . '

Natasha was cornered by the arm-chair. Miss Franklyn seemed about to burst into flames.

'*Since* I am only meeting you both for the first time yesterday and today I really could not be saying which of you is my friend,' she said. 'I did not know which of you is nicest. But surely it is wasting time a little to be getting so angry with poor old Gresham? She is only being a poor ham fat?'

'Ham fat!' snarled Miss Franklyn. 'That's what you think. That woman is the devil incarnate, that's all. I say, she's a fiend in human form.' There was a pause.

'You mean she's not nice?' said Natasha innocently.

'I would like to kill her,' said Miss Franklyn. And she abruptly turned her back and stared into the looking-glass.

The dim white dressing-room, reflected behind her, made a background to her uncertain blonde prettiness. Natasha felt a chill run up and down her back.

'I would like to *kill* her,' said Marylyn Franklyn again.

III

Miriam, fascinated by the haphazard rehearsal that continued on the stage, had remained in the front of the house. Under her watchful and cynical eye the Tottenham Tots had performed their Post-Horn Gallop. Harry and Banjo DeFreeze had entered, screaming in their wheelbarrow, looking even more odd in chocolate-chalk stripes than they would 'on the night' in scarlet sateen. Hampton Court had fretfully announced that he was unable to do any of his 'bits'.

'Why not do your chorus song then?' said Banjo DeFreeze helpfully, rubbing his hand across his curly hair and falling into an indolent attitude that suggested irresistible sex magnetism.

'Yes, why not?' said Harry.

'Might give us a chance to join in too,' said Banjo.

'That's right, we'd see how it'd go on the night,' said Harry.

'Oo, do, Mr Court, do,' called out a Tiny Tot that had crept back out of the woodwork.

'Oo, yes, *do*,' echoed its companions.

And simpering slightly, Hampton Court forthwith climbed upon the stage and sang out at the echoing emptiness of the Theatre Royal and the cold appraisal of Miriam Birdseye, the following little song. Miriam afterwards told Natasha that she considered it a fair specimen of its kind.

> *H-A-P-P-Y spells contented,*
> *That's what we all are!*
> *Mum and Dad, and Auntie Jane*
> *When-you-see-them-frowning-tell-them*
> *Don't complain!*
> *H-A-P-P-Y spells contented,*
> *That is what we are.*
> *The bad old world, ain't it a shame?*
> *Is full of mis-er-ee and pain,*
> *For-ev'ry-day-of-sun-there-are*
> *Three of rain.*
> *That is how things are.*

At this point Miriam, who was listening breathlessly to every word, beating time with her foot, became aware of someone sitting beside her in the stalls. She turned her head. It was Banjo DeFreeze.

'Pretty terrible, eh?' said Banjo, raising one thick black eyebrow.

('Mum and Dad and Auntie Jane,' sang Hampton Court desperately, in the distance.)

'Still, I suppose someone's got to do it, eh?' muttered Banjo DeFreeze. 'Now a really good song like "Chick, chick, chick, chick, chicken, lay a little egg for me" is too good for 'em. Too clever, really. They don't pick it up quick enough. Don't you agree?'

Miriam turned her head to look at Banjo and encountered a bold black eye. There was also a flash of jet white teeth in the dark. She hastily looked away again.

'Yes,' she said.

'Now the thing about *Panto*,' said Banjo DeFreeze, edging a little closer, 'is that it's the kiddies' revue, see? And if you please the kiddies and their mums and dads, without teaching 'em anything their mums and dads don't want them to know . . .'

Banjo's knee arrived near Miriam's.

'And then you send 'em home satisfied, see? And they come again. Follow me?'

Miriam followed him only too well, and said so.

'Now the big thing about Panto,' said Banjo DeFreeze, 'is that you have to keep the theatre full for fifteen weeks and if you don't have them coming back again and again, in a little place like Newchester you can't keep the theatre full. Follow me? Now, that's why,' went on Banjo, gently sliding one large hand along the arm of the stall between them, '*that's* why we need funny men in this business. More than we do glamour pusses like you. Follow me?'

It was many years since Miriam had been described as glamour puss, and she said nothing.

'Shall I explain further?'

Banjo DeFreeze's curly head, smelling slightly of hair grease and eau-de-Cologne, shampoo and cold cream, arrived almost on her shoulder. His mouth was about half an inch away from her ear.

'There's a very excellent book about Panto, which you ought to read,' said Banjo. 'That's if you're really interested in Panto. Called *I Remember Chirgwin*.'

Something tickled Miriam's ear. She rose to her feet and coldly dusted off her skirt. As she did so she dusted off one of Banjo's hands.

'I'll do no such thing,' she said.

'Why ever not?' said Banjo, aggrieved. 'It's a good book.' And he repeated the title. *I Remember Chirgwin*.

'I know it is,' said Miriam. 'I wrote it myself.'

IV

The wild wet day had deteriorated into fog and drizzle. Natasha escaped from Miss Franklyn and went up the main shopping street, Northshire Street, towards a haberdasher's called Atkins and Marshall. It was possible for her to walk up the street without getting her feet and legs soaking wet. It was dark, although it was now nearly noon. Many of the motor-cars, splashing in the centre of the street, skidding on the tram-tracks, had their sidelights on.

Natasha now had her future narrowed down to a fifty-fifty chance. If Atkins and Marshall had pale-blue satin and a good supply of maribou in stock, all right. Natasha would buy it and would run up an alternative costume to Milady's Powder-Puff. She would use the wardrobe mistress's sewing-machine (the wardrobe mistress, a Mrs Furbinger, had said she would be delighted) and she would appear in the pantomime. But nothing, certainly, would induce her to appear in rose pink and a plastic knob. It is significant that Natasha was not even faintly worried by the dance which she would have to perform as Milady's Powder-Puff. The 'Dance of the Fée Dragée' had been good enough for Diaghilev and it would damn' well have to be good enough for Newchester.

Atkins and Marshall was an old-fashioned shop on the right-hand side of the Northshire Street tram-tracks. It had the most confused window display Natasha had ever seen. Lace, hats, feathers and trimmings of one sort and another jostled one another behind the plate glass. Collars, insecurely stuck to the glass with paper stickers, festooned the foreground. Wreaths of pink daisies, blue daisies and white daisies (marked, insanely enough, 'Acceptable Gift') hung drunkenly in diagonals across the glass, like a weird Christmas decoration. White cardboard boxes formed a background for this confusion.

Surely, among all this insane profusion, Natasha would be able to find some maribou. She clicked back the old-fashioned door, and a bell jangled somewhere above her head. A young gentleman in a tail coat leapt forward at her. Evidently, in spite of the muddle, the shop paid. Indeed, it was full of customers. Bewildered, Natasha found herself asking the young gentleman in the tail coat for maribou, and then she found herself propelled gently along, past counters of green and scarlet cord and ribbon, past scarves and cardboard heads wearing hair-nets and, once, a plastic lady's head dressed in a coquettish fur-felt beret, labelled 'Peaks and Tams to Taste'. Above her head Natasha could hear a little sloping wooden track, that squeaked and groaned continuously, while wooden balls, containing change and bills and receipts, bowled swiftly backwards and forwards between the counter and the cash-desk.

The young man swept up a tall chair, rapped her with it behind the knees and said 'Pleasure!' He then disappeared. Fascinated, Natasha wasted five minutes observing wooden balls in action. The young ladies also had a catapult with which they started them on their journey. Then she remembered the maribou. She woke with a jerk from her swoon and found Tom Atkins, the Lord Mayor of the City, at her elbow. He looked amiable but puzzled.

'Well, little lady,' he said, 'what can I do for you? Can I help you at all? It is Mrs DuVivien, now, isn't it? Who is going to stay with me over Christmas, and help me to celebrate it. What can I do you for?'

He had been going on like this for some time before Natasha realized that in all probability she was speaking to the Atkins part of Atkins and Marshall. She frowned, trying to concentrate.

'Maribou,' she said. 'That is it. Maribou. And also pale-blue satin.'

V

'Well,' said Mr Atkins, 'the maribou is easy. Definitely. But the pale-blue satin ... Well, wait now ... ' He turned towards the counter with an old-fashioned gesture of introduction. 'Here is Miss Burston. She will serve you with maribou.'

Miss Burston had evidently been crouched behind the counter in an attitude like a Greek runner. She now sprang smartly forward and whipped an emerald box on to the counter. She flipped off the lid. Inside, wound on a deep-sea fishing tackle of cardboard, were yards and yards of maribou.

'How much would Madame require?' said Miss Burston. Her eyes were anxiously on Mr Atkins. Miss Burston was faded and hopeless in black with a beige woollen cardigan. Her hair, equally, was beige. Natasha suddenly heard herself saying that she wanted a good deal of maribou. Some yards, certainly. She couldn't say how much exactly. Miss Burston smiled pityingly. No doubt she was faded and hopeless, but at least she knew how many feet there were in a yard.

'What is Madame wishing to make?' she said.

Her tone subtly implied that Natasha would be perfectly unable to make anything at all.

'A fancy dress,' said Natasha. 'I want to make an underskirt, in order that I may go to a ball as a powder-puff.'

Outwitted, Miss Burston looked down her nose. Between them they decided that thirty yards of maribou would be enough. The maribou was parcelled up and paid for. A lady (more *chic* and a better thing altogether than Miss Burston) sprang forward in reply to a call for 'Cash, please, Mrs Hurley,' and, glancing brightly everywhere but at what she was doing, scribbled an indecipherable collection of initials against Natasha's purchase.

Miss Burston screwed up the bill and the carbon copy and Natasha's five-pound note and put everything into a wooden ball. She put the ball above her head into a little cage and pulled a lever that lifted the cage and set the ball in motion, rolling it astonishingly towards another lady (also in black and a beige cardigan) who sat remotely, high above the shop in the cash-desk. She dealt with many, many wooden balls in the course of five minutes. Natasha, watching the wooden balls crashing in and out upon their journeys reflected that had she attempted to deal with even *one* wooden ball and its terrifying contents, her face would have worn the agonized expression of a bolting blood mare, rolling eyeballs and all. At this moment Mr Atkins spoke again.

'The blue satin,' he said, 'is rather different. You had better come to my office. Miss Burston will send the maribou along.'

And Natasha meekly followed him through the various departments of the shop to his office, a little box of beaver-board, set in the background, directly under the cash-desk.

'Come in, come *in*, little lady,' he said genially enough, and opened the door. Darling Natasha suddenly felt the oddest sensation. She felt that Mr Atkins was not everything that he appeared to be.

VI

Mr Atkins pulled up a chair and sat down behind a fine mahogany desk. At his back a heavily frosted window looked down upon the back lanes of Newchester. The top part of the window was plain glass. The letters T. K. and I. appeared, back to front, in gold. Natasha, puzzling up at them, realized that they would form part of the words 'Atkins and Marshall', heavily etched upon the window.

'Now then, little lady,' said Mr Atkins.

Against one wall there was a very large-scale map of Northshire, done in painted plasticine. It showed, in high relief, the Quaritch Hills, the River Tame, Newchester and its environs. Fascinated, Natasha now approached it and ran a finger lightly along the neat blue serpent of the River Tame.

'Ah,' said Mr Atkins, 'you're looking at my map. Fine piece of work. Done locally. At the University. They did it very well, too.'

He stood proudly and looked over Natasha's shoulder. He, too, traced the course of the river with his stubby thumb.

'There's Baley's Mount,' he said, laying his thumb upon the nearest of the Quaritch Hills. 'An' here's my home, Bayleyside, where you'll be going this evening.'

There was something reassuring about Mr Atkins' map. Natasha, looking at it, wondered why she had shuddered as she came into the cosy little office.

'You're cold,' said Mr Atkins, as though he read her thoughts. He switched on a radiator. He took a key from his waistcoat pocket and began to play with it. He sat down again on his chair. 'About this blue satin,' he said heavily.

On the desk at his elbow was a photograph of a young woman with a waved head. She had turned sideways and simpered over her bare shoulder at the moment when the photographer had taken his photograph. Written across her were the words, 'Yours Ever, Kidder'. She was at least twenty years younger than Mr Atkins. Behind, on the wall, was a calendar called 'Full Cry'.

'You'll need clothing coupons for that, y'know,' said Mr Atkins. 'Got any?'

Natasha shook her head.

'Ah,' said Mr Atkins. And he reached down to a drawer in his desk, inserted the key in the drawer and drew it out. Inside there appeared to be several of those little pink books which, marked 47/48, 48/49, have dictated our lives during the last five years.

'There now,' said Mr Atkins. 'You just take one of these and pop along to my satin counter and buy what you want. You'll soon find Tom Atkins is a man of his word. Then you meet me again at six this evening.'

Natasha rose to her feet and began to say thank you.

'See you,' said Mr Atkins behind her, 'at six.'

5

Natasha was reluctant to return to the Theatre Royal to assist in further fantastic lunacies. She had never believed the stories told her by theatrical friends of the circumstances that attend the putting on of a pantomime. They had sounded so unlikely. Now, it seemed, these stories were all quite true. Natasha was mildly astonished.

She decided to go back to her hotel room. Here she spent a happy day, crouched on the floor with a pair of sharp scissors, cutting out and lightly tacking together the pale-blue satin dress of Milady's Powder-Puff. And by degrees, as she snipped and laid various pieces cut on the bias against other pieces equally cut on the bias, inevitably she forgot the twisted, angry face of Marylyn Franklyn. She forgot Dandini and her obsession. An obsession which was murderous.

II

Miriam, also, was thankful to escape the rest of the rehearsal. Even *Miriam's* enthusiasm for the Theatre was inclined to become exhausted when the Theatre was represented by such things as Vivienne Gresham's patriotic song, Act II ('That's what we're fighting for!'), sung against a dim view of Surrey, with all the flowers ever known coming simultaneously into bloom in the foreground.

Miriam came blinking into the half-dark of Atkins Street, amused at the way in which she and Natasha had become involved in Hampton Court's pantomime.

'I don't know, I'm sure,' said Miriam, and scowled ferociously at a photograph of Hampton Court, dressed as Humpty Dumpty. 'I hope to heaven *this* doesn't develop into one of darling Natasha's murder dramas ...'

For her dear friend Natasha had already been inexplicably mingled up with four distinct murder dramas.*

At five minutes to six Miriam and Natasha were sitting meekly enough in the wide front hall of the Saracen's Head, their suitcases packed beside them. Their feet were folded like gentlewomen. All about them, to their mild surprise, surged a press of gentlemen. They moved restlessly up and down the hall and cried out to one another 'Guy!' and 'Slingsby!' and 'Warren, old man.' Most of them wore bowler hats and some of them wore heavy melton cloth overcoats.

'I did not know there were so many navy-blue gentlemen in England,' said Miriam, and beckoned to a waiter. She asked him who they all were. He smiled kindly.

'It is the Conservative Congress, madam,' he said.

'A Congress of Conservatives,' said Natasha, pleased. 'There will be a pride of lions next.'

'They have been lunching in the Vandyke Room,' said the

---

*Death before Wicket, Murder, Bless It, Death Goes on Skis, Poison for Teacher.

waiter and lingered, watching Natasha's inconsequent beauty with dazed happy eyes. 'Mr Atkins,' he volunteered suddenly.

Natasha smiled like a cherub and the waiter became her slave for life.

'Is that *our* Mr Atkins?' she said.

'I expect so, miss,' said the waiter gallantly. 'He is the Conservative Candidate. Oh yes, miss, I expect he is your Mr Atkins.'

And he went away, reverently, his little silver salver clenched against his black trouser leg.

'How I wish everyone would call *me* miss instead of madam,' said Miriam crossly.

'Your servant, miss and madam,' said a pleasant baritone behind Miriam's head. 'I've been sent by our host to collect you. My name is Shelly. I am a Communist.'

Natasha sprang from her chair, startled.

'Sent by whom?' said Miriam, keeping her head.

'Mr Atkins,' said Shelly, 'I am to drive you all to Bayleyside in my car. Tom's has broken down.'

He seemed genuine enough. He was a tall young man, with curly hair and an air of crumpled elegance that was instantly appealing. He wore a yellow woollen waistcoat. Several buttons were loose and dangling on his coat. He was clean shaven. There was a little ragged hole in the knee of his tweed trousers and Natasha loved him at sight.

'You had better not be saying that you are Communist *here*,' she said slowly as Timothy Shelly picked up their suitcases and walked before them into the street. 'You will be torn up like wild *dogs*. These gentlemen are all Conservatives.'

Two very broad-shouldered gentlemen in slate-blue and grey

elbowed past them in the revolving door, and said, 'Well, see you next June, Freddie,' to each other.

'Also,' said Natasha, and stopped for a second on the top of the steps. She looked across the bleak wetness of Atkins Street at the Theatre Royal. 'Also I am a White Russian.'

In the twilight several Tottenham Tots could be seen hurrying away from the theatre, carrying dancing slippers in bags. Their shrill voices came unpleasantly towards them across the shining pavements.

'Well, so am I, more or less,' said Timothy Shelly. 'My grandmother was Princess Namalitzin.'

And for some reason or another, Natasha did not pursue this subject further.

Timothy Shelly's car was a large American vehicle with a long seat in front and a long seat behind and plenty of room for everyone. Tom Atkins was already sitting in front when they appeared. He did not offer to move. Disgruntled, the two ladies climbed into the back. Tom Atkins slewed round in the front seat and laid a confidential arm along the top of it. He began to talk, as Miriam afterwards said, like an A.A. itinerary.

'We shall leave Newchester by the West,' he said. 'And make up the valley of the River Tame towards the Quaritch Hills. Pity it isn't a nice day. We'd've been able to stop and see the Roman Fort.'

Timothy Shelly swung to avoid a tram and swept between two lots of cyclists, past a dripping-wet war memorial, a public park and a wide open space where some boys were returning from a football game. Their boots swung round their necks like yokes.

'Fascists,' said Timothy Shelly. 'The Italians were. The

Romans, I mean. Even in those days.' His voice was, perhaps, slightly pompous.

'Well,' said Miriam firmly, 'I am Italian. My grandmother on my father's side.'

'So am I,' said Timothy Shelly instantly; 'by my grandfather's governess. A sad unfortunate story which reflects no credit on our name.'

'Don't be an ass, Tim, old lad,' said Tom Atkins, and laughed thickly. 'Always joking he is, ladies. Don't you pay any attention to *him*.'

They left behind them the rows of terrace houses, and their unfortunate dirt-clogged fronts and greasy gardens. They began to pass City Building Schemes and rows of council cottages. Here and there among them, swallowed up by strips of unhygienic brick, and equally unhygienic pavement, were fine Georgian or Queen Anne Mansions, left futile, in two acres of unproductive soil. Many of them had already been turned into Orphanages or Cripples' Homes and proclaimed the fact, shamefaced, with hoardings and dark-green, gold-lettered notices. By and by the tram-tracks ceased and then the houses, and then they were stealing along Westward, through the purple countryside towards the last streaks of the fading day. Timothy Shelly had switched on his headlights and the hedges leapt out, black and bold above him as the sky seemed to disappear.

'Well, ladies,' said Tom Atkins happily, squirming round again in the front seat, 'welcome to Bayleyside. Welcome to Liberty Hall.'

III

Liberty Hall, or Bayleyside, as I should really prefer to call it, was a thoroughly foolish pretentious house with a flat Victorian face that had looked across the River Tame with bland conceit for about eighty years. 'No one calls on Bayleyside' had been a saying in Newchester in the nineteenth century. It was still the truth. There was a white gate that stood open, and a small park, and a very intricate drive, much messed about by bushes, and hens, and sheep and a cow. 'Bayleyside is self-supporting,' Tom Atkins was often heard to say. And then there was a rather tiresome oval of gravelled drive, where most motorists found it very difficult to turn. Timothy Shelly stopped and switched off his engine.

'Think I'll leave the thing here,' he said. "S'easier.'

Tom Atkins opened the door and got out, crunching the gravel. Instantly, in the wet dark, there was the barking and leaping of dogs and a sudden oblong of bright orange light with a female figure standing against it at the top of some steps.

'Oh, *good*,' breathed Miriam, on Natasha's right. 'That will be *Kidder*. I have been looking forward to her all day.'

As Kidder stepped backwards into the lighted hall of Bayleyside she revealed herself as an edition – or perhaps one should say a ten-years-older reprint – of that photograph already seen by Natasha, sitting on Tom Atkins' desk. There was the well-waved head, that now appeared as a rich auburn. ('Dye,' muttered Miriam in Natasha's ear. 'I know, for I once went that colour.') There was the arch glance and the merry smile, the pearl studs in the ears. The bare shoulders were covered now by a pale pink twin set ('Braemar,' said

Natasha to herself, as she shook hands), and the firm white column of a throat rose from three loops of rich pearls. She greeted her husband on the mouth and he responded with enthusiasm. 'Oh, lor', said Miriam quietly, 'I can't stand much of this.'

'You poor dears,' cried Kidder. 'You must be frozen. Come into the lounge.' Her eyes were all for Shelly.

Two wet and smelly little dogs preceded them. Their toenails scrabbled on the edge of the floor. They seemed to be terriers. The carpet was not fitted to the walls and the surrounds had been left bare. The door that swung to behind them, shutting them away from the rest of the world for ever, it seemed, was weighed with a heavy rep curtain that slid slightly to and fro on a curtain rod. It acted as a moderately effective draught excluder.

'Ha!' said Tom Atkins, striding along ahead of them. 'A fire. Come along, Mrs DuVivien. Come along, Miss Birdseye.'

'And we'll all have a little drinkie before the meal?' said Kidder. She performed a little dance among the dogs in front of a tray of glasses, decanters and bottles. The glasses were most depressing. They were decorated with small, painted cocks of vulgar appearance. Cowed, Miriam accepted the fact that she was about to have a drinkie in the lounge. She turned towards the fire. She had been vaguely aware of an ape-like figure lounging. It rose, shaking cigar ash in all directions. Hampton Court.

'You know Hampton, don't you?' said Kidder, tinkling among the glasses. 'And Tim you've already met. So now you know the whole party.'

She straightened her back and laughed.

'Tom called me up at lunch-time and said I could expect to have you with me over the holidays and all. So we'd better get used to one another. Sherry, Mrs – er . . . ?'

She turned to Natasha, who was stretching her long, beautiful hands carefully towards the blaze.

'My friend,' said Miriam abruptly, 'only drinks champagne.'

'Good,' said Timothy Shelly in the doorway. 'I thought these two bottles would come in handy.'

And he whirled forward with a bottle of champagne under each arm. He began to undo the wires. Kidder Atkins was delighted. She went bouncing out of the room to get champagne-glasses, agreeing with Shelly that champagne was the only aperitif. And through the general bustle and noise of wires breaking, and glasses being brought, Natasha and Miriam were able to look around them. They sat side by side on a very ugly sofa, upholstered in brownish brocade, on a dark terracotta carpet. The mantelpiece was marble and embarrassing. Natasha looked hastily away. It held more photographs of Kidder Atkins as a Petty Officer Wren, and Tom Atkins as a Special Constable.

The room was comfortable, if hideous, and the fire was hot, and as Natasha drank her first glass of champagne she said to Kidder that it was most *kind* and sweet and very, very generous of her to have two strange actresses – or worse – one strange actress and one strange dancer in her house over Christmas and the New Year. Such was the excellence of Timothy Shelly's champagne that everyone applauded and laughed at this not very remarkable speech, and Kidder said again that Natasha and Miriam were welcome, welcome.

'It's lonely out here, you know,' said Kidder. 'And Tom and

I, we don't care for fossilizing. So we're glad to have you. We are, indeed.'

Miriam said not at all.

'You liven the place up,' said Tom, and briskly drank his champagne.

'And it needs it,' said Hampton Court suddenly and very viciously. 'A more nasty, unpleasant house and sillier people than you I'll never see. Never stayed in worse.'

There was a frightened silence. Kidder said 'Oh, dear,' rather loudly.

Her husband said, 'Now then, Hampton, old lad, drink up, or have a brandy, and don't be a damned fool.'

Miriam looked at Natasha and winked and both began to giggle. And then, to Natasha's surprise, she found Timothy Shelly beside her, filling her glass again.

'Strange man,' he said coldly in an undertone. 'Has to be the centre of attraction, no matter what. Expect he'll pass that outrage off as a joke. Very odd.'

A lady in an overall poked her head round the door and said that dinner was served. The party went anxiously towards the door, eyeing Hampton Court, who swaggered slightly and spread his arms as he waved the ladies before him. Natasha complained fretfully to Miriam that they would have to run the gauntlet of the dogs, who were now waiting for them in the hall.

'My stockings,' said Natasha, 'will, of course, be ruined.'

'Impossible beast,' said Shelly.

Natasha wondered if he could mean Hampton or the dogs.

'Jump!' said Miriam. 'Jump over their heads. Then they can't reach you.'

Taking her own advice she bounded happily ahead of the other guests into the dining-room.

'High spirits,' said Hampton Court sourly, following them.

IV

Hampton Court remained sour during most of 'the meal', as Kidder continued to call it. Everyone drank warm Bovril in very broad, shallow soup dishes, and were encouraged by Kidder to pour sherry into it. Finally they ate a vast and extremely good apple-pie. It was studded inside with small blunt black nails which, on examination, were discovered to be cloves. But for the lady in the green overall, there were no maids. She had obviously cooked the dinner with Kidder's help and with the help of Hampton Court's confidential maid, Sary, and she now served it, plonking dishes down in front of Mr Atkins with a loud sniff that could well have been described as olde worlde. Spirits were plentiful and of a rather obviously good quality. Neither Natasha nor Miriam dared touch them. Natasha murmured that she might spoil the taste of the champagne. Miriam announced that she was already stinking.

Hampton Court drank two stiff whiskies and progressed from sourness to coarseness and finally to picking quarrels. He sat and poked mouthfuls of duck into his round moist mouth. He, as usual, lacked charm.

He was prepared to lead the conversation in any subject. Most of his conversational roads brought him back to Hampton Court. By the time that Miriam had tried to fling the light conversational ball with a discussion on 'roller skating' and they had all learned how Hampton had conquered the 'Drop 3

Waltz' on the old Queen's Rink in '26; and Natasha had equally attempted 'hunting' (as being suitable for a house-party), and they had all heard how Hampton had gone out with the Belvoir; and by the time that Tom Atkins had told Hampton to 'Pass your plate, old lad', Natasha was utterly sick of the sight and sound of him.

'It is because he is quite stupid and ignorant,' said Timothy Shelly in her ear. 'And very common. It is just as well he goes on talking about himself. He knows something about that at all events. When he talks about anything else he is quite pathetic.'

'I find him pathetic in any case,' said Natasha with a sigh.

'You do?' said Timothy. 'That is very interesting. *All* human beings are very, very distressing I find. All this scrabbling to make a living and trying to build cities and running up wars. Oh, it's dreadfully sad.'

He watched her very carefully. Natasha's lovely eyes filled with tears.

'Oh, I so *agree*,' she said.

'Got Banjo and Viv and Harry coming in after,' said Tom Atkins. He said it through a large and imperfectly concealed mouthful of apple sauce and potato and tinned green peas. 'We might have a game of cards and a yarn.'

'Vingty!' cried Kidder. 'Anyone any more greens?'

'We might have a drink,' growled Hampton Court.

'Could anyone please be telling me what is Vingty?' said Natasha gravely.

Timothy Shelly silently helped himself to more green peas and watched her lovely profile in dumb admiration. One pea fell from the silver spoon and went bowling away across the shining table like a very small green cannon-ball. Timothy Shelly put down the spoon with a sigh.

'Vingt-et-un,' said Hampton Court with a frightening sort of controlled fury, 'is a thoroughly stupid game, depending almost entirely upon chance, played by cretins in third-class railway carriages.'

Timothy Shelly's fine elbow, in its slightly frayed tweed, slipped suddenly on the table near Natasha's.

'I *like* Vingty,' said Kidder Atkins, flushing. 'And there are too many of us for bridge.'

'Enough for two tables,' said Tom Atkins. 'Bring on that apple-pie. Wherever is Miss Burns?'

Miss Burns, Natasha imagined, was the lady in the green overall. She appeared with the pie and there was a small interlude of plonking and sniffing before Timothy Shelly leant his elbow firmly on the table and turned towards her and said:

'Perhaps the ladies do not care for bridge?'

He continued to stare without shame at Natasha, who was blissfully aware of him. He had somehow contrived to make everyone else at the table foolish and rather vulgar.

'Miss Birdseye,' she said, with demurely lowered eyelids, 'plays only *Poker.*'

Timothy Shelly bent a little forward, to catch this remark the more clearly.

'What about you?' he said. 'Are you a simple girl at heart? Long country walks with the dogs? *Yarns* with our host over the log fire?'

Natasha looked at him gravely.

'I am a simple girl at heart,' she said. 'But I quite detest dogs.'

V

It was Miriam who afterwards declared that Hampton Court first introduced the subject of murder at that table. Natasha, although remaining polite, and prepared to discuss such persons as Banjo and Harry DeFreeze, would only have liked to discuss one person at the party. And that one person was, oddly enough, Timothy Shelly.

'Heaven knows why Hampton Court brought murder up,' said Miriam afterwards in their bedrooms before going to bed. 'Because one supposes he has never committed a murder. Although I wouldn't put it past him. So why does he mention it? I am putting it very badly. Do you see what I mean?'

Natasha remarked absently that she was dissatisfied with her face. Definitely.

'Even so,' she added, leaning forward, 'Hampton is finding a lot to say. With or without personal knowledge.'

And she went into a daze, surveying herself in the glass without enthusiasm.

'And murder in relation to Kidder.'

'And Mr Shelly . . . ' said Natasha, with a gentle sigh.

'And ourselves,' said Miriam, and scowled.

Natasha suddenly realized that Miriam was on the verge of being extremely cross with her. She tried to pull herself together.

'I am expecting that was it,' she said. 'One of these unsavoury characters.'

'Timothy Shelly,' said Miriam, raising one eyebrow.

'No,' said Natasha gravely, 'Mr Shelly is not unsavoury. He

is spotlessly clean. Clean but tattered. I expect he sends his clothes to cleaners and laundries a lot . . . '

She was silent again, considering the private life of Mr Shelly in relation to her own. Miriam smiled broadly.

'All right,' she said, 'I won't tease you. But tell me what you were going to say?'

Natasha came out of her dream with a little leap.

'Oh!' she said. 'I am only going to say that quite possibly one of these unsavoury people has heard of what we did for Radcliff Hall School. Or the Flahertés. Or something. And so they wanted' – Natasha paused for a second – 'the *lowdown* on murder.'

'We didn't do much for the Flahertés,' said Miriam. 'But I see what you mean.'

Natasha, bending her starry head, moved the things on her dressing-table. Miriam began to reconstruct the dinner-table conversation bit by bit.

'Hampton Court said he had been talking to a man in a pub about the neatest way to murder a person,' said Miriam, 'and that he'd take the person out in a rowing-boat on a dark night and give them a crack on the top of the head with the oar. *That* doesn't sound as if he'd ever heard of "*Birdseye et cie, we detect anything*".'

This had been the name of Miriam's detective agency.

'And Timothy Shelly was *saying*,' said Natasha, suddenly taking some interest, 'that you would have to be very, very strong and skilful to be coping with a rowing-boat *and* a victim and give *Timothy* drugs any time. Or poison. Isn't he sweet?' concluded Natasha happily.

'And Kidder said "how morbid",' said Miriam, with a delighted snigger.

'And that is where that horrible Banjo and Viv and Harry arrived,' said Natasha.

'Don't mind *Harry*,' said Miriam. 'Poor little thing; he's quite harmless. It's Banjo who is so terrible. Like a thick black animal. And Vivienne. Vivienne. Well, I suppose I am unnaturally biased about principal boys who have pantomimes of their own.'

'A principal boy without a pantomime is like a man without a moustache,' said Natasha. 'My poor Miriam. How sorry I am.'

The two friends were silent for a moment, thinking of Miriam's grief.

'And that,' said Miriam finally, 'was when we moved out of that bad dream of a dining-room into that nightmare of a drawing-room.'

'Of course Timothy Shelly has no moustache,' said Natasha inconsequently.

'I say,' said Miriam, 'what about that pink oil painting of Kidder in the dining-room? What about *that*?'

They stared round the bedroom, which gave a hundred other incredible examples of the taste of the Atkinses.

'Yes, I *know*,' said Natasha. 'But *we* are not in the best of taste ourselves, either, to laugh at people who have been so offully kind to us.'

Miriam frowned and pouted.

'And so the conversation about the murder went on,' said Natasha hastily, getting up and swathing herself in a pale-blue dressing-gown. 'What was it that Vivienne Gresham was saying?'

'Harry DeFreeze said the whole thing was damn' silly because no one wanted to murder anyone, any way, so it was a waste of time, and Banjo DeFreeze said ... I say, wasn't he rather tight, or wouldn't you think? ... that hundreds of people wanted to murder Hampton Court, particularly children who were taken to the pantomime by their mothers and fathers. I thought that was rather good myself. Perhaps someone *will* murder Hampton Court.'

Miriam also got up as Natasha took off her dressing-gown and sprang into bed.

'Murder Hampton Court?' said Natasha vaguely. 'Oh, I don't think so. This bed is really quite comfortable. You'd never think it to look at it. He certainly seemed very excited about something. Perhaps he is *frightened*.'

The springs creaked as Natasha curled up like a little cat.

'He certainly seemed very excited about something,' she said.

Miriam stood at the door, looking tall and slender.

'He is an ape,' she said. 'An ape dressed up. That is all. Good night.'

And she went out of the room and turned out the light. For the Atkinses (although exceedingly kind) did not provide their guests with bedside lights. And Natasha, lying in the dark, remembered in hazy detail the people who had made up the scene around the dining-room table. For they had used the dining-room table, covered with a green baize cloth, for their game. Banjo DeFreeze, as banker, cutting swiftly and dealing with terrible commonplace thumb gestures; Vivienne Gresham, Harry DeFreeze, sometimes biting his thumb and sometimes the edges of the cards. Hampton Court, winning a good deal of money, blaspheming a little whenever he lost. And Timothy Shelly. Tall, ironic-looking, with his beautiful twisted smile. Perhaps a little pompous. And surely, Natasha asked herself, he had a definite softening of his glance whenever he looked at her? Natasha fell asleep.

VI

Miriam, returning to her room, was vaguely annoyed by her friend's refusal to concentrate on the 'murder' conversation. Miriam had felt there was something indefinably wrong with those interminable games of Vingt-et-un. There was something not quite *right* about Banjo DeFreeze and his tragic brother, and their woman, Vivienne Gresham. And Timothy Shelly, even, for Natasha had an unfortunate love of wastrels. They had all appeared galvanized by satanic purpose, electric round the green-baize table. Their faces saying things like 'Five and Under' and 'It's a Natural' should have appeared innocent. They had seemed old and evil, like vampires. Even Kidder, in her pink twin set, had invested remarks like 'I'll twist you', and 'I'll buy', with an uncomfortable intensity they did not deserve. And she had often glared at Timothy Shelly.

'I am starting a cold,' said Miriam sharply to herself. 'Imagining such things. I must have a temperature.'

She was annoyed because Natasha had gone dreamily to sleep thinking of Timothy Shelly. Timothy Shelly, indeed! Miriam wondered what *he* was doing in the house of the Atkinses?

She twitched back the curtains and stared out at the faintly moonlit, rolling magnificence of the Northshire moors – the Quaritch Hills – that lapped up to Tom Atkins' back door.

'It must have been that conversation about murder,' she said under her breath, 'that made me think of everyone in

67

terms of it. I *wish* people wouldn't talk about things they don't understand.'

Miriam rested her head against the cold window. She ran one finger down the pane in a series of dismal squeaks.

'So Hampton Court thinks he would smack someone on the head in a rowing-boat,' she said. 'Or Timothy Shelly would poison someone. And Banjo DeFreeze would shoot. Or so he says. And his brother would use a knife. Or am I just getting a temperature?'

Miriam Birdseye spoke to the unheeding Quaritch Hills.

'I wonder how *I* would commit a murder if I wanted to?' she said.

She was silent a long time, considering this hypothetical absurdity, while the pale moon rose higher and, eventually, wore a ring of many colours like a nimbus. To show that it would rain tomorrow.

6

In time Natasha and Miriam grew used to the life at Bayleyside. Each day they drove into Newchester with Tom Atkins, and every second day Kidder came too. When Kidder was not there no one spoke. The car would bowl along with a well-bred hiss past soaking wet fields and copses, undisturbed by chatter, or back-seat driving or outspoken thoughts. While Mr Atkins' wool-gloved hands lay impassively on the steering-wheel, Natasha and Miriam had a quiet half-hour to collect their energies and vitality for the rehearsal ahead of them. Miriam nagged the aching tooth of her secret ambition by attending all rehearsals.

But when Kidder accompanied them into Newchester 'to do her shopping and change her library book', there was conversation, and it was of a most devitalizing sort.

On the day of the Dress Rehearsal (Christmas Eve), there had been a light fall of snow. Kidder had bundled herself into the car, remarking that at any rate there wouldn't be a full graveyard this Christmas. Natasha, shuddering, said it was quite cold enough for a full graveyard.

'No! No!' cried Kidder. '"Green Christmas fills the grave-yard", that's what I always say.'

She nodded brightly round the car and her husband agreed with her.

'That's right, Kidder,' he said, slipping his clutch slightly, bowling out of the white-painted gate of Bayleyside, turning South along the Tame Valley. '"Green December fills the churchyard." Now then, dear, what are you doing this morning? Where shall I drop you?'

Kidder was wearing a squirrel coat with a brightly checked suit and a very dressy hat. She sighed and lay back and re-arranged baskets and wraps and scarves around her.

'Well,' she said, embarking happily on a description of her day's activities, 'of course I have the turkey to pick up ... and twelve more Christmas Cards to buy and send. Nutson, Mawd and Pander had some awfully cute photographs of Beauty Spots ... I ran out of the Official County Borough Council ones,' she went on happily, turning to Tom Atkins; 'with the picture of you in your robes and chains of office and the little bow of Newchester regimental ribbon—'

'Good heavens!' said Miriam involuntarily. It was seldom that Miriam ever addressed any remark to Kidder. Kidder now turned to her gratefully. Beyond the windows the landscape rolled away towards Newchester. The line of trees beside the road were warped and stunted by other Decembers. The snow lay in faint patches on the grass.

'Yes?' said Kidder.

Miriam's mind thrashed around, searching for a way out of her difficulty that would not be rude to her hostess. The car was a little warm world in itself, apart from the world.

'I was just thinking,' said Miriam eventually, 'of that conversation we had the first night Natasha and I were staying with you. Do you remember at all? At dinner. Hampton Court said the best way to murder anyone would be to take them out in a rowing-boat on a dark night.'

Bright white signposts flickered against dark woods. The hedges below them were purple. The snow in the middle of the road had turned brown in a double track.

'I certainly remember,' said Tom Atkins, with a thick cosy chuckle. 'And I remember thinking too, at the time, how little we all know ourselves. Because, d'you see, if ever there was a lad would have to commit murder with a few thousand people looking on, Hampton Court is the boy.'

The sky was sullen with a threat of heavy snow to come. The sun must be struggling up behind curtains of thick mist and fog.

'I am so *sure*,' said Natasha, 'that you are right. But what motive could anyone *ever* have for killing another person? It is always worrying me. Unless, of course, they are mad people,' she added vaguely, looking out of her window.

Her breath made a little fog of its own on the glass, within the world, yet not of it.

'Oh,' said Mr Atkins briskly, 'jealousy, ma'am. Jealousy and passion and hate. And greed. The usual things.'

'The Seven Deadly Sins,' said Miriam gently. 'Lust and anger. Any of them, in fact, barring sloth.'

She blew on her mittened hand.

'I think people usually do it for money,' said Kidder suddenly, surprisingly. 'Money and security. Financial security, I mean.'

The car was no longer cosy. Kidder's voice was rough and passionate, altogether too unacademic for the subject under discussion. There was a moment of disquiet when Natasha felt the skin on her shoulder-blades crawl gently. The world within the world was breaking up.

'Goodness,' said Miriam, sucking her thumb through her mitten, '*that* doesn't sound a good reason to me. Security is just a state of mind. You don't get *that* by killing someone.'

The envelope of peace that had been torn by Kidder's hysteria re-formed itself among them, restored by Miriam's amiable drawl.

'*You* can't, maybe,' said Mr Atkins. 'But our Kidder *could*. I expect that is what she means.'

He laid his hand in its babyish woollen glove on his wife's. She sat very still. Natasha was instantly aware that this gesture had quietened the atmosphere.

II

The dress rehearsal began at 2 p.m. and fell very flat indeed.

The theatre was packed, but with a 'paper' audience. The little gold houselights and the white paint, the charming Regency interior seemed a mockery this afternoon. No theatre should ever house such people. Sitting on the tip-up red velveteen seats, where on Boxing afternoon there would be tier upon tier of white-socked children, were reporters, theatre cleaners, cloakroom attendants and their relations. Naturally, because they had not paid for the seats, they were as *blasé* as hell. Their lack of enthusiasm presently communicated itself to everyone in the company. Everyone gave a bad performance.

Vivienne Gresham, as Hampton Court said to anyone who cared to listen (and this was usually Miriam Birdseye), was quite filthily bad and her every word deserved to be her last.

'If this goes on, Miss Birdseye,' he hissed, standing in the wings, 'I shall sack her and leave it to your good nature to step into the breach. Look at her now! She deserves to be *murdered*.'

Vivienne Gresham, dressed in black with white ruffles at throat and wrist, and a good deal of imperfectly powdered white wig hanging down the back, was having an altercation (in rhyming couplets) with Miss Esmeralda Greenaway, The Fairy Queen of Starry Nights. Vivienne Gresham, for some reason best known to herself, had hitherto been quite inaudible to the audience, who were starting to say such things as 'Speak up, can't you?' and 'Ten to One on Old Mother Riley.'

Miss Greenaway was saying, quite chattily:

> *"Tis plain this magic Princess has your heart,*
> *Now listen, Prince. You'll win her, 'spite of art.*
> *Send messengers to ride o'er land and sea –*
> *Where'er the slipper fits, why then 'tis she.'*

The orchestra in the background moaned steadily away at a waltz called 'Hearts and Flowers'.

'She's damnable, *damnable!*' said Hampton Court very loudly, and was clearly overheard by everyone in the theatre. 'I'll not stand for her another day!'

Prince Charming never replied to the Fairy Queen. Vivienne Gresham halted in her tracks, glared across at the wings where Hampton stood, and then marched briskly up to him.

There was deadly silence.

She then struck him a heavy blow across the cheek and returned to the centre of the stage.

'—!' said Hampton Court, rubbing his cheek. He stood

there a second. Then he turned. He left Miriam alone in the wings. He went away. And it must be admitted he, too, went with murder in his heart.

III

Five minutes before this Harry DeFreeze sat in his dressing-room. His shaking hand plucked at his flat, thin hair. He was writing a letter. Harry drove the pen sadly up and down across the paper. It was horrible, yellowish paper, with little faint red lines ruled on it. Harry hated it. The pen did not work well. It sputtered and spat and flung up great thick drops of ink, like black blood.

> *For a long time, Viv* (wrote Harry), *I have been quite fed up. I know I got my divorce and that ought to have been enough. I should have cut adrift from you. I should not of stayed, watching you torture me with Banjo and hundreds. But I couldn't do it.*
>
> *I suppose I loved you once, Viv, I can't remember. It is all so sad. But I am sick of you and the mess you make of other people's lives.*
>
> *You are a callous bitch, that's all, and I'm going to end it, once for all.*

Poor Harry DeFreeze licked up the little shiny envelope and addressed it to Miss Gresham. He made a blot. A tear fell on it. It ran slowly down, smearing the envelope. He was very, very sorry for himself. He went out into the passage and walked towards Vivienne's dressing-room. He pushed the door and looked in. He hated her bitterly.

There was no one there. The place smelt slightly of stale powder and Guinness and grease-paint and sweat and shoes. There was a pair of shoes lying in the middle of the floor. There was a photograph of Banjo on the dressing-table. Harry hated everyone until he was consumed by it and his blood seemed to be running white hot. Two tears quivered on his cheeks. He must not waver in his resolve. He controlled his chin. He saw his face in the looking-glass as he propped up the envelope. It was weak, weak. Sick and weak. He felt very ill, but he *must* do it.

'I *will* do it,' whispered Harry DeFreeze.

He stepped out into the passage. He went along towards the light board.

IV

On the stage the story went on. Vivienne Gresham was about to sing her number 'Searching for Love, Searching for Love', and then set out to look for the lady who fitted the magic slipper. The Fairy Queen sank down through the floor on the stage-trap platform, singing bright advice to Prince Charming as she did so. Vivienne Gresham remained on the stage, at the top of an utterly meaningless flight of steps, heavily illuminated by limes and therefore slightly blinded by them. This was the first full lighting rehearsal.

The script called for her to approach the footlights, still singing, until she was joined by the Twenty-four Tottenham Tots. Everyone then suddenly burst out singing 'Blue Skies, Nothing But Blue Skies From Now On.' To reach the Tots, Vivienne had to walk over that part of the stage where the stage-trap platform (returned from its journey with the Fairy Queen), was let into the floor.

But the platform had not returned. In the centre of the stage there was a neat and yawning hole, unnoticed by anyone.

Vivienne Gresham walked straight down the steps, followed all the way by a little pool of limelight, singing hard. She crashed, head over heels, through the open trap into the sub-stage. And, as it happens, she broke her neck.

BOOK TWO

———

ENTER MIRIAM, DISGUISED AS A PRINCIPAL BOY

Confusion followed this horrid moment in the Theatre Royal. The curtain was rung down, ordered by Hampton Court. He (everyone afterwards said) kept his head remarkably well. Two mothers, however, of the Tottenham Tots, who were waiting in the wings to wrap overcoats round their children at the end of 'Blue Skies, Nothing But Blue Skies', became hysterical. They collapsed, weeping at the dangers of Life on Tour. 'Only wish we'd gone into *Where the Rainbow Ends* at Shepherd's Bush Empire,' they said to each other tearfully.

The stage manager, Tony Gresham, did not behave any too well, either. The audience could hear him screaming, 'Mum, Mum, I swear it wasn't my fault, I swear I didn't do it! Mum! Mum!' long after the safety curtain had clanged into place and the police ambulance had driven up and the *Newchester Evening Mail* had burst into the building through the stage door to take flashlight photographs.

'I am olways thinking what *wonnderful* opportunities there are being for people to be behaving so magnificently in these moments,' said Natasha. She was holding delicately to the banisters of the stone staircase that linked the dressing-rooms with the stage. The naked electric light glinted on her beautifully groomed hair and more vaguely and more occasionally on glimpses of pale-blue satin under her dark woollen tartan dressing-gown. (Natasha had a great many dressing-gowns, but this tartan one was the warmest of them.)

'You mean behave like ladies and gentlemen?' asked Miriam beside her.

Our two friends were shocked, but it must be admitted that they enjoyed the excitement of this moment; and they were conscious of sweeping through it with gloriously tightened nerves.

'I suppose I do,' said Natasha, and she sighed.

'Look at Tony Gresham, for example,' said Miriam.

He came weeping towards them. His face was white and drawn, and tears streamed most despairingly down it. His hair was covered with dust. His hands hung loosely at his sides, useless, white as pale fishes.

'Tony weeps very easily, however,' said Natasha, for Miriam's benefit. 'Be blowing your nose, Tony.'

'Haven't a hanky,' said the stage manager and sniffed against the back of his hand. He helplessly spread dirt across his face with his knuckles. 'Oh dear, oh dear, oh dear.'

And he sank on the stairs at their feet and put his head on his knees. The heavy tramp of feet, moving rhythmically, taking the same length of stride, vibrated the stone staircase. Tony lifted his ravaged face.

'What is it?' he said. 'What are those footsteps?'

'It's the police, dear,' said Miriam, comfortably.

'Oh!' said Tony, and suddenly stared fearfully from one to

the other. 'Where will they take her?' he cried wildly. 'Where will they take her?'

Miriam dropped on the steps beside him and put her kind long arm round his neck.

'Darling Tony,' she said. 'Poor sweet. Please don't cry so, darling. Look, your eyes will be awful tomorrow. She's OK. Honestly.'

'But she's dead,' wailed Tony. His head fell with a thump on Miriam's utterly unmotherly bosom. 'Dead,' he repeated. And he suddenly looked up into her face with a gay, little boy smile. 'And I bet you'll be Prince Charming,' he said.

II

The drama dragged itself out, lengthened and continued far beyond the end of the time the rehearsal had been billed to stop. The police ambulance left, its electric bell rattling. A hundred Christmas shoppers, with gaping mouths, paused to wonder what was going on. The wardrobe mistress, Mrs Furbinger, saying she had a son of her own, took Tony Gresham home to his lodgings and gave him aspirins and warm milk. The Tottenham Tots then drove off in their char-à-banc (the driver of the vehicle had had a free pass for the rehearsal and he was angry because he had been balked from seeing the whole show), and Natasha slowly changed, announcing as she did so that her dress needed alteration. Miriam 'talked' to her during all this, which meant that she sat in the dressing-room in silent sympathy. Then, feeling that their feet did not belong to them, they walked numbly upstairs to the stage door.

Outside the winter night was wreathing the street in brown

and amber fog, lit by the street lamps. The sun had gone and darkness was falling from the sky, hazy and beautiful where it reached the street.

Here stood their host, Mr Tom Atkins, in deep conversation with a big policeman. The policeman was in plain clothes. He carried a brief-case with A.P.R. on it in small letters.

'Sorry to trouble you, Mr Atkins, sir,' he was saying as Natasha and Miriam approached, 'but the point is we, that's to say, the *Crown*, you know, we always like to have a witness of some social *standing* . . . '

'Who said Lord Mayors didn't count?' hissed Miriam in Natasha's ear.

'Sh . . . ' said Natasha.

The policeman stepped politely to one side and Tom Atkins showed his teeth at Miriam and Natasha. Natasha was startled to see the grief and horror and distress in his eyes. She had not known that he was so sensitive.

'I won't keep you, ladies,' said Tom Atkins, and turned towards the big policeman. A strip of neat yellow moustache in the middle of the policeman's face looked like pig's bristles.

'Sergeant Robinson,' said Tom Atkins, and waved a hand at Miriam and Natasha. With this unconventional introduction they had to be content. A flame of interest leapt in Sergeant Robinson's eyes.

'Well, I *was* there during the whole performance,' went on Tom Atkins, 'but at the time M-M-Miss Gresham fell – I *think* I must have been going through the pass-door. I heard someone *scream*, certainly . . . '

Tom Atkins paused and looked desperately worried. He did

not seem to be searching for words. He seemed to be puzzled about something.

'That would have been Dandini who screamed,' said Miriam. 'A very hysterical lady.'

The cold fog from the street seeped in towards them and Tom Atkins coughed, turning away his head. On the pavement snow glimmered faintly.

'Dandini was screaming?' said Sergeant Robinson, wrinkling ginger eyebrows. 'Who is Dandini?'

'Rather an unpleasant woman called Marylyn Franklyn,' said Miriam.

Natasha said nothing, but she continued to stare at Tom Atkins with enormous eyes. They were like pools in her milky face.

'Very well, Sergeant,' said Tom Atkins. 'If you think I'll *help*, you can call on me for your inquest.'

'Certainly will help, Your Worship,' said Sergeant Robinson. He suddenly stood to attention. 'Per'aps you'll be kind enough to call at the station some time and sign a statement.'

Outside, very gently, snow began to fall. Flakes swirled and scattered in the stage-door light. Sergeant Robinson, who had been outside the door, stepped under cover. Flakes of white became drops of water on his collar.

'What time, Sergeant?' said Tom Atkins. 'Remember this is Christmas Eve.'

The traffic seemed to hush as the snow fell. Cars hooted, and somewhere a tram clanged.

'Very well, sir,' said Sergeant Robinson. 'As soon as ever you can. Right away would be fine. Get it over with. *If* you can spare the time?'

There was a new smell in the fog, brittle and rather exciting. Yet the evening seemed warmer and more comfortable.

'Shall have to make time, shan't we, ladies?' said Tom Atkins. 'Since the Crown demands it.'

He smiled his tom cat's smile. Miriam shrugged her shoulders. Tom Atkins murmured something about 'picking Mrs Atkins up at Marny's'.

It was this moment that Hampton Court chose to come jittering and swearing out of the dark passage behind them. He was still dressed in vivid pink plush jodhpurs as Buttons, the Baron's servant.

'For God's sake, Miss Birdseye,' he said, roughly, 'I need you. Come and help me. This flipping Marylyn Franklyn is in sobbing hee-bees in her dressing-room on account of how I've made you Prince Charming and not *her*. Damn it. It's the only *thing* will save this show.'

'This show has the kiss of death on it in any case,' said Miriam.

'Oh, for Jeez sake, can it, can't you? That your idea of a bright crack?' said Hampton Court.

'I do *think*,' said Miriam, dangerously, 'that you might have asked me first, before telling old Franklyn. I could have *told* you this'd happen ... '

But the light in Miriam's eyes was brilliant and exciting, and it had been put there by something more than anger.

III

'I will be coming with Mr Atkins to the police-station then,' said Natasha, with her sweetest smile.

Sergeant Robinson jumped a little, but said that he was charmed, he was sure.

'Anything,' said Mr Atkins, 'to hurry you up. Mrs Atkins an' me, *we* don't want our Christmas dinner spoilt giving evidence. We have Christmas dinner midday tomorrow,' he said, turning to Miriam and Natasha. 'When are you goin' to have the inquest?' he concluded, stepping out into the snow. Natasha followed him and Sergeant Robinson followed Natasha.

'Soon as possible, sir,' said Sergeant Robinson. 'Boxing Day, most likely.'

'Quite so, quite so,' said Tom Atkins.

Natasha and he paced away with the Sergeant. The two men walked one on either side of her. She trotted a little to keep up with them. Sergeant Robinson looked as though he would like to stroke her. Miriam and Hampton Court stood under the stage-door lamp and watched them go.

And then Timothy Shelly suddenly loomed out of the ground at their feet. He looked untidy, as usual, and he wore no overcoat. One ragged curl of beige hair fell forward on his forehead and he tossed it back.

'Where is she going?' he said urgently. 'Where are they taking her?' His voice cracked slightly and he snatched Miriam by the arm.

'Hey!' said Miriam crossly, and shook it off.

'*Why* is Natasha going away with those men?' said Timothy Shelly.

'To the police-station,' said Hampton Court maliciously, watching Timothy Shelly through eyes like a snake's surrounded with intricate scales. 'For questioning,' he said, and turned away.

85

Timothy Shelly gasped and held himself up by the door jamb. He looked as though he were going to be sick.

IV

The police-station stands four square to the whole of Newchester. It is a big white building, with fire-escapes and a little collection of flats for married policemen and their wives and children. It is built around a courtyard that is a suntrap. During the late war many young gentlemen and ladies in the A.R.P. sunned themselves here, and there were some strange lobsterish forms to be seen in the lunch break, sitting about on the running-boards of cars.

This Christmas Eve, however, when Natasha and Tom Atkins and the Sergeant walked across it, the courtyard was quite dark. The snow lay loosely on unattractive packing-cases and on an old motor tyre which someone had left in a corner. Their feet left neat footprints, hardly discernible against the whiteness. Natasha sniffed the brittle air. A crystal of snow melted in her hair.

'This way, miss,' said Sergeant Robinson, unnecessarily holding her delicately under the elbow, leading her under an arch. A door swung abruptly inwards and showed bright lights and warmth and noise and stuffiness. Chains of Christmas paper in pink and yellow had been draped, criss-cross, about the reception office. There was a nasty pink and purple paper bell pendulant from the electric light. There were several policemen with their helmets off, sitting among furniture that consisted mostly of strips of teak and mahogany. There were also some green tin filing cabinets. One of these policemen looked up as they came in. He had a yellow pencil behind one ear.

'The Inspector wants you when you're through with the Theatre Royal, Swiss,' he said. 'Oh, and the *Evening News* want some dope about what they're calling "the Death Fall".'

'OK,' said Robinson laconically. 'Important?'

Tom Atkins, walking beside Natasha, suddenly bristled. Natasha wondered if he would have made any more impression on these policemen if he had worn his chains and robes of office.

'Apparently,' said the policeman with the yellow pencil, 'robbery with vi'lence out towards Gospond an' a case of grievous bodily harm out Faunton way. Oh, and that book of tickets you had for the Police Ball, Sandy wants the vouchers.'

Natasha stared around her, fascinated by the lack of interest in crime. The Christmas decorations were inclined to add to this impression, if anything.

'OK,' said Robinson again. 'In here, please, Your Worship.'

His Worship, Tom Atkins, Lord Mayor of the City of Newchester on the River Tame, took a deep breath and held his hat against his chest as though he were entering a tomb. Instead, they came into a comfortable little office, warmed by a roaring gas-fire, decorated with pale-blue streamers and several sprigs of mistletoe. There was a cluster of Christmas cards (chiefly dogs wearing tartan bows, with pipes in their mouths) on the little iron mantelpiece above the gas-fire.

Sergeant Robinson took off his hat and his belted tweed overcoat and hung them on a hat-rack shaped like a jungle tree. Tom Atkins went on wearing his overcoat defiantly. There was a knee-hole desk in a corner of the room. Robinson sat down at it now. The telephone jangled harshly and he picked it up. He waved them to two hard chairs that faced the desk.

'*Jack-in-Office*,' said Tom Atkins quite distinctly, although under his breath, as he sat down.

Natasha looked at him startled. The look of distress in his eyes had gone. A clear, hard hatred was fixed there. They seemed suddenly hard and sharp and suspicious.

'Why?' said Natasha. 'I thought as being Lord Mayor you would be so keen on all of this? You and the Magistrates? Is that not so?'

The Sergeant went on talking to his Inspector on the telephone. The gas-fire went on roaring. The evening, dark and impenetrable as ink, stared through the window-pane. Sometimes a soft flurry of snow beat against the glass as gently as doves' wings.

Natasha wondered why Tom Atkins suddenly hated the Sergeant. He seemed a good and competent man. He seemed on the side of Law and Order. He had quite a nice little ginger moustache. He seemed sincere and reliable. Natasha was already, she thought, quite fond of him.

Sergeant Robinson put down the telephone in his sincere, reliable way, and began to take Tom Atkins' statement. To do this he filled in a form, writing carefully, with his head cocked on one side.

'But look *here*,' said Tom Atkins, suddenly very excited and cross; 'is all this necessary? I mean, until the coroner has determined how M-Miss Gresham died, you won't want any statements, will you?'

The gas-fire seemed to grow hotter and hotter. Natasha restlessly crossed one beautiful leg over the other.

'Seems more satisfactory to have it on this form, sir. Then I have something I can go on.'

Sergeant Robinson's tone could hardly have been more deprecating, more aware of His Worship the Lord Mayor and all that he implied. The inside of Natasha's calf began to burn and she recrossed her legs.

'But it seems so unnecessary. I mean, *surely* I'll only have to tell the story in my own words to the coroner on Boxing Day ... you only picked on me because I was—'

'Lord Mayor?' said Sergeant Robinson.

'Quite so,' said Tom Atkins.

'It makes it all smoother for the coroner, sir, who will probably be Bertram Kelvin, K.C. He *likes* statements. I'll take it all down in shorthand if you like, and if you find it easier, sir? If this other will hold up your arrangements at all?'

He was *all* deference and sincerity. Natasha wondered why Tom Atkins was making such a fuss. Perhaps he had wanted all the policemen to spring to attention when he came in.

The hot little box of a room suddenly was filled with a sense of panic and conflict, while Tom Atkins wriggled inside his overcoat, giving the impression that he was trapped. Natasha almost felt she had ceased to exist. She became, in her mind's eye, as small as a fly on the wall. Sergeant Robinson, his smooth ginger head bent over paper on his desk, wrote rather sideways, twisted in his chair. Tom Atkins was acutely uncomfortable and sweated freely.

'You are an *ass*,' murmured Natasha. 'Not to be taking off your overcoat.'

'"On the evening of the twenty-fourth,"' droned Sergeant Robinson, his head on one side, the tip of his clean, pink tongue showing between his teeth as he pursued his upstrokes and down-strokes, '"I was standing at the back of the pit-stalls watching the performance" . . . '

'It was more similar to a dress rehearsal,' said Natasha.

'Quite so, quite so,' said Tom Atkins.

'"And I moved down the side gangway of the stalls towards the pass-door" . . . Why did you do that?' said Sergeant Robinson, looking up.

'I don't know . . . Why the hell shouldn't I? I wanted to go behind, I suppose . . . I can't remember,' said Tom Atkins all in one breath.

Sergeant Robinson stared at him.

'These two ladies,' Tom Atkins began to explain, 'who are staying with me . . . they are *performers* in the pantomime, you see. I meant to find out when – er – that's to say, what *time* they would be ready to come out to Bayleyside. Er – my house . . . ' he concluded lamely. 'Can I take my overcoat off?'

'Oh, do so,' said Sergeant Robinson airily. 'Do so by all means. '"Towards the pass-door,"' he wrote, '"with the intention of asking the two ladies who are staying with me when they might be ready to go home." And then what, sir?'

'Then there was this terrible scream.'

'Dandini,' said Natasha, in her slow grave voice.

'*Before* you went through the pass-door, or after?' said Sergeant Robinson.

There was a pause while Tom Atkins looked unhappy and twitched his tie straight. Then he took a deep breath and said, '*Before*,' as though he were spitting out a mouthful of some unpleasant food. Sergeant Robinson turned to Natasha.

'Madam,' he said, 'you are a performer in this piece. You must know the Theatre Royal pretty well by now?'

Natasha drooped her lovely head.

'What goes on inside the pass-door?'

'What is going *on*?' Natasha was indignant, as though Sergeant Robinson had accused her of nameless indecencies. He grinned and played with his fountain-pen.

'Yes, what *is* there just inside it? What stands there, in the way of scenery and that?'

Natasha thought for a little while.

'It is the prompter's corner,' she said finally. 'The switchboard. I think the switchboard for the lights is on that side.'

'Yes, miss,' said Sergeant Robinson, 'it is.' He bowed his head and looked at Tom Atkins. 'Switchboard works footlights, floodlights, batons and also controls the star trapdoor an' platform,' he went on, in a quick gabble. He was reading from a piece of paper. 'See what I'm gettin' at, sir?'

'I might if you told me,' said Tom Atkins angrily.

'You are perhaps meaning did Tom – er – Lord Mayor – er – did Mister Atkins see anyone just inside the door when he came through?' said Natasha excitedly. 'Because otherwise you must be blaming the accident on negligence of stage manager (Tony Gresham, her son, by the way), or assistant stage manager, Miss Breath ...'

Natasha spoke very fast and her eyes shone. The Sergeant watched her very carefully.

'Rather unpleasant woman in navy slacks,' he said slowly. 'Miss Breath wasn't i/c lights, Gresham tells me. She was i/c props. All the same, you have something there, miss. I must congratulate you on your—' But upon what Sergeant Robinson was about to congratulate Natasha we shall never know, because at that moment there was a thundering of feet outside in the passage and a heavy bang on the door. Timothy Shelly burst into the room. His face was flushed by the cold evening. His hair was hopelessly tousled. His blue eyes were blazing.

'I swear Natasha didn't touch that switch,' he said. 'I swear Natasha didn't. I was standing right where I could see Natasha all the time and I *know* . . . '

'But surely,' said Tom Atkins restlessly tucking his short legs into safety under his chair, 'surely the coroner will bring in a verdict of Death by Misadventure or mishap or whatever you call it? And even if the whole thing *is* proved to be due to the gross negligence of the boy, Anthony Gresham, he would never be charged with manslaughter? Why ... ' Tom Atkins, who had been addressing Natasha and Timothy Shelly and the Sergeant as though they were a public meeting, once more became human and nervous and fretful. 'Why, he's her son ... ' he ended shakily, and blew his nose on a white pocket handkerchief.

'Excuse *me*,' said Sergeant Robinson, 'I think we need a window open.'

And he got up and opened the little window at his back. There was a small ridge of snow, blurring along the ledge. Beyond it was fog and street lights and street noises, the sound of traffic passing.

Timothy Shelly slowly regained his composure. His breathing became normal as he blushed and moved from foot to foot.

'Why, come and sit *down*,' said the Sergeant, returning to

his own swivel chair. 'Kind of you to come along to help me. Really most public-spirited. *Do* sit down.'

He indicated another uncomfortable little chair with a grand gesture. Timothy Shelly dropped into it. His manner was curiously compounded of defiance and eagerness, and surprise at the intensity of his own feelings. He looked up humbly at Natasha, who regrettably winked at him with the eye furthest from Mr Atkins. Timothy Shelly instantly laughed and put up his hand to hide his mouth.

'Now then, sir,' said Sergeant Robinson, drawing another sheet of paper towards him; 'your name, if you please? Full name.'

'Timothy Bentinck Shelly of Dranrocket, County Cork,' said Timothy.

'Ah, an Irishman,' said Sergeant Robinson pleasantly.

'Certainly not,' said Timothy Shelly sharply. 'I'm an Englishman. I'm just giving you my permanent address, that's all. It's my mother's house.'

'Ah!' said the Sergeant. 'I see. Occupation?'

'Er – *writer*,' said Timothy nervously.

'Journalist,' said the Sergeant firmly. Timothy made a movement of protest, but checked himself. 'Married or single?' said the Sergeant.

'Widower,' said Timothy rudely. 'You can work it out for yourself.'

Natasha noticed with some surprise that Timothy also seemed angry and miserable when closely questioned by the Sergeant. His statement, translated from his uneasy monosyllabic replies into the euphonious roll of police-station English, said that Timothy Shelly, who had been backstage during the performance, because of his interest in the *production*, had been sitting on the stone stairs that connected the dressing-rooms with the stage, reading Tolstoy's *War and Peace*. At this point he glared anxiously at Sergeant Robinson and dared him to suggest that a stone theatre staircase was not the best place in the world to sit to read one of its greatest masterpieces.

'And you didn't move?' he suggested.

'No,' said Timothy Shelly crossly.

'Until?'

'Until I heard Miss Franklyn scream from the stage. Mrs DuVivien was already in the wings waiting for the orchestra cue for her dance—'

'Mrs DuVivien?' said Sergeant Robinson.

'This is me,' said Natasha demurely.

'I *see*,' said Sergeant Robinson with a (Timothy Shelly thought) maddening grin of complete understanding.

'So I came on to the stage as well,' went on Timothy Shelly lamely.

Sergeant Robinson now leant back in his chair looking at him brightly, with his head on one side. He did not write anything down.

'And there were lots of people milling about and shoving, and that damn' woman screaming and Hampton Court—'

'Ah,' said Sergeant Robinson abruptly, 'it's Mr Court's production, isn't it?'

'In a manner of speaking it is,' said Tom Atkins.

'What do you mean "in a manner of speaking"?' said Sergeant Robinson.

'Well, I'm financially involved too,' said Tom Atkins. 'In fact,' he ended, 'mine is the backing.'

'The power and the glory,' murmured Timothy Shelly.

But there was quite a long pause in the little room. Everybody moved their feet and Timothy Shelly blew his nose, explaining to Natasha as he did so, that he hated warm rooms with draughts shooting through them from open windows, and he was sorry he had made such an ass of himself.

'I thought you needed rescuing,' he said and looked sidelong at Natasha, like a bird. His hair stood up on the top of his head in a fawn cockatoo's crest.

'No,' said Natasha.

'So you stand to lose a packet by tonight's little carry-on?' Sergeant Robinson prompted Tom Atkins pleasantly.

'Actually the reverse,' cut in Timothy Shelly. 'Miss Birdseye will make a *far* better Prince Charming than Miss Gresham ever did.'

'So far as I know,' snapped Tom Atkins, snubbing him, 'Miss Birdseye has not yet promised to fill the gap.'

Outside some shrill little voices were suddenly raised in screaming and breathless information about 'Good King Wenceslas'.

'How odd it is being,' said Natasha inconsequently, 'that this old man who is once looking out of a window and that is absolutely oll I know about him.'

'He was deep and crisp and even for a start,' said Timothy.

'No, no,' said Natasha. 'That was his page.'

'So there you were in the dark,' said Sergeant Robinson ponderously, turning back to Timothy who jumped nervously. 'Do you know where the switchboard was in relation to yourself?'

'I think so,' said Timothy carefully.

'Could you draw a plan?'

'It might not be accurate.'

'Well, *try*.'

Sergeant Robinson suddenly seemed a little fed-up with his public-spirited witnesses, who were too inclined to make facetious jokes among themselves about carol singers. Tom Atkins said again that it seemed an awful trouble to take over an *accident*.

'I am expecting,' said Natasha gently, 'that Sergeant Robinson has been having offul trouble in his time with insurance companies.'

Sergeant Robinson looked startled and grateful, and Timothy Shelly drew his little plan.

II

'Now,' said Sergeant Robinson looking at Timothy Shelly's plan which he had finished drawing, neatly and very fast.

He had long, brown hands with strong thin fingers and blunt, sensitive fingertips. They were attractive.

'Now,' said Sergeant Robinson again. 'This *lever* – it works the trapdoor, or platform, or whatever it is that wasn't there, which Miss Gresham fell through?'

'The star trap,' said Natasha. 'Yes, it does. It is being rather big and stiff and old-fashioned, like a railway brake lever. It creaks rather.'

'Does it?' said Sergeant Robinson casually. 'Didn't anyone ever order it oiled?'

'I do not know,' said Natasha.

'I believe Hampton Court did,' volunteered Tom Atkins. 'He mentioned it at dinner the other night.'

'Did he?' said Natasha.

'Perhaps you weren't there,' said Timothy kindly.

'It was certainly oiled today all right,' said Sergeant Robinson.

Natasha was silent, furrowing her lovely brow. That something was not quite *right*, somehow, she was now positive. She already knew that one night, in the dark, very soon, she would wake, her eyes wide with fierce surmise, and realize all that had not, at the time, appeared to her significant. Darling Natasha knew her sympathies and her sensitivities far too well. She sighed now and brought her mind back with a jerk to Timothy Shelly. He was putting the names and approximate positions of the various persons on the plan.

As Timothy Shelly put in his last spot and wrote alongside it in elegant calligraphy 'Vivienne Gresham', a clock outside struck the half-hour.

'My oath,' said Tom Atkins, standing up, 'half past five. Must get along. Our family retainer will give notice else. May we go, Sergeant?'

'Do, do, by all means, Your Worship,' said Sergeant Robinson smoothly. 'And if you remember anything else, and you, sir, and you, madam, just pop in and ask for me. Robinson, they call me. That's right, old Swiss Robinson will see you through.'

Timothy Shelly gave a little gasp.

'Swiss' Robinson stood up. Much to Natasha's alarm he now offered her a large pink hand to be shaken.

'You'll have to sign that in court again, sir,' he said chattily to Tom Atkins, holding on to the door handle as they went out into the merciful draughtiness of the corridor. 'We might have occasion to use your plan, too,' he said patronizingly to Timothy Shelly.

Timothy Shelly merely scowled. But as Natasha afterwards said to Miriam, this was really rather sweet of him.

III

The journey back to Bayleyside was exhilarating.

When they reached the Theatre Royal stage door they were told lugubriously by George that 'Mr Court and Miss Birdseye 'as went off a long time ago. Went 'ome, in fact, in Mr Court's car.' The fact that they had not, therefore, to deal with Hampton, augmented by the feeling that they had recently been released from prison, loosened all their tongues, and until they picked up Kidder they chattered merrily to one another about nothing at all. Even when they had Kidder with them they continued for a long time to be gay, vying with one another in describing the accident to her.

'Where were you, Mother, when it happened?' said Tom Atkins, and turned his head to look at his wife.

'Yes, yes, how did you first hear? *Do* tell us,' said Timothy Shelly.

'Be making a story of it,' said Natasha.

They both leant eagerly forward. There was a great tension and gaiety in the air. Kidder Atkins moved her shoulder restlessly.

'I think I was outside Nutson, Mawd and Pander,' began Kidder slowly.

'How curious,' said Natasha.

'Quite a lot of people often are,' said Timothy Shelly, laughing wildly.

'Sh!' said Tom Atkins.

'Yes. That's right; I told you. I had to buy Christmas cards for special people, you know, with skis and that on them—'

'Nuts. I bet they are all old-fashioned sailing-ships saying "A Cargo of Good Cheer for Xmas",' whispered Timothy Shelly.

'And some suitable for *anyone*, without verses,' said Kidder. 'Or mottos. And I saw a man come dashing out of the street where the stage door is. I never can remember the name of that street, Tom. What is it again?'

Tom Atkins growled something that no one could hear.

'That's right,' said Kidder; 'and he came bawling out, screaming for a doctor. A doctor or a policeman. That was what he said he wanted.'

'Seems reasonable enough,' said Timothy.

'Oh, I don't know. Not in the middle of Christmas shopping. Well, I stared. And Mrs Doctor Symington, who was with me, *she* stared. And Mr Nutson, who had carried the cards up from the basement and was having a chat with us both, he stared too. And Mrs Doctor Symington said she was a doctor's wife.'

'She would,' growled Tom Atkins. 'Snob.'

Natasha was startled.

'Oh, Gladys is a decent enough sort, dear, and after all, doctors are wonderful, fighting for humanity and all . . .'

There was a pause, punctuated only by the purr of the engine and the noise of the horn as Tom Atkins hooted for a lonely crossroads. The country, as usual, was obscured by the light mist on the windscreen and the car windows.

'On second thoughts,' murmured Timothy Shelly, 'I bet the Christmas cards were rabbits dressed as human beings washing each other and putting each other to bed.'

'Very nasty,' said Natasha gravely. 'Or ladies in crinolines with watering-cans. Or stage coaches.'

'Oh, I'll give you stage *coaches*,' said Timothy. 'I mean they are "downright Dickensy", now aren't they? How I loathe Dickens. Damn his eyes!'

At this point Kidder Atkins sprang round from the front seat in a frightful rage. Natasha, who thought for a moment that she was about to swing into a violent defence of *Little Dorrit*, was horrified to see that there were two enormous tears glittering in her eyes. Her handsome face seemed slightly parboiled and Natasha suddenly wondered if she and Mrs Doctor Symington and Mr Nutson had all lunched together, and lunched rather well.

'Oh, all right then, *mock*!' she shouted confusedly. 'It may seem all right to *you* that there's a woman dead in the Theatre Royal, and other people mayn't have good taste like you have, but other people think Christmas sacred, so there, and the thought matters most and, speaking for myself, I am terribly upset for Vivienne Gresham and that poor young man, her son. No matter what other people may be—'

'Here, I say, old lady,' said Tom Atkins in the shocked silence that followed this little speech. Kidder obviously had only stopped because she had run out of breath. She evidently had a lot of other things to say. Timothy Shelly opened his mouth to apologize and pacify her.

'Oh, *you* needn't speak, you dirty Communist!' she cried explosively. 'Useless wastrel, living in other people's houses, eating their meat ration.'

'Here, Kidder, calm down, can it, old girl,' said Tom Atkins anxiously.

'And you're no better, Tom Atkins, filling our house with theatrical folks at Christmas. Yes, indeed. *You* know what's wrong, *you* know ...'

The silence in the car was now ghastly. Timothy Shelly asked Natasha in a low voice whether she thought Mrs Atkins was about to pick holes in her own scheme of interior decoration.

'It ought to be full of young folks, Tom, and you know it. Christmas is the children's festival ...'

And to everyone's horror, Kidder burst into muffled and unattractive sobs, weeping copiously into Tom Atkins' rough tweed sleeve which he now put round her. Driving clumsily with his other hand, he turned in at Bayleyside gates. He appeared unmoved, but in the windscreen Natasha could see the same look of fear and anger that she had observed in his eyes earlier in the police-station.

In the dark Timothy Shelly grabbed at Natasha's hand. His own was warm and dry and reassuring. They sat hand in hand all the way up the drive to the front door of Bayleyside.

When they got out of the car there was no fog and the stars were blazing like lamps. Timothy Shelly looked at Natasha in starlight as though he had never seen a human being before.

IV

Kidder ran away from them up the steps. She opened the big front door with a latchkey, fumbling a little with the lock and swearing to herself in the dark. She disappeared into the house and the door slammed behind her.

'I'll help you put the car away,' said Natasha and Timothy Shelly simultaneously.

'Thanks very much,' said Tom Atkins uneasily.

In silence they climbed back into the car and in silence they remained as it turned laboriously in the carriage sweep. The headlights stabbed a way through dark bushes and damp trees, until it stopped in the carriage house. Then Tom Atkins switched off the engine. They sat for a moment in complete silence. The garage was brilliantly lit and unfriendly. They might have been at the bottom of a coal-mine.

'Forgive the wife,' said Tom Atkins nervously.

He went on sitting behind the steering-wheel.

'When she gets like that she doesn't know what she says.'

'Oh, not at all,' said Timothy Shelly.

'She wanted children, you see,' said Tom Atkins. 'And we can't have any. And any little thing sets her off—'

'Like the accident at the Theatre Royal, for example?' said Timothy Shelly brightly.

'Yes, that's right,' said Tom Atkins heavily, switching out the lights. 'Any little thing.'

V

As they came out of the carriage house and made their way round the front of Bayleyside they were greeted by the glorious noise of untrained children's voices, singing perfectly in tune. It disturbed all their hearts. It was the carol singers from the village. They must have come up the drive when Tom drove them round to the garage. They were drawn up outside the front door in a semicircle. Their feet were lit by a pool of golden light from a hurricane lamp.

Natasha and Timothy stopped dead. Natasha was frozen by

beauty. Tom Atkins went solidly on, fumbling in his pocket and jingling slightly as he sorted out his change. Even this, however, did not spoil the moment.

The carol singers sang:

> *In Dulci Jubilo*
> *Now sing we all io . . .*
> *He, my love, my wonder,*
> *L'ith in precepio*
> *Like any sunbeam yonder.*
> *Alpha es et o.*

'Poor Kidder, poor Kidder,' said Timothy Shelly slowly. 'In her barren home.'

3

It is unsuitable to spend Christmas week in a house overshadowed by death. It is often done, of course, but this does not make it any easier. And when the death is both unnatural and violent there is an uncomfortable undertow of suspicion directed by the guests at one another, that can only be accentuated by paper hats and caps, Christmas trees, roast goose and exploding bombs containing 'Novelties and Jewels'.

At Bayleyside the week began with the Christmas midday dinner, when Tom Atkins drank a smooth half-bottle of Scotch whisky before dinner, and sat through it, unable to carve or say anything except 'Quite so, quite so.' Kidder kept up a flow of badinage that was even more distressing. It obviously rose from an unrealized passion for Timothy Shelly and showed itself chiefly in bickering over second helpings and excited demands for games of 'Hide and Seek' and 'Sardines'. Natasha dared not catch Miriam's eye. Miriam, when she was not murmuring her part over and over to herself under her breath, laughed heartily at Hampton Court.

Hampton, too, was in an advanced state of jitters about his unrehearsed Principal Boy. He had been drinking far too much. His face was a pale white, his speech was wildish and rather rude. His tongue (if anyone had wished to observe it) was furred. He swayed a little in his chair and cracked a walnut. He looked at Tom Atkins with snake's eyes.

'Peace on Earth an' Goodwill toward Men,' said Hampton. 'And that goes for the DeFreeze boys too.'

'Qui' so, quite so,' said Tom Atkins.

Banjo and Harry had been asked to dinner. They seemed fairly conscious that their odd little party had been reduced to two for ever. Banjo had taken everything in his stride and was enjoying himself hugely. He was pulling crackers with Kidder, showing all his teeth in a rush of sexual satisfaction, and quite often he touched anyone he could reach with the palm of his hand. No one but Banjo gained any satisfaction from this.

Harry DeFreeze on the other hand was deeply distressed. He sometimes said, 'I'm on the waggon,' in a low voice when he was offered a drink. Otherwise he said nothing at all. He sat silently by Miriam, furtively feeding pieces of turkey to the dogs.

'That's right,' said Banjo. He read aloud a terrible cracker motto about 'A kiss in the dark from a boy I know'. He reached forward a large white hand, covered with little black hairs, towards Kidder.

'Bet *you've* got some peace and goodwill at last in *your* homestead, eh, old Harry?' shouted Hampton Court. 'Cheaper buying shrouds than fur coats, eh?'

The conversation trailed away into an uncomfortable trickle. Timothy Shelly, his elbow conversationally propped among the glasses, told Natasha how to tie a Jock Scot.

'Eh?' said Harry DeFreeze. He dropped a nut on the floor and ducked his head. 'Eh? Didn't quite catch what you ... Haven't been quite the thing lately. Sorry. Bad company. Very.'

Tom Atkins might have been able to help with soothing interjections and speeches like 'Dry up, Hampton, old lad.' But his eyes were glazed and he swayed to and fro at the top of his own dinner table. Hampton continued briskly with his outrage.

'No, but seriously.' He pushed his plate aside and swigged at his glass, which now contained port. He glared round the table. His elbows were square amongst a wreckage of nutshells. 'We're all better off without Viv, aren't we? Harry gets some peace and saves a packet of dough. Banjo doesn't lose anything. Miss Birdseye gets a damn' fat part in a damn' fat panto. And *I* gain a very charming Principal Boy.'

Hampton rose to his feet. Miriam said nervously that 'Mum's tum was nothing like right.' Timothy Shelly gave Natasha some fascinating details of the hackles and topping of an eighteenth-century fly called 'The Black Dog'. Banjo DeFreeze pinched Kidder's knee. Harry DeFreeze and Tom Atkins remained immobile. Two large tears wandered down Harry's nose and splashed on to his dessert plate.

'*Ladies and Gentlemen*,' said Hampton Court firmly, looking up at the ceiling. 'Out of the ashes, Phœnix-like, the show goes on. I give you *Miriam Birdseye*, coupled with the names of the great ones of the past ... '

'And *that* isn't very complimentary, dear,' said Miriam coldly. 'The Phœnix is at least two thousand years old.'

II

The little procession of people that streamed across the dark hall to the drawing-room, drunkenly banging into one another, could best be described as a 'rout'. Tom Atkins led the party and somehow managed to give the impression that he would drop on all fours any minute now. Natasha and Timothy Shelly came last, deep in conversation. Miriam waited for them by the little brass gong. He was laboriously teaching Natasha the elementary principles of salmon fly-tying.

'What do you say these things are called, Timothy, my dear?' asked Natasha in her slow, grave Russian voice. 'The tag and the tail and the butt? It does not seem *likely*. And, my *dear*, the hackle?'

Her voice rose and became almost shrill in its disbelief.

'The throat, the body, the wings and the hook,' said Timothy Shelly fondly. 'It's quite usual, I assure you. It's like heraldry when you get used to it.'

Ahead of them Kidder Atkins gave a scream and ducked under Banjo DeFreeze's encircling arm.

'And you really use this incredible stuff to be making *flies*,' said Natasha, astonished. She read from the little note-book that Timothy had handed to her. 'Lead-coloured pig's wool from under the ear. I did not know that pigs *had* wool.'

'Oh, there are much more amusing things than *pig's wool*,' said Timothy Shelly. He flipped over a page or two. 'Look here. Hackle from the rump of a blue game hen. Dubbing of hare's flax or mixture of fur from ear and face of hare.'

'Ear *and* face of hare,' said Natasha solemnly. 'It is like *Macbeth*.'

Banjo DeFreeze now advanced purposefully on Kidder with a heavy branch of mistletoe.

'*Macbeth*?' said Timothy Shelly. 'Why *Macbeth*?'

'Eye of newt and toe of frog,' explained Miriam Birdseye. 'Look, darling, do you mind if I crouch with you two on the sofa? I'm terrified. I don't know which frightens me most, that awful Banjo or that *macabre* Hampton Court. And I *can't* learn my part. I've forgotten everything. And Hampton ought to be rehearsing now. It's absolute hell. He won't take any trouble.'

Miriam rolled pale-blue eyes in great agony. Natasha smiled at Timothy Shelly.

'Tomorrow is your first night, of course,' said Timothy Shelly, and held the door open for them both. The two ladies almost ran into the drawing-room and sat side by side on the sofa. The room looked quite pretty. There was a little Christmas tree in the window, glowing with frost and witch balls and little candles. Beyond it the dark Quaritch Hills made a shadowy background. Inside, the firelight flickered and Kidder quarrelled with Tom Atkins, who wanted to turn on the lights.

'Can't see a damn' thing,' said Hampton Court.

'But you will have lots of time before tomorrow to learn your words, surely,' went on Timothy Shelly, sinking on to the sofa between them.

'I don't see how I can,' said Miriam. 'There is this godawful dinner on the stage this evening for the Tottenham Tots and their mothers and the stage-hands.' Miriam looked up anxiously at Hampton Court, who was straddling the fire-place. He did not seem to hear her. 'So that's the end of this evening,' went on Miriam. 'Of course, the party should have been cancelled. Definitely.'

Natasha sat silently on the sofa, with her lovely head slightly on one side. Banjo DeFreeze and Kidder began to pass round the room, like things in a séance, carrying very small cups of lukewarm coffee. Tom Atkins complained again about the lack of light, choked and spilled his coffee suddenly on his trousers. He left the room in a great rush. Kidder followed him, clucking and vexed about his carelessness. As the door shut behind them Banjo DeFreeze slowly advanced towards the fire-place, speaking in a low, slightly hoarse voice.

'After all,' he said, 'I bet we're all dying to discuss Viv's death and whether it was an accident and all. Well then, let's. I thought Hampton was damn' right, speaking up as he did at dinner. Honest, he was, you see. Why, look, it must be a *record* that someone can die suddenly like that and leave everybody so pleased ... '

Banjo's teeth flashed in the firelight. A muffled sob from his brother Harry, standing by the Christmas tree, had interrupted him. Banjo was annoyed.

'Don't pay any attention to my brother,' he said. 'He's had a nasty shock, that's all. He hasn't known what he's been at for years, let me tell you. When Harry pulls himself together and thinks what Viv's death'll mean to him in the way of freedom and that, he'll be a new man. He was *haunted* by that old tart. That's what.'

Tears poured down Harry DeFreeze's face quite unchecked. He hid his face in the heavy, dark brocade curtains. His narrow shoulders shook. Banjo swore softly and sat in an arm-chair near the fire. He drew his legs under him as though he were going to spring. He had a cigar in his right hand, together with a glass of brandy, and he put his empty coffee-cup on the floor between his feet.

'There now,' said Timothy Shelly quietly. '*There* we are.'

Natasha and Miriam sat rigidly, wondering what impossible thing Banjo could say next.

'Now let's see,' said Banjo gaily, 'where were we all when it happened? We were all on the stage, weren't we, or in the wings? Yes. I can remember us . . .'

He nodded round the circle, as though he were checking names on an imaginary list. Harry came slowly towards the circle of firelight. Natasha and Miriam glanced fearfully at each other across Timothy Shelly's elegant legs. Hampton Court glowered down at Banjo, furious because he was monopolizing the conversation.

'What's it matter to you, Mr Smart Pants DeFreeze,' said Hampton, 'where we all were? Hey? That'll be found out by the coroner fast enough. All in good time. You'll see.'

'Oh well,' said Banjo easily, looking up at Hampton with his cigar between his teeth. 'Oh well, I always like to know what I'm in danger of. Don't you?'

There was a gentle menace behind the words. Hampton snorted and used a very rude word.

'Well, for example,' said Banjo, 'who's responsible for the flipping switchboard? Hampton, because it's his panto, or Tony Gresham because he's Hampton's stage manager?'

Banjo leered round the room, and Hampton growled out again that it was for the coroner to decide.

'Don't be an ass,' said Miriam. 'The lights are obviously Tony Gresham's. And that includes the star trap. Hampton would have knocked hell out of Tony Gresham if anything had gone wrong any other day. Wouldn't you, Hampton?'

Miriam grinned ingratiatingly at Hampton Court. The

effect was very like the Southern aspect of the cathedral of Notre Dame.

'Taken out his liver with a rusty penknife,' said Hampton round his cigar.

'So the poor boy killed his own mum,' said Banjo, a prehensile hand on each knee, his brandy-glass now empty on the floor with his coffee-cup. 'Funny the way these things work out, isn't it? It's a funny old world—'

'Oh, don't be so silly, Banjo,' said Harry DeFreeze suddenly. 'You can't blame anyone for negligence if it's proved to be an accident.'

It was so long since Harry had said anything at all that everyone was astonished. A complete silence fell on that squalid drawing-room, with its pretty Christmas tree and its dreadful atmosphere of unhappiness and mistrust. And at that moment the door opened and a shaft of yellow electric light intruded from the hall. There stood Miss Burns in her green overall.

'It's a gen'man,' she said, 'from the insurance. Wants to see a Mr Anthony *Gresham*. He's out here in the hall.'

'Claret Jay. Body claret seal's fur, ribbed with oval gold thread,' said Natasha dreamily.

'Out in the hall,' said Miss Burns firmly.

III

'I'll handle this,' said Banjo DeFreeze. He suddenly whipped a pair of horn-rimmed glasses out of his pocket and put them on. They were fine, big, expensive glasses that lived in a green leather case.

'I'll see to the insurance agent,' said Hampton Court.

They started towards the door simultaneously, clashed hips and apologized rudely. Hampton Court dropped his cigar butt in a sodden little heap on the floor. It slowly began to burn a hole in the tomato-coloured carpet. Hampton angrily turned on the lights as he went. Natasha and Miriam blinked at each other, and at Timothy Shelly, startled. Harry DeFreeze blew his nose on a white handkerchief with a blue border, wiped his eyes and sniffed.

Banjo and Hampton burst out together into the hall, with Hampton slightly in the lead. A little man in a crumpled waterproof was standing by the gong. As they came up to him he coughed and put a soft felt hat on the table behind him. He held out a visiting-card. Banjo took it and examined it minutely, as though it were a rare postage stamp.

'My name's Court,' began Hampton truculently, before anyone else had time to speak.

'Pleased to meet you,' said the man in the crumpled waterproof.

'And Gresham is my stage manager,' said Hampton. 'Anything concerns him, concerns me.'

'What bunk,' said Banjo, handing back the visiting-card. 'If Tony Gresham got married you wouldn't even be allowed to kiss the bride.'

'I'm from the Save Our Souls Insurance Company,' said the little man, peering from Banjo to Hampton and back again. '*Beaver* is the name. We have an arrangement whereby clients—'

'Well,' said Hampton unkindly, 'you don't think you're going to sell *me* anything, do you?'

'SOS advertises in Kwikbind pocket-books,' said Mr Beaver.

'What *is* all this?' said Banjo kindly. 'Come to the point, old man.'

He laid the flat of his hand warmly on Mr Beaver's shoulder.

'Why, you poor fella, you're wet through and through,' he went on. 'Come into the drawing-room. *Hardly* the way to spend Christmas. Selling insurance . . . '

And kindly and gently he propelled Mr Beaver into the drawing-room.

'I'm a single man,' said Mr Beaver. 'Don't go in for festivities and that. Bed-sitter.'

He blinked a little at Natasha, a little more at Miriam, and most of all at the glass of brandy which Timothy Shelly now thrust into his hand.

'Sorry our host isn't here to welcome you,' said Timothy.

'He passed out,' said Hampton Court, with a harsh little chuckle. 'Now. What is it you were selling Mr DeFreeze and me?'

Mr Beaver drank a little brandy and colour mounted in his thin cheeks.

'Wasn't selling anything,' he said firmly. 'Trying to find Gresham. Told by stage-door keeper he was out here. Anthony Gladstone Gresham. Took out a one-day accident policy in the name of his mother, Vivienne Rose Atkins Gresham, for one day, i.e. Christmas Eve. Understand from wireless this lady died yesterday. SOS want me to investigate.'

Mr Beaver drank deeply at his brandy and sat rigidly upright.

'What sum did Save Our Souls contract to pay Mr Gresham in the event of his mother dying on Christmas Eve?' said Timothy Shelly. He was very tall and slender, leaning against the fire-place.

'Three thousand pounds,' said Mr Beaver, and gulped.

'And the premium?' said Banjo sharply. He was still wearing his glasses and he was a little piped down in consequence.

'One penny,' said Mr Beaver, and finished his brandy.

4

The consternation that followed Mr Beaver's announcement cannot be exaggerated. Banjo DeFreeze, Hampton Court and Timothy Shelly thought it the worst and most suspicious thing they had ever heard. Natasha and Miriam leapt at Mr Beaver and soothed him with little speeches. 'Poor Tony? Why, he's heartbroken. He wouldn't hurt a fly.' And 'I will take you your wager of one penny to three thousand pounds if you wish that this boy will never be claiming.'

In the end Mr Beaver drove away in his Morris 8, full of brandy, with one of Tom Atkins' cigars burning brightly in his mouth. He was unconvinced that Tony Gresham would make no claim on his company. He was bound for 148a Leazes Gardens, Newchester. The house-party had given him this address as Tony's. 'Stays in lodgings, does he? Oh, with old Ma Hitch? I know *her* . . . ' had been Mr Beaver's sinister comment. Now the house-party waved him goodbye from the top of the steps outside Bayleyside. The dusk grew deeper and deeper each minute. The sullen clouds, gathered on the Quaritch Hills, smelt bitterly of snow and still more snow. The whining of the cold wind and the faint, retreating noise of Mr Beaver's engine died away.

'No sign of *Tom*,' said Banjo DeFreeze. He took off his glasses, folded them and shut them away in their green case. 'Suppose he did pass out? And where is Kidder? Kidder Atkins? I haven't seen her for hours ...'

Banjo stood in the hall and looked anxiously up the big mahogany staircase. His short thick neck strained backwards as he did so. He was no longer in good form. Bayleyside seemed empty and shadowy as a tomb.

'Dear Harry has been disappearing also,' said Natasha at the drawing-room door. 'Poor little thing. I am supposing it is too much for him after everything else, hearing that his *son* has taken out an SOS Accidental Policy like this.'

'Son?' said Banjo contemptuously. 'Son? Don't be a fool. *Harry* hasn't any son ...'

He snorted and came striding towards her with quick, jerky steps. Natasha backed nervously into the drawing-room. The fire was dying. Miriam was on her knees, coaxing flames and cheerfulness from the ashes.

'Well, if Tony Gresham isn't Harry's son, whose son is he?' snapped Miriam. She lifted her face from the coal-box. A long smear of black now ran up and down her nose like a tattoo mark. Her fingers were filthy.

'Yes,' said Hampton Court. He sat on the sofa and crossed one small leg over the other. 'Who is Tony Gresham's father? I've always wanted to know.'

There was a pause. Everyone in the room felt his or her nerves tighten beyond screaming. Then Banjo crossed negligently to the fire-place and kicked the tongs clattering into the grate.

'As a matter of fact,' said Banjo, 'Tony is *mine*. My boy. My son. Any objections, any of you?'

And he spun round upon them, his thick black brows screwed up together like a hairy caterpillar, his two fists clenched. He seemed prepared to fight the whole world if necessary.

II

How the party managed to drag themselves to the motor-car to drive once more into Newchester to take part in the Tottenham Tots' and stage-hands' dinner, no one knows. Timothy Shelly drove them because he was sober. Natasha was sad because she was not able to sit beside him. But how the rest of the party felt and at what particular moment Tom Atkins reappeared, is a mystery that no one would like to explain. Tom's hair was damp and it had been arranged down the sides of his forehead in two blank, flat curtains. He wore no hat. His eyes were heavy with sleep and his face seemed leaden and stupid and run to heavy fat. Otherwise there was nothing to tell anyone that Kidder had been pouring water on him for the last half-hour. 'Quite so, quite so,' said Tom Atkins. 'You drive, Tim boy.' And he climbed into the back of the car and fell asleep between Natasha and Miriam.

Of course Kidder had reappeared as well. She sat in the front beside Timothy Shelly and Hampton Court, every inch the Lady Mayoress, occasionally twisting her head to glance at 'the boys', as she called Banjo and Harry DeFreeze. They were sitting in the little occasional folding seats. Miriam and Natasha were transfixed, Natasha by the idea that Banjo would presently try to creep upon her knee. They sat in complete silence, wondering what could happen next.

'You're very quiet, Miss Birdseye,' said Kidder. Her voice was challenging.

'I am frightened,' said Miriam. 'Don't know a word of Prince Charming and we open tomorrow, that's all.'

For the remainder of the journey Hampton Court and Miriam conducted a rehearsal (words only), discussing the amount of support that 'Cinders' (as Hampton Court elegantly called her) could be expected to give to Miriam.

III

If Natasha and Miriam had thought Christmas Day dinner at Bayleyside was horrid, it was only because they had not yet encountered true beastliness. They had not yet endured Christmas night dinner with the Tottenham Tots.

A large trestle table had been laid on the stage in front of the opening set, 'The woods outside Prince Charming's Palace'. 'Jesmond Dene in spring,' murmured Banjo DeFreeze, looking at it. Round it there were set sixty hard little wooden chairs. Several cold roast turkeys and cold roast geese were laid haphazardly up and down the table. It had evidently been a white Christmas on the black market. There was a crate of beer standing incongruously in front of a glade of brilliantly blooming bluebells. Somebody had wittily muddled up a cardboard chicken and a string of rubber sausages from the Baron's Picnic Scene, Act I, with the rest of the food. The Tots roared their approval of this. The beer was opened for their mothers and the stagehands, but soon several Tots had drunk their mothers' beer and soon the stage was a litter of turkey and goose bones, torn cracker-covers and discarded paper hats and caps. The Tots considered paper hats 'daft', and quite a lot of them demanded gin.

Presently Hampton Court, who had been waiting in vain for his individual bottle of champagne to be lowered on scarlet Christmas ribbons from the flies, thumped on the table and stood up. There were cries of 'Go it', and 'Who's King of the Castle?' and from the wild gaiety of George, the stage-door keeper, it was suddenly obvious to one and all that Hampton Court would never be able to drink *that* bottle of champagne.

'Hush,' screamed Hampton. 'I will have *hush!*'

He was wearing a tartan poke bonnet with pale-blue paper streamers and he looked obscene.

The Tottenham Tots cheered him. Dawn O'Day (whose real name, it will be remembered, was Ginger) suddenly flung a pineapple chunk. Banjo DeFreeze, wearing a fez, banged with his knife and fork on the table and cried out, 'M'*lord*, Ladies and Gentlemen, pray *Silence* for His Highness,' and choked into his glass of beer. Several Tottenham mothers were quite horrified, and one of them (a Mrs Cole, from Penge) left the theatre in a huff, taking her daughter Maureen with her. She never appeared in pantomime again.

'*Hush,*' repeated Hampton Court. 'We are gathered together—' – as he glared around him; the cheering Tots and the iconoclastic Banjo were silenced – 'today for the purposes of goodwill and good cheer, previous to undertaking that great adventure, that hardy British perennial, the Christmas panto. Folks.'

'Soaks,' said Banjo to two Tots in stitches.

'Some of you feel it was not in the best of taste for me to hold this dinner in the circumstances—'

'Too right I don't,' said George, the stage-door keeper, through a haze of Cliquot.

'Got it in one, smarty,' said Banjo, and pulled two simultaneous crackers with Dawn O'Day and Dreme Child.

'But, folks, the show must go on. Kings will die. Kings will succeed. Principal boys will perish. In their stead will come other principal boys to flourish. From the ashes, phœnix-like, the theatre always rises. Ladies and Gentlemen; the show must go on. I give you Miriam Birdseye . . .'

There was a spontaneous explosion of applause and horror and sheer excitement. Someone started a gramophone that played 'Hearts of Oak' in a crazy fashion. Miriam was too aghast to stand up and say anything but 'Thanks very much.' She was even too distressed to add her customary wisecrack about the Phœnix being two thousand years old.

'Shut that damn' thing off,' shouted Hampton, and the gramophone screamed to a halt. Sixty glasses were still held high. Sixty faces looked up at Hampton, fascinated by his filthy showmanship.

'But,' shouted Hampton, '*before* we drink the health of this great little old trouper I will ask you for half a minute's silence to remember "Viv". Our Viv. I think I may call Vivienne Gresham, "Our Viv". She is now one with Mrs Siddons, Miss Bernhardt, Duse and Marie Lloyd. She awaits with them, Ladies and Gentlemen, the Call Boy of the Stars . . .'

And to everyone's surprise and to the disgust of Miriam Birdseye, who felt she was being made a fool of, Hampton lowered his head, folded his little hands in front of him and turned down an empty champagne glass on the table-cloth.

'I cannot remember witnessing a more thoroughly degrading spectacle,' said Timothy Shelly.

IV

Even taking into consideration the overstrained nerves of the company there was no excuse for the excesses that followed. There was no excuse for Mr Jenkins, the conductor, to pursue Cinderella round the stage, leaping and praising her contours, forcing her to hide behind Miriam and say, 'He's a man old enough to be my father, Miss Birdseye.' There was no excuse for Dandini, who threw a plate at little Dawn O'Day. Above all, there was no excuse for Miriam to sing 'That's what we're fighting for'.

Finally everyone was grateful to Harry and Banjo DeFreeze who turned this shambles into a charming interlude. As the china began to break and the blood to flow, they had hurried out to their dressing-room and, accompanied by a sobered Mr Jenkins, they went effortlessly through their world-famous eccentric dancing act 'Four Feet that Beat as One.' Dressed as elegant civil servants in double-breasted white satin suits and white bowler hats with neatly folded umbrellas under their arms, they flicked through a series of spectacular arrangements of 'The Birth of the Blues', 'Waiting for the Robert E. Lee' and 'I can't give you anything but love, Baby'.

Their faces were immobile and unsmiling, the upper part of their bodies supple but unbent, their feet capered wildly, double beating and shuffling and tapping. They never missed a beat. Harry, of the two of them, was the more indolent and the most inspired. On the stage he became a thing possessed. Banjo, his bounding vitality furiously restrained, seemed to try too hard. He had less natural grace. Yet, such was the magic of their twinkling feet that the sordid stage that had been all littered with turkey bones and paper, became an enchanted place, where love and heartbreak and sheer joy of life were danced by Harry DeFreeze with contemptuous ease.

And when Banjo stopped and mopped his brow and Harry went on alone, dancing his solos, 'Frankie and Johnny' and 'She was Poor but she was Honest', and 'The Rich man rides by in his Carriage and Pair', the Tottenham Tots stood on the table to screech their approval. Harry was so neat, so deft and, above all, so *funny*. His feet, performing an hilarious jig as the two drunken 'parents in the country' who had drunk 'the cham-pagne that she sends them, but they never speak her name,' was as brilliant as anything that Natasha had ever seen. She, too, thumped her approval on the person standing beside her.

'Harry!' she yelled, and 'Harry *DeFreeze!*' And then she added, more quietly: 'Poor little Harry. Who would have thought he had it in him?'

The person she was thumping was Timothy Shelly.

'The Fairy Queen of Starry Nights is going to sing next,' he whispered. 'Shall we go?'

And when they had left the Theatre Royal it was as though Atkins Street had been turned into a *décor* for a romantic ballet. Timothy Shelly hummed the first two bars of Chopin's Seventh Prelude. They came into the starlight, and Natasha's heels slipped on the pavement. His hand, under her elbow, helping her, was impersonal.

'What are you thinking?' he said, and added vaguely: 'Lord, the moon is so *bright* tonight . . .'

Natasha looked up at the theatre portico. It made a fine classic shape against the sky. On the other side of the road chimney cowls, like strange snail shells and periwinkles and hermit crabs, spun and turned and made odd shapes against the wind in the sky.

'I was expecting to be seeing a witch up there,' said Natasha.

'On Christmas Day?' said Timothy Shelly. 'Oh, *come* . . .'

Natasha laughed. The frost on the pavement was like a spider's web and very beautiful.

'Very well,' she said. 'I was thinking of this unfortunate Gresham boy who has insured his mother, and lost her, and who is presently interviewing that Mr Beaver. I *do* wonder what is happening between them.'

Timothy Shelly sighed.

'And you want to go and see what is happening more than anything in the world?' he said sadly.

'Oh yes!' Natasha was excited.

'Very well,' said Timothy Shelly. 'May I always be able to grant your wishes as easily.'

V

The streets and squares of Newchester had never looked more lovely. The light snow that had even fallen on the tram-tracks, covered all the hideous scars in the city's face; and the steel cables overhead shone and glittered like tinsel. 148a Leazes Gardens was the first-floor flat of a Georgian house that looked on to a public garden, planted in the form of a square, paled off with iron railings like shining spears. The light that glowed from the windows was red against the blue light of the moon and the silver snow. The trees in the square were black and sharp, and a statue of a little girl glimmered beside a fountain.

'148a, Hitch,' read Timothy Shelly curiously. 'And 148b and c appear to be Hitch as well ...'

'I am expecting she is owning the whole house and is turning each floor into a flat to let it off to theatrical persons,' said Natasha.

'Listen,' said Timothy Shelly.

Through the dark square wandered the beginnings of Debussy's 'Clair de Lune'.

'Appropriate,' said Timothy Shelly, fingering the knocker. 'I don't like to ring the bell. It might be in the wrong key.'

'Knock then,' said Natasha, with her sweet smile that was so like a pretty cat's. 'Knocking is always so dr-ramatic.'

Timothy Shelly beat on the door. Natasha's foot tinkled against a milk bottle. It fell with a tiny crash on to the pavement.

'Oh dear,' said Natasha, and bent quickly. 'No,' she said; 'it isn't broken. There is a note inside it, however, which has fallen out ...'

Timothy Shelly also bent down. He struck a match and held it cupped in his hand. They were nice hands.

'What does it say? "Please leave two pints tomorrow, I got company",' he said, straightening his back. Natasha stood up too, reading the piece of paper.

'Something of the kind,' said Natasha. 'But it is in such curious handwriting for a landlady. So *musical*. The capital letters are like bass and treble clefs, it is strange ...'

And she held the paper out to Timothy Shelly, who took it and burnt his fingers on the match and threw it away into the blackness, a glowing red spark to fall with a hiss in the gutter.

'Oh, I don't know,' said Timothy. 'Perhaps Tony Gresham is a good, kind little lodger and he wrote the note for old Mum Hitch?'

Above their heads the music died away in a flutter of petulant wrong notes. They heard a hoarse, middle-aged woman's voice call: 'OK, Tony, ducks. I'll go. I'm at the end of me seam.' Then there were flapping feet (evidently in bedroom slippers) on stairs and a wheezing noise. Then the music began again. This time it was the 'Catédrale Engloutie'. Bolts scraped, the door cracked. It opened cautiously inwards, an inch or two at a time.

'Who is it?' said the hoarse voice.

'It is Miss Nevkorina from the theatre,' said Natasha quickly. 'And Mr Shelly come to see how Mr Gresham is—'

'And wish him a happy Christmas,' said Timothy Shelly, pressing forward.

'Oh, I didn't see it was *you*, Miss Nevkorina. Come in. Yes. Mrs Furbinger it is, of the wardrobe. Yes. Mrs Hitch popped out over to her niece's for supper. They've a party. Yes. And I agreed I'd stop here with Mr Tony. He really shouldn't be left. For a bit of company, like. He's been ever so cut up since you know what . . .'

Mrs Furbinger went ahead of them up the stairs, bending slightly forward, talking all the time. She had difficulty in breathing.

'I brought me machine an' a mince pie or two my daughter 'ad made, and Tony and me's been as cosy as cosy. We had the King at three o'clock. And since then he has had his piano, of course . . .'

They came to a turn in the staircase. A stuffed duck in a

glass case sat foolishly on a weird mahogany waggon. Above it there was a cuckoo clock with a painted china face. It was broken.

'I been getting on with the alterations to your costume, dear,' she said to Natasha, flinging the information over her shoulder. 'You'd done the tacking ever so nice. Now you've come round you can try it on. Here's the parlour . . .'

She opened a door ahead of them. Natasha and Timothy found themselves propelled into the 'parlour' without any sense of initiative.

It was a big room, and once upon a time before someone partitioned it off, it had had good proportions. There was a gas-fire that roared and illuminated a heavy rug and a foot-stool, and there were red window curtains. One of these was drawn back and the pale moon glared in. Natasha had an impression of bric-à-brac, small tables, low arm-chairs and plants in pots, teeming in the darkness. The only light was by an upright piano with a puckered green silk front. It was a standard lamp with a crimson silk shade. This light was reflected in a looking-glass over the gas-fire. Stuck round the looking-glass were hundreds and hundreds of decayed and tinkling photographs of dead principal boys and girls. Later, when Natasha was able to examine them she found they were all signed and Mrs Hitch had added in capital letters 'Passed on' and a date. Most of them had gone a pale fawn and had curled at the edges from the heat of the fire.

> 'Golden lads and girls all must
> Like chimney-sweepers come to dust,'

murmured Timothy Shelly.

Tony Gresham was sitting at the piano. As they came in at the door he stood up. He held a glass in his hand.

'Happy Christmas,' said Timothy.

'We are coming to see how you are,' said Natasha.

Mrs Furbinger died away in the distance, muttering and grumbling and wheezing like a summer storm. Tony Gresham lifted the standard lamp round the stem in both hands and brought it forward. Some more of the room came to life. There was a sofa, heavily upholstered in turkey carpet. Natasha and Timothy sat on it.

'There's beer,' said Tony Gresham. 'And whisky. And a little gin, and some of Mrs Furbinger's mince pies.'

There was a pause while Natasha explained that she didn't drink, and Timothy said thank you, he would have some beer.

'It was kind of you to come,' said Tony. He shuffled the piano-stool forward.

'We are coming,' said Natasha hesitantly, 'because of this Mr Beaver of the SOS Insurance Company, and we are thinking—'

Tony Gresham flew into a little rage. He gestured round his head as though he were swatting at a wasp, and a lock of golden hair fell into his eye. He tossed it back angrily.

'*That* dreary beast,' he said. 'My dear; came *pushing* in here when Mrs Hitch and I were trying to eat our turkey. And he talked a lot of *bilge*. *We* thought he was trying to get a free Christmas dinner.'

'How awful for *you*,' said Natasha with her head on one side.

'How boring,' said Timothy Shelly.

'You're quite right, it *was* boring,' said Tony, and opened a bottle of beer. He poured it out and handed the glass to Timothy. 'My dear, we put him in here. All among the—' He looked round him and giggled faintly. 'All among the *dead*. I interviewed him *after* the turkey. Mrs Hitch gave him a mince pie.'

'What was he wanting exactly?' said Natasha.

'He wanted me not to claim on a perfectly good insurance policy, if you please,' said Tony indignantly. 'Returned me the coupon I'd filled up and asked me to forget all about it, that's all. My dear, I was *livid*. I'd forgotten all about the damned thing until he produced it and waved it about.'

'And now?' said Timothy Shelly.

'I'm damn' well going to take advantage of it,' said Tony. 'Why shouldn't I? Three thousand quid, indeed. We could put on some decent *plays* for that.' There was a slight pause. 'The mater would have been the first one to say "Put on some decent plays, Tony",' concluded Tony Gresham lamely.

'Have you got this coupon?' said Timothy Shelly. He held out a hand full of magnetism.

'Yes,' said Tony. He hunted in his hip pocket. 'He gave it back to me. Ah. Yes. Here it is.'

He drew out a small, flimsy piece of paper, headed with a picture of a life-belt engraved SOS. Natasha held it up to the light. Timothy Shelly looked over her shoulder.

'Hey,' he said, after a minute or two. 'This isn't *your* handwriting, is it? At least, it's not the same writing as that in the milk bottle downstairs.'

Tony Gresham looked surprised and rather angry. However, he had apparently decided that Mr Shelly could do no wrong.

'No,' he said. 'No. That's right. It's not *my* writing. Would that make the claim illegal?'

He sounded anxious, but not at all guilty. It was difficult to guess what emotions lay behind this white, nervy face and what motives controlled his words.

'Would it?' he said.

'It is all depending,' said Natasha, 'on whose writing *this* is ...' And she looked up at Tony with hard, candid eyes.

'Well, *that* ought to be all right from the insurance company's point of view,' said Tony, eagerly. 'Banjo filled it up. You know. My father. Banjo DeFreeze. It was his idea, actually ...'

5

It was most alarming to witness the outburst of hysteria that followed Timothy's gentle attempt to explain why public and police opinion would go against Tony, were he to claim his three thousand pounds. Tony's nerves seemed to break one by one, until he became once more, under their eyes, the abject, weeping boy of yesterday.

'Oh, now, Tony dear, do not be crying so,' said darling Natasha. 'Your eyes will be all *cerné*. You must please yourself, of course.'

Timothy Shelly leant his elbow on the mantelpiece and said he hoped that nothing he had said had upset Mr Gresham?

'Oh, no, no, *no*,' said Tony rapidly, the tears streaming down his face like rain. 'No, no. I just can't help this, that's all. I wouldn't cry for choice. Don't be silly.'

The door opened and now Natasha could vaguely see Mrs Furbinger, looming towards the firelight. Hers was a fat and cosy shape, not unlike Mrs Tiggy Winkle. She evidently wore a black cardigan, stretched tightly from a cameo brooch of Queen Victoria, at her throat.

'Been doin' that on and off, he has, since,' she said, with

gloomy relish. 'Can't help it, he says. Ah well. Good cry never did anyone no harm. Want to try your costume, dear?'

Tony Gresham stopped crying. Natasha, standing up, wondered out loud why, when one was invited to have a good cry, the tears dried themselves at the source. Tony Gresham said it was because the moment they were invited they became a scientific necessity instead of a romantic absurdity, and Mrs Furbinger left the room. Timothy Shelly said slowly that he would sooner be a scientific necessity himself.

'Ah,' said Tony Gresham, looking at him with large, bright eyes. 'But *you* are a true romantic.'

'You two romantic young gentlemen will be quite oll right, then,' said Natasha gaily, going towards the door, narrowly avoiding a small object in her path. On examination it proved to be a church hassock, upholstered in brown carpet. 'If I go and try on my little dress? I can see that Tony will not be crying unless you, Timothy, discuss the murder.'

The warm room, overloaded with the spoils of the Victorian and Edwardian eras, suddenly became cold. A chill wind that stole up everyone's back with a stealthy *frisson* silenced them. Yet Tony Gresham did not burst out crying again. He sat bolt upright on the sofa and all the blood in his body rushed to his face, where it flamed in the firelight.

'Murder?' he said. '*Murder*? There's no question of *that*, is there?'

He looked at Natasha with wild dismay. Natasha, also, was startled.

'Did I say *murder*?' she said. 'How very odd. I didn't mean to.'

Mrs Furbinger waited for Natasha in the kitchen. Mrs Hitch was evidently a large, warm, comfort-loving personality. A big, glossy, tinted photograph above the fire-place in a green plush frame showed she was once a beautiful woman and had played in *Dick Whittington*. The photograph was signed 'Dolly Hitch'. It wore the tights and thigh-length boots of this famous Lord Mayor of London. Natasha looked at it wonderingly, and she looked, too, at all the other *objets d'art* that were spread about the mantelpiece. There were fans, made of straw and peacock's feathers. There were little china shoes filled to the brim with crimson plush, with 'A Present from Bognor Regis' on the toe; and there was an evil-looking yellow frog about twelve inches high with a perpetually gaping mouth. There were also three books, lying one on top of the other: Zara's *Dream Book*, Napoleon's *Book of Fate* and the *Rubáiyát of Omar Khayyám*, bound in limp purple suede. There was no dust. Natasha found the whole thing reassuring. There was also a pack of playing cards, the cardboard a little frayed at the edges with constant use.

'Old Ma Hitch was a beauty in her day,' said Mrs Furbinger, observing Natasha's cool, incurious glance. 'Drink ruined her all right. Saw them ring down on her in Leeds. Yes, in *Floradora*. Eh, what an artist. Had to be carried to her dressing-room. That's right.'

Natasha paid little attention to Mrs Furbinger's monologue, and even less to her appearance, to which she was well-used. She had got to know her quite well in the last week, at the theatre. She was fascinated by Mrs Hitch's kitchen and she wondered if the Earl of Kensington had ever sat here. There was an enormous black-leaded range, where a coal fire roared and glowed and where a kettle steamed. There was a red, grey and blue clippy, raggy mat in front of it. There were two deck chairs to sit in, and on the kitchen table (which had a green woollen table-cloth) there was an enormous bird-cage that looked like the Crystal Palace. Inside was a very fine grey parrot, with old scaly eyes and a harsh voice. Natasha, who adored parrots, crossed the room to talk to it. It regarded her with a cold angry eye and said a rapid sentence composed entirely of four-letter Anglo-Saxon words.

'I am so *sorry*,' said Natasha gravely. 'I am mistaking you for a bird.'

The parrot cackled harshly.

'You shut up now, Poll,' said Mrs Furbinger. 'Gets on me nerves. Best put his cover on.'

His cover was green baize. The bird squawked angrily as he was shut in and darted out a black, leathery tongue. Natasha said she would miss him.

'And here's your costume, dear,' said Mrs Furbinger, suddenly shaking out a shower of pale-blue satin and white maribou. 'Looks quite nice, I must say. Quite the powder-puff. Goin' to try it on?'

Natasha stared round the kitchen, reflected that Timothy Shelly and Tony Gresham might come in at any minute, and said sadly that she thought she had better wait until she got back to Bayleyside.

'Please yourself,' said Mrs Furbinger.

Natasha discussed how much money she owed her. Money changed hands and Mrs Furbinger seemed pleased. Natasha folded her dress. Mrs Furbinger produced a brown paper hat-bag with 'Atkins and Marshall' printed on it in a fine sloping hand.

'Well,' she said, 'there's one person OK then. Tomorrow, that's to say. Yourself.'

Natasha was horrified.

'Why do you say *that*?' she said, very distressed. 'You are sounding as though something dreadful is going to happen tomorrow.'

A slow smile crossed Mrs Furbinger's stout grey face and left no trace behind it. She patted her smoothly parted hair. She was perhaps a little frightening. Her round face suddenly appeared like a curtain between Natasha and the truth, between Natasha and the future.

'We aren't at the end of *this*,' said Mrs Furbinger. 'Deaths never come singly.'

She sounded very pleased about it.

For some reason Natasha temporarily recovered from her distress. She gravely agreed.

'I, too am very superstitious,' she said. 'What signs have *you* had? I am saying such a strange thing just now in the parlour. I am calling Mrs Gresham's accident a *murder*. What do you think of *that*?'

Mrs Furbinger was quiet for a long time, watching Natasha blandly through the rings of fat that surrounded her little black eyes. She sat down in one of the deck chairs and poked the fire before she replied.

'Oh, it was murder right enough,' she said, quite casually. 'I'm not one to meddle with fate.'

Natasha was astonished.

'But *why* are you believing this? What reason can you possibly have?'

Childishly clairvoyant herself, Natasha quite often refused to admit the gift in others. Mrs Furbinger did not reply. She put down the poker in the grate and looked at her fat, slippered feet.

'Tell your fortune if you like,' she said.

'How?' said Natasha, suspiciously. 'With cards?'

Mrs Furbinger was contemptuous.

'Cards!' she said scornfully. 'No, indeed. Tea-cups.'

She reached a little brown tea-pot from the hob and poured out a cup of tea.

'I am not having to drink it?' cried Natasha, fearfully. She backed against the kitchen table.

'No, no, dear. Swill it round and pour it back ...'

Natasha obeyed Mrs Furbinger, wondering. The swollen tea-leaves swirled and danced and finally settled in little shapeless clumps on the inside of the china cup. The moisture drained from them. Suddenly they were no longer shapeless. They became coaches, witches, unicorns, lions, coffins, gravestones, churches. They made a little misshapen world inside the cup. Natasha looked into it, wondering.

'Show me, dear,' said Mrs Furbinger, comfortably. 'Ah, yes.'

Her manner suddenly changed. Her voice seemed harder and more metallic and might have belonged, suddenly, to a different person.

'You've been married,' she said, in her difficult sing-song. 'You fell out of love. Your husband is gone. You don't want him back. You have a new life and a new man. You want both ...'

Natasha's wide eyes grew wider still.

'There's trouble here, though,' said Mrs Furbinger. 'And death to concern you. But it does not touch you.' She suddenly resumed her old, comfortable tones. 'Perhaps it's Vivienne Gresham,' she said.

Natasha did not speak. She went on looking at Mrs Furbinger with enormous eyes, like a cat. Mrs Furbinger's voice again became unnatural and disembodied. Her face, too, had become different. It was sharp-featured, hard-eyed.

'There's another coffin here,' she said. 'That makes *two*.'

She came out of her trance, blinking. Her features returned to their comfortable normality.

'That was the sign that I had, too, dear. That's why I said troubles don't come singly. We *all* better watch out.'

Natasha looked at her curiously.

'We are all right?' said Natasha, finally. 'Or so you say? You and I? It does not concern us, any of it?'

Mrs Furbinger agreed and put the cup on the table. A little jet of gas in the coal puffed and wheezed and whistled between the bars, sometimes blazing out bright and yellow, sometimes dying to a faint trail of smoke.

'That boy up there, though,' she said, watching Natasha with eyes as blank and hard as pebbles, 'he's not all right. That poor boy. He's in it up to the hilt.'

'Who?' said Natasha, bored. 'Tony Gresham?'

'Oh no, dear, not *him*,' said Mrs Furbinger. 'The other one. The tall boy. *Your* boy.'

'*Timothy Shelly?*' said Natasha, with a wild surmise.

'If that's his name,' said Mrs Furbinger.

III

Left in the warm darkness of the parlour with Tony Gresham, Timothy Shelly sat on the sofa like a heap of pleasant bones, dressed in tweed. He wondered what the hell he could say to Gresham, as he called him in his mind. He had better not mention the accident, for a start. And, arising out of that, he had better not mention Pantomime. Christmas, too. Tony Gresham would not care to talk about festivities, no matter how careful the approach. By the time Timothy had considered and rejected (out of sheer sensitivity) as many as fifteen subjects of conversation, Tony Gresham had slouched back to the piano and was sitting on the piano-stool, scowling at the transcription of 'Clair de Lune'. This was a little tattered at the edges and gave the impression that it had been clamped to the rack of the piano for some days. It was held up by decorative clips that turned smartly inward, grasping its two lower corners. Tony Gresham broke the silence, and he did not break it with Debussy.

'I say,' he said, fingering Middle C. It was yellowed and a little chipped, like an old tooth. 'I say, do *you* think my mother was murdered?'

Timothy Shelly wondered what to say.

'It hadn't occurred to me,' he said, slowly, hoping for the best, 'until that charming Mrs DuVivien mentioned it. Who would benefit by her death?'

'Are you in love with her?' said Tony Gresham sharply. He struck a diminished seventh with his left hand, resolved it and continued in quite a different, conversational tone of voice. 'I mean, I suppose *I* would over the insurance. Financially, that's to say. But I'm very upset, really, dear. And then Miss Birdseye got Prince Charming, which she's always wanted to do as much as *The Wild Duck*.'

Timothy sat very still, shocked, considering Tony Gresham's first question. He hardly heard his other remarks.

He supposed he was. There was a tremendous attraction about her, certainly. A sort of remote, intellectual quality. Above the obvious magnetism. It couldn't be analysed. Well, it *might* be analysed. He wouldn't care to analyse anything so exquisite or enchanting. To take the heart from a fairy-tale, the glamour from a music-hall, the excitement from speed.

Tony Gresham had now revolved on the music-stool, like a clever little gnome on a circular toadstool with a screw-winding apparatus, and said:

'Why don't you say something?'

He pouted and giggled in rather a malicious way. He began to play an obvious Nocturne by Chopin. He played it with irony, but otherwise very well and delicately. The notes trickled from his fingers like drops of water. Timothy Shelly sat on the sofa with his head flung back. He decided it was difficult to be really cross with little Master Gresham.

'I expect those two boys, your father and your uncle, were a bit sick of your mother just the same?' he said, suddenly harsh. He wanted to *hurt* Tony Gresham. But he did not interrupt the Nocturne. It went smoothly on, sliding under Tony's hands like a river, a cold, heart-breaking river with the moon shining on it.

'Yes,' said Tony. 'I thought of that, too. I suppose Mother looked an awful old bag to you, dear. But I couldn't help being fond of her. Not that I've had anything to do with her for three years since I've been at Stratford. She admired one so. But Banjo. My father . . . '

The Nocturne halted. The silence was abrupt and terrifying. Tony Gresham struck the piano violently with his clenched hand. 'I *hate* him,' he said, in a passionate whisper. 'I hate him, I hate him, I *hate* him . . . '

It was at this precise moment that Natasha re-entered the room.

IV

'Hatred is so unbecoming to the face,' said Natasha, vaguely. 'One should always say enthusiastic things about *everyone*. One's face remains better so.'

She crossed to the sofa and picked up her bag. It was a very nice bag with a shoulder strap. She said amiably that they would have to be going now. Tony Gresham stood up and slowly faced them both. He just about came up to Timothy Shelly's shoulder.

'I will come some of the way,' he said, 'if you don't mind. I really feel very jumpy.'

He bit one of his finger-nails and looked distressed and drawn.

'I'm so *sure* you do. But we are going out into the country, you know,' said Natasha. 'You cannot be coming out to *Bayleyside* with us.'

'Bayleyside!' cried Tony Gresham, explosively. '*That* old dump. And Kidder. I say, what about *Kidder*?'

They moved to the landing at the top of the stairs and Timothy began to go down them. Here the darkness became chilled and there was a faint smell of old mutton fat, creeping towards them up the stairs. Tony Gresham, behind them, fumbled for an electric light switch and swore. There was a click and then they saw there were red glass beads hanging from the light shade.

'*You* know Bayleyside, then?' said Timothy, and paused with his hand on the banister. There was a heavy carved knob at the bottom, in the hall. And the inner front door was of painted glass, with a yellow glass handle.

'Are you ever staying there?' said Natasha, puzzled.

'Staying there,' said Tony, with a contemptuous sniff. 'I should just about say I *am*, dear. Why, I would be staying there now if I hadn't determined not to. Determined to be independent and separate for once in my life.'

There was a picture on the stairs of a bishop, looking out of a window.

'Good heavens,' said Timothy Shelly.

'Why are you so surprised?' said Tony. 'Of course I didn't suppose anyone knew that Tom Atkins was my—' Tony Gresham suddenly stopped and bit his forefinger and looked as though he were going to cry again.

'Your what!' said Natasha, very gently. 'You cannot be saying your *father* again, Tony. Because you have already told us and so has Banjo, that Banjo is your father.'

'Swine!' cried Tony, passionately. 'With his horrible ape-hands and his white teeth. I hate him. Mother hated him, too,' he ended, on an uncertain note.

In the hall there was an umbrella stand of blue and white Japanese china. There were umbrellas in it and Natasha identified a green silk Edwardian sunshade.

'No?' said Timothy Shelly. 'But what about Tom Atkins? What's he to you? Or what were you going to say he was?'

'Oh ...' Tony Gresham was vague. 'My patron, I suppose. Yes. That's it. A patron of the arts, is Mr Atkins of Atkins and Marshall.'

They were in the hall now and Tony Gresham was opening the front door for them. There was a large chalk drawing of a monk tapping a beer barrel on their right. Natasha recoiled from it.

'A patron of the arts,' she said. 'He was never giving *me* this impression.'

'No, dear?' said Tony Gresham, sharply. 'Well, suppose you ask yourself why *Shelly* is staying with him, then. And why are you staying with him yourself, dear?'

Tony Gresham, having reached the end of this speech, flung open the front door and looked out into the white, glimmering square. He shivered.

'I don't think I will accompany you, after all,' he said. 'Thank you for coming. Most kind. Most kind. See you tomorrow. The call's for four-thirty. Curtain up at seven. Sleep well, *romantic* Mr Shelly—'

And Natasha and Timothy heard the door shut softly behind them.

'Now what on earth was all *that* about?' said Timothy Shelly. He rubbed his right hand through and over his untidy hair.

'I do not know,' said Natasha.

There was a pause.

'Why *are* you staying with Tom Atkins?' she said.

They could hardly hear their feet on the pavement. The

snowfall was light, but it was enough to hush the ringing of their heels.

'It must have been snowing since we went in,' said Timothy. 'Funny. I didn't notice any clouds.'

Natasha suddenly stopped and faced him. She was in the light of a street lamp. Her strange Russian face, with its slanted cat's eyes and high cheek-bones, was thrown into all manner of weird planes and shadows.

'Look,' she said. 'Timothy. Why are you staying with these terrible Atkins?'

Timothy Shelly laughed.

'Does it matter?' he said. 'Do you mind?'

There was a pause. The wind stole along the gutters beside them and a piece of dirty paper fluttered nearby, to contaminate them.

'Yes, it matters. Yes, I am minding,' said Natasha. 'That odious Tony has made it seem that Tom Atkins is meeting you at Frinton-on-Sea and is taking a fancy to you ...'

Timothy Shelly went on laughing. Natasha stamped her foot.

'Oh!' she said.

'Very nearly right,' said Timothy. 'Except it was Bexhill-on-Sea, and it was *Mr* Atkins' sister.'

The paper twirled in the draught and danced away to the other side of the road. It had not touched them. Distance lent it witchcraft. It became as beautiful as spray thrown by a great wave. Natasha laughed too.

'Very well,' she said. 'It is all a nonsense. What about Banjo?'

'Yes, indeed,' said Timothy. 'Why, if he did fill up that policy application, why did he pick on Christmas Eve of all days?'

'We should ask him,' said Natasha.

Ahead of them, against the sky, the tall wings of the South African War Memorial made a brave pattern.

'We should ask him tonight,' said Natasha.

'Oh, for heaven's sake!' said Timothy. 'I really have had enough of this nervous detective work. Can't we have tonight for ourselves? Can't we ask Banjo tomorrow?'

And they agreed to ask Banjo tomorrow. But tomorrow was too late.

6

Boxing Day dawned with all its miseries. It dawned with rain and sleet and a general thaw that made everyone in Bayleyside rheumatic. It crept on towards afternoon with swollen streams and gutters that overflowed and slates that loosened themselves to fall crashing about the ears of the postman, the newspaper-boy and the baker, as they queued up for their Christmas 'boxes', Tom Atkins was generous to the messengers of his fellow tradesmen. They left Bayleyside on their bicycles, or in their little vans, with bright, happy faces. Each one of Tom Atkins' house-party, however, was miserable.

Tom Atkins had a hangover and he stamped into his study and slammed the door, where he evidently had a mysterious telephone conversation with someone that quite obviously made him angrier still. Kidder said she did not feel at all well. She was sure it must have been the turkey stuffing. Hampton Court was in his usual filthy mood. Natasha and Miriam had stage fright. As the day went onwards, weeping, and as four-thirty stealthily approached, our two friends both went white and drawn. Their hands shook as they clattered their knives and forks at lunch. It was a dismal meal of cold turkey and even colder plum pudding. They felt sick. They pushed away their plates untouched.

The only person who was in a gay and sunny mood was Timothy Shelly, who had gone out rough shooting with a neighbour and had returned at about three o'clock soaked through and through and very cheerful. He had a gun tucked under one arm and a pair of hares swung from his other hand.

The neighbour, whose name was Otter, and who makes no other appearance in this story, was voluble about Timothy's prowess with shotgun and revolver. It seemed that Timothy had shot the hares with a revolver, when they were running, and it was the keenest thing that Mr Otter had ever seen, by jove. He drove away in his old-fashioned D-nosed Morris Cowley, and Timothy Shelly ran up the steps of Bayleyside towards Natasha.

'Oh, Timothy, we *missed* you at lunch,' said Natasha, dispiritedly. 'Those poor hares. Do be taking them away. I suppose you will use their faces and so on, for catching other wild things, such as salmon.'

Natasha, who had brightened considerably at the sight of Timothy Shelly (and, indeed, he did look extremely jolly), resumed her tones of deepest mourning. She was glum again, as though the cares of the world lay on her shoulders.

'What *is* the matter, darling Natasha?' said Timothy.

They were in the hall, and he was standing in his stockinged feet, shaking bright drops of rain in all directions.

'What *can* be wrong, my own? Please tell me ... '

Natasha turned away.

'It is, I am supposing, nerves.'

'For the First Night?'

Natasha turned back towards him.

'Yes, *that*. And then there is also something else. There is a feeling under oll, under everything, that something far worse is going to happen. I do not know. I am in a state.'

Natasha shook her lovely head.

'What is that in your pocket?' she said. 'Is it, perhaps, a *baby* hare?'

'No,' said Timothy. 'It's a revolver. I often take one rough shooting. You can sight and fire so much quicker than you can with a shotgun.'

'I thought revolvers are being very inaccurate?'

'They are inclined to be.'

'I am expecting you are a very good shot,' said Natasha, admiringly. Timothy shrugged his broad damp tweed shoulders. Natasha's black mood left her. 'You must *change*,' she said, and ran her long hand over his forearm. 'You will catch a terrible cold. You will die. And everything then will be quite impossible.'

'Ah!' Timothy looked gaily down at her, with pleasure skipping about in the pupils of his eyes. 'You would *mind* if I died? You think I am important to you?'

'You are a compensation,' said Natasha gravely. 'That is oll that I can be saying just at present.'

II

Afterwards, in his bedroom upstairs, as he peeled off his soaking wet woollen stockings, Timothy looked at his damp, pink feet and dried them with a big rough bath towel. He wondered what Natasha had meant by 'compensation'. He was not at all pleased. Compensation for what? Compensation for the dreary house-party? Compensation for some other ghastly love-affair he knew nothing about? Compensation? For the beastly pantomime? Timothy Shelly shook his head.

He hunted out a clean, dry pale-blue shirt and a navy-blue suit that he seldom wore. It was very clean and, unlike most of his suits, well-pressed. He suddenly decided to wear a frivolous little bow tie, whose predominating colours were red and blue. It suited him, but he made a face at himself in the looking-glass. He combed his hair and tried to smooth out the curl and failed. He really looked *very* tidy. So tidy, really, he didn't feel at all like himself. And then, possessed by some momentary impulse of sheer devilry, he slipped his revolver into the outside pocket of his suit. Perhaps he would get a chance to show Natasha … He looked at himself again. It pulled one of the shoulders out of shape and spoilt the set of the coat over the hip. But Timothy preferred himself that way.

III

Hampton Court drove them into Newchester at seventy miles an hour, on the crown of the road, sometimes sliding across to the right-hand side of the road to take a left-hand turning. Every time he did this Natasha and Miriam gasped a little and clutched each other in the back.

'I suppose those gad-damned useless DeFreezes'll manage to get to the theatre by themselves,' said Hampton. The car skidded lightly on the wet road that was running with thawed snow and slush. He blasphemed. 'Or do you think I ought to call for them?'

Timothy Shelly was in the front. From time to time he

winced at the blasphemies, or imagined that his last hour had come. He waited a second before he replied.

'I thought Harry was pretty well cut-up yesterday,' he said. 'But not Banjo. Banjo ought to get Harry there all right. Where are they staying?'

'At that other hotel,' said Hampton. 'With Viv. I forget its name.'

There was an uncomfortable silence. The unbearable restraint, which had pursued them all day, redoubled itself and clutched at their throats. Hampton seemed unaware of it.

'When is the blasted inquest, anyway?' he went on relentlessly. He spun the steering-wheel to avoid two pedestrians very narrowly. They seemed to scream and wave their fists at him. 'I thought that Sergeant – Whatsis—'

'"Swiss" Robinson,' said Timothy, shutting his eyes as the great car rocked to a halt by some traffic lights.

'Um. That's it. I thought Sergeant Robinson said it was today.'

'I don't think he can really tell,' said Timothy. He opened his eyes again as they roared down Northshire Street. The thaw was unpleasant in the city. Heaps of grey and grimy snow were piled high in the gutters. They twirled past the South African War Memorial with its gallant angel's wings. Timothy remembered his mood of the night before and sighed. Some shops were lit, in spite of it being a Bank Holiday, and oranges and chocolate and cigarettes shone under the light like a precious cargo. 'Perhaps the inquest will be tomorrow,' said Timothy.

'Sergeant Robinson had better not interfere with tonight, that's all,' said Hampton Court, and added a string of choice blasphemies. The car skidded to a halt in front of the Theatre

Royal stage door. 'Tonight's the night, mark my word. All Newchester will be here.'

His miserable passengers opened the doors and tumbled out on to the pavement. Miriam, who had gone extremely green, clambered out and held herself up by the door jamb.

'What's wrong, old thing?' said Hampton Court. He called out over her shoulder: 'Any post for me, George, before I put the car away? Got stage fright, Miriam? Bear up, old girl.'

Miriam leant into the car and slapped his face hard. It rang like a pistol shot. The gallery queue, which was already forming, began to talk amongst itself, wondering what it could be.

'That's for your driving, you beast,' said Miriam. 'I swear I'll never drive with you again.'

Hampton Court sat behind the steering-wheel, smiling unpleasantly, feeling his cheek.

'Why,' he said in his nastiest tone of voice, 'how very odd . . . *Vivienne Gresham slapped my face, too.*'

IV

The pantomime at the Theatre Royal was quite the most important theatrical date in Newchester's year. Important London actors and actresses might open in plays by significant playwrights 'prior to London production'. Musical comedies and revues might appear 'straight from London's West End'. Their impact was absolutely nothing beside the impact of the Boxing Day performance of *Cinderella*. A man's social position in the city was judged by the number of seats he had taken, and the part of the house in which he had taken them. Mr Tom Atkins, for example, ranked high. He had the two front rows of the upper circle for the staff of Atkins and Marshall. He and Mrs Kidder Atkins and Timothy Shelly (the only members of the house-party who were not by now members of the *Cinderella* Company) were snug in orchestra stalls. Kidder was restless because Timothy Shelly had not yet appeared to sit in his seat. She said anxiously that he would be late, and miss the overture, and she turned her handsome head backwards and forwards from entrance to entrance, looking for him. Here middle-aged ladies in black with white collars and cuffs dealt out sheaves of programmes and maintained an appearance of unyielding *hauteur*. No Timothy appeared among them.

And Newchester poured in. It poured in, chattering, in musquash coats, waving programmes. It poured in, distressed and anxious, with children in white ankle-length socks. It opened boxes of chocolates and crackled cellophane. It filled all the seats of the Theatre Royal in a mood of happy anticipation that nothing could disturb. And such is Newchester's firm self-satisfaction and ignorance, very few people in the audience had heard of Miriam Birdseye before. They complained fretfully to one another about the absence of Vivienne Gresham, whom most of the adults could remember from their childhood.

Adults who were accompanying children were, of course, unable to discuss the accident, and as there had been no newspapers published since Christmas Eve, very few of them were in possession of all the facts. A late edition of the Newchester evening paper had carried the story on Christmas Eve, but very few people had been in the centre of the city at that time to buy it. Accordingly the audience sat and read their programmes with little disappointed faces, wondering who Miriam Birdseye was, and was it really true that Vivienne Gresham was very ill. (And some said, dead.) There was, as yet, no suggestion of anybody getting their money back.

This malaise and indifference to the sparkling name of Birdseye communicated itself in subtle fashion to poor Miriam, who sat trembling in her dressing-room in hunting pink.

The orchestra began to tune their instruments.

'Oh,' she was saying desperately to Tony Gresham, 'I don't know one word of this wretched part. Not one word.'

She struck an attitude and read from the book:

> *'Thank you, my people, for cheering me, your Prince,*
> *As you all know, I've not been hunting since*
> *My father died. But now today*
> *We'll hunt Monsieur Reynard. Hoick Holla,*
> *Tally Ho. Forrard Away!'*

She turned to Tony Gresham who had looked in, as a good stage manager should, to comfort and wish luck.

'Tony, it doesn't even scan—'

'Now, Mum,' said Tony, crouched on the floor by her knees. He was, most surprisingly, a tower of strength. 'Don't lose your head. No one ever listens to the words, anyway. You shout whatever you think, dear. You'll be all right. It's the songs that count . . .'

'But I don't know the songs either,' said Miriam miserably as her heart turned sickeningly over. The overture began in the distance. With a trembling hand she fixed another beauty spot on her chin as the call-boy thundered on the door.

'*Overtures and beginners, please!*'

'Thank God my legs are all right,' said Miriam, and stretched them out, considering them gravely in their scarlet silken tights and high-heeled shoes. 'I shall have to get by on my legs.'

'Darling Mum, I must go,' said Tony. 'You'll be all right. You'll see.'

'Thank you, my people,' said Miriam abstractedly. 'Oh lord. I don't even know the words of the *songs*.'

The door slammed behind Tony Gresham and the call-boy came clattering back along the line of dressing-rooms.

'Five minutes, please, Mr Court!'

'Five minutes, please, Miss Franklyn!'

'Five minutes, please, *Miss Birdseye!*'

'Oh . . . oh . . . oh!' said Miriam. 'I think I'm going to be sick.'

'That's right, dear,' said her dresser. She had come back into the room and was running her eye over Miriam's first change; valet-style bottle-green coat, Act I Scene iii, the Baron's kitchen.

V

It was too late for tears. The pantomime had begun. Mr Jenkins, unrecognizable in a white tie and white carnation, had rapped smartly on the little glowing platform in front of him. The houselights dimmed. Mr Jenkins' baton was electric and in the dark a little star shone at its tip. The orchestra played bravely through the villagers' dance, the hunting music, most of the 'point' numbers and the motif dedicated to the Fairy Queen of Starry Nights. They also played Cinderella's own personal abandoned moaning music (the fireside of the Baron's kitchen), and (for some reason best known to Mr Jenkins and

Hampton Court) 'Don't sit under the apple tree with anybody else but me'. Mr Jenkins had turned and bowed to Kidder and Tom Atkins. And then the rustling and the whispering died and the animated buzz turned to a sigh as the red curtain slid upwards. Hampton Court's mammoth production of *Cinderella* unfolded itself at last.

First there was a beautiful woodland scene. Every tree was in full leaf. There were bluebells and wild roses blooming profusely. A number of decorative peasants walked about arm in arm, singing one of the folk songs of their country, apparently, too, in the language of the country. A horn blew. The peasants, startled, rushed anxiously from side to side, going through all the gestures of listening very intensely. A first-class peasant, in a straw hat with velvet ribbon, called out in a high voice, 'The hunt is up!' And there came in view four gentlemen in scarlet coats and elaborate hunting horns, leading two exhausted Dalmatian dogs. Behind them was the field; a splendid turn-out of squires and squireens in eighteenth-century hunting dress. The horns blew again, this time a fanfare. A confused cry went up: 'The Prince! The Prince!'

And the entire company drew back to disclose Miriam, who sauntered into view through the trees, acknowledging their cheers. She had not one word of Hampton Court's original book in her head. She struck an attitude and declaimed in ringing tones:

> *'Thank you, my people. Can you tell me why*
> *You are all hunting foxes in July?'*

There was an instantaneous roar of laughter that drowned the remainder of her speech. The Tottenham Tots, hearing their entrance cue, behind a confusion of tally-hos and yoicks, burst cheerfully on to the stage to do their hunting dance. Miriam stalked cheerfully to the wings through a line of knees performing the *salut d'armes* in time to the 'Posthorn Gallop'.

Miriam's dialogue with Cinderella passed uneventfully, for it was in prose, and it had been rehearsed. She changed places with Dandini without mishap and Dandini's song 'Prince for a Day' passed to lukewarm applause. And then came the moment when the entire stage was again at Miriam's disposal.

Lights dimmed and the limelight played on Prince Charming as, in fairly unhappy couplets, he should have talked to himself about his newfound love for Cinderella.

> *(The shy young maiden of the woods,*
> *I'll tell the world that I find her the goods.)*

But of course, Miriam's mind went blank again. Nevertheless she did not falter. In a beautiful resonant voice she announced to an astonished Mr Jenkins:

> *'Come gentle night, come, loving black-browed night.*
> *Give me my Cinders. And, if she should die,*
> *Take her and cut her out in little stars,*
> *And she will make the face of heaven so fine,*
> *That all the world will be in love with Cinders.'*

At this point Mr Jenkins, delighted, flung up his baton to bring in his orchestra. The roar of applause behind them was reassuring. Miriam began Charming and Cinderella's duet 'Out of my dreams', and Mr Jenkins mopped his brow. He hissed to the first violin that she would get no cues from Miss Birdseye tonight and to keep her eye on the stick, for heaven's sake. The first violin nodded grimly, with her chin on her instrument. The drop-curtain fell into place for a howling audience who could not understand why they were so excited. And here were the Baron's evil daughters, skipping about in the kitchen, 'tidying up'.

The orchestra settled back in their seats and turned over the pages of their music and the audience settled down to a good 'laff' as Banjo and Harry DeFreeze bounced about being highly humorous among the kitchen properties. As usual Banjo went too far. He poured a small can of whitewash over Hampton Court (certainly not in the script). Hampton drew himself up, hissing obscenities.

'The kiddies love it,' said Kidder as the house rocked all round them.

'Quite so,' said Tom Atkins.

VI

The pantomime went on and gathered pace. It was impossible for anyone to be angry with Miriam Birdseye. Her rhyming couplets were so clever, her speeches from Shakespeare were so apt, her voice was so beautiful, and her legs so symmetrical, that the audience could do nothing but adore her, and scream its adoration. So, with reservations, did her fellow artists.

'It's all very well, dear,' said Dandini sourly, 'but what will happen tomorrow night?'

'It's a wonderful performance, dear,' said Banjo. 'Peters! Just pop over to The Saracen for a Guinness for me and my brother. He'll be right out when he's done his solo.'

(Harry was dancing 'She was Poor but she was Honest'. The audience seemed to have been chloroformed, it sat so still and sighed so often with pleasure.)

'It's a divine performance, Miriam,' went on Banjo. 'Divine.'

And he embraced her heartily. And Miriam did not recoil from him. She went down to her dressing-room dizzy and plastered with applause and excitement. And on the stage the music changed to cue in Cinderella, alone by her fireside.

And Banjo went into *his* dressing-room and began to change for his next entrance.

Peters, his dresser, found him half-changed when he came back with his two glasses of Guinness from the Saracen's Head. For Banjo was lying on the floor in a dreadful heap, like a bundle of old clothes. In the middle of his forehead there was a neat blue hole. He was quite dead.

BOOK THREE

———————

EXEUNT UGLY SISTERS

I

Poor Banjo's dressing-room looked as though a powerful typhoon had struck it. A chair was overturned. His make-up and various sticks of grease-paint were spilled on the floor. Falling, he had evidently grasped at a drawer in the dressing-table and the contents had fallen all about him in a hideous little heap.

Now he lay on his back with his legs twisted oddly, one leg under him. His right hand grasped the handle of the little drawer and was flung out to one side pathetically. The objects from the little drawer lay round his head.

Later, Sergeant 'Swiss' Robinson made an inventory of these things when he was summoned from the front of the house. He arrived very promptly, in a dinner-jacket. He had been sitting in the dress circle with Mrs Robinson. 'Swiss' Robinson's list of the scattered objects read:

Two postcards of Paris beauties.
Two packets of Players (20s.).
A cork-dropper from a bottle of angostura bitters.
A hare's foot.

A letter from a young lady dated 22 December, from 15 Leazes Gardens, on pink, deckle-edged writing paper signed 'Doris'. It thanked Banjo for the good time he had given her 'Last Night'.

A small, red penny note-book with nothing written in it at all.

A traveller's ration book, inscribed Benjamin D. Pilkington.

An unnamed book of clothing coupons.

'The whole thing may be meaningless,' said 'Swiss' Robinson, when he had made his list and straightened his broad shoulders. 'But on the whole I've noticed in the past that *nothing* is meaningless. No matter how small.'

He stamped about the dressing-room, drawing chalk marks round the body, stepping gingerly so that he should not disturb it.

'Poor chap,' he said, and added (a little indiscreetly for Hampton Court was standing just inside the door): 'shot by a heavy-type revolver bullet. No one must leave the backstage part of the theatre. I will conduct a search directly for the weapon.'

Hampton Court blanched. His eyes were furiously pinpointed with worry. He asked if the show might go on.

'I locked the pass-door at the *start* of the performance,' he said anxiously. 'And I stand to lose a helluva lot of dough if this show shuts down. That locked pass-door would clear all the audience, now, wouldn't it?'

Hampton looked worse than bizarre, lounging in his plush jodhpurs in that dreadful setting.

'But how can you do *Cinderella* with only one Ugly Sister?' said Robinson obstinately.

The dressing-table had been swept quite bare when Banjo fell. There were smears of powder on it, perhaps where his hand had dragged. There were his various changes, hanging on hooks and coathangers in a corner. His hunting costume. His ball dress. His comic stays. His white satin suit and the bowler hat that went with it. Among these bright trappings his day lounge suit (navy blue with a thick white chalk stripe upon it) appeared colourless.

'I'd make an announcement from the stage,' said Hampton, 'that Banjo is very ill and let Harry carry on as *both* Ugly Sisters.'

'Heavens,' said 'Swiss' Robinson, very shocked; 'you've got it all taped, haven't you? But won't he – Harry – be a bit upset? I mean, the feller was his brother, wasn't he?'

He scrubbed a hand up the bristles on his neck and stared at Hampton. In the distance they could hear Mr Jenkins, playing manfully through the Entr'acte. 'Swiss' Robinson looked as though he would like to hand the whole decision on to a higher authority.

'My dear sir,' said Hampton Court, and drew himself up, 'Harry DeFreeze is a *trouper*.'

'Swiss' Robinson shrugged his shoulders.

'Please yourself,' he said coldly. 'As long as me and my men can carry out our investigation, and no actor, or anyone who was behind the scenes here for a minute this evening, is allowed to leave the theatre now, I dare say the Chief Constable will have no objection.'

'Isn't the Chief Constable Mr Tom Atkins, in any case?' said Hampton Court.

'No, sir,' said 'Swiss' Robinson. 'He was Chief Constable last year, sir.'

And mentally he made the note (perhaps a little unprofessionally, for it was an opinion based on an imperfect working knowledge of psychology) that Hampton Court was an inhuman baboon person.

'While the "show goes on",' he said slowly, 'I'll go an' see George. Your door-keeper. And Banjo DeFreeze's dresser.'

'Peters,' said Hampton Court, and nodded.

'If that's what he's called,' said Robinson. His manner was distinctly lukewarm.

II

So far as 'Swiss' Robinson could judge Banjo DeFreeze had been shot through the forehead at 8.45 p.m. At that moment the stage was full (it was the tableau of milady's dressing-table) and, apart from the principals, the entire company and Natasha were supposed to be on the stage singing a full-throated chorus called 'Going to Vanity Fair'.

George, at the stage door, had heard the shot. He was quite positive that no unauthorized person had entered the building before or after this time. When he had heard the shot he had been on the telephone. Yes, whoever he was talking to would know exactly what time *that* was and give him a check. Huh. As well as an alibi. (George had moistened his lips.) He had been talking to Mrs George at the time, as it so happened. And they had both commented. They had thought it was a car backfiring in Atkins Street. He couldn't say anything else except Mr Banjo had had two telephone calls that afternoon. No, he hadn't heard him take them. They were entered in the little book here. George was very sorry about the whole thing, he was sure.

His little glass cabinet was searched. He had a packet of turkey sandwiches, a tin jug of tea (very sweet), a pair of dry slippers and a pad for taking down messages. There was no sign of a revolver.

Banjo's dressing-room was locked and the call-boy was on his rounds, calling the beginners for the second half, before Natasha returned from her small triumph, carrying a large basket filled with dark red roses. They had been handed to her from the orchestra pit at the end of the dance of the Fée Dragée, which had stopped the show. (This had happened at 8.40 p.m. precisely.) She came downstairs with her basket now, quite unaware of everything that had happened. She looked tired, but incredibly beautiful in her famous pale blue and maribou, and found terrible chaos and anger raging in all the dressing-rooms.

'Hampton Court expects us to go on with his blasted show,' screamed Marylyn Franklyn on the staircase. 'In conditions like these. It's a disgrace.'

'What conditions?' asked Natasha vaguely. 'The little ponies?'

The little ponies were two vicious little skewbald Shetland slugs who were waiting to be led on to the stage by the silent gentlemen who had controlled the Dalmatian dogs. Behind them trailed Cinderella's magic pumpkin coach, illuminated by fifty-six fairy lights, which lit up when one of the gentlemen pressed a switch. The ponies were behaving exactly as one might expect in these circumstances. One of them had bitten a gentleman in the fleshy part of his arm. The other had nervously disgraced itself.

'The ponies!' snorted Marylyn Franklyn contemptuously.

'The ponies, indeed. Didn't you know Banjo DeFreeze was shot?'

Natasha looked vague.

'So many people in this pantomime are being shot and so *much of the time* that I should not have been thinking one drunk more or less would be making any difference,' she said slowly.

Marylyn Franklyn flew into an even more violent rage.

'Not *drunk*!' she screamed. 'Shot! Dead. Murdered. Killed with a revolver. Shot through the forehead.'

Even Marylyn was satisfied with Natasha's reaction to this sentence. Her white hands flew to her mouth. The basket fell and the roses spilled like blood all the way down the stone stairs while Natasha stayed, trembling, on the top step.

'A revolver!' she said slowly. 'Oh no, not a *revolver*. Anything but that.'

III

And so Hampton Court bounced out to the footlights and made his announcement about Banjo DeFreeze's sudden serious illness, and how there would only be *one* Ugly Sister for the rest of the pantomime. Several doctors, although none had been called for, rose from their seats and officiously left their wives and families, to spend the remainder of the evening in the saloon bar.

Sergeant 'Swiss' Robinson, waiting for the arrival of the photographer from Newchester Central Police-Station, wondered again and again if he had made the right decision in allowing the show to go on. He was almost sure he had *not*. He went about his routine duties in Banjo's dressing-room, gloomily and methodically, surveying the unhappy wreckage. He examined the chairs and the dressing-table for finger-prints. There were hundreds of them, all smeared, all covered with face powder. None of them were distinct enough to use as evidence. He searched Banjo's jacket pockets for further letters. He found two bills (one from a dentist), a receipt for a year's rent from a block of service flats in London called Porpoise Court, and a postcard from 'Doris' saying that she would 'definitely be with mum for Christmas, longing to see you again, Banj, old boy.' He generally went over the room with a fine toothcomb. There was, of course, no sign of a revolver. It was only when he heard the dreadful strains of Hampton Court singing,

'H-A-P-P-Y spells contented.
That is what we are,'

in the distance that he recollected something. In 'Swiss' Robinson's youth pantomime comedians had sometimes thrown presents to the audience, wrapped up in coloured paper. My God. If one had an accomplice and could throw fairly accurately . . .

His suspicions were suddenly violently aroused. 'Swiss' Robinson leapt up. He locked the door behind him. He rushed upstairs towards the stage.

IV

Hampton Court, looking very like a pink squash rackets ball, sprang about the stage, encouraging the left side of the stalls to sing against the right side of the stalls, the ladies to sing against the gentlemen, the gallery (merely) to sing. He was going over remarkably well. Every now and then a shrill scream of eldritch laughter from a young lady in the gallery proved it. The house, full of sympathy for the game little troupers, carrying on in the face of illness, had evidently decided that they were little troupers themselves. They had settled down to five minutes' steady self-entertainment. It was a little embarrassing.

Robinson stood in the wings and scowled. His good idea had been a waste of time. Hampton Court was not flinging revolvers (wrapped in cellophane and marked 'Do Not Open Until New Year's Day') to an accomplice in the audience.

Robinson looked at his watch. It was well past nine o'clock and there was still plenty of pantomime to be got through. The Shetland ponies, stamping softly somewhere near him, reminded him that the ballroom scene was getting very near. First Hampton would do his best to make everybody cry, as Buttons failed to get into the ball, and Cinderella swept past him ...

Wait a minute. Where *were* the ponies? How had they got here? They couldn't have come through the regular stage door and down those stone steps.

He went in search of a groom and found a taciturn creature with a long upper lip. In the daytime he worked in a riding stables called 'Mayes'.

'Get here?' said the groom. 'The ponies come down th' other side, like. We put a ramp down them stairs there, see? The carriage is all ready here and then we hitch them up, like.'

'*Which* other side?' said Robinson. 'The other side of *what*?' He was still angry and nervous.

'T'other side of th' dressin'-rooms,' snapped the groom.

'You mean there are *two* stage doors?' said Robinson slowly.

'Naw,' drawled the groom. 'Gittup, you little scone!'

(This last remark was addressed to the pony, which laid its ears back flat on its head and showed one long, yellow tooth in a miniature sneer.)

'What d'ye mean, "naw"?' snapped Robinson.

'Keep yer hair on,' said the groom. 'On'y meant there was one stage door—'

'No, no,' cried Robinson, greatly excited. 'Are there two entrances backstage? Two ways people can get in?'

'In a manner of speakin',' said the groom maddeningly, wiping his nose with the back of his hand, 'you might say there *was . . .*'

In the pause that followed this heavy remark Tony Gresham appeared. With a hissing of sibilants that sounded like a Queen Cobra, he asked them to be 'Quiet, please. *Do* give Mr Court a chance.'

'Except that it's nearly always locked,' concluded the groom, as though Tony were not there at all.

V

Excited and puzzled Robinson plunged downstairs again, determined to interview Peters, dresser to the Brothers DeFreeze.

He could hear there was turmoil in Harry's dressing-room. He could hear it as he turned the corner of the stairs and came along the passage. Harry's dressing-room had always been next door to his brother's. There were five dressing-rooms on the ground floor of the theatre. They were assigned to Hampton

Court, Marylyn Franklyn, Banjo, Harry and the starring lady (Miriam Birdseye in this instance), in that order, reading from left to right.

Robinson hesitated before he knocked on the door. He read Harry's visiting-card, which was elaborate and Olde Englishe in design. He was glad he did not knock. Just as he was about to do so, the call-boy appeared from nowhere, rapped smartly and disappeared along the passage, calling as he went:

'Brothers DeFreeze, stage, please!'

Robinson effaced himself as Harry came out of his dressing-room. He was livid under his make-up, which was white and red, like a clown. He plunged towards the stairs, carrying his skirts in each hand, showing elastic-sided boots and red and white striped stockings. He was in his yellow satin ball dress and scratch wig, ready to sweep spectacularly into the ball. Even Robinson thought he looked ill. He turned the corner of the stairs and came face to face with Hampton Court.

Hampton was sweating and happy, conscious that he had done his very best with 'H-A-P-P-Y spells contented!' He was in a mood where he would have kissed Kidder Atkins. He was on his way to change from pink plush jodhpurs to white satin jodhpurs. But as he passed Harry on the stairs he said, 'Go it now, kid!' and slapped him gaily on the shoulder. No doubt he meant it kindly. It was hardly a tactful gesture. Harry started as though he had been stung. His face went even more peaked and spiteful.

'If you don't *mind*,' he said slowly, with heavy sarcasm, 'I have some *work* to do.'

He brushed Hampton on one side. Hampton was *furious*. As Robinson heard his cluck of rage he glanced round him for cover. He dived into Harry's dressing-room, and there, with the door ajar, he eavesdropped in a most ungentlemanly way.

'What's the matter with you?' said Hampton coldly. 'You'll draw double salary. Nothing to complain of . . .'

In the dressing-room a little man with a fawn, twitchy face approached Robinson who put his forefinger to his lips.

'OK, OK,' said the little man, obviously Peters, the dresser. 'I only want to listen, too—'

'Why, you big *baboon*!'

That was Harry screaming, and out of control.

'Since you're still at it . . .' That was still Harry. '. . . You can instruct your call-boy in proper calls. No more calls for the *Brothers* DeFreeze. Banjo is dead, you understand? Dead. Dead. *Dead*!'

Hampton Court seemed unmoved by Harry's hysteria.

Peters clucked sympathetically in Robinson's ear. 'Nasty temper when he's roused,' he said.

'Baboon, am I?' said Hampton unpleasantly. His voice rasped dreadfully. Every word he said was distinct. 'What about your letter to Viv, eh? Saying you were going to end it all? The night she died? How about *that*? How you were sick of her deceivin' you with Banjo an' hundreds of others? What about that?'

In the pause before Hampton Court continued. Robinson became aware of Peters, who went 'Tchk! Tchk!' in his ear.

'Don't you suppose Mr Blasted officiatin' Robinson'll like to hear 'bout that? Before you start callin' *me* a baboon, you'd better find out where that letter got to. It about amounts to a confession of *murder*, that's all.'

'Tchk,' said Peters.

'Murder!' screamed Harry. 'What the hell d'you mean? Viv

murdered? I swear I didn't murder her, whatever I said in that letter. I was—'

'Ah,' interrupted Hampton Court. 'But who shot Banjo?'

'*On the stage, please, Mr DeFreeze, please!*'

The call-boy had evidently come back and was calling Harry from the stairs. From Harry's dressing-room Robinson and Peters could hear feet pattering furiously on the stone stairs up to the stage. Someone swung up the passage and into a dressing-room and a door slammed. Robinson waited for Peters to say something.

'Tchk,' said Peters. 'Well. I always did say Mr Harry was a dark horse.'

VI

'Don't you *like* Mr Harry, then?' said Robinson. He sat down on the hard little wooden chair that Harry used when he was making up. He stared up at Peters.

Peters was a neat little man, in shirt-sleeves and a black waistcoat. His hair was brushed upwards, like a lavatory brush. His eyes seemed weak. He blinked continuously at Robinson, while he hung Harry's white satin suit on a coat-hanger and put away his white bowler hat in a cardboard hat-box. He smoothed the nap of the bowler hat very carefully as he did so.

'I was Mr *Banjo*'s dresser,' he said demurely.

'You're a Newchester man,' said Robinson, suddenly accusing.

'That's right. Newchester bred and born. Accent gives us all away every time.' Peters seemed quite unperturbed about it.

'But you toured round with B— I mean, you toured with the DeFreezes?'

Peters considered for a second before he replied to all Robinson's questions.

'That's right. And glad to,' he said eventually. 'Good job t'was, dressin' both of them. Specially in the summer on the Halls.'

'*But* you arrange to come to Newchester – come home for Christmas, eh? Is that it?'

'Sometimes. *Sometimes*,' said Peters, with a secret smile. 'Last year we was in Sheffield.'

It was Robinson's turn to pause, then:

'You married?' he said abruptly.

'That's right,' said Peters, startled.

'Your wife lives here in Newchester?'

'That's right,' said Peters.

'At 15 Leazes Gardens and you have a daughter called Doris?'

'Now how the hell did you know that?' said Peters, without any pause at all.

2

'Swiss' Robinson's interview with Peters did not last long.
When Robinson discovered he had a daughter called Doris,
Peters looked at him with new respect. He did not seem distressed at the thought, however, or to realize that, as Doris's
father, he was in a significant position. Did Peters know that
his daughter had been flirting with Banjo? Peters' mouth grew
hard and tight and disapproving. With girls of today there was
no knowing where they'd stop. Robinson took this to be an
answer 'Yes *and* No.' He ploughed on with routine questions
about Banjo's day to day behaviour.

Apparently Mr Banjo was the flashy type. But good-hearted.
Yes, he took a drink. No, Peters hadn't no idea if he had any
enemies. He couldn't say he was sure. Mr Banjo had quite a
few men friends. They went to the races and that. He was a
ladies' man, really, but nothing startling. More of an artist than
anything, really, Mr Banjo. Loved the Theatre . . .

Robinson looked up with interest.

'What do you mean, "loved the Theatre"?' The idea that
someone might work for something other than money was new
to Robinson.

Peters considered.

'Well,' he said slowly, 'he spent a lot of time here. Good pros always do, you know. He was never late on a call. Nor missed a performance. The other artists, yes. Mr Harry, even. Mr Banjo, never. Not even when he had the gastric flu real bad. I remember him saying to me, "Peters," he said. "Peters. I just can't seem to get warm."'

Robinson cut across some frothy reminiscences of Banjo's symptoms on this occasion. It seemed it had all taken place in Leeds three years ago.

'Was he regular in his habits? You could count on him doing the same thing day after day?'

'Oh, he was regular in the Theatre, Mr Banjo.' Peters paused and scratched his head for a second before he went on. 'There was one thing. Always arrived at four for a 6.30 performance and twelve noon for a matinée. Opened his post and popped out to tea and lunch, whichever ... He got a lot of letters,' concluded Peters wistfully.

Robinson made marks on Harry's dressing-table with a powerful thumb. Peters took down Harry's next change from the rail in the corner. It was a highly humorous pink flannel house-coat, worn for trying on the slipper. This episode was to take place in front of a drop-curtain consisting of portraits of the Baron de Broke's ancestors.

Did Mr Banjo arrive at four today, Robinson wanted to know? Funny he should ask that. Actually today Mr Banjo had come in at noon like as if for a matinée. He was in a bit of a fuss about some telephone call. He had put it through from the stage door. He worked the switchboard himself. That was Mr Banjo all over.

'Where was George?' said Robinson sharply.

'How the hell do I know?' Peters was angry.

Robinson realized he had made a tactical error and tried to soothe the little man.

'OK, OK,' he said. 'Don't fuss yourself. It might help, that's all, if I knew who he was talking to, see? Would it be a local call? Did you hear any of it?'

Peters *had* heard some of it. He couldn't say who it was to, hows'mever. Seemingly it was a business call, though. Mr Banjo made a date with whoever it was.

'Really? Any idea where? Or what time for?'

'Reely couldn't say.' Peters was cold. 'When Mr Banjo went out he always said, "See you in church" or "Just popping across the road." But it was more in the way of a pleasantry, like.'

'Quite,' said Robinson. 'Which did he say on this occasion?'

'See you in church,' said Peters, slowly and solemnly.

II

Natasha arrived downstairs in the dressing-room that she shared with Miss Esmeralda Greenaway, the Fairy Queen of Starry Nights. Miss Greenaway was not there. She was up on the stage, giving Cinderella a last warning about midnight:

> *Remember, Cinders! When you hear the clock*
> *Begone! Or you will get a shock.*
> *Your jewels will go, in shame your cheeks will burn*
> *As to vile rags your lovely satins turn . . .*

Miss Greenaway's dressing-table, with its powder and grease-paint, its telegram of good wishes, its piece of Christmas cake and glass of sherry, its photograph of her late husband, a squadron-leader in the Australian Air Force, all pointed to a precise and genteel nature. Nothing was spilled. Everything was neat and, where it could be polished, shiny. Timothy Shelly sat in a chair in front of the looking-glass and played with the photographs. They were stuck around the edge of the glass like a decoration.

'These,' he said, without looking up, 'must be her children. And that must be her husband. He looked like a Kenneth.'

Natasha gazed over his shoulder.

'He *was* a Kenneth,' said Natasha. 'Oh, Timothy, I spilled my roses. I was so *upset* ...'

Timothy Shelly looked at her in the looking-glass and grinned crookedly.

'Did you read ...?' he said. He stopped and blushed.

'Oh!' Natasha was excited. She searched among glossy dark leaves and smooth, wired florists' stems. 'Then they *were* from you. Is there being a card or something?'

'Somewhere,' said Timothy carelessly, as though it were of no consequence.

Eventually Natasha found it. It was a little envelope, no bigger than a visiting-card. She tore it open. Written very, very small, as though with a mapping pen, was a little verse.

Natasha
> *Was it the wind that called so gay*
> *And left my heart like aspens stirred?*
> *As though some laughing, maddening word,*

Hardly remembered in the day,
Would come like music in the night . . .

'Oh, *Timothy*,' said Natasha. She turned towards him with the card in one hand and the wreckage of the roses in the other.

'It isn't finished,' said Timothy, and scowled. 'It will probably take about eight years to finish.'

Natasha smelt her roses. Her eyes reflected the excitement of the dressing-room and the bright lights round the looking-glass. In her eyes Timothy Shelly could see himself. Where would he be in eight years' time?

'I'll go out in the passage,' he said, 'while you change.'

'No,' said Natasha sharply. 'I shall not change for a little. This' – she waved the poem – 'this puts everything out of my head. Coming down I spill the roses because Banjo has been shot. Sergeant Robinson ... Banjo is dead ... and Sergeant Robinson is interviewing everyone. Timothy, you must give me your revolver.'

She held out her smooth hand.

'Carnation, Lily, Lily, Rose,' whispered Timothy.

He ran his hand through his hair and a lock fell forward on his forehead in disarray. He patted his right hip. His face changed. Then he rubbed his eye-sockets furiously and became wild and distressed.

'Natasha!' he cried. 'I can't. I haven't got it ...'

III

'I was watching Miss Natasha Nevkorina dance, you know,' said Harry DeFreeze smoothly. He was repairing his clownish make-up with a big powder-puff and some rouge. 'I couldn't have heard anything up there on the stage. Not even an elephant gun.'

He touched some rouge on the tip of his nose and etched in the lines round his mouth.

'What time does Miss Nevkorina do this *toe dance?*' said Sergeant Robinson. His voice, now and hereafter, was offensive.

Harry DeFreeze looked at him curiously.

'What on earth do you mean?' he said. 'I don't know what time she does it. This is the first run-through of the pantomime. And it's not a toe dance. Miss Nevkorina danced for Diaghilev.'

'Whoever he may be,' said Robinson lightly. 'Sounds Russian to me.'

Harry DeFreeze's eyes went to very small points like pins. He put on his red wig. There grimaced back at him from the glass the warped female face of Mania, the Baron's daughter.

'There were quite a number of people in the wings, watching her,' said Harry. He was incongruously dignified. 'And they seemed to consider it a bit better than a toe dance.'

'*Who*, for example?' snapped Robinson.

'Oh, really,' said Harry testily. 'I've told you I was watching her dance. Her boy-friend, I expect. That Shelly. My brother may have been there, too, for all I know.'

Harry DeFreeze bit his lip and winced. Robinson watched him narrowly.

'But you were watching the dance yourself. You're certain of that?'

'I've told you so,' he cried. 'My God! I've told you so. Isn't it enough to lose one half of the best act a fellow ever had, and to lose the top of the bill in consequence, *and* one's ex-wife all in one week without you blasted bobbies coming trampling all over me like this?'

Weeping, Harry dabbed at his eyes.

'There!' he said, in angry, twitching triumph. 'You've made my mascara run . . .'

'*DeFreeze Brothers, please.*'

The call-boy's voice was outside the door again.

Harry's miserable gargoyle of a face worked terribly. His narrow chin trembled.

'I-will-not-cry, I-will-not-cry, I-will-not-cry,' he muttered. He bit his under-lip. He wrapped his flannelette house-coat round his narrow hips and picked up a fan. It was a foolish ugly thing of arsenic green feathers. He sailed towards the door. Never had the trappings of a funny man seemed more tragic and incongruous.

'My brother Banjo,' he said suddenly, to no one in particular, 'was never late on cue in his *life.*'

The door slammed behind him.

Sergeant Robinson was left with his eyes starting from his head.

'Raving,' he said. 'That's all – raving mad.'

IV

'You have not got the revolver?' Natasha was angry and indignant. 'What can you *mean*, you have not got it? How extraordinary you are. You have it when we leave Bayleyside. You are showing off with it before that terrible drive we have with Hampton Court in that *dangerous* car. You have it when we are coming into the theatre. I know you have it coming into the theatre. It spoilt your appearance, bulging like that in your pocket.'

Timothy Shelly seemed horrified.

'I know I had it, too,' he said vaguely. He was not drunk. 'What have I done with it?'

'You know what I should do?' said Natasha slowly.

Timothy hardly seemed to care what Natasha would do. But he inclined his head and said 'What?' morosely.

'I should be going and telling Sergeant Robinson what an utter bloody fool I am and how I am losing it. And I should go and tell him now, before he is coming to me with it in his hand . . .'

'And have him tell me I shot Banjo with it?' said Timothy Shelly coldly. 'Thanks very much . . .'

V

In Harry DeFreeze's dressing-room Robinson's exasperation with that odd sense of values known as the 'artistic temperament' did not last long. Presently he sighed. And then he laughed, looking towards Peters, the dresser, for comfort. He got none. As the door slammed behind Harry, Peters' narrow shoulders shrugged slightly. He did not even turn his head. Robinson sighed again and asked Peters which was Mr Court's dressing-room.

'Last one along on this level,' said Peters, without moving. 'On the right.'

So Robinson went out and along the passage. He was suddenly aware that he was tired.

He was also, he thought, improperly dressed for a Police Investigation. This dinner-jacket had always cut him under the arms. Mrs Robinson, too (her name was Bella and she was a bit of a bitch), would be properly fed up with him. As Bella imagined that he had only been called round as a result of his own curiosity, to make further inquiries about Vivienne Gresham, she would assume that he had gone out and was drinking his head off with his fine theatrical friends. Well, let her assume. That sort of suspicious nonsense was enough to drive any man to drink ...

And incidentally ... mightn't there be a connection between the two deaths? There was definitely something not quite right behind the scenes of this pantomime. There was definitely something. What could one call it? The kiss of death?

Sergeant Robinson dismissed all these thoughts as idle nonsense. He told himself he had been over-working.

He pushed open Hampton Court's door without knocking.

Hampton was bent over his dressing-table, furtively putting something away in a drawer. He looked round guiltily. He concealed something behind his back. Robinson saw it clearly reflected in the looking-glass. It was a half-full bottle of gin.

'Oh,' said Hampton Court sourly. 'It's only you. I thought – well, never mind. Sit down. Only got ten minutes before my next call, though ...'

Hampton was changed into a navy-blue page-boy's suit covered with silver buttons. He looked incredibly debauched. A cigar, half-burned down, lay spilling its ash on the dressing-table. Its exotic fragrance mocked its drab surroundings. An older cigar, that had burned a hole in the carpet some days ago, lay where it had fallen, cold at Hampton's feet. Hampton's dresser was evidently not fussy about cleaning. All along the top of the dressing-table were old brown marks of burns, and interlocking rings, where glasses habitually were set down. Robinson, a neat, clean man with a neat clean mind, was disgusted by squalor. He reflected that it was unfair to accuse Hampton Court of all this damage. Clearly other people had used the room before him . . .

'You need an ash-tray,' he said mildly.

'I've got one,' said Hampton Court. He slapped it down from the window-sill to the dressing-table. Written round the edge of the rim was 'The Great Northern Hotel, Leeds'. Robinson lit a cigarette and put a match neatly into the ash-tray.

'Well?' said Hampton Court belligerently. 'How're you getting on? This is what we pay our rates and taxes for, remember.'

'Fine – fine,' said Robinson easily, blowing smoke about. 'Considering.'

'Considering what?' snapped Hampton Court. 'Our feelings? You don't think of *them* much. You don't give *them* a thought.'

'Now, Mr Court,' said Robinson. 'You know I'm only doing my duty.'

'Have a drink,' said Hampton instantly.

'Not on duty, Mr Court,' but Robinson looked wistfully at

the bottle of gin. His tongue seemed cleft to the roof of his dry mouth. His whole system screamed for juniper berries. 'The thing is *this* ... I've collected quite a lot of individual statements. And it's pretty obvious to me that by the end of this evening we shall have enough data to show where all of your ... ' Sergeant Robinson coughed, searching for the right word, 'your artists,' he discovered finally, 'where all your artists were when this shot was fired. That's to say, enough to see who is telling the truth. Or who is telling lies. And to make a picture.'

'Ah,' said Hampton, drinking the gin that remained in his glass. 'The truth always checks. I've noticed that.'

He poured himself another stiff gin. He emptied the remains of a bottle of tonic water on to it and began to gulp it down far too fast. Robinson moved restlessly in his chair.

'Ah,' said Robinson, in his turn. 'Now, here's my plan. When I have collected all your individual statements as to movements, et cetera, I shall call a big meeting of all the lot of you.'

'To check up,' said Hampton, and nodded his ape's head. 'Check up the truth. Truth always checks.'

'Exactly,' said Robinson. 'Now which room do you suggest would be big enough? Do you have a green room in this theatre?'

It seemed warmer in Hampton Court's dressing-room than in Harry DeFreeze's. Robinson moved restlessly and found an electric radiator behind him, playing slap on to his broad shoulders.

'Big enough for what?' said Hampton, a little stupidly. 'I don't ever recollect a *green* room in any theatre I ever appeared in.'

'Big enough for the entire company,' said Robinson. 'Anybody who might have noticed anybody, Tots included.'

Hampton considered for a minute, looking vaguely at his changes, which hung against a wall, concealed by a drab and anonymous curtain.

'The only place that is even remotely big enough,' he said finally, with a 'take it or leave it' air, 'is the Tots and Chorus dressing-room. It runs all the way along the floor below here. Space of three rooms this size in it.'

He waved a hand expansively around his head. Robinson suddenly observed a bunch of about fifteen latch-keys on the dressing-table.

'That will do fine,' said Robinson.

'But look here!' Hampton, having made his helpful suggestion, was suddenly angry again. 'Look here. We'll be stuck in the theatre until three in the morning if you take individual statements all round the company like that. To check in public?'

Robinson wondered why any man could possibly want fifteen latch-keys.

'I must remind you, Mr Court,' said Robinson, suddenly official, 'that murder is a very serious business and needs the most drastic remedies. And depend upon it, I shall get all the statements of your principals before then. And, remember, I'm not at all sure I've done the right thing at all in allowing you to continue with the show like this. The Chief will tell me it is irregular. And the Chief will be right.'

He smoothed his moustache and was reassured by its familiar feeling. He considered the latch-keys all the time that he was speaking. One for his own flat. One for his girl-friend's . . .

185

'*What?*' Hampton was appalled. 'Interview us while the pantomime is still going on?'

One for the garage. One for another little establishment. Twelve little establishments. No, that really went too far . . .

'That's right.' Robinson was quite unrepentant.

'But – so confusing. Don't know what I mightn't say – in a hurry. No time to think. My solicitor . . . '

Hampton's tongue galloped loosely away along a track of excuses. But he seemed disturbed.

'All the more chance that you tell the truth, if you speak in a hurry,' said Robinson. And it was suddenly his turn to smile unpleasantly.

VI

In her dressing-room Natasha was still in a rage.

'Where did you lose it, Timothy? You ought to know if you think. *Think*, think, think.'

Timothy Shelly sat with his handsome head in his hands. He was the very picture of despair.

'If I knew, my dear,' he said gently, 'it wouldn't be lost. Now would it?'

VII

Sergeant Robinson stood up, looking gloomy. He felt that Hampton Court's little electric radiator was about to set him seriously alight. He wriggled his red-hot shoulders, positive that he would shortly be able to smell singeing flesh as well as scorched cloth.

Hampton Court showed uneven teeth and said, 'Well?' on a thin note. 'Why not interview me as to my whereabouts?' he went on. 'Hey?'

'Oh,' said Robinson vaguely. 'I don't think I'll bother to do that.' He baited him gently. 'The truth always checks, sir, don't it?' He grinned broadly at Hampton Court, whose face went black with rage. Then Robinson suddenly felt, with keenest pleasure, one of the seams in his tight, blistering dinner-jacket give way with a tiny crash. At last he was able to move his arms.

'One thing, though,' he went on amiably, 'which seems to me to have a direct bearin' on the death of Mr Banjo DeFreeze. One thing I would like . . .'

Hampton looked up at him with his mouth fallen open in a silent question. His brow was still overshadowed by clouds of temper.

'The letter that you possess of Mr Harry DeFreeze. Apropos the death of Miss Vivienne Gresham, his late wife.'

Hampton blasphemed. He said he had no such letter. He said he had no idea what the hell Sergeant Robinson was talking about. He said Sergeant Robinson was a 'mean, up and down chimneys, listening at keyholes, sneaking sort of a policeman'. In fact, he behaved very like Humpty Dumpty in *Alice in Wonderland*. Sergeant Robinson was unmoved. He held out one broad, pink unemphatic palm; and presently Hampton Court, thoroughly fed-up, put the letter in it.

'Thanks,' said Robinson coldly, and started towards the door.

'But look here,' said Hampton in a quick and passionate rage. 'Look here. I don't know at all the legal position regarding that document. I don't believe that you're entitled – not for one moment.'

And he studded his protests with a selection of adjectives that I must, I find, suppress.

'Neither are you, Mr Court, neither are you,' said Robinson. And he shut the door of the dressing-room smoothly behind him, with the subtlest and most insulting of double clicks.

3

Marylyn Franklyn sat in her dressing-room. She was very frightened. She was haunted, and she was wondering how she might best conceal from Sergeant Robinson the fact that she and Banjo DeFreeze had been having an *affaire*.

Marylyn's thin, twisty blond face peeped back at her, blank, from the looking-glass. It was spiteful and white with fear. In her mind's eye she was still overshadowed by Banjo. She could not believe she would not see him if she turned her head. There he would be, large and powerful, mastering her with easy humour and cheerful familiarity, overpowering her fears with smooth commands and (sometimes) with restrained physical violence. If she turned her head. She went on looking in the glass.

She shivered and covered her eyes with her hand. Then she began to hunt furiously through her handbag. There was a lot of obvious evidence in existence because Banjo had always thought it unnecessary to conceal anything he did. Marylyn had fought a losing battle against his large, dark nature.

For she was a married woman. Her husband, Paddy, would (she always told her lovers) 'murder' her if he detected her indiscretions. And her daughter (aged seventeen, called Maureen) – her daughter's innocence had to be protected at all costs. It was to keep Maureen and Paddy (she told herself) that she slaved on the unrewarding stage and faced the heartbreaks of failure. The truth was, however, that her life was spent in a series of insincere, unreliable amorous adventures, and it was easier to conceal them from Maureen and Paddy if she had a profession to cover them up. It was not the first time, for example, that Marylyn Franklyn had scattered the unpleasant contents of her mock leopard-covered bag and destroyed the relics of a guilty love. Marylyn, a poetess in her way, described this as 'a bit of fun between two good sports'.

Here, then, with tattered powder-puffs and aged lipsticks and dusty, clogged kerbigrips, and broken compacts made of gilded tin, were gathered the pathetic remnants of Banjo DeFreeze's last attachment. There was a Movisnap, taken in Atkins Street, Newchester, by one of those errant young gentlemen with Leica cameras. It showed Marylyn in a fine big Robin Hood hat with a pheasant's feather, and the leopard skin waistcoat that matched this bag. It must have caught the photographer's eye. And Banjo was leering horribly and whispering indelicately in her ear.

Marylyn sighed and tore it up. The fragments fell sadly in the waste-paper basket on top of an old beef sandwich and the paper belonging to a Mars Bar. There was a menu of a dinner of Oddfellows, where Banjo and Harry had been guest artists and had performed a dance or two as a Cabaret. Marylyn had gone as Banjo's partner and everyone had signed the menu. Mr Atkins had been there, she remembered. And that old Vivienne Gresham had gone with Harry. Funny the way Harry had gone on and on, even after he'd divorced her. No accounting, there wasn't really.

Marylyn remembered that dinner all right. Bit different from this Christmas when Lord Flaming Mayors had found themselves too blasted stuck-up for her.

The boys had had a success. And so had Marylyn. Two Oddfellows had invited her home with them 'for a bit of sport'. Oddly, Banjo had been *furious*. High-pitched, angry words had passed between them. Perhaps it had been a bit much, going home with them like that. Still, it was nice that Banjo cared enough to be jealous. And as for That Vivienne Gresham.

Marylyn drew in her thin mouth and sucked her sharp teeth, shuffling the Oddfellows' menu up, dragging the waste-paper basket towards her with her foot. Someone tapped on the door as she tore it up.

'That you, Gert?' she called. And she added, almost automatically, under her breath, one of Banjo's old jokes. 'Gertie gets dirty after eight-thirty.'

She giggled sadly.

But it was not Gertie, her dresser, with the Guinness that had been ordered so long ago from the Saracen's Head. It was Sergeant Robinson, rubbing his blond moustache with his thumb. Quite a nice-looking fellow, the Sergeant ...

'Come along in, dear,' said Marylyn gaily. 'Come along in.' And she swept everything back into her handbag. Money, compacts, powder, lipstick, hairpins, all lay jumbled in a frightful coil of dust, smelling strongly of *Soir de Paris*, in the bottom of her bag.

'May I sit down?' said the Sergeant. The dressing-room was slightly scented. It was different altogether from any of the others he had been in.

'Please yourself, dear,' said Miss Franklyn. 'You can always shut your eyes when I change ... '

Sergeant Robinson flinched and shut his eyes involuntarily. Then, like a brave man, he opened them again. Marylyn was dressed for the ball, returned to valet status, in scarlet livery with silver cords. She had an elaborate white stock. In the ball-room scene, Dandini, the prince's confidential servant, would be expected to mingle with the guests and help the Mount Charles Male Voice Quartet (now dressed as footmen) to hand drinks about among the guests. Hampton Court would run amok, making difficult jokes about 'wanting soom of that in a moog'. Dandini would be expected to deal with him.

'Change?' said Robinson. 'You look very nice as you are, my dear.'

He drew a chair towards him and stood, holding it by the back, looking down at her, blinking. Marylyn Franklyn bridled.

'Go on,' she said vivaciously. 'You know damn' well I have to change for the march past of the Clans. I will say that for Hampton. He *does* dress his pantos regardless ... '

Sergeant Robinson sat heavily in a chair and drew it slightly forward. He did not care to ask of what Hampton Court was regardless when he dressed his pantos. Taste, perhaps?

'Don't people care for Mr Court's pantomimes as a general rule, then?' he said mildly.

Miss Franklyn considered. She licked the tip of a finger and she rubbed it delicately over her eyebrows. They appeared as neat and as narrow as a butterfly's antennae.

'Well, no – not reelly,' she said. 'After all, he's not the Littlers, now, is he?'

Sergeant Robinson agreed that he was not.

'Nor Tom Arnold. Well, I suppose beggars can't be choosers, I always say. What did you want to see me about, Sergeant?'

Sergeant Robinson looked around him. He turned to a scrutiny of Miss Franklyn's face. He watched a wary expression that flickered, like lightning, in and out of Marylyn's pale eyes. The woman was obviously terrified of something. Robinson crossed his fingers.

'So hopeless,' he said thickly and (he hoped) amorously. 'Talking to you here. In fact we can't, I mean. Talk, that's to say. There are hundreds of things I want to know. Feel it in my bones. You're the only one who can tell me. Definitely.'

Marylyn Franklyn looked pleased.

'Well,' she said. 'My digs are scarcely ... I mean, I'm staying with old Ma Hitch in Leazes Terrace. Frankly they aren't fit to ask a fellow back to. Well, you know what I mean?'

The apprehension was still there, however, but it was drowning slowly in a pale wave of interest. Interest and satisfaction. Sergeant Robinson was very reassuring.

'Oh,' he said. 'I didn't mean ... You know, we can talk very well over supper. That is, if you'd care to join me? If you're free, that is?'

Marylyn Franklyn, leaning forward to stick a beauty spot on her narrow chin, considered deeply. A more honest woman, who felt the sickening fear in her heart, and who had noticed in herself the nervous trick she had acquired of glancing furtively over her shoulder; a more honest woman might have asked herself if she could ever be free again. But Marylyn Franklyn straightened her shoulders and swung one silk leg provocatively over the other.

'Oh yes,' she said briskly. 'I'm free all right. Very kind of you. I'm sure.'

Robinson moved in his chair and did his bovine best to look rapacious.

'Good,' he said. 'Then we can have a jolly good old chat. Any particular spot you'd like? I feel like a steak, myself.'

'You look like one,' said Miss Franklyn vivaciously.

Her fear and caution were relentlessly washed away by Robinson's manner.

'Well,' she went on gaily. 'I like the Newchester myself. One can always get a nice steak at the Newchester. But' – for a half-second fear showed itself again in the white of her rolling eye – 'but you're a policeman?'

Robinson sighed.

'We're human,' he said. 'Don't fuss yourself about policemen, my dear young lady. We're more human than most, actually . . . '

Marylyn Franklyn's face brightened considerably.

III

The call-boy had rapped his imperious summons on Marylyn Franklyn's door, and cried her five minutes, and Marylyn had said 'No peace for the wicked' before Robinson spoke again.

'I'm sorry,' he said, 'that you aren't comfortable in your

lodgings. Old Mrs Hitch has quite a good reputation for comfort. In fact, a *very* good reputation for comfort.'

Marylyn's resentful reserve thawed further.

'It's not that, dear,' she said rapidly. 'Not that at all. Old Ma Hitch runs one of the best lodging-houses north of Derby. No, dear. The fact is that Tony Gresham is staying there too—'

Robinson was all polite attention.

'The stage manager?' he said. 'Is something wrong with him, then?'

'Wrong with him?' cried Miss Franklyn, and promptly exploded into one of her strange outbursts. 'My God! Little stuck up queen. Thinking himself too high and god damn mighty to speak to anyone else. Playing the piano all day long. Debussy be sugared! He only does it to upset me. Chopin! My eye!'

Robinson made sympathetic noises and said that he, too, hated *Inspector* ... But Marylyn Franklyn was really not fascinated by Sergeant Robinson's Inspector. Her rage was fully wound. She went on, frothing at the mouth with fury.

'Who the hell is he to give himself airs, I'd like to know!' she cried. 'We'll have him playing Benjamin Britten and Bach next. It makes me laugh when I think whose child he is, really.' And she did, indeed, stop for half a second and give a little venomous laugh. 'Fancy Viv Gresham's son eaten up with Bach, Beethoven and Brahms. Honestly! It gives me the sick, *I* can tell you.'

Robinson, murmuring sympathetically, suggested that Miss Franklyn knew Miss Gresham pretty well, then?

'*Know* her? My whole life's been dogged by her, ruined by her. My God. We were at school together!'

And she picked up a lipstick pencil and gave herself a new and angry set of scarlet lips, round her snake-like mouth. In the centre of them her two front teeth, with their sexual gap, seemed like sharp gravestones. Sergeant Robinson was immensely relieved when the call-boy saved him from a further five minutes of Marylyn Franklyn. She went gaily to the Ballroom Scene, blowing Sergeant Robinson a kiss as she went. When she was safely gone he shuddered delicately, and picked up the leopard-skin waistcoat that lay in a heap in a corner on the back of a sofa. He wanted to find out what manner of woman he had asked to supper. The satin backing of the waistcoat was stained by something. The Sergeant did not like to consider what sort of stain it might be.

IV

When he came out into the passage, Sergeant Robinson met Natasha and Timothy Shelly. They looked, as we might expect, drawn and mistrustful of each other. Timothy was particularly sheepish. The Sergeant, who was quite delighted to see Natasha, hardly suppressed a little cry of joy. Natasha was elegant. After the squalor of Marylyn Franklyn's dressing-room she seemed like a fragrant breeze from a warm summer's day.

'The sweet South,' said Timothy Shelly, not entirely inappropriately. 'That breathes upon a bed of violets, stealing and giving odour—'

'Warm South,' corrected Sergeant Robinson, who had 'done' *Twelfth Night* in School Certificate.

'Mr Robinson, Sergeant, sir? We wish to be speaking to you,' began Natasha, in a rush. 'We are in great straits.'

'No?' said the Sergeant gallantly. 'I am perturbed. Perhaps you have been informed that no one may leave the theatre, or perhaps one of my men has forbidden you to do something?'

'Oh, are there being policemen posted at the entrances?' Natasha was still wearing her pale-blue satin and her maribou, but over it she had cast her beaver coat. She seemed to brighten at the thought of the policemen at the entrances.

'There are, indeed,' said Sergeant Robinson.

A brilliant smile shone in Natasha's eyes. She was warm and alive and exciting.

'Then it will be quite all right,' she said happily, and held out her hand. 'Come, Timothy,' she said, and turned away. Shelly, as though compelled by some magnetic star, turned away with her.

'Hey!' cried Sergeant Robinson crossly. '*This* is no way to go on. You come to me with a cock and bull story you're in trouble—'

Natasha spun back and her eyes blazed.

'Well, and so we were!' she cried. Her beautiful features contorted themselves into an expression that on any face should have been called a scowl.

'In trouble?' snapped the Sergeant. 'I absolutely *insist* on being told what it was.'

Timothy Shelly stood all this while like a zany and gazed at Natasha. Fragments of Shakespeare and Herrick and other tender lover's poets rose to his lips, and went away again unspoken, or stayed, trembling in his eyes. Now he suddenly jerked himself from his dream and said abruptly:

'Trouble, Sergeant? Oh, the *lady* wasn't in trouble.' He

struck a little attitude and went on speaking rapidly. The words tumbled over themselves, making very little sense. 'Oh, certainly not. It was I who was in trouble. You see, I came into the theatre with a revolver. And I've lost it. Yes indeed.'

He stopped speaking. The Sergeant's mouth fell open and his eyes seemed to dart out as he looked at this large, decorative, untidy young man.

'I should say,' he said slowly, 'that you *are* in trouble.'

'But not *now*!' Natasha was suddenly excited. Almost she beat upon the Sergeant's broad bosom with her clenched fists. 'But since you are now having policemen on the entrances the danger for Timothy is oll right. It is oll over.'

'Why?' said the Sergeant coldly. He was, in any case, a little jealous of Timothy Shelly.

'Because, you silly man, the revolver cannot now be leaving the theatre. Not with the murderer, at oll events. And my poor idiot Timothy is absolved.'

The Sergeant suddenly grinned.

'Well, ma'am,' he said slowly. 'I *do* see what you're drivin' at. Thousands wouldn't. But that doesn't exonerate your friend, I'm afraid.'

'Why not?' Natasha was passionate. Timothy Shelly had returned to his dream. He hardly appreciated the efforts that Natasha was making for him.

'Because in the end we shall find the weapon. The revolver. And if it turns out to have been fired (which seems more than likely) I think Mr – Mr Shelly, is it? – I think he will have a nasty half-hour explaining that he didn't fire it.'

Timothy Shelly shrugged his broad shoulders.

'You seem quite calm,' said the Sergeant. Envy crept into his voice.

Timothy Shelly closed one eye.

'But I *ought* to be all right,' he said. 'Oughtn't I? I mean, I never fired it. Innocence will out.'

'Do not be being such a fool!' cried Natasha, infuriated beyond endurance. 'It is not *innocence* will out. It is murder.'

V

'Very well, then,' said the Sergeant, and he could not help laughing. Natasha was so earnest and so anxious to please him, and she was also so genuinely concerned for Timothy Shelly that she touched his susceptible heart. 'Very well, then,' he said kindly. 'Why not let's sit down somewhere and talk this whole thing out? When did you last have the revolver? Where can we go?'

He turned round and round in the passage ineffectually, while his shoulders blocked the way. Timothy Shelly, clutching at his fawn hair with one anxious hand, suggested Natasha's dressing-room. Natasha shook her head.

'Miss Greenaway will be returned,' she said. 'This is being the first half finale, this Ballroom Scene. My dressing-room will not be being empty again for such a long time.'

Timothy Shelly pulled his upper lip. He was suddenly helpful.

'I thought the Fairy Queen of Starry Nights appeared at midnight and stood under the clock, waving her wand,' he said, gently mocking Natasha, and, with her, all pantomimes. 'While Cinderella runs madly about the Ballroom in the half-dark, tearing off all of her finery.'

'That is quite perfectly true,' said Natasha. 'I am forgetting I believe she does. But after *that*, there will be the interval, and *that* will be being terrible, as no one will be on the stage at oll, but oll will be behind the scenes ...'

Her eyes were wide with the horror of them all.

'Milling round and getting in the way and talking,' said Timothy Shelly gloomily. 'And all of them wondering who shot Banjo out aloud.' He shuddered. 'Terrible,' he said.

His shoulders suddenly slumped under the weight of it. His hands dragged in his trouser pockets. Sergeant Robinson became a little restless. He led the way to Natasha's dressing-room, thumping with his feet and whispering something to himself under his breath about people who were too sensitive. Timothy returned to his daze. Natasha walked along beside the Sergeant, saying nothing at all. The dressing-room (as they had surmised) was empty. The Sergeant came straight to the point.

Where had Timothy Shelly first missed the revolver?

When he was talking to Natasha just now.

Why was that?

'Well,' said Timothy, 'she knew I had a revolver, you see, and I think she, very sweetly, was worried that you might accuse me of – shall we say – letting it off?'

The Sergeant said sourly that that was not to be wondered at really, when Timothy came to think of it. Timothy bowed his head, and the Sergeant asked if he could remember at all where he actually remembered having it last?

Timothy considered.

'I had it in the car. And I came into the theatre with it.' His forehead wrinkled like a map as he tried to concentrate and remember what had happened. Suddenly, miraculously, it cleared. 'I was in a bit of a state about some flowers I had ordered,' he said finally. 'They hadn't come, and I went out to the florist to get them.'

Natasha blushed.

'And you took the revolver with you?' said the Sergeant coldly.

There was a pause.

'Do you know,' said Timothy, 'I don't think I did. I believe I put it down somewhere. Oh, good. That lets me out, doesn't it?'

The Sergeant was very angry.

'Now, look here, young man,' he said briskly. 'This is no way to go on. In the first place to lay a revolver down some-where – or to say you did – does not, as you put it, "let you out". In the second place, I should like to see your licence for this firearm. In the third place, where did you lay it? Or, at least, where are you going to *say* you laid it? And in the fourth place allow me to remind you we are investigating a murder. Maybe *two* murders. Kindly dismiss all thoughts of levity.'

'Firearm,' said Timothy inconsequently. 'What a strange thing to call a revolver.'

VI

Eventually Timothy made quite a statement. By the time that Miss Greenaway had come back from all the excite-ment of the Ballroom Scene and her dialogue with Prince Charming:

FAIRY QUEEN:	Ah, Cinders! See I warned you in my rhyme
	What would befall if you forgot the time.
CHARMING:	Where is that girl with whom I danced that waltz?
DANDINI:	Don't look now, she turned out to be false.
CHARMING:	Nevertheless, she has left something here.
	A slipper! Well, I'm blowed. Of crystal clear,
	A *lovely* slipper. Friends and subjects all,
	Who came invited to my Christmas Ball.
	Here now I swear, before Tom, Dick and Harry
	Whoe'er this slipper fits, that girl I'll marry.

By the time that Miss Greenaway had returned from these breathtaking incidents, Timothy had admitted that he put the revolver down in George, the stage-door keeper's little box, behind the telephone switchboard. That no, he hadn't drawn George's attention to it, and hadn't thought it necessary. That he had rushed to the flower-shop and come back with the roses in time for Natasha's dance, and that (in all the excitement of delivering them) he had utterly forgotten about the revolver. Could the Sergeant blame him? He was very sorry, but please, couldn't the Sergeant see how it was?

The Sergeant appeared unimpressed. Natasha, however, glowed with pleasure. She became quite angry with 'Swiss' Robinson and his scepticism; at one point she asked him, in a fury, if he had any knowledge of the truth *at all*, if he was so *crass* as to remain disbelieving of Timothy. Sergeant Robinson shrugged his shoulders and bit a pencil.

'How do you explain, then,' he said kindly, 'the fact that

when we searched George's little hutch there wasn't even a whisper of a revolver?'

Timothy muttered that he didn't know everything. Natasha burst out in a frenzy, her hair floating forward into her eyes, her colour mantling her cheeks like the sunset at high tide, and ebbing almost as fast – Natasha burst out that the Sergeant was hell, hell, *hell*, and she would never speak to him again.

'Can you not be seeing what happened, crass?' she cried. 'This poor Timothy leave the gun in George's office, which is stupid of him, I admit. And while he is gone away in this romantic and beautiful manner, the murderer takes it and shoots Banjo dead—'

'Hey! Hey!' said the Sergeant. 'Hold your horses, ma'am. Till we find this gun we don't even know it has been fired. We certainly won't know *if* it has fired the right shot. Now, don't be previous. There may've been another gun in the theatre, and Mr Shelly's gun, when found, may be clean. Any way of telling if it's yours, sir?' he ended, turning to Timothy, who said crossly that it had his initials on it.

'But meanwhile,' said the Sergeant, 'since you two people are so anxious to aid and abet the law, maybe you'll tell me something about Miss Gresham's little boy, Tony. Is Mr Harry DeFreeze his father?'

'No,' said Timothy eagerly, delighted by any questions that led away from himself and his revolver. 'I'd always imagined that, but apparently he was Banjo's. Banjo claimed it. So did Tony.'

'I see,' said the Sergeant reflectively.

But what he saw, or what significance he attached to this intricate relationship, Natasha and Timothy never knew. It was at this precise moment that Miss Greenaway came into the room, still declaiming in her thick, rich contralto:

'Ah, Prince, God Bless You. I am glad you said it.
These noble sentiments do you great credit.'

4

The great Ballroom Scene came to its spectacular conclusion. Miriam stood at the top of the steps, silhouetted against the starlit back-cloth by a blinding white limelight, and held the slipper triumphantly above her head in a gesture of determination. The curtain fell. The house went wild. Miriam took her solitary bow.

The company clattered anxiously down the stairs to its dressing-rooms. The Tiny Tots (and their mothers) were particularly anxious.

There is probably no more gossip-ridden stratum of society than that composed of theatrical mothers or duennas. And these mothers had been presented with a positive surfeit of talking subjects in the death of Vivienne Gresham, and, now, the death of Banjo DeFreeze. This twofold drama had almost silenced them. They stood huddled together in the Tots' dressing-room, like sheep in a pen, and whispered fearfully among themselves with one eye on the door. Here, Hampton Court had pinned a notice:

This dressing-room will be required for Police Interrogation at the end of the performance. Everybody will be required to attend.

Hampton Court.

The over-theatrical signature, with its elaborate 'H' and 'C,' and its ornate, wedge-shaped flourish, had annoyed the mothers of the Tottenham Tots before now. They remained together and hardly troubled to dress their offspring for their next number. The second half of the pantomime was mostly comic, and it mostly took place in Baron de Broke's old mansion, Hardup Hall. The Tots were changing for their big number, when they sang 'That's what we're fighting for' for no apparent reason in the middle of the woods, dressed as wooden soldiers.

Ginger and Nobby (Dreme Child and Dawn O'Day) rather enjoyed these garments, and they now began to climb into them, without waiting for help. Their duennas were (they could see) completely disorganized.

The big dressing-room was long and grey and cold. There was a table that ran down the middle of it. Supported in the middle of the table were various looking-glasses, at an angle. This table was used by the Tottenham Tots. Bare electric light bulbs dangled from the ceiling, or swayed in the wind. Against the walls were further tables, each with its own looking-glass improperly lighted. These tables were at the disposal of the ladies of the chorus, the eight Royalettes, as they were always called.

The whole room was under the sway of Mrs Furbinger, the Tiggy-Winkle shaped wardrobe mistress, who was so good at telling fortunes. She was answerable eventually, as well as to

Hampton Court, to the Great Madam Cariocola of Tottenham, who turned Tots out of her dancing school like day-old chicks from an incubator. This Christmas there were no less than two hundred and twenty-eight Tots appearing in provincial pantomimes in Liverpool, Dungeness, Blackpool, Newchester, Stafford, Derby and Birmingham ... It is really impossible to give the full details of Madame Cariocola's enterprise.

Mrs Furbinger, suffering slightly from gastric trouble, looked benignly round the room through small, gold-rimmed glasses. She hoped none of the Tots was sickening for anything this year. It had been so dreadful when there had been that whooping-cough epidemic. In the far corner Ginger and Nobby were pulling their tap dancing shoes out of the green tin lockers that lined the walls, quarrelling mildly, as usual. Near them Mrs Furbinger observed there was a small, sickly Tot called Bertha. Ginger and Nobby had been in trouble before for bullying Bertha. Old Ma Furbinger moved towards them. In spite of her gastric trouble she was surprisingly light on her feet. Ginger and Nobby were still in front of the lockers. Bertha was crying quietly because one of the tin plates had come off her tap shoes.

'Now then, Dawn! Now then, Dreme!' said Mrs Furbinger. Ginger and Nobby were so unused to their real names that they seldom recognized them. They continued to struggle into their shoes and sateen trousers, swearing at one another, and not looking up. Round the room, behind them, the snarling of other Tots, also changing, sounded like the noise of beasts in Regent's Park.

'Dawn! Dreme!' called Mrs Furbinger, more earnestly. 'Why now, look, you two, you've lef' the tops of your lockers in a perfect disgrace. All them old coats piled on the top. Disgoosting. You two are the worst two Tots I ever 'ad to do with ...'

And Mrs Furbinger contemptuously twitched the two coats (one scarlet with a white fur collar, the other purple with brown) to the floor, and started back from them with a sharp cry.

Underneath, on the tops of the lockers, snoring in a strangulated fashion, was the Lord Mayor of the city, Thomas Atkins, of Bayleyside. He was evidently extremely drunk.

Mrs Furbinger flew straight into a terrible rage, induced by terror. She had obviously been given a frightful shock. She screamed curse words and threats. Beast that he was, he had lain here all this time, amongst these innocent children (here Nobby leered horribly and kicked Ginger on the ankle), intending heaven knows what lecherous orgies. He was disgoosting. He had better be off, and directly, before Mrs Furbinger prosecuted ...

Tom Atkins swung his feet down off the lockers towards the floor.

'Quite so, quite so,' he said.

II

'Well, and wot abaht *that*?' said one Tottenham mother to another Tottenham mother.

'Narsty ol' beast,' said the second Tottenham mother.

'Lyin' there pretendin' to be asleep. Pretendin' to be drunk, too, I shouldn' wonder—'

'Narsty ol' beast.'

'No better than 'e ought to be. Ol' Peeping Tom. Lord Mayor, is 'e? Well, wot can be expeck from Newchester?'

'Newchester ain't West Hartlepool,' remarked a third Tottenham mother. A severe wrangle started about the relative percentage of vice in North Country towns and cities. The dressing-room was in a state of turmoil when Hampton Court burst into it, panting, wearing his highly-buttoned 'de Broke' livery.

'I want to draw your attention to my notice!' he screeched, bouncing up and down on the spot. As usual a rag of cigar was clenched in his teeth. 'The room must be cleared,' he screamed. 'And *tidy*. So that Sergeant Robinson can conduct his investigations.'

Mrs Furbinger stepped forward. Her black cardigan, tightly stretched from her cameo brooch of Beethoven, heaved tumul-tuously. Her gold-rimmed glasses danced with rage.

'Better clear out your smart aleck friends, then,' she snapped.

'That's right,' and 'Dirty Old Man' and 'Peeping Tom,' remarked various other mothers unpleasantly. Mutiny seemed imminent. Those who were not moving up and down the room, snarling and growling now withdrew into a corner, and sniffed. The Tottenham Tots, disconcerted by this panic among their elders, were gathered sullenly into a heap. They were kicking one another's shins at the other end of the room. The lady whose monotonous remarks of 'Narsty ol' beast' had punctuated the early part of the scene, suddenly became very excited and wagged a fist under Hampton's nose. He recoiled, shrieking to Mrs Furbinger.

'What exactly has happened, Mrs Furbinger?' he said unsteadily. 'Why are you all so upset?'

The fact that a certain amount of hysteria might legitimately follow upon two violent deaths did not seem to strike him.

'It's the Lord Mayor!' cried Mrs Furbinger. 'As 'e calls himself. Coiled up on the top of them lockers, 'e was. Tight as any little ol' hedgehog, he was. No 'arm done, I dessay. *But*,' with heavy sarcasm, 'you might arst him not to do it again.'

Hampton was aghast.

'Mr Atkins?' he said. 'Really, *Mr Atkins*? Then I suppose he'll have to come to the Police Investigation.'

Mrs Furbinger snorted.

'Investigation?' she said contemptuously. 'I don't care about any Police Investigation. It's your Lord Mayor investigating my *Tots* I'm afraid of ...'

III

In the front of the house there was also a certain amount of vulgar consternation.

When the fathers and mothers of the various white-socked children, who made up the greater part of the audience, left their seats, and their children unattended, and surged towards the bars they were surprised to find policemen there. The policemen were seated, ponderously, with their helmets on their knees. One or two of the thirstier fathers and mothers found the bars a little overcrowded with policemen, and their fellow-townsmen and women, and they made an attempt to surge on, across the road to the Saracen's Head and The County. Here, to their alarm, they were stopped politely by further policemen, in shining black mackintosh capes. They said that 'No one must leave the theatre until the end of the performance without a written permit from the Sergeant.'

Kidder Atkins had sat too long alone in the three stalls without Tom and Timothy. She had sat longer than she cared to think about, and she had come into the foyer for company. She became quite tearful when she found all the exits blocked. She had been fast enough out of her seat and into the bar to obtain a double gin and tonic water for herself. She drank it now, morosely, in the foyer at the top of the velvet stairs, and looked down at the heads of the policemen as they bent deprecatingly, averting 'panic'.

'Just a routine check-up, madam,' one of them was saying, for what it was worth, to a lady in musquash who had a small boy by the hand.

'But the child's poo-ly. He'll *have* to go home,' said musquash. 'Can't sit in damp drawers. He'll catch his death.'

'You'll have to see the Sergeant, madam,' said the policeman, painstakingly polite. 'And get a pass. Then I'm *quite* sure it will be all right.'

Kidder could stand her loneliness no longer. Behind the policeman's head she could see the brown, brittle fog of Atkins Street, and dimly the bright lights of the public bar of the Saracen's Head. Across the road, even if she did wet her bronze satin court shoes nipping through those piles of slush and muck, she might find Tom or Timothy, or both. It would be worth it. She would learn what 'went on'. And the ghastly panic that welled up in her throat might be drowned in gin, and still more gin. Kidder stuffed one fist in her mouth and stifled a scream. Oh dear, to pull this off she would need to be very calm. Very calm, indeed. She drank the remains of her gin and tonic, and made her way down the stairs to the entrance, flirting ever so slightly with her hips, from sheer nervousness.

'Good evening, Bartram,' she said lightly, to the young blond policeman who had been so polite to the musquash mother a moment before.

'Good evening, ma'am. You'll have to see the – oh! It's you, Mrs Atkins. I didn't see you.' The young policeman coughed and shuffled his feet. He was a little embarrassed, mostly because his name was Truscott.

Kidder came nearer to him and gave the impression by the unbridled movements of her stomach that she was about to swarm up him and down the other side, as though he were a chandelier. He moved backwards uneasily. An electric bell shrilled furiously in the bar above them, indicating that the Grand Christmas pantomime was about to begin all over again.

'What's the matter, Bartram?' said Kidder. 'Why are you all here on duty? What happens to our houses while you're all here? What a chance for the burglars, eh?'

She was forceful and jocose. Only her blue eyes, flickering and darting, betrayed her uneasiness.

Truscott was disconcerted. He could tell the Lady Mayoress nothing without telling several other ladies and gentlemen, who were drinking in every word, with obvious flapping ears. The electric bell shrilled again.

'Look, ma'am,' he said despairingly. 'You'll miss it *all* if you don't go back. The Sergeant'll be round directly an' I'll speak to him about a pass for you, if you like . . .'

'Really?' Kidder rolled her eyes alarmingly and swung her stomach about.

'Yes, really. You go along inside now, and come back in quarter of an hour. And you'll see ...'

Kidder consulted her fantastically expensive emerald and diamond watch.

'Nine-thirty,' she said. 'Very well. I'll come back at nine-forty-five.'

'That's right, ma'am,' said Truscott. 'You do that.'

He spread his arms wide and attempted to drive the crowd upstairs again.

Slowly the mass of chattering people in the foyer oozed upstairs. The queues came out of the bars and the ladies' cloakroom. The good children who had been sitting still, swinging their legs and crinkling cellophane and toffee papers, watched the drop curtain and its weird, bright advertisements ('Buy Hobbsy Hats for smart snap brims at Atkins & Marshall. Hobbs. Hobbs. Hobbs') until one curtain slid slowly up and showed the authentic crimson. Mr Jenkins came back and the houselights dimmed. And everyone in the audience sighed, ecstatically.

IV

And the pantomime continued. In the leafy summer glades outside the Prince's Castle the same carefree peasants strolled and sang to one another about the news of the day. Inconsequently, the Tots danced on to the tune of 'The King's Horses, The King's Men', and performed an elaborately meaningless tap dance, dressed as wooden soldiers, knocking one another down and finally falling, with a heavy rattle of synthetic musketry, one upon the other.

Then the peasants walked on again, arm-in-arm, and made way for Dandini, who came down the middle of the stage, waving a vast proclamation. Behind her came a Tot, dressed in a turban, with a blackened face, carrying a cushion with the slipper on it. Marylyn Franklyn was in a state of sexual anticipation (due to the imagined interest of Sergeant Robinson) and she flung her words at the audience with more zest than usual.

> 'Oyez, Oyez!' she cried. 'Come neighbours all!
> Give ear to what has happened since the Ball,
> Baron de Broke is bankrupt. On his ancestral hall
> The broker's men will very shortly call.
> Prince Charming is in love, and gives his oath
> Before you all that he will pledge his troth
> To any maiden that can wear this shoe!
> Come, try your luck! And see if it is you!'

Several maddened villagers in straw hats and poke bonnets came bounding forward coyly and made ineffectual dabs at the slipper. The Fairy Queen of Starry Nights (pile of faggots, Black Macroom cloak, steeple hat and loose sequins peeping from under the whole) suddenly appeared at the side of the stage and uttered some pretty smart prophecies about the Prince and Cinderella. The whole chorus sang an impassioned song about the difficulties of obtaining footwear (not one word of which was distinguishable) and Miriam Birdseye (black and silver) swanked in for her comic scene with Buttons, Hampton Court. Miriam would (she said) teach him how to woo his sweetheart.

The house now rippled with more sophisticated laughter (for

Miriam was really being extremely funny, and rather coarse), and Mr Jenkins began to bob up and down in the orchestra pit to get a better look. Kidder Atkins, however, was inattentive. She sat glumly in her stall, every now and then holding her wrist-watch up to the light. The lights had gone down and the Tots had rejoined Miriam on the stage for the Patriotic Song ('A grey-haired lady in a shawl, That's what we're fighting for ...'), before the hands of her watch showed 9.45. Then she rose to her feet and tiptoed out, stumbling heavily over the feet and legs of her immediate neighbours, to the Foyer and the Atkins Street entrance.

V

Robinson began to do his methodical round of the theatre. He thought of his policemen in terms of pickets, posted at the various entrances. The first picket he visited was the stage door. Here a very large and extremely reliable officer named Bowes was standing rigidly to attention. Robinson asked for his report.

Bowes said that at 21.30 precisely a young gentleman with very blond hair, in a yellow slip-over, had tried to get out, and had become angry and abusive when prevented. He wouldn't give his name, but when calmed down by the stage-door keeper he had been called 'Mr Gresham'. Various other people had been surprised to see Bowes at the stage door. No one else had become violent. For example, His Worship the Mayor had come upstairs at 21.35. When told that he might not come past, he had wandered sadly away, whistling and banging against the walls. He had had no shoes on. Also, if the Sergeant would pardon *him*, Bowes had observed that His Worship had had a breath on him you could cut with a knife. Whisky, Bowes had thought.

'Where did this Gresham feller go?' said Robinson.

'One of the dressin'-rooms, Sergeant. Star dressin'-room he said.'

Robinson looked over Bowes' shoulder along the dim passage.

'Miriam Birdseye's dressing-room,' he said. And he retraced his steps.

VI

Miriam, at that moment, was standing in the middle of the stage, dressed as a beefeater, lit pink, and singing:

> *'A cottage and a spinning-wheel*
> *And roses by the door.*
> *The chapel bells at ev-Er-ning,*
> *That's what we're fighting for.'*

Consequently when Robinson's brisk, neat knock sounded on the door, she was not at home.

But the door yielded easily enough. Robinson stood massively inside another dressing-room. He was heartily sick of them and their claustrophobic atmosphere. But this dressing-room was different from the others. Since Miriam had moved into it, it seemed gay; and it had charm. A large reproduction of a Marie Laurencin hung on the wall. There were hundreds and hundreds of Christmas cards littered about the dressing-table. Some of them were very *recherché*, indeed. Others were

216

theatrical. There were photographs and telegrams, and a very odd little collection of china feet (decorated with roses and violets) marching from left to right amongst silver-backed hairbrushes. Robinson halted irresolute. Somebody, beyond the red woven curtains that had been drawn across the clothes-rail, was weeping bitterly.

'Come out, Mr Gresham,' called Robinson blithely.

The weeping stopped.

'Come on out, Mr Gresham,' repeated Robinson. 'I won't eat you.'

There was no reply, but a muffled oath and a little crash, and an agitated trembling of the curtain. They all betrayed the presence of Tony Gresham. Robinson yawned noisily and settled down on Miriam's chair. It creaked.

'Take your time, then,' he said idly. '*I* don't mind. I'm in no hurry to give you your pass. That's what you want, isn't it?'

The curtain moved delicately aside. Tony Gresham's tousled blond head appeared, looking as though it were full of dust and ashes. His yellow slip-over was crumpled and woebegone. His eyes were red-rimmed, and his cheeks stained with dust and tears.

'Pass?' he said. 'Then you *will* let me leave the theatre?'

Robinson looked at him and spoke cautiously.

'Probably,' he said. 'If I'm satisfied with you.'

Gresham's face fell. He stepped into full view, scowling. He was filthy dirty and his hands were twitching.

'Why do you want to leave the theatre?' went on Robinson. 'Is it urgent?'

'Yes, it is,' said Tony, all in a rush. 'I can't stop crying. I just *can't*. And Hampton will be *vile* to me if I miss a cue. And I can't go on ... I can't go on without ...'

Robinson crossed his legs and tried to look paternal.

'How long have you been taking it?' he said sharply.

He traced patterns among the china feet and the silver brushes. Tony Gresham began to bluster pathetically.

'Taking *what*?' he cried. 'What the devil? Bullying me like this – a poor orphan ... Damn you, it's only medicine! I was prescribed it at first ...' He suddenly flung his head back and became less incoherent. 'Why shouldn't I take benzedrine?' he said.

'Difficult ever to pull yourself together and be a real person if you depend to that extent upon drugs,' said Robinson. 'However, that's your business ...'

'It certainly is,' snapped Tony.

'But I expect I have some somewhere,' continued Robinson mildly.

'Oh, don't *bother*, thank you very much,' said Tony Gresham, offensively polite. 'Miriam has some somewhere, I'm sure. She'll give me some when I come back.'

Robinson sighed.

'Oh, do come off it,' he said. 'Why did you *really* want to leave the theatre?'

He leant forward and suddenly became intense.

'Is this anything to do with it?' he said, and twitched a large manilla envelope out of Tony Gresham's hip pocket.

'Hi! Give me that!'

Tony jumped futilely, trying to reach it. Robinson, tantalizing him, held it just out of reach.

'Anthony Gresham, Esquire, Poste Restante, c/o G.P.O., Newchester,' read Robinson slowly. 'Writin' to yourself, eh? *And* getting in a stew through wanting to post it, eh? The night your father was shot. The week your mother died.' He paused for a second and then went on ponderously. 'I think we'll read this letter that you're so anxious to post, my boy. *I* think you need Uncle Robinson's advice.'

He slid his powerful thumb under the flap and tore the envelope open. Inside there was a piece of cheap writing-paper, ruled off in faint red lines. There were also about sixteen pages of clothing coupons.

'Well, well,' said Robinson, pleasantly, and unfolded the paper.

' . . . !' screamed Tony Gresham. ' . . . !!' He struck furiously on Robinson's arm, his face contorted hideously from its usual prettiness by fear and rage. 'You're exceeding your duty all right. You wait till I call up Banjo's solicitor. Leave that alone, you filthy beast, that's my father's—'

'Last Will an' Testament,' said Robinson coldly. He spread the sheet of paper upon his knee. It was the usual printed form that is supplied in cheap stationers. With his left hand he idly protected himself from Tony's childish attack. 'The Last Will and Testament of Banjo Pilkington DeFreeze,' read Robinson slowly, from the heavy Germanic letters at the head of the paper. 'To My Boy Tony, whom I had by Vivienne Gresham and who is consequently known as Tony Gresham I give an' bequeath my entire fortune of which I die possessed, viz. £4,000 in Transvaal Copper. £394 5s. 6d. in my current account, and my half-share in the Limited Company known as DeFreeze Brothers. I am in my right mind.' The signature had been witnessed by someone called Leslie Phillips, waiter.

He had signed it 'Banjo Pilkington DeFreeze'. When Robinson had deciphered the date below it he was startled. It was 26 December. He had made his will that day.

5

Miriam burst into the dressing-room, tearing off her ruff and clambering out of her beefeater's doublet, hat and wig in a slight panic. But she did not seem displeased to find Robinson and Tony Gresham glaring at each other across her dressing-table, like two tom cats on the top of a fence. She had discovered *far* worse things, she assured them, in her dressing-room in the run of *Absolutely the End*, during the American invasion. A harassed and anonymous dresser took away the doublet and rammed Miriam into a bottle-green eighteenth-century coat.

'Look,' said Miriam, bending forward to stamp her foot into a high-heeled scarlet patent leather shoe with a *diamanté* buckle. 'Look, Sergeant Robinson. I want to see you. Can you possibly wait here until I come back? I shan't be long and I have a terribly long time off stage until the finale. You know. I shall have to come back here and change into highland dress, but you won't mind that now, will you?'

Sergeant Robinson coughed and said he was pleased, he was sure, and the dresser fled, slamming the door behind her and tucking the beefeater's shoes into a cardboard box. Evidently it was a change that had been effected in the wings.

'What happens now, then?' said Robinson, fascinated and bewildered by the extraordinary lives led by these pantomime artists. After all, he told himself, two of them were now dead. It was surely his business to find out how they had lived.

'Oh, slapstick, slapstick,' said Miriam airily.

'Baker's man,' said Tony Gresham vaguely.

'Everyone's a bit fed-up because of there only being one Ugly Sister and very few cues given at all by Harry DeFreeze in consequence. And now these two Broker's Men, Mic and Mac—'

'Hampton,' said Tony Gresham suddenly. 'Hampton has given Mic and Mac *carte blanche* to *ad lib* in the Baron's Kitchen. Isn't it *dreadful*?'

Miriam paused in the act of tucking her hair into a superb white wig with side curls.

'No!' she cried, horrified. 'You can't mean it. Well, we'll be lucky if this pantomime is over by one in the morning. *Very lucky.*'

'I do think it's mean of him,' said Tony solemnly. 'Not fair on the other artists.'

Robinson sat abruptly in the arm-chair provided in the star dressing-room for visitors. It was quite comfortable and (in his own mind) he decided he would stay there for quite a long time.

'What do you mean by *ad lib*?' he said slowly. 'And why has Hampton Court given Mic and Mac *carte blanche*? Why should the timing of the pantomime be affected by it? And why are you both so angry?'

Miriam Birdseye exchanged a quick, subtle glance with Tony Gresham.

'Look,' she said. 'Tony. Be a darling. Explain to the Sergeant and keep him here until I come back. *I must talk to him.*'

And she swept out of the door, dressed for her visit to Baron de Broke's kitchen. And all the things on her dressing-table rattled viciously, and a pretty white Staffordshire figure that had been standing on a plinth above the Marie Laurencin shuddered violently, toppled dangerously and fell forward. With a supple cricketing gesture Tony Gresham caught it.

'Well held, sir!' cried Robinson heartily.

II

Tony Gresham began to explain to Sergeant Robinson the horror of allowing two unbridled comedians like Mic and Mac complete licence in the Baron's Kitchen scene. The door creaked and jerked, and then opened a couple of feet.

'*Miriam!*' said Natasha's beautiful voice in a half-whisper. 'Miriam? Can I come in? Timothy is with me.'

'Yes, dear, for heaven's *sake* do,' said Tony Gresham rapidly and testily. 'Miriam will be *delighted*. I am just trying to explain about Mic and Mac, dear. Also,' he added, and his voice became hard and unpleasant, 'also, the Sergeant has found a little document, my dear, and he has been third-degreeing me about it, and it looks as though Banjo, my dear papa, killed himself. He and no other.'

The door opened wider and Sergeant Robinson was able to see Natasha. His expression changed to one of sheerest pleasure. She was changed into a superb highland ball dress – a white crinoline with a sash of scarlet tartan. Timothy Shelly, now thoroughly crumpled and bewildered, towered behind her.

'You are not meaning that this poor sexy Banjo commit *suicide?*' said Natasha. 'No murders?'

She sounded so disappointed that Robinson began to laugh quietly.

'No, dear,' said Tony Gresham quickly, a little exasperated. 'No dear. Not exactly *that*. But we've found Banjo's Last Will and Testament and it is dated today . . . '

Natasha came into the room with a whirl of miraculous grace.

'So he must have been knowing that he might be going to die to write it,' she said, inclining her lovely head. 'I am seeing what you mean.'

'Who did he leave his money to?' said Timothy Shelly, and Tony abruptly put one hand on his hip and looked through his long lashes at Timothy, and said: '*Me*, as it so happens, dear. Any objection?'

And he put out the tip of his pink tongue.

Robinson rose heavily to his feet.

'Miss Nevkorina?' he said miserably. 'My chair?'

'Not at oll,' said Natasha. 'I will be sitting here on this little hard one and so I shall not be creasing myself.'

And she sank, with a beautiful drift of white tulle skirts, on to Miriam's little hard-backed chair. Robinson sat back with a sigh of relief.

'And, incidentally,' he said grimly, 'I'm afraid that Mr DeFreeze's making his will today doesn't really point to suicide. So consequently we're unable conclusively to rule out the possibility of murder—'

'Conclusively to rule out,' murmured Timothy Shelly. 'To conclusively rule out. To rule out conclusively.'

'Why not?' Tony Gresham leant back against the curtains.

'Yes, why not?' said Natasha. Her eyes were very wide open

and fixed upon Sergeant Robinson, and he took out his white silk handkerchief and mopped his brow.

'Because, madam,' he said, 'if Mr Banjo had shot himself in the forehead the weapon would still have been there, in the dressing-room. And it has been removed, do you see? And we are *still looking* for it. Remember?'

Timothy Shelly's face fell.

'Oh, we are, are we?' he said sadly. 'What a pity.'

Then he was silent, sinking cross-legged to the floor, idly tracing patterns with one long, slim forefinger on the toe of his large, hand-made, badly-kept shoe. By and by he took a fountain-pen out of his trouser pocket and a folded piece of paper from his waistcoat and he began to make notes on it. Natasha, looking over his shoulder, observed the words:

> O, it is well for those
> Who undertake great enterprise,
> That they do not know
> The nature of love.

and looked hastily away again. Tony Gresham was speaking.

'But surely it is a bit *odd* that Banjo made that will the day he died, now, isn't it,' he said.

'Oh yes,' said Robinson. 'It is very odd, indeed.'

'It is more perhaps,' said Natasha tentatively, 'that he is knowing something dangerous was going on and he is making his will just in case.'

Timothy Shelly looked up from his pen and paper as she spoke and smiled most brilliantly. Tony Gresham also suddenly sat cross-legged on the floor, Sergeant Robinson replied.

'That is a remarkably sensible suggestion,' he said.

'I can hear Miriam's feet approaching,' said Tony Gresham. 'I must say we are doing this pantomime under remarkably difficult conditions.'

III

'Well,' said Hampton Court, complacently enough. Miriam Birdseye was standing beside him in the wings. 'They seem to be eating it up, in spite of everything.'

Miriam smoothed the skirts of her flared coat and glanced uneasily into the theatre at the maddened house, which was rollicking with Mic and Mac (the men in possession) and Harry DeFreeze in the Baron's kitchen. They were 'washing-up'.

'It's all very well, Hampton,' said Miriam coldly. 'But you're not a pro. You've had no experience. Frankly, those two, Mic and Mac, will go *too* far. *I'm* not looking forward to my entrance, I can tell you. I shall get a bucket of whitewash in the face.'

Hampton Court sniffed.

'It's not likely,' he said. 'Really, Miriam, you are an old fuss. In their contracts I particularly specified that no one was to get any whitewash on them. Barring Mic and Mac, of course. They're to be fined if anyone else does. See?'

It was Miriam's turn to sniff.

'Dear me,' she said. 'You *are* an innocent ape financier, aren't you? How long do you think they're going to keep that up? Why, they'd probably consider it *worth* a fine.'

Hampton was very angry.

'All right, then,' he said in a fury. 'We'll *all* get covered with

225

whitewash, *I* don't mind. You'd better make your entrance quickly. Before the real shambles starts.'

'A real shambles,' said Miriam haughtily, 'must include blood.'

Hampton rang the bell that was supposed to represent the front-door bell of Hardup Hall. He rushed on to the stage with a typical comedian's glissage. He called out 'Cinders! Cinders!' and 'There's someone at the door!' All the world knows that the funny bits of a pantomime are written (in the best Shakespearian tradition) in prose. Cinders (from the opposite wing) answered him, and made her entrance. She, too, was a little apprehensive.

The Baron's kitchen already presented a hideous spectacle. Mic and Mac were performing a little dance among a lot of broken crockery and Harry DeFreeze was standing on the table, displaying a lot of elastic-sided boot and red-and-white-striped stocking. When Hampton rushed in, Harry DeFreeze called out loftily that the de Brokes had 'no times for callers. They were going to paper the kitchen and whitewash it. Weren't they boys?' Mic and Mac (mercifully tongue-tied comedians) hung their heads and shuffled their feet. Hampton Court remarked with elaborate nonchalance that he thought the caller was the Prince. He looked like the Prince. He might not be, of course, but . . .

'Charming!' screamed Harry DeFreeze, bounding to the floor. 'Not *Charming*! Then we must tidy up.'

Even Miriam, standing bored and angry in the wings, waiting for her entrance cue, was moderately amused by Mac, Mic and Hampton Court tidying up the kitchen. The house, of course, were ecstatic. When Miriam and Marylyn Franklin finally made their entrance, all the broken crockery had been brushed hastily under the table, and Mic and Mac were sitting, soberly, on seatless chairs. Even so no one had anticipated the roars of happy laughter that would overwhelm Harry DeFreeze's simple statement that he would not try on the slipper. Until, that is, they looked at the cushion, carried by Dandini, Marylyn Franklyn. On it, instead of the slipper, was a large Army Service pattern revolver.

6

At that moment (or so it was said afterwards) Miriam's sleight of hand would have made her reputation as 'Miriam, the Girl Illusionist' on any stage. She turned to the wings, caught up the slipper where it lay twinkling on the floor, and pocketed the revolver all in one sinuous movement. Perhaps 'pocketed' is hardly the word for Miriam's movement. She actually concealed the revolver in the stiff folds of her capacious cuff. The scene went on. The slipper fitted Cinderella. Miriam delivered herself of a number of astonishing couplets of recognition and pleasure, invited everyone to her wedding and escaped back to her dressing-room. Her friends were greeted by her in a manner that they did not expect.

'*Everyone must go!*' cried Miriam, bursting in. 'Except the Sergeant. The Sergeant and Natasha can stay.'

'I *do* call that mean,' whined Tony. 'I was in on the *discovery* of them after all—'

'Them?' said Natasha, puzzled.

'Everyone except the Sergeant and Natasha and Tony, then,' said Miriam, and gazed round her to see who was left. Timothy Shelly rose humbly to his feet and said he would be outside.

Miriam promptly relented. Everyone could stay. But how, with so many people in the room, should she change for the March Past of the Clans?

Timothy gently suggested that the three men might wait outside in the corridor until Miriam called them in. Natasha, a woman, might even be an asset in changing into highland dress?

It was agreed. Sergeant Robinson got up and stumped out, followed by Tony and Timothy, and Natasha rose in a great billowing swoop of tulle and sank again into Miriam's arm-chair. The tulle drifted into place much more slowly than Natasha.

'You are a graceful creature, Natasha,' said Miriam sincerely.

'It is that sort of remark which has been getting you where you are today,' said Natasha. 'Now do not be wasting time in putting on that vulgar highland bonnet. Be telling me all about it. And what is being the matter?'

'Well, this for a start,' said Miriam.

She took the revolver from her sleeve and wrapped it in a handkerchief and laid it delicately on her dressing-table.

Natasha was greatly impressed.

'Oh hell!' she said simply. 'Are there any initials on it?'

'I didn't look,' said Miriam, surprised. 'I thought only about finger-prints.'

She unwrapped the revolver again, very carefully. There on the butt were the initials T.S., entwined with formal flowers and leaves of a rather Victorian fancy.

'Is it being my poor Timothy's?' said Natasha. 'It is exactly as I was afraid of. Has it been firing?'

Natasha was so upset and so distressed, and so concerned for Timothy Shelly that her English completely disintegrated and emerged from her mouth in any order, laden with unnecessary participles.

Miriam coldly slipped the safety-catch and 'broke' the revolver.

'How very odd,' she said.

There was only one shell in the chamber. It had been fired.

II

'But that isn't all,' went on Miriam. 'That's only the half of it. This evening, when I was changing into the beefeater dress – you know, my dear, I had never actually worn it before, only fitted it. It had been, as I thought, hanging here on Vivienne Gresham's clothes-rail all the time ...'

Natasha was silent, looking dumbly down at the revolver, wrapped in its handkerchief, where it now lay in her lap.

'I suppose there can be being no doubt,' said Natasha. 'No doubt at oll that this revolver is being darling Timothy's?'

Miriam looked up. She looked peculiar because she was only wearing a wig and a pair of white satin tights. The effect was like a French poodle, clipped in an advanced manner.

'No doubt whatever, I should say,' said Miriam. 'But listen, dear. I found these *clothing coupons.*'

'Clothing coupons?' repeated Natasha, without interest. 'How many?'

'About three thousand,' said Miriam. 'In little books. In the lining of the beefeater's doublet. Like wadding. I haven't got them all out yet. They're in little books—'

'Little books?'

'Oh, Natasha, do pay *attention.*' Miriam was beginning to

lose her temper. 'Ration books. Of clothing coupons. You know the way they are. Little *pink* books—'

'Oh?' Natasha was still vague.

'Yes. It's obviously the basis of some gigantic swindle and someone has hidden the books, at some inconvenience to themselves, in the beefeater's costume.'

'It is obviously not being darling Timothy.'

Miriam put down her sporran on the dressing-table with a meaningless monosyllable of exhaustion and fury.

'Tchk!' she said. 'Darling Timothy, indeed. Who said it was darling Timothy?'

'It is only,' said Natasha in her slow, sweet, charming voice. 'That as it is Timothy's revolver which has been found, and which has been fired in this alarming manner, I think it might be well for me not to be married to a gentleman accused of murder. Or, at most, manslaughter. I might not mind *that*. And, of course, it is obvious to one and all that *sweet* although he is being, dearest Timothy never even heard of a clothing coupon.'

Miriam put her white satin Highland bonnet hat on top of her wig at a becoming angle. She powdered her nose.

'I see what you mean,' she said. 'About Timothy. But *are* you going to marry him?'

'I am,' said Natasha simply.

'But has he asked you?' said Miriam.

'He has not,' said Natasha.

III

Miriam was extremely gay, in sporran, plaid, cairngorm and order of the garter, superimposed upon white eighteenth-century garments, when the gentlemen re-entered. Tony Gresham, in fact, exclaimed, 'Mum! You're Bonnie Prince Charming!' and embraced her before anyone could stop him. Timothy Shelly said he thought that was a very fine wig, and Sergeant Robinson, with instinctive social tact, remarked that Miss Birdseye certainly knocked *him* in the Old Kent Road. Miriam shrugged eloquent white satin shoulders.

'How are they getting on up there?' she asked, with an inclination of her head.

'Up there, dear,' said Tony, 'they are still *ad lib*-ing. Hampton is standing in the wings with a stop-watch. Harry DeFreeze is on the top of the step-ladder. Mic and Mac have emptied several buckets of water over each other. There have seldom been such bestial scenes in this theatre.' He sighed delicately.

'In fact,' said Miriam, 'I'm safe for ten minutes more.'

'Oh yes,' said Tony. 'Ten minutes, certainly.'

So Miriam began her story in chronological order, describing in some detail the discovery of the clothing coupons. The Sergeant (as we may expect) was very interested in this. He wanted to see *everything* and spent one or two precious moments unpicking the lining of the beefeater's doublet to find two or three more ration books that had escaped notice. Natasha began to breathe more freely. There seemed a distinct possibility that no one would mention the revolver for a little while, and she would have a chance to make a plan for Timothy. Then there came a sharp rattle of long, pear-shaped finger-nails on the door.

'*Coo*-ee! It's *mee*-hee!' called a voice of indescribable vivacity.

'Marylyn Franklyn,' said Tony Gresham. And someone groaned.

IV

Marylyn's highland dress was a fantastic conglomeration of kilts, glengarry, sporran and plaid, all worn slightly wrong.

'Hardly a valet's dress,' said Timothy Shelly vaguely, looking up at her.

'More of a gillie, reely,' said Miriam.

'I say, Miriam, old sport,' began Marylyn excitedly. 'When I saw the revolver on that cushion you could have shot me with it. You could really. Oh, hallo, Sarg.' She waved an airy hand at Sergeant Robinson who had (of course) leapt forward like a bull at the word 'revolver'. Marylyn attached no such academic interest to his movement, and she smiled in a provocative manner and stuck out one hip under her kilt. 'You were quick on to the ball, Miriam, weren't you?' said Marylyn.

'What *is* all this, ladies?' said Robinson. His eyebrows were joined together in a thick, fair, busy line. He was angry.

'I was just going to *tell* you,' said Miriam, pouting. 'Only you went on so about the c—'

'*What?*' screamed Marylyn. 'Haven't told him yet? I *say!*'

She looked from Miriam to the Sergeant with the greatest suspicion, and Miriam bridled angrily on her chair.

'How very queer,' said Marylyn. 'It's the very first thing I thought of. Where's the Sarg got to, I said. I must tell *him* about this.'

Marylyn Franklyn somehow made this simple sentence bristle with indecencies.

'Why, Sarg,' she went on gaily, 'she found the revolver. Or rather, *I* did. Rather a lark, eh? It was on my little cushion.'

Marylyn Franklyn here tittered in a suggestive manner and

closed her right eye several times. Timothy Shelly shuddered and looked away. Sergeant Robinson replied ponderously.

'May I see the firearm in question, madame?' he said. And he held out his pink, capable hand.

'Oh, the *firearm*?' said Miriam, picking it out of Natasha's lap, where it lay harmlessly enough. Natasha gave a little cry and reached out a hand for it. Then she sighed and looked down and let it go. 'Certainly. Here you are. T.S. on the butt. All wrapped up in a handkerchief against finger-prints. And only one shell in it. And that a used one . . . '

Timothy Shelly suddenly rose from the floor in sections and dwarfed everyone in the room.

'Hey,' he said. '*Only one shell?* That's ridiculous. When that revolver left Bayleyside this afternoon there were six cartridges in it . . . '

V

Natasha sighed and told herself that there was, perhaps, a limit to ingenuous honesty. She was inclined to look with affection at Timothy, nevertheless. He stood so very straight and he answered the Sergeant so very carefully, as he formally identified his property, and said firmly that he had a licence for it. The licence was not, however, upon him. He would produce it tomorrow, if the Sergeant wished? It was at Bayleyside.

It was impossible to tell if the Sergeant was satisfied with Timothy's replies. He said that he wondered what could have become of the missing cartridges. This was a preoccupation shared by everyone present. A tremendous pattering of feet up and down the stairs foretold the end of the terrible slapstick scene in the Baron's kitchen. Even Hampton Court hurried past to his dressing-room, thinking that there should be some cutting before the following night. The call-boy raced by, calling the finale. Everyone but Timothy Shelly and Robinson went out into the passage.

'*I shall see you all again*,' shouted Sergeant Robinson after them. 'Almost immediately. In the Tottenham Tots' dressing-room. Or so I understand!'

No one replied; or the thunder of feet on the stairs drowned any polite rejoinder anyone may have made, as the Tots and the Royalettes and all the local girls who had played the parts of first, second and third-class peasants rushed up to make their final entrance in the Grand March Past of the Clans. Miriam and Cinderella (that anaemic, throaty and almost anonymous young lady) had two entrances to make. One, strolling in the half-dark when Miriam said, chattily:

> *Well, Princess Charming, now that we are wed*
> *Where shall our honey-mooning feet be sped?*
> *Don't you think, darling, it might suit our health*
> *To be in Bonny Scotland for the Glorious Twelfth?*

The other, a little less foolish, with everybody else in order down the mighty staircase.

This staircase, decorated with heather and bluebells, had been erected while slapstick raged in front of the drop-curtain. Around it the stage presented its usual appearance. Birch trees waved, and the back-cloth showed a sky of tender blue above purple mountains, as Mr Jenkins swung the orchestra from 'The Road to the Isles' *via* 'All the Blue Bonnets are Over the

Border' to 'The Skye Boat Song', 'Hieland Laddie' and 'Loch Lomond' in what he called a 'gigantic Scotch Switch'. The first batch of Royalettes came swanking down with claymores at the carry. They paused at the top of the steps, four buxom young ladies in lemon-coloured tartan with canary velvet coats. Their leader announced, in tremendous tones, 'Mac-Far-r-rlane!'

And now they followed thick and fast: 'MacTavish!' and 'Mackintosh', 'Duff' and 'Gordon', 'Angus' and 'MacBean', until the eyes spun and the head danced a reel with Mr Jenkins and his specially imported bagpipes. Here came the male voice quartette, in sober black velvet and Royal Stuart, carrying bag-pipes that they were, rather obviously, not playing. And here came the first and lowest of all the comedians, Baron de Broke in tartan trousers and a dreadful Tam O'Shanter, announcing himself as 'Huntley and Palmer'. Then Mic and Mac in the hideous clothes they usually wore in the summer months in their music-hall act (tartan scarves and so on), singing drunk-enly that 'Glasgae belonged to them'. Then Harry DeFreeze in a comic tartan crinoline.

And then Beauty, following hard upon the beasts, Natasha, all alone, red roses in her hands that matched her scarf. Then, angry because his ovation was not as big as hers, Hampton Court in tartan jodhpurs. (Hampton Court also carried a shot-gun, which he fired, amid lurid screams, to bring down a rubber pheasant from the flies.) Harry DeFreeze's sensitive little face flinched as he stood, chasseying, by the side of the stage with the other principals. Banjo could not hear the clapping and the shouting ...

Miriam and Cinderella (whose name Natasha had at last

236

remembered as a 'Miss Betty Byng') came last and delivered their final shaming couplet:

> *Ah, Mr Jenkins! Let the people sing.*
> *And lead us in 'God Save Our Gracious King'.*

Whereupon the whole cast and the orchestra came to attention and bellowed out the National Anthem (in theory). In practice, however, the crashing of the tip-up seats all over the auditorium quite spoiled the effect. Mr Jenkins, spinning round on his plinth, kept his drums rolling as long as he dared. Even so the singing was distinctly ragged. It was punctuated here and there, too, by helpless giggling. For the spotlight, which should have been trained first upon Mr Jenkins and his orchestra, and then (spectacularly) up and down the full-throated ranks of the *Cinderella* Company, the spotlight had missed its target.

It had been trained instead upon the back of the orchestra pit, and here it had discovered the greenish twitching face of the Lord Mayor of the City, Thomas Atkins. He was helplessly stuck between the first and second violins.

VI

Kidder Atkins did not witness the latest social indiscretion of her husband. She was waiting with Police Officer Truscott (whom she continued to call Bartram) on the steps of the grand portico under the labels: Dress Circle, Boxes, Stalls E-D. Truscott fidgeted about. He knew his orders well enough, and he also knew how often orders had to be countermanded (on the officer's own initiative) to avoid annoyance to a public figure. Kidder was a fine and public figure, indeed, in her oyster satin and her musquash, swinging her beaded bag, and every now and then touching her ears where her pearl studs glimmered.

'Sorry, I'm sure, madam, to cause you this inconvenience,' said Truscott anxiously. 'The Sergeant must be greatly held up to be so long.'

Kidder handed Truscott a dazzling smile. On the walls Mrs Siddons (as Viola), Sarah Bernhardt (as Pelléas), Mrs Patrick Campbell, Marie Lloyd, seemed old and faded beside Kidder in the flesh.

'What do you suppose it is?' she asked Truscott.

'That's keeping him, madam?' he replied, in his gentlemanly way. 'Couldn't say, I'm sure. Don't even know why we're here. We were called out all of a sudden. "Emergency call at the Royal". And when we got here Sergeant Robinson give us our orders.'

On the other wall Sir Henry Irving (in *The Bells*), Sir John Martin Harvey (as Hamlet), Alan Ainsworth, George Alexander were boring. Kidder knew them by heart. They did not help her now.

'Oh.' Her face went slowly white and her neck was suddenly dyed an unbecoming crimson. 'Sergeant Robinson? Isn't he in charge of the accident, too?'

'Accident, madam?'

The floor was made of black and white squares like a chessboard. Truscott had been counting the squares, up and down, and now he fancied he might play checkers on them. Truscott had been in the Navy. He wondered if Mrs Atkins were sport enough to play. He doubted it.

'Yes, yes.' Kidder was testy. 'The accident to the Principal Boy, Miss Gresham. My husband told me all about it. Actually I was in Atkins Street at the time.' Kidder's caution suddenly broke and she tried to impress this young policeman. 'Talking to Mr Mawd of Nutson, Mawd and Pander. Of course it was a terrible thing for my husband, you know.' The three double gins suddenly lent their wings to her tongue. 'Him being so close to the pantomime and so forth.'

'Yes, I suppose so.'

Truscott was all polite attention.

'Put up half the backing,' said Kidder. 'That's why we're here tonight. My money, actually.'

Truscott was very impressed.

'As matter'f fact,' Kidder was confidential, 'reason why I put up half backing was to oblige. Oblige his sister, Vivienne. Vivienne Gresham. My husband's sister. Imagine that. Talented family.'

Kidder giggled and Truscott said that he, too, had a sister-in-law on the stage.

'The Old Vic,' he said. 'Not the same sort of thing as Miss Gresham, of course. She's only just beginning, is Mavis. Walking on and Shakespeare. That kind of thing.'

Kidder said the stage was ever so interesting.

'Mind, Miss Gresham was a real artist,' said Truscott. 'Real loss she'll be. Particularly to Newchester. Yes. We loved her here. She was one of the real old-fashioned Principal Boys. *I* shall miss her,' Truscott said. 'I loved Miss Gresham, madam.' And he sounded most genuine.

'Did you?' said Kidder. 'I thought she was common.'

VII

Sergeant Robinson eventually reappeared at a quarter past ten and told Truscott that everyone could go home. Kidder, who had been trotting backwards and forwards between the saloon bar and the door and Truscott, was belligerent. She approached Robinson, and her handsome face seemed boiled and red and shiny. Her eyes were bloodshot.

'I have a serious occurrence to report,' she said. Her speech was very furry now. 'My husband left my side at the commencement of the performance, and he hasn't been back since. Also, Mr Shelly—'

Truscott faded delicately away.

'I have them both, madam,' said Robinson. 'Backstage. If you would care to step round and join us.'

'I mus' get my wrap,' said Kidder, and she went upstairs towards the saloon bar, swaying slightly.

Robinson followed Truscott down the steps of the portico towards Atkins Street. The fog was brittle and tasted slightly of soot.

'Odd,' said Robinson. 'What other wrap can she want? She's wearing a fur coat already.'

'She's drunk, Sergeant,' said Truscott.

'Oh heck,' said Robinson. 'So it runs in the family, does it?'

Truscott whistled.

'Old Atkins bein' brother to the old girl, Gresham, d'you mean, Sergeant?' he said.

'What's that?' Robinson sounded quick and angry. 'Who told you?'

'Oh, sorry, I'm sure.' Truscott was aggrieved. 'Mrs Atkins did. *I* didn't know it was Official Secrets Act.'

'Don't be a fool, man.' Robinson was rough. 'But you're not to tell anyone else, see?'

Truscott saw Kidder coming round the bend of the staircase; he turned his back and walked sadly away as Kidder came sailing magnificently downstairs.

'Ready, Sergeant?' she cried.

She seemed a little sobered.

She proceeded with Sergeant Robinson towards the stage door, leaving Truscott wondering what the hell was going on and the hell he was going to do now. After tilting his helmet on to the back of his head and scratching at his forehead, he walked back to the Central Police-Station, where he spent the rest of the night playing billiards. He told himself he was thoroughly fed up with the Force.

7

The Tots' dressing-room was oppressive with a sea of faces.

By the time that the principals: Miss Birdseye, Hampton Court, Mic and Mac, Baron de Broke, Cinderella, Marylyn Franklyn, Natasha and Harry DeFreeze; *and* His Worship the Lord Mayor; and Timothy Shelly had been packed into the room on top of the Royalettes and the Twenty-Four Tottenham Tots, there was only about a square foot of space left for Sergeant Robinson and Kidder Atkins. Tom Atkins had been taken gently out of the orchestra pit by Mr Jenkins and the leader of the first violins, a kindly little Central European jew called Ephraim Golder. Ephraim Golder had been the first person to notice Tom Atkins. Tom was now standing just inside the door, apparently bewildered but tame.

'Mus' get back to Kidder,' he said at intervals. 'Po'r Kidder, all 'lone in stalls. Qui' so.'

Mr Jenkins (whose name, by the way, was Bob) was very, very kind to Mr Atkins. As it so happened Mr Jenkins' relaxation was consumption of very, very large quantities of gin. He knew only too well how Mr Atkins was feeling. His sympathy was tinged, however, with envy, because Mr Jenkins had not had a drink since six o'clock.

'Never mind, old man, never mind,' said Mr Jenkins soothingly. 'Mrs Atkins will be here directly. I know she will.'

Ephraim Golder was suddenly very angry. His early kindness, evaporating, left nothing but irritation. He was teetotal, and he fiddled in the Theatre Royal orchestra to pay for the musical education of Rebecca, Samuel, Isaac and Naomi Golder, his children. He wanted to get home to them, particularly to Naomi, his favourite child. At intervals, kicking one short leg against the other, he said:

'Ai, ai, Mr Jenkins. This fellow Robinson, he must release me at once, isn't it. I must be going home. Please see ...'

II

The remainder of Mr Jenkins' orchestra, now in threadbare overcoats (men) or dark evening dresses under waterproofs (women), stood about in the passage and waited for a decision to be made about them. They clasped their instruments in canvas cases with the exception of Miss Vandaleur, the 'cellist, who had left her 'cello downstairs at the stage door. Opinions in the orchestra were evenly divided. Family men and women were anxious to return home as soon as possible, but they wanted something a little better for discussion than fifth-hand gossip. Bachelors and spinsters were avid with excitement over everything. If necessary they would have been prepared to pay quite large sums to stay and see what was going on.

Consequently, when Sergeant Robinson returned with Mrs Atkins and announced that he was sorry to keep them from their suppers and their beds, but it was all in the interests of Justice, Ephraim Golder was the only person who complained.

'Ai, ai,' he said. 'Sergeant. They are vaiting for me with hot steaks. They will all be spoiled.'

'Terribly sorry, Mr Golder,' said the Sergeant, speaking very slowly, as he always did to Jews and foreigners. 'Terribly sorry. I'm afraid we can't spare you, on account of how you may turn out to be a material witness.'

Pacified by this polite and energetic use of his name, Mr Golder relaxed and allowed himself to be led, muttering, into the big dressing-room. Everyone seemed to be sitting against the wall on the floor. There was a thunder of discussion that died down the instant the Sergeant came in, and began again as soon as everyone could see that he wasn't going to say anything.

There was a little disturbance when the lady viola, a Mrs Beddowes, and her daughter, Miss Nancy Beddowes, a second violin, clashed their instruments together in their wooden cases and sat down on top of Bertha, the sickly Tottenham Tot, who screamed her head off. Bertha was soothed and given a toffee Rolo to suck. She now presented a very unwholesome sight.

Kidder Atkins, coming into the room with a swift intoxicated rush, glared round her for a long time before she discovered Tom Atkins, sitting at the back of the room. She went straight to him and they began to quarrel passionately in low voices.

'I can't help it, I tell you,' Tom Atkins kept saying. 'I can't help it. This fellow Banjo was murdered and they wouldn't let anyone leave.'

'What were you doing here in the first place?' said Kidder bitterly. 'Which of them is it that you want? The Russian or Birdseye?'

'What a *frightfully* carrying voice dear Kidder is having,' Natasha said to Timothy Shelly.

'I don't know which I hate most,' said Timothy, suddenly bitter. 'Her or her drunken beast of a husband. I wish I were safely back in the County Hotel, where I *started* this Christmas—'

'Oh, were you staying in The County—' began Natasha eagerly.

Sergeant Robinson banged on the table and made an announcement.

'I'm terribly sorry,' he said, 'but I'm afraid I can hear the Police Ambulance at the door. I shall be about five minutes.'

'I know those five minutes,' called out Hampton Court offensively.

'Ai, ai,' said Mr Golder.

III

With Sergeant Robinson no longer in the room there was a general relaxation all round, and various horrid scenes among the Tots. Natasha had changed into her tweed coat and skirt, and was therefore content to sit on the floor with her knees up to her chin, talking to Timothy Shelly in low, intimate tones.

'Of all the horribly unsympathetic backgrounds for you,' he said. 'This room and those children. Really!'

The green tin lockers, slightly chipped, were behind them. A small soiled tape, belonging to an under-garment of a Tot, peeped out of one of them. Timothy Shelly indicated it with a hopeless gesture of disgust.

'It doesn't even act as a foil to you,' he said. 'The whole thing is fantastic.'

He turned back to Natasha and looked at her for a very long time. His hand moved a little towards her, but he halted it. A little world seemed to grow up as he looked, like a magic bubble. The Tottenham Tots and the Royalettes (thought Timothy) had never existed at all ...

'They are not there at oll, dear Timothy,' said Natasha, as though she read his thoughts. '*I* do not notice them, either. But then I am, perhaps, a little short-sighted. It makes everything so beautiful. I am very lucky.'

For Natasha the Tots were halo-ed and wore nimbuses of gold. There was danger, too, somewhere in the haze.

'It makes *you* very beautiful,' said Timothy Shelly. 'If I touched you, this bubble might break. Shall we break it?'

'No, it would not,' said Natasha. 'But do not try.'

'No,' said Timothy.

'Why doesn't that Sergeant come back?' said a flat, North Country voice on their right. Natasha vaguely discerned that it was Kidder who spoke.

'Tell me,' said Natasha, '*please* why are you staying in Newchester at oll. I do not believe you were picked up by Tom Atkins' sister in Bexhill-on-Sea?'

'It is a long time ago,' said Timothy. 'And I had not met you. It is such a long time now, *because* of you. Perhaps this is eternity?'

Kidder Atkins moved savagely in the distance.

'You're drunk,' she said to someone, angrily.

'Never be minding oll that,' said Natasha. 'Why were you staying at Bayleyside? And why did you start at the County Hotel? Why are you in Newchester at oll?'

The precious bubble quivered and shook, on the verge of breaking. Timothy Shelly clasped his hands and they showed white round the knuckles.

'I came to divorce my wife,' he said. His warm and pleasant voice had gone hard and ugly. 'To get her to agree to let me arrange it. And as her brother lives up here, too, I got him to try and help me. And I went to stay with him.'

Natasha could hardly speak.

'Did she? I mean, was she?'

'No,' said Timothy coldly. 'She was *not* co-operative. She was not a nice woman. *Particularly* she would not set me free because my brother had died and I became Sir Timothy.'

A Tot began to sing in a whining voice that there would be 'Blue Skies, nothing but Blue Skies from now on'.

'She was bloody about it,' said Sir Timothy Shelly.

The same Tot screamed suddenly and said it had broken a tooth. It was Nobby. Mrs Furbinger advanced down the room to slap it and tell it not to tell lies.

'Sweet, darling Sir Timothy,' said Natasha, who had gone whiter than paper. 'Tell me now, very slowly. Was your wife, who would not divorce you, being Vivienne Gresham?'

'Yes, she was,' said Timothy Shelly.

IV

Sergeant Robinson supervised the removal of poor Banjo DeFreeze from his dressing-room. Watching the ambulance men struggling with the stiffening corpse, after he had marked the old position of the body with chalk marks, Robinson reflected gloomily that when his time came he would prefer it *not* to overtake him on duty. He would like to be ready for it. Perhaps one should be ready all the time ... The window of the dressing-room was now open. Even the fog, scented with soot and Newchester coke fumes, was a relief. He wondered vaguely about Banjo, as he followed his remains downstairs. He couldn't say *why*. There was something about these DeFreezes or Pilkingtons or whatever they chose to call themselves, that was withdrawn and secret. His mind raced away on a chain of circumstantial reasoning. He abruptly halted it. That was exactly what he had been taught *not* to do. He had been taught method, and sanity and deliberate building up of legal justification on *facts*. He had not been taught to behave like a clairvoyant.

It was these theatricals. They would get anyone down. They were making him, ponderous old 'Swiss' Robinson, lose his head. But why had Harry DeFreeze decided on that particular day that his ex-wife's progress over the broken bodies of men foolish enough to make love with her must be stopped? If that was what he meant? And why had he written a letter about it, if that was what he meant. Robinson fingered the letter in his pocket.

"'You're a callous bitch, that's all",' he quoted to himself. "'And I'm going to end it, once and for all".'

The ambulance drove carefully away. Its engine broke the silence outside the stage door. The crowds had long ago gone from the theatre. There had been no noise in the narrow street until the engine started up. The ambulance jangled its bell for the corner of Atkins Street. The silence surged slowly back with a faint acrid smell of exhaust fumes. Could Harry have discovered that Miss Gresham had re-married? Could it be something like that? Robinson turned and found Bowes at his elbow.

'Sorry to disturb, you, Sergeant,' said Bowes, 'but it did seem to be urgent. A child actor has broken a tooth, biting on a bullet. A revolver bullet, unexploded. It was hidden in a packet of toffees. Child called Dreme Child.'

Sergeant Robinson stared at his subordinate. He wondered how long it would take before the solid and completely immovable Bowes would be disintegrated by the values of the Theatre.

'Extraordinary,' he said laconically. 'When?'

'Just now, Sergeant,' said Bowes. 'It seems that there are four other cartridges in the packet. They *are* a service revolver type.'

'Making five in all,' said Robinson. 'So there's still one missing. Can you lend me your notebook and pencil, Bowes?'

And he wrote, in a carefully sloping hand, in P.O. Bowes' notebook. 'Interview wardrobe mistress, Mrs Furbinger, about clothing coupons.'

'And now,' he said, in a thoroughly theatrical manner. '*On* to the Public Enquiry!'

Bowes looked at him as though he were slightly dotty. He certainly felt light-headed.

V

Dreme Child had been pacified by Mrs Furbinger, who had confiscated the toffee packet.

'But it's a front tooth, damn it all,' the child had wailed, weeping copiously, for in spite of her toughness she was vain, like anyone else. 'I shall look *awful*. Oh, why, why should this have happened to *me*?'

Many people sitting in that room had asked themselves this question in the last week. Natasha was asking herself at that moment. Timothy Shelly was gripping his thin wrists tightly, and saying over and over again: 'Well, I can't help it. It's the truth. If she's ever going to like me at all she's going to like me *because of* (not in spite of) the truth. I can't help it.' Tony Gresham was also asking. And his natural uncle, Harry DeFreeze, who could so easily have been Tony's father.

Harry and Tony sat side by side on the table and swung their legs. When Sergeant Robinson came in, the extreme tension of their nerves was obvious. Harry was sitting, biting his finger-nails, flicking his lighter, fidgeting his feet. Tony was chattering like a monkey to anyone who cared to reply. At the moment Marylyn Franklyn had chosen to sit beside him, and they talked; which is to say that they pursued two irrelevant monologues.

'I must say,' Marylyn was saying, 'I thought it *very odd* that Birdseye didn't tell Sergeant Robinson about the revolver. That seems to me most suspicious, I must say. It's quite as though she had something herself to conceal . . .'

'I do think,' Tony Gresham was saying querulously, 'that all those clothing coupons are a bit *much*. I mean – we've all swindled to a certain extent in our time, and I've had a book or two, *personally*, but I do think two or three thousand . . . ! Really! I expect they're forged . . .'

It was at this moment that Sergeant Robinson re-entered the room. He took the packet of Rolo toffees from Mrs Furbinger. Everyone was very disappointed in the matter-of-fact manner in which he handed them straight to P.O. Bowes, telling him to take care of them. They had expected further dramas.

George, from the stage door, came in timidly, poking his head round the door first, like a gnome. He was wearing a bowler hat. Tony Gresham moved up for him, and he sat down beside him on the table.

'Now, folks,' began Robinson heartily. Tony Gresham shivered. 'I really am desperately sorry to have kept you here so long—'

'Not at all, not at all,' said Tom Atkins.

'But you are going to be the greatest help to me. I must ask you first of all to listen to some rather boring facts. But I hope (and believe) that they may clarify *all* our minds as to the events of tonight, and help us to interpret them.

'First, then. In the last ten days two people, well known to you all, have died in a violent fashion in this theatre. They were both principal players in this pantomime. They had (at one time) been man and wife. Whether there was any connection between their deaths is another matter ...'

Here Bertha, the sickly Tot, screamed and burst into tears, and Mrs Furbinger growled out that it was a sin and a shame to expect kiddies to listen to such talk.

'Secondly,' said the Sergeant firmly. 'All of you gathered together here were present in this theatre on the occasions when both these people died. Third ...'

The Sergeant paused, for he had been interrupted again. Tom Atkins was on his feet, still in his socks. He was swaying to and fro.

'Kidder!' he said. 'My wife. She wasn't here either time. Kidder. You should let 'er go home.'

251

'Would you please sit down, Mr Atkins?' said the Sergeant quietly. 'Mrs Atkins asked to attend this enquiry. I have not detained her.'

Tom Atkins lowered his eyes and shuffled his feet and apologized, collapsing on the floor again beside his wife.

'What a family,' said Timothy Shelly.

'Sh ... ' said darling Natasha.

'Third,' pursued the Sergeant. Everyone was breathless with excitement at the public humiliation of the Lord Mayor. They were leaning forward, drinking in Robinson's every word. And Robinson tasted the dangerous pleasures of public speaking. He became, perhaps, a little over-excited and indiscreet. 'Third,' said Robinson, 'I have not the slightest doubt in my mind that Banjo DeFreeze was murdered.'

The intake of breath all round the room on this word would have satisfied a politician. Robinson gazed around him, well pleased. This was it, all right. This was life, power, glory.

There was an angry tap on the door. Bowes went out. Robinson feeling the tension grow, was not altogether ill-pleased. He waited, mentally gathering up the nerves of his listeners into a little bunch as he did so. Bowes came back, looking perturbed.

'Yes, yes,' said Robinson sharply. 'What is it, man? Speak up.'

'It's Mrs Robinson, sir,' said Bowes. 'And she seems very angry.'

VI

It took Sergeant Robinson a very long time to recover the complete attention of his audience. Those who had not broken down, sniggering, at the spectacle of pride and its fall, were now bored at the Commonplace of husbands and hen-pecking wives. Marylyn Franklyn said to Tony Gresham that the Sergeant was a much smaller man than she had imagined.

'No man who was not a fool allows himself to be hen-pecked. Ergo, Robinson is a fool.' Timothy Shelly said this out of the corner of his mouth to Natasha.

'Really?' said Natasha. 'And what about yourself? If ever there was being an old hen ready to peck I should have said it would have been being Vivienne Gresham?'

'Not at all,' snapped Timothy Shelly. 'She was very fond of me. She said so all the time. *Peck* me, indeed.'

'Well, she is being hen-pecking poor old Harry,' said Natasha. 'Look at him.'

Harry did, indeed, present the appearance of a pecked neurotic. His fingers twitched. His hands shook. He hardly made any attempt to control himself at all. Timothy suddenly laughed.

'All right, darling,' he said gaily. 'She was absolute hell. I *loathed* her.'

'Why on earth were you marrying her, then?' said Natasha, as she registered the word 'darling' with a stab of painful excitement. She would recall that later, hugging it to herself, tonight before she went to sleep. There was no time now to consider it. Timothy, she knew, was in danger.

'I can't think,' said Timothy. He laughed again, happily, deep-throated. It was a very pleasant sound. 'I can't think. Can you?'

'I cannot,' said Natasha.

Timothy suddenly became serious.

'Oh, I was a complete *ass*,' he said. 'It was my children. I thought she was, you know, a motherly type. She said she would make a home for them ... And I believed her.'

VII

Robinson returned in a hurry from his interview with his wife. He seemed perturbed. He was flushed round the gills. He began, once again, to address his public meeting. His voice was harsh. He no longer had any pleasure in the sound of it.

'You were all,' he said, 'present at the two occasions when death visited this theatre. First when Vivienne Shelly, commonly known as Gresham, crashed to her death ... '

(Sensation – not at the words 'crashed to her death' – but at the word 'Shelly'. Natasha's hand stole out and held Timothy's. He looked at her wildly, with gratitude. His eyes were bright with affection.)

'Second when Banjo Pilkington DeFreeze died as the result of a revolver shot wound in the forehead. What I want you to tell me, all of you, before you go home, is *where* (to the best of your knowledge and belief) the following people were, on both these occasions. As you file through the door you must tell Police Officer Bowes, who will write down your statement. You can then be allowed to go home.'

He paused and looked blandly round the room.

'This is not,' he said firmly, 'a completely legal undertaking. If any of you refuse and say you would rather speak to your solicitor first you will be quite within your rights. It will, however, considerably hold up the enquiry. And it will delay the law worse than the law delays already.'

He paused once again.

'So far as I am concerned,' he said, 'everyone may go except you, Mrs Furbinger, Mr Harry DeFreeze and Sir Timothy Shelly.'

(Sensation again at the words 'Sir Timothy'.)

'Here is the list of people whose whereabouts I want you to check.

Sir Timothy Shelly	Thomas Atkins
Harry DeFreeze	Marylyn Franklyn
Anthony Gresham	Hampton Court'

VIII

The people rose to their feet, whispering and shuffling. Ephraim Golder said he wished to see his solicitor first, thank you very much. Esmeralda Greenaway (The Fairy Queen of Starry Nights) said the whole thing was a lot of rot and everyone knew Viv Gresham had died of an accident, but *she* wasn't afraid of the law. She advanced on P.O. Bowes with a firm and vigorous step. He stood his ground most nobly.

'Darling Timothy,' said Natasha slowly, 'what became of the mother of your children?'

Timothy Shelly's face softened as he looked at her. Golden light fell on his untidy hair from the unshaded swinging electric bulb. The magic bubble began to grow again around them.

'Helen?' said Timothy. 'She died. She died in London in the Blitz, 1941, September.' There was a pause. 'Dust has closed Helen's eyes,' he said slowly.

8

'Well?' said Sergeant Robinson. 'Where was it you said you wanted to go?'

Marylyn Franklyn was inclined to be sulky. She did not suppose, she said, that the Newchester Grill would have kept steaks as long as this. For anyone but their regular customers, that is.

'Aha,' said Robinson nauseatingly. 'But if a little bird had rung up and said how late we were going to be, and if the little bird had definitely specified steaks, and if the little bird had been a regular customer, what then?'

Marylyn Franklyn was still inclined to be sulky. She said there was no point (in that case) in making fun of a girl. Pointless, she called it. And in silence they walked up to the corner of Newchester Street and Atkins Street where the bright red neon lights of the Newchester Grill still glowed and glittered through the fog. The doorman saluted Sergeant Robinson and called him by name.

'Don't worry,' said Sergeant Robinson, in a tone of voice that can only be described as 'arch'. 'Mrs Robinson's gone safely home.' He took her elbow, and pressed it, reassuringly. 'Nothing like it, eh?' he said.

They came through the revolving door into a hall whose walls were papered with paper arranged to look like birchwood, knots and all. Marylyn Franklyn's temper seemed to improve. The glitter of chromium from the downstairs bar ('Ladies unaccompanied not allowed') seemed to work upon her like a charm. She went meekly upstairs, ahead of Robinson, drawing her dark green coat tightly round her hips. Her pale hair hung over her collar in a heavy metallic curl. Robinson, observing her from below, saw that her stockings were slightly splashed with mud along the seams. Also her heels were worn down on the right-hand side. She was not a dainty girl.

II

The grill-room upstairs also glittered with chromium. The chairs were scarlet leatherette. The tables were round. At the back of the room there was an unpleasant bar with a chromium rail for the feet, a looking-glass that multiplied all these horrors by fifty (it was cut up into fifty fragments, each a foot square), and a neat little round-about man in a white linen coat. His name was Les and he sometimes passed betting slips. He saw Sergeant Robinson and bowed. He breathed on a glass and polished it with a napkin.

'Well, Marylyn, old girl, if I may call you that,' said the Sergeant, and came swiftly to the point, 'what'll it be?'

'A small port,' said Marylyn.

A waiter with a blue chin tucked them into a scarlet leather alcove. There were small lights with scarlet and yellow shades. The tablecloths were white, and there was a good deal of clattering cutlery.

'A small port and a pint of bitter,' said Robinson to the waiter. 'And the menu,' he added. And he winked.

When the drinks came, Robinson drank smoothly, thirstily, staring boldly at Marylyn over the top of the glass. Marylyn said, 'Cheers, dears,' and sipped. But she sipped fast. Her glass was empty and another small port was ordered for her before Robinson said anything, except, 'I like mine rare, and a bit overdone for the lady,' and 'Chips, o' course,' and 'I can't see any point in vegetables, can you?' As Marylyn's third small port approached, in the middle of a round silver tray, brought in person by Les, Robinson put a warm hand on Marylyn's chipped, varnished nails, and said:

'Well, little lady, so you were at school with the deceased Vivienne Gresham?'

Les, who had been waiting to pass the time of day with the Sergeant, and generally make him welcome, faded away.

'Fancy,' went on Robinson. 'She must have been in the Sixth form when you were quite a little kiddie, eh?'

A crackling and spluttering from the grill suggested that their steaks were now under the flame. Marylyn's face was now a pale, pale mauve under her powder. The combined effect of the port and the hot grill-room was unattractive.

'That's right,' said Marylyn. 'Vivienne was always ever such a nob.'

The flames from the grill and the gentleman in the white hat who watched over it were reflected a hundred times in winking chromium. Les had gone back to the bar and was looking gloomy behind the till.

'Nice school, was it?' said Robinson. 'I went to the Haberdasher's Usk myself.'

Presently the manager would come and the chairs would be put on the tables, ready for Les to sweep the room. But Robinson would be allowed to stay if he wanted to, because he was a 'regular' and a policeman.

'Reely?' said Marylyn. 'Viv and I were at a convent. Very nice, I suppose, North of the City,' she said, and waved a claw. Les jumped and looked startled. 'Very nice port, here, I must say.'

Robinson smiled, and his smile suggested that it was from his own personal cellar, arranged entirely to please Miss Franklyn. Their steaks came, and for a long time no one said anything except 'English mustard or French?' and 'Cruet?' They were both hungry and they were both frankly greedy people. It is unnecessary to describe them eating. When the steaks had been taken away and the Sergeant was eating biscuits and cheese and Marylyn Franklyn was eating an ice, Robinson began again.

'I suppose you knew her brother, Tom, all right, as you were at school with her?'

'Oo,' said Marylyn. 'Yes, I will have a liqueur. Thanks, I'll have a *crème de menthe*. Fancy you knowing old Tom was her brother. That's not a thing *he* likes known much.'

'No?' said Robinson.

Sergeant's expenses hardly stretched to liqueurs. However, perhaps as a result of this little meal he would be drawing C.I.D. Inspector's expenses before he was much older.

'Tom Atkins was my first boy-friend,' said Marylyn dreamily. 'I was little Maggie Franks in those days. He was ever so much older than me, of course.'

'Of course . . .' said Robinson.

'Quite a scene about it in the Atkins family there was, because they *said* I was a jewess. Well, well, well. Times change, don't they? Look at Palestine. Thanks. Cheers, dears.'

And the *crème de menthe* followed the small ports. No one else was in the grill-room now. The grill flickered and Les began to count his takings. The very modern clock above the looking-glass showed half past ten.

'So you're a local girl too, are you?' said Robinson. 'Have another?'

'Don't mind if I do,' said Marylyn Franklyn. 'Yes, we're all local. Little Tommy Atkins. Little Vi Atkins. (Viv Gresham, I ask you?) And little Maggie Franks. Ah well. Paddy would *murder* me if he knew I were here tonight with you. Paddy's my husban'. 'S Australian.'

'He ought to meet Mrs Robinson,' said Robinson. 'They'd get on.'

Marylyn Franklyn lowered her eyes and looked sideways for a match. The butt of her cigarette was already stained a deep crimson with lipstick. Robinson struck a match, trying not to look at it. Really. The things one did for England. He sighed and Marylyn Franklyn misinterpreted it.

'It's all right, big boy,' she said. 'Paddy won't catch us.'

Robinson felt cornered.

'Tell me something,' said Marylyn, narrowing her eyes. She put her head on one side and looked at him winsomely. 'How did you ever find out old Viv was *Lady Shelly*? Is it true?'

She rolled the words 'Lady Shelly' round her sharp teeth more fulsomely than she had rolled her port and her *crème de menthe*. Robinson winced.

'Identity card,' he said shortly.

'Oh, I see,' said Marylyn. 'Alimentary, my dear Watson.' She laughed merrily. 'Quite a good one, that, eh? I had it last year as Dandini in Bradford, "Elementary" "Alimentary", see? It was a better panto than this one ...'

She observed that Robinson was not listening and wondered whether to appear hurt. She decided to keep that line until later.

'You never asked *me*,' she said coyly. 'If you knew where any of these six people were when "it" happened.'

'No point,' said Robinson, suddenly unpleasant. His mind was grappling with a past he had not known where little Maggie Franks was slighted by the Atkins family. He wondered how long a grudge like that could last. 'Did you know Banjo DeFreeze well?' he said abruptly.

Marylyn shivered. It was as though a cold wind had stolen through the grill-room and laid uncanny fingers on the nape of her neck. Did she know Banjo well?

She saw his thick curling hair. His broad prehensile hands. His black eyebrows and twinkling eyes, like an animal's, so bright Marylyn could feel his hand on her arm *now*. My God, did she know him well. She looked down horrified. It wasn't Banjo's hand. It was Sergeant Robinson's ...

'I said, "Did you know Banjo DeFreeze well?"' said Robinson. 'Didn't you *hear*?'

The room spun back to its proper position. The chill air departed. Marylyn felt her blood start beating again in her heart, in her wrists, in her face ...

'Yes, dear,' said Marylyn rapidly. 'No, I didn't hear. No. *He* wasn't a local boy. He came from London, I think. Old theatrical family, the Pilkingtons. *You* know ...'

She gulped at her liqueur glass and left a stain of lipstick on the rim.

'Indeed?' said Robinson. So Banjo had had this one, too, had he? Perhaps they had eaten here as well.

'Haven't you got a Christian name at all, Sarg?' said Marylyn. 'I'd like to use it, if you have.'

Robinson was thoroughly sickened.

'Call me "Swiss",' he said. 'Everyone does. Old "Swiss" Robinson, they call me.'

He paid the check. Les was obsequious as they went out. Robinson reflected he had paid dearly for these little pieces of information. He began to hate Marylyn and her conceit and her boring, genteel, dirty ways. He slouched behind her, suddenly wanting to hit her. The cold fog struck at them on the stairs and she shivered.

'I am batchy,' she said. 'Not taking off my coat in there. I'll catch me death. You'll see.'

'Better have a taxi,' said Robinson, loudly patronizing. 'There's one on the rank. It *is* Mrs Hitch's, isn't it?'

'You *have* a memory, dear,' said Marylyn Franklyn, admiringly. 'Or perhaps you're just interested in little me?'

'Have to on my job. Can't be writing in a notebook all the time,' said Robinson ungallantly.

'Sorry, I'm sure. Squashed flat,' said Marylyn. She coquetted with her heels on the kerb.

Robinson was fed up. He wanted to escape home to his wife. He wanted to allow all these facts (which had nothing at all to do with one another, as far as he could see) to simmer and set and form a pattern. He wished like hell he could leave the silly bitch flat to see herself home. He wished

she would clear off by herself in the taxi and leave him . . .
He wondered how on earth the night would end and how
he could escape.

Robinson, my boy, he told himself, standing on the kerb
waiting for the Tametaxi to swirl up beside him. Robinson,
this is just the moment when you'll get a break, if you plug
on. Something may happen to make sense of the whole thing,
'Swiss' old boy. Press on. Press on.

So 'Swiss' Robinson pressed on, into the taxi behind
Marylyn Franklyn.

III

'148a Leazes Gardens,' said Marylyn Franklyn in a lordly voice
to the Tametaxi driver.

'Huh,' said the taxi-driver. 'Old Ma Hitch.'

This silenced Marylyn Franklyn.

All the way to Leazes Gardens, twirling round the corner
into Newchester Street, still dominated by twinkling traffic
lights, Marylyn and the Sergeant were silent. They were huddled, each in their separate bundles, staring out of the windows
of the cab at the deserted streets. Where Natasha and Timothy
had found things lovely and had noticed against the sky the
pattern of pride made by the wings of the war angel on the
memorial, and had been charmed by the fog, filtering upwards
from the gutters, Marylyn saw only Woolworth's closed, and
Atkins and Marshall with the shutters up, and the last bus
going to the country, leaving many sad passengers dejected in
a queue.

The taxi swerved across the tram-lines, under the glittering strands of the overhead cable, into the dark square of Leazes Gardens. Here was 148a. Here was the Sergeant's next decision. He paid off the taxi and turned back to Marylyn, jingling the money in his trousers pocket.

'Coming in?' said Marylyn gaily. She had evidently forgotten her horror of Tony Gresham, Bach, Beethoven and Brahms. 'I expect Ma Hitch has some beer.'

'I don't mind if I do,' said Sergeant Robinson, with hardly a second's hesitation.

IV

There was no music in 148a Leazes Gardens. Marylyn let herself in and groped, cursing, for the electric light switch. The dark hall sprang into relief about her as she went ahead, past various dank waterproofs and hats that made strange shapes in the shadows. She came to the kitchen door and stood outlined against it. Here everything was sweetness and light.

The parrot cage was shrouded in green baize. Tony Gresham and Mrs Furbinger sat on either side of the kitchen table, which this evening wore its red frieze cloth. They were laying out the Major and Minor Arcana with a set of very old German tarot cards. Cups, swords, pentacles and wands were littered in a terrifying profusion about the table. As Marylyn and Sergeant Robinson stood at the top of the steps and looked down on their bent heads, one neat and grey and grasped in curls, the other fair and vulnerable, Mrs Furbinger picked up the nine of swords with a little cry of horror. It showed a woman in bed weeping. Nine drawn swords dominated the darkness behind her.

'There,' she said, 'Tony. Not that I think it has anything to do with your legacy from Mister Banjo. But I knew I done wrong sewing up them clothing coupons for your poor dear mother in that old costoom. I shan't have a moment's peace till I tell the Sergeant all about it.'

There was a very faint smell of kippers. It was easy to guess what Tony had had for supper.

'But look, Mrs Furbinger,' he was saying earnestly. 'Here is the hierophant in the great Arcana.'

'That signifies the Pope,' said Mrs Furbinger. 'That denotes that all will be accomplished as be wished for the querent for the greatest good.'

'What is this frightfully upsetting gentleman standing in this box with all that armour?'

The old-fashioned stove twinkled with black-lead. The curtains were drawn closely, excluding the rest of the world.

'That is the chariot of victories with *urim* and *thumim* like, on both shoulders and all the earth under him. But look at this three of swords . . . '

She gave a long sigh, compounded of bronchitis and apprehension. The kettle on the hob also puffed and wheezed and blew out its little plume of steam.

'I think *all* the swords are terrifying,' said Tony and covered his eyes with his hand. 'I don't know which frightens me most. That one with the man face down, I think, transfixed with swords on the seashore . . .

The cards made sinister shapes on the warm red cloth in the friendly room. They represented a future that was fearful and menacing. It was dangerous, like madness. In this kitchen everything was safe.

'You'll get over it in time,' said Mrs Furbinger comfortably. 'I was just like you over the tarot cards at the start. Particularly the three of pentacles with them beggars in the snow and that stained-glass window. Fair gave me the creeps, I can tell you. But I'm altogether over it now ...'

And she dealt them out in three packs face downwards, muttering, 'To your house, to your heart, what's bound to be.'

'Good evening, all,' cried Marylyn from the top of the steps. 'Hullo, Mrs F. Is Ma still poorly?'

Mrs Furbinger looked up blandly, still holding the cards in her mottled paw. Tony Gresham scowled and looked away.

'Been in bed all day, seemingly, Mrs 'Itch 'as,' said Mrs Furbinger comfortably. 'But she's under the doctor now. It's the stone, he says.' Mrs Furbinger was quietly pleased, savouring her gloomy news. 'She'll 'ave to be cut for it, Doctor says. It's in a very nasty place.'

Tony Gresham stretched forward in a rather futile effort to clear up the cards and several of them fell on the floor.

'Very good of you to be helping out, I'm sure, Mrs Furbinger,' said Sergeant Robinson, advancing into view behind Marylyn. Mrs Furbinger was startled.

'Little friend to all the world, is ma,' said Tony.

'Now,' began the Sergeant. He sat down sideways on the table. His hip nudged the fool (a pleasant Renaissance figure, holding a rose and a satchel, stepping over a cliff) and the five of pentacles (an odd little figure, apparently roller-skating in front of a formal version of a city) which both went fluttering to the floor. 'Now, Mrs Furbinger,' he continued. 'About these clothing coupons.'

The Bayleyside kitchen presented a different aspect.

Here, Sary O'Driscoll, Hampton Court's self-styled 'confidential maid-servant', was ironing. She was a stout, conceited, idle creature. She used all the intelligence she had for avoiding hard work. Miss Burns was thoroughly irritated by Sary, whom she dismissed from her mind as 'Shanty Irish'. She felt she would be very glad when Sary was out of 'her' kitchen. Hampton Court was leaving Bayleyside that night, after an interminable Christmas stay, to occupy a suite at the Great Northern Hotel, Newchester. Miss Burns would be glad to see the back of them.

There was a heavy wooden table that seemed to occupy most of the room; Sary was resting her elbow on it now. There were three burst arm-chairs that surrounded an Ideal boiler and there were various pulleys and washing-lines in the ceiling, where Sary hung Mr Court's shirts and 'pantsies'. She liked telling Miss Burns how superior her last place had been to Bayleyside.

Miss Burns was annoyed by all this. No one enjoys being despised. It had the oddest effect on Miss Burns. She constantly showed off and boasted about the cleverness and the social position of Thomas Atkins.

'A finger in pract'c'lly every pie in the city. A very liberal man is Mr Atkins.'

Sary *looked* at Miss Burns. She spat on her iron and tested it with her plump forearm. She was wearing her hat (a brown velvet work-basket) because she and Mr Court would presently be driving back into Newchester, after he and Mr and Mrs

Atkins had eaten. She had already made great copy out of the fact that they would be driving about in a Rolls-Bentley.

'Where I was last back in Ireland now, with my own sort,' said Sary suddenly, 'Mr Thomas's shirts were too hard to do, him being such a fine big man. So I always sent them to the laundry.'

Miss Burns sniffed.

'Oh,' she said. 'I wouldn't wash anything for Mr Atkins. Indeed no. The laundry's for washing, I always say.'

'Mr *Court*,' said Sary, 'won't *have* his shirts laundry-washed.' Sary looked contemptuously at Miss Burns. 'Time that black-market joint of yours was to be coming out of the oven, child. If they're coming back for this late supper we've all heard so much about. Though hot meat at this time of night'll be laying heavily on their stomachs like lead, God knows.'

'Ai don't know why you call it black market, ai'm sure,' said Miss Burns, suddenly extremely genteel. Her sniff, too, said plainly enough 'Irish trash'.

'I don't know what you'd be calling it, but where there's only two in family and two ration books and a Baron of Beef in the oven, I believe I'd be calling it black market ... '

'Just shows how much you know,' said Miss Burns, sniffing furiously. 'We never lack for anything here. You know Atkins and Brady, the big butchers on the corner of the Poultry Market. That's our little concern, and—'

'Really?' Sary was impressed. 'I thought he was only the haberdashers, like.'

'Oh *no*,' Miss Burns was shocked. 'Mr Atkins practically *owns* Newchester, as you might say.'

Sary suddenly wanted to know who Mrs Atkins was before

marriage. Her last mistress, Mrs Thomas, had been a lovely person. Not that Mrs Atkins put her in mind of Mrs Thomas at all, but . . .

'A Miss Franks,' Miss Burns believed.

'Oh.' It was Sary's turn to sniff. 'A jewess.'

'Ai couldn't say, ai'm sure.' Miss Burns suddenly took the joint, crackling and sizzling from the oven. A cloud of blue unappetizing smoke filled the kitchen. 'She came from the Coast somewhere, I believe. "Kidder" they called her. Kidder Franks. Played tennis for Northshire, I believe. Very nice people.'

'Interestin',' said Sary.

In the distance, penetrating the foundations of the whole house, came the deep purring of the Rolls-Bentley, approaching the drive.

'That'll be Mr Court now,' said Sary proudly. She put down the iron and folded up the shirt and went briskly to pack it on top of Hampton's suit-case.

'Terrible thing,' said Miss Burns, 'about Miss Viv Gresham getting her neck broke like that.'

'Them that leads bad lives come to bad ends,' said Sary. 'Yes, it was a terrible thing. Mr Court was saying when he drove me into Newchester to do some bits and pieces of shopping for him, he was saying to *his* way of thinking it wouldn't be an accident at all.'

The noise of the car engine came nearer. It became a part of their conversation.

'No!' Miss Burns was horrified.

The noise was outside in the yard, turning. A great white light blazed on the window from the headlights of the car.

'He said that Miss Gresham had a peck of enemies and there was very little sympathy for her at all. He said lots wanted her out of the way. He'd drink taken and you know how his way is . . .'

Miss Burns was very impressed. Outside, doors slammed and voices were raised. Neither Miss Burns, nor Sary, ran to the back door. They were fascinated by their own conversation.

'But who would want her out of the way? What a terrible thing to say—'

'Just what I said myself. Mr Court said Mrs Atkins did, for one.'

'*No!*' Miss Burns did not attempt to defend her employer's wife.

'For a reason he wouldn't mention. And that Miss Franklyn who's in the panto, her with the painted face . . .'

'I believe she's cousin to Mrs Atkins,' put in Miss Burns timidly.

'Indeed.' Sary swept on, hardly registering the fact. 'And Mr Harry DeFreeze evidently. For he'd once been married to her and didn't care for her way of life. And her son, Mr Tony. Mr Court has a *very* good brain. You know. Legal. Oh, and that Mr Shelly . . .'

'Mr Shelly, indeed!' Miss Burns was furious. 'I'm surprised Mr Court didn't put *himself* on the list as soon as Mr Shelly. Why, Mr Shelly wouldn't hurt a fly. Why, the other day, when I was coming upstairs with Mrs Atkins' tray, he helped me with it, as kind as kind. And no need to, either. He's a *gentleman*. There now. There goes the drawing-room bell. That'll be Mr Court, I don't doubt.'

The jangling of the old-fashioned bell marked 'drawing-room' showed that someone was certainly in the drawing-room, demanding drinks.

'Crippen had a heart of gold, they say,' said Sary.

9

When Natasha and Timothy Shelly left the Theatre Royal they were both extremely hungry. For this reason Timothy was not as good-tempered as usual. He was 'on edge'. His emotional nerves, drawn as tight as he could bear them, might (he felt) fly apart at any minute, like violin strings. When this explosion came how would it leave him? Weeping, perhaps. Helpless, certainly. It was not reassuring.

'Well, I am surprised that you are not being arrested,' said Natasha. 'The way you are going on in there.'

'You can't arrest someone without a warrant,' snapped Timothy. 'And without a motive,' he added, as an afterthought.

Natasha looked up at his proud head. He looked like an eagle. He was so *young*, she thought suddenly.

'You need feeding,' said Natasha. 'Soon you will be no longer an eagle, but a thrush. All eyes and beak.' She stopped dead and stared about her. 'What is this place. It smells of food. Newchester Grill? And you *do* have a motive for one of them.'

'My God!' Timothy steered her away. 'We can't go there. Full of beasts drinking gin. No. You must have candlelight. Candlelight and claret. I have arranged it.'

They turned away from the hard, shiny doors of the Newchester Grill down strange twisted streets. They were steeper than any Natasha had walked, since she came to Newchester.

'This is the old part of the city,' said Timothy. 'Some of these houses are very early indeed. There's nothing later than Queen Anne, I believe. Down here is a little public-house in the day-time where Josef's wife (they are French) will cook us a meal at night.'

'How do you know?' Natasha craned back her head and looked up at a wrought-iron lantern that etched an elegant pattern in the fog. 'How do you know she will?'

'I asked Josef, when I gave him the chicken this morning. I couldn't face another meal at Bayleyside.'

'Oh, neither could *I*!' said Natasha fervently.

'Here we are,' said Timothy. 'It's called "Pudding Chare". Extraordinary, isn't it?'

They were in a narrow lane, quite near the river. Natasha could smell the air from the sea. The tide was evidently 'on the turn'. Every now and then, some miles away, at the mouth of the river, came the baying of a fog-horn. Its deep music released some of the emotional knots in Timothy's nerves. He beat on a door ahead of them with careless abandon. A window creaked open above his head. A male foreign voice said it had given them up. Josef, evidently. Bolts shot back. A woman, bobbing in a continental manner, said she had put the other guest in the parlour. She hoped that was right.

'Other guest?' said Natasha. She could not keep the disappointment out of her voice.

'Old Miriam had no other way of getting back to Bayleyside except in my car, you know,' said Timothy gently.

'I was being quite forgetting Miriam.'

As Timothy had promised, there was candlelight in the parlour. There was also firelight, flickering and reflecting itself in dark wood panelling and silver plate. In front of a magnificent sixteenth-century fire-place there was a round table, set for three, with a bottle of wine, already opened, keeping itself *chambré*.

The wide bay window was uncurtained. They could see Miriam sitting there, breathing deeply, and looking out at the arch of the great bridge over the River Tame, where it hung like a magic bow in the fog. Every now and then it was lit by a great blue flash, as a tram-car passed over it.

'It is really very beautiful, Timothy,' said Miriam. 'It was kind to bring us here. I thought Newchester so *awful*. And I'm not enjoying the pantomime now these murders have happened. I am bored by murders. They are *all* Natasha's fault.'

'How could that be? Miriam, *really*.' Timothy was very shocked.

'I don't know,' said Miriam sadly. 'There are always dramas round Natasha and me.'

'Yes, indeed,' said Natasha.

'Mrs Josef said the chicken would be ten minutes after you arrived, and I must say I'm absolutely ravenous. That patriotic song takes far more out of one than one would imagine. "That's what we're fighting for", indeed.'

Miriam rattled happily along about the pantomime, hardly listening to anything she said. Her large pale-blue eyes were full of affection whenever she looked at Natasha and Timothy. His eyes were only for Natasha, who sat beside her friend in the window and congratulated her most sincerely on the evening.

'You were being superb,' she said. 'It was a personal triumph for you. The Littlers will be going green when they hear. The Littlers,' explained Natasha, turning to Timothy, 'would never allow darling Miriam to be Principal Boy. Particularly *Jack and the Beanstalk*. They will be mad to have her now. You will see.'

'We must drink some wine,' said Timothy.

Peace poured slowly into their veins.

'Why don't you call yourself Sir Timothy, Timothy?' said Miriam suddenly. Timothy seemed, if anything, pleased by the question.

'I was for a short time, a communist, so I gave it up. I am no longer a communist, but I am not yet used to the form.'

'That hardly seems to me a reasonable explanation,' said Miriam, in the accents of Lady Bracknell in *The Importance of Being Earnest*. 'I suspect you of frivolity. Why didn't Vivienne Gresham call herself *Lady Shelly*? *She* was no passionate devotee of Marx.'

'No, indeed,' said Timothy. 'But it took her a long time to find out she *was*. My brother died only about a year ago. Of war wounds. I was very fond of him. His name was Percy.'

'Was *he* being married at all?' said Natasha.

'No,' said Timothy. 'Luckily. Unmarried and no children.'

II

'Your children, Timothy, where are they?' said Natasha suddenly, after they had eaten the chicken and while they were eating the Camembert provided by Josef.

'No!' said Miriam. 'I don't believe you. He's got children,

too.' She fell into exaggerated attitudes of wonder. 'It's fantastic. What are they? Boy twins?'

Timothy was now in a very good temper. He was full of excellent food. His darling Natasha was there. He was rid of the dreadful Atkinses for the time being. He was really quite fond of Miriam Birdseye. No one knew where he was and he could not, therefore, be interrupted by persons whom he disliked. He smiled delightedly.

'They are with my mother in County Cork,' he said. 'There are two of them, certainly. But not boys. They are both girls. Caroline and Harriet. I like them. They are quite nice.'

'Is your mother nice, too?' said Natasha.

'I don't know,' said Timothy. 'Was yours?'

'Perfectly frightful,' said Miriam. 'I hated her. Mine, I mean. I never met Natasha's.'

'Caroline Shelly,' said Natasha, 'is being a very pretty name.'

'Harriet is pretty, too,' said Miriam, with her mouth full. 'What relation are you to the poet "Bird thou never wert" and all that?'

'None at all,' said Timothy. 'The name's spelt differently. I wish I were.'

And leaning back he said, very slowly:

'Thy dawn, o master of the world, thy dawn,
The hour the lilies open on the lawn,
The hour that grey wings pass beyond the
         mountains . . .'

'But that isn't by Shelley,' said Miriam. 'That's by James Elroy Flecker.'

'I know,' said Timothy. There was a pause. 'Do you two girls *really* think I killed Banjo DeFreeze?'

III

Hampton Court stood at the drawing-room door and shouted as loud as he could for 'Sary!' She replied from the basement, with a cheerful screech, 'Yes, Mr Court!' Presently she came, bouncing a little and breathing rather heavily.

'Sary,' said Hampton. 'Are we packed? We're leaving directly. Tell Miss Burns that Mr and Mrs Atkins don't want any supper.'

Tom and Kidder sat on each side of the fire, looking uncommonly stupid. Their faces, against the background of terracotta arm-chairs, were pink and glazed, half-cooked looking.

'Qui' so, qui' so,' said Tom Atkins. He fumbled with his lighter. Kidder appeared to be speechless.

'Thank you, Mrs Atkins,' said Hampton, 'for having me. I'll give you a ring in the morning to see how you get on.'

Kidder nodded. Tom Atkins made the foolish gesture of accompanying Hampton to the front door, and sank back in his chair, apparently defeated by demon drink.

'There now, Lord love us all,' said Sary, selfrighteously. 'And if that isn't that great black-market Baron of Beef wasted.'

'Not a' all,' said Kidder.

'C'n have it cold,' said Tom Atkins. And he nodded and slid further and further down his chair.

'You're only expecting a knighthood, Tom, old lad,' said Hampton, and shrieked with laughter at his own wit. 'Go along quickly, Sary,' he said, turning to her. 'Get Miss Burns to help you with the bags. I'll see you in the car.'

IV

The Rolls-Bentley's engine roared purposefully as they rocked down the Bayleyside drive between the dark yews to the Newchester Road. Hampton, with his hands clenched on the steering-wheel, as usual pushed the car along far too fast. The feeling of synthetic power lent wings to his brain. Sary, sitting beside him, her stout hands in network gloves clenched fast upon his dressing-case, glanced fearfully at the speedometer. It wagged its way to seventy miles per hour, and hung there, quivering ecstatically.

'Well, Sary,' said Hampton. He slashed the great car over to the wrong side of the road to take a left-hand bend. 'Well, now. What would *you* say if you heard Mr Banjo DeFreeze had been shot in the forehead, eh?'

'Oh Lord, love us all,' said Sary.

'Yes, and the Sergeant announced that in his opinion it was definitely murder . . . ' Hampton's voice was excited. When he was in this mood Sary was usually afraid of him.

'Lord love us,' she repeated. 'Whatever else can happen now at all?'

The main road sprang up at them, outlined in white and black. It poured away under their tyres like a stream of thick treacle. Outside the city the night was clear of fog. The moon (thought Sary) was like the eye of God, so bright and revengeful.

'I'd rather not say what can happen now,' said Hampton Court. 'But *someone* is going to be arrested.'

The car swung and scrabbled on the crown of the road as Hampton dragged it round a corkscrew turn. The headlights shone on the scared white faces of two cyclists, who jumped, terrified, into a ditch, to safety. Sary, used to such phenomena, sat still. Every now and then she glanced at Hampton. The country round them had been drained of colour by the moon. Hampton's face, too, was white and dead and angry.

'Would that be why we're leavin' Bayleyside in such a hurry, Mr Court?' said Sary.

'It is,' said Hampton, catching the idiom from her. 'God help us all, it is.'

A signpost, tilting drunkenly, indicated, Newchester 7 miles.

'Who do you expect to be arrested, now, Mr Court? Are you in any danger of it at all, yourself?'

Sary's eyes were like currants thought Hampton, glancing at her in the driving mirror. Silly blank meaningless currants.

'Would we be stayin' in Newchester?' she went on. Her voice seemed to register terror. She sat so still. She could not be frightened if she sat so still. 'Are you goin' on with the panto, Mr Court, neither good nor bad?'

The speedometer needle dropped to fifty. Hampton slashed round a bend. It soon mounted again, however, to seventy. And there it stayed until they stopped, rocking, outside the Great Northern Hotel, in the heart of the city. The fog had closed down upon them long before this, but it made no difference to Hampton's speed.

'How can I reply to all your questions, Sary?' said Hampton in a soft, pious, suety voice. He leant out, signalling to the hall-porter to take the luggage. 'Which interests you most?'

Sary considered.

'Who would ye ever expect to be arrested at all, Mr Court?' she said finally.

Hampton stood on the pavement with his feet rather wide apart. He rocked slightly on the balls of his toes as he replied to her.

'There are evidently six people whom the Sergeant considers involved,' he said. 'And I am one of them.' And he laughed bitterly and a little crazily. 'I think, though,' he said, 'that he will be hard put to it to find me a motive.'

V

Sergeant Robinson stood outside Mrs Hitch's door in Leazes Gardens, thoroughly fed up. Mrs Furbinger, when attacked about the clothing coupons, had hardly been helpful. She had said that Vivienne Gresham had given her the books and had asked her to sew them into the doublet for her; and the matter had lain heavily on her conscience ever since. She had offered no explanation as to *why* Vivienne Gresham had asked her to do this, nor where she had got the coupons *from*. She added a number of irrelevancies about the Queen of Pentacles and the Star and the Moon to which Robinson paid little attention. Tony Gresham had remarked that he personally betted they were forgeries, and had received a blank, blue stare from Robinson.

No one was happy, and Marylyn Franklyn had annoyed Mrs Furbinger very much by dropping a spot of grease on a tarot card called the Tower. This showed a very unpleasant little reproduction of a Northumbrian peel tower, being struck by lightning, with people falling out of the windows. It denoted (or so Mrs Furbinger said, in rich, wheezing tones) madness. Sergeant Robinson had decided that this was his exit line. He had escaped, angry and uncomfortable, with one more impossible piece to fit into this jig-saw puzzle of a case.

He began to walk towards Northshire Street in a bad temper. It was all these interlocking relationships that made everything so difficult.

'Banjo,' he said to himself. 'And Vivienne. Silly names they both have.'

He saw them side by side in his mind. Around them, with horrible hooks to clutch at one another and grab, he saw the other members of the *Cinderella* Company and their relationship to each other.

He found that he had stopped at the end of Leazes Gardens. He looked up at the church tower of St James the Less, which overhung the square. Through the fog he could see the lighted clock face. It showed twenty minutes before midnight. Bowes would have already tabulated the positions of everyone in the theatre. Bowes was a good man. If he, Robinson, got his step to inspector, Bowes would probably be sergeant ...

Something was holding him, rooted, by the railings of Leazes Gardens. It was something more than a three-year-old habit, left from the time when P.C. Robinson walked Leazes Gardens on his beat. It was something he had remembered. About Banjo DeFreeze, the ladies' man. He had gone around with Doris Peters, the dresser's daughter, who lived at 15 Leazes Gardens.

He went back along that black street. He thought about Banjo, the ladies' man, who had successfully run two women at the same time. At least Marylyn Franklyn had been passionately jealous of Vivienne Gresham. So she was probably unaware of the existence of Doris Peters. Suppose she found out?

But a woman of her type would hardly kill a lover. On purpose, thought Robinson wryly. She ought to have gained and become Principal Boy on Vivienne's death, if Miriam Birdseye hadn't stepped in. No. The logical choice for Marylyn's second corpse would have been Miriam, not Banjo.

For some reason Hampton Court here spun into his mind.

Of all the people in this lunatic set-up, Robinson understood Hampton least. That bad, mad simian personality that had smouldered, like one of his own cigars, through tonight's performance. One really couldn't tell what a fellow like that would do next.

Robinson stopped in front of the door of 15 Leazes Gardens. He was struck by his own unprofessional behaviour. He, old 'Swiss' Robinson, had been thinking like a silly schoolgirl. Running away with theories before he had walked about with facts. The truth, as that dirty beast H. Court kept saying, always checks. OK. Let him get some more truth. Robinson lifted his right hand and thundered with the knocker on the door of Number 15 Leazes Gardens.

VI

A light showed blank above the door before Peters opened it. He was wearing a grey alpaca jacket. He was very rude.

'Look here,' he began furiously. 'An Englishman's 'ome is 'is castle. W'y couldn't you come and ask your blasted questions at the theaytre, like a gentleman? I'll not answer one of them. I'm sick of you . . . '

He made to shut the door in Robinson's face. Behind Robinson the clock of St James the Less slowly struck the three-quarters. The fog muffled the beating of the bell, and the sound only came faintly to them.

'Long past me bedtime,' said Peters, as Robinson put his foot in the door.

'And mine,' said Robinson. 'Don't want to see you. Want to see your daughter, Doris.'

Peters came slowly out on to the pavement. The door swung to behind him, but the latch did not click.

'Look here,' he said, in a low, hoarse whisper. 'Doctor's just gone. Had to give Doris a sleeping pill. Orders are "Don't disturb until tomorrow mornin'." and I *won't wake the kid*. See?'

He thrust his face to within an inch of Robinson's.

'I see,' said Robinson thoughtfully. 'She was upset, of course, by Banjo's death?'

'Oh *no*,' said Peters, heavily sarcastic. 'Took it in her stride. On'y lost a fiongcay, that's all. They grow on ev'ry tree.'

But he looked uneasy, and as he spoke his eyes searched Robinson's, as though he were hoping for a clue to his reactions.

'Did she say anything? Before she went to bed? Before she took the sleeping pill? Come on, man. Spit it up. Doris'll thank you for telling me. See if she don't. Why, I might never even have to interview her, if you tell me . . . '

The moisture on the pavement glimmered all round them. The fog seemed to press in like damp wool. A faint gold crack of light reminded Peters where his house was.

'You silly blasted bloated interfering fool of a flatty,' said Peters. And he stepped backwards and opened the door and slammed it in Robinson's face.

BOOK FOUR

─────────

FLOURISH – EXEUNT OMNES

I

Constable Bowes sat in the outer office at the Newchester Central Police-Station, ponderously methodical, everyone's first choice for advancement to Sergeant.

He held the lists in his right hand that had been drawn up from the evidence gratuitously presented by the people in the Tots' dressing-room that night at the Theatre Royal. It was late. Sergeant Robinson had not arrived. Bowes sighed and looked at the clock. It was ten past twelve and he could not go until Robinson released him.

The reader would find these lists as exasperating as Bowes had found them, compiling them. They showed the whereabouts on each important occasion, with several cross-checks, of the entire *Cinderella* Company. With the important exceptions, that is, of Shelly, Franklyn, H. DeFreeze, Court, Atkins and Gresham. Some of these people had been prepared to vouch for the whereabouts of one of Robinson's suspects at the time when Banjo (or Vivienne) died. Almost immediately, others sprang forward to contradict their statements. For all practical purposes Constable Bowes' patient analysis might never have been made. It was obvious that it would be a waste of time collecting depositions.

II

By and by Police Constable Truscott came into the room, carrying a billiard cue. He asked Bowes why he was so down in the mouth. Bowes didn't know. He thought it was a bit much, being kept hanging around, not knowing what went on. And then being expected to be brilliant all the time. Like an educated pig. He, too, thought the Force was getting him down.

Truscott balanced his billiard cue along the top of a tall, sloping wooden desk, of the type used exclusively in police-stations and old-fashioned shipping offices. For some reason known to themselves, these organizations consider that clerks work better standing up.

'I'd sooner be an educated pig than called *Bartram*,' said Truscott, idling with the ink-pot. It was the strangely shaped type of pot that can be stood upside down without spilling. 'Dame in a musquash coat called me Bartram for forty-five minutes tonight, and I didn't like to contradict her. Who's Bartram, anyway?'

He picked up the cue, sighted along it, and hit the ink-pot a little tinkling crash. The ink-pot sidled along the desk to a red ink-pot and kissed it delicately.

'Cannon,' said Truscott, and repeated his question louder. 'Bowes!' he said sharply. 'I said "Who's Bartram?"'

Bowes was miserably reading the telephone directory.

'Wish blasted Robinson would come,' he said. 'Then at least I'd know where I *was*. This theatre case is the rock bottom. No one ever tells me *anything*. One hangs about. One never gets any expenses out of them. Who's Bartram, you say? He was a policeman, too. Got six months for black-market dealing. Nasty case. Lot of city councillors involved, they say. Bartram didn't split, apparently. Paid plenty of dough to keep his mouth shut.'

Truscott suddenly hit the ink-pot very hard and brought it crashing to the floor. It lay there, a little pool of scattered glass and spreading ink. A tiny stain on the scutcheon of the police-station floor.

'Dough, eh?' said Truscott. 'Damn. Now I've smashed the thing—'

'It must've been too full, that's all,' said Bowes. 'Oh, no. It's broke. Well, there's some blotting-paper.'

He bent down, cheerfully enough, to help. He was glad of any interruption.

'How do they know Bartram made any dough?'

'He's bought a hotel in Scotland,' said Bowes amiably. 'Waitin' for him, they say, when he comes out. Nice tidy little sum. All ex-policemen keep pubs.'

Truscott whistled enviously.

'Coo-whow!' he said, on a cuckoo's liquid note. 'Could do with a basin full of that.'

They bent together and mopped up the ink with blotting-paper. As they stooped, creaking in their stiff tunics, breathing heavily, pinched round the throat, the telephone rang. Truscott stood up and wiped his hands. Thinner and more agile, less dependable than Bowes, he reached the telephone first.

'Yes, Sergeant. Yes, Sergeant. He *is*, Sergeant. Both of us? And an ambulance? Yes, Sergeant.'

He put the receiver back and turned to Bowes.

'Well,' said Bowes angrily, 'three bags full, Sergeant?'

It was, after all, Bowes who had had the job of compiling those abortive lists.

'Sergeant Robinson,' said Truscott slowly, with his eyes starting from his head like lobsters', 'wants us both at the theatre directly. Harry DeFreeze, the dancer, has committed suicide, he says.'

III

Bowes and Truscott began to dress for the street in a leisurely fashion. They discussed the weather, the necessity for waterproof capes. The alternative of wearing a greatcoat. They were still tidying the great wooden desk, had blotted the ink, and were about to fetch one of their colleagues to guard the outer office in their stead, when the street door opened with a sharp click and a young woman swanked in. There is no other word that describes her behaviour. She was wearing a transparent scarlet waterproof with a hood. Under it her fair hair showed almost lint white round her thin face. Her eyes were blue and blank like a kitten's. She was pretty in a delicate, fragile way.

'Looks T.B.,' murmured Bowes to himself, slowly adjusting his helmet. 'Yes, miss?' he said out loud.

'I want to *see* someone,' said the girl. She had a commonplace little voice, all over-laden with affectations of manner and pronunciation. 'I want to see someone who is in charge of the *Banjo DeFreeze Murder Case* . . . '

She said the last four words with a sophisticated drawl of embarrassment. She hitched herself up to a high stool and crossed her legs. They were thin, like match-sticks. She wore rubber overboots, with clip buttons, to protect her from the damp. Bowes and Truscott stared at her from behind the wooden shelf that separated them from the general public.

'What's your name, miss?' said Truscott.

Bowes shut his mouth, which had fallen very slightly open.

'Miss Doris Peters,' said the girl.

IV

Truscott looked at Bowes.

'Shall I take down this young lady's statement?' he said. 'You go along to Robinson? And I'll follow you? You'd better mention this . . . ' He turned back to Doris. '*Who* do you allege has been murdered, miss?'

Behind her pretty little head, in its scarlet hood, the reflection of traffic lights showed that the fog was gone. It was now a really wet night. The snow would all be washed away by morning.

'Banjo DeFreeze,' said Doris Peters. 'My fiongcay. He knew his brother was going to kill him.'

'Brother?' said Bowes. He halted just inside the door on his way to the street.

'Yes, yes,' said Doris angrily. 'They're a dancing turn. You know. DeFreeze Brothers, Four Feet that beat as one. My father dresses them . . . '

Bowes came slowly back into the room.

'Your father does what?' he said, standing with his feet rather apart. 'Oh, wait a minute. *I* see what you mean. You mean your father is a dresser at the Theatre Royal . . . '

Doris was furious at this evidence of police obtuseness.

'Yes, yes,' she said. 'Banjo *knew* someone would try and kill him. He told me. We had lunch together.'

'Where did you have lunch, miss?' said Truscott. He took

off his helmet and leant confidentially on the wooden shelf between them.

'Malinowska's,' said Doris, and named a respectable Polish restaurant near the theatre.

Truscott wrote it down. Bowes tiptoed heavily to the door and went out into the wet winking street. The cold air swallowed him as the door opened. A fresh draught came into the hot room. Doris pulled back her hood. She emerged looking younger. She had a page-boy bob.

'*He* is stupid, isn't he?' she said to Truscott. She indicated Bowes with a shrug of her scarlet, shiny shoulder. She showed a mouthful of sharp, narrow white teeth like fishbones.

Truscott said he didn't know, he was sure, and smiled back.

'You and Mister DeFreeze had lunch,' he continued, 'at Malinowska's. What then?'

Truscott's fountain-pen was red, she noticed. Almost the colour of her waterproof. He had a signet ring.

'Well, Mr DeFreeze was worried,' said Doris, watching his slow, competent hand moving rhythmically across the paper, taking down every word she said. 'Not at all his usual bright self. I told him she'd be out for his blood if she saw us lunching ...'

'She?' Truscott paused, with his head on one side.

'Miss Marylyn Franklyn. A woman who's in the show with him, actually. That was what brought "it" up ...'

Truscott nodded and went on writing busily. His fountain-pen went laboriously across the paper. Soon, he thought, he would make sense out of all this. Perhaps this *brother* was the one who Robinson thought had committed suicide. He had said DeFreeze all right. But he thought Robinson had said

'Harry'. Doris became confidential. She leant forward across the wooden shelf and a great waft of 'White Lilac' came to him. The wooden shelf became damp and dark where her waterproof touched it.

'I mean . . .' said Doris. 'I do think no matter *what* a girl has done, et cetera, she should think of everyone else. I mean, murder isn't very nice, is it?'

And she pursed up her thin little mouth and shook her head. Truscott, laboriously finishing the sentence about 'mentioned Miss Franklyn', agreed that no, murder wasn't very nice. He pushed aside the notebook, and looked up at her. Doris drew a quick breath, and went back to an upright position. She re-crossed her legs.

'Well, anyway,' she said, 'Banjo was worried. He told me everything, you know, always.' She went on anxiously, looking at Truscott to see how he was taking her. 'He said I was his real pal. He told me all about Marylyn Franklyn. I didn't mind at all. Honest.'

Truscott did not dare to interrupt her. He was afraid that a tactless word from him might end the spasmodic flow of information. Not that he understood it. It seemed to make very little sense.

'You said,' he said eventually, 'that Mr DeFreeze was of the opinion that someone was after him? Do you know who?'

Doris Peters shook her head.

'Or why?'

She looked trapped, Truscott cursed himself.

'Do you think,' said Doris, worried, 'that there is any doubt that Banjo was murdered?'

'Why?' said Truscott.

The dull room, the green tin filing cabinets, the little drying pool of ink were suddenly a non-existent background. Doris Peters, bravely trying to help justice, law and order, filled Truscott's immediate vision.

'I don't know,' she was saying. 'Murder isn't *nice*. I don't want to tell you anything unless it's necessary, I mean, but Father said he was *shot* . . . '

Truscott sat up straight. The short dark hairs at the back of his neck bristled with a sudden thrill. Sergeant Robinson had said that Harry DeFreeze had taken an overdose of barbituric. OK. This *must* be the other brother. He felt on safe ground.

'Your father,' he said cautiously, 'knows as much as any of us.'

Doris Peters promptly came to a quick decision.

V

'Very well, then,' she said. 'Dad said not to come. Dad said I would only get myself deep in this and best left alone. Dad said I'd lose my good name. That was to stop me coming here tonight. But, of course, I wouldn't listen to him.'

Doris tossed her pretty head and laid a red patent-leather bag on the counter.

'It was these clothing coupons,' she said brightly.

Truscott stared at her.

'I know it was very wrong of me,' she said hastily. 'But Banjo used to give them me. And any customer who wanted something, *you* know, and hadn't any, I'd pass them over the counter to her. Or pin them to the bill. It's quite easy. Of course there are *some* people you can't trust.'

'I see,' said Truscott, and wrinkled his nice, fresh young face.

He wondered what the blazes this had to do with anything. 'I see, Mr DeFreeze gave them to you. Where did he get them from?'

'I don't know.' Doris was miserable. 'He never told me.'

'Was his brother in it, do you know?'

'No. Yes. I'm sure I don't know. Banjo used to keep them in the seams of his stage clothes. Particularly when he had women's clothes to wear. Crinolines and that ...'

Doris was bitterly disappointed in herself.

'And where do you work, my dear?'

Truscott did his best to sound brotherly. He did not succeed. Doris simpered.

'Aren't you just awful?' she said, with a bright titter. 'Atkins and Marshall, acksherly. In the Ladies' Gowns.'

VI

It was Truscott's turn to come to a decision. He clapped his helmet on the top of his head. Newchester is a city that clings to her helmeted policemen. She is proud of some obscure tradition about the Chartist riots in the Northshire mills, when a man's life was saved by a saucepan. This anecdote has, perhaps a little unnecessarily, been worked into the archives of the Newchester Police.

'Miss Peters,' said Truscott, 'you will save everyone a lot of time if you will come along to the theatre now. Would you do that?'

Doris Peters' face was suddenly sharp with terror. She slid down from her stool and looked up at him. One hand rose to her mouth.

'Banjo!' she said fearfully. 'I don't want to see Banjo dead . . .'

Truscott laid a friendly hand on her forearm.

'Quite OK, my dear,' he said, in his spurious, brotherly fashion. 'Your late fiancé is in the infirmary on a nice marble slab. It's only his *effects* I'd want to show you . . .'

Doris, for some reason, was reassured at the thought of Banjo on a marble slab.

'Oh, I don't mind seeing his *effects*,' said Doris happily, 'That's all right. But I've never seen a *body* and I don't think I ought to start with someone I like, somehow, do you?' She looked up at him. 'I suppose you've seen hundreds,' she said.

'One or two,' Truscott admitted modestly. He struggled into his stiff cape. Doris's eyes shone, transparent with admiration. Truscott thought she was quite a pretty little thing. There are few expressions more attractive to one than open-mouthed admiration.

Truscott and Doris Peters left the police-station side by side, well pleased with each other.

VII

Robinson sprang at Bowes with a little snarl as he arrived.

'You didn't hurry, did you?' he cried, accusing. 'And where's the ambulance?'

'Coming,' said Bowes laconically. He was late. He knew the Sergeant had had no supper. He made allowances for Robinson's bad temper but, like a parlourmaid, he was not going to be put upon.

'Why are you late?' persisted Robinson.

'New evidence just come in,' said Bowes shortly. 'Name o'

Peters.' Robinson stood rigid, astonished. 'Know her, Sergeant?'

'Supposed to be in bed with a sleepin' pill, that's all,' he said rapidly. 'Poppa told me. Been at the house just now.'

'Kind of rum,' said Bowes. 'Truscott was takin' down her statement. Seemingly she was engaged to the first brother what died. Banjo. Or so *she* says.'

Robinson led the way to Harry's dressing-room.

'Clever of you to call at the house, Sergeant,' said Bowes, following him.

'It's nothing,' said Robinson lightly. 'Poppa dressed these two, that's all. Thought there might be a connection. Didn't know what. This one – Harry – looks like a real suicide job, all right. He's in bed with a sleeping pill, too.'

Over Robinson's shoulder Bowes saw into Harry DeFreeze's dressing-room. It was neat, pathetic, quite anonymous. On a hard antique sofa opposite his clothes-cupboard lay Harry's body, covered with a coat. An ungummed letter, shakily addressed to 'The Coroner', leant against the dressing-table mirror. Beside it was a large brown bottle labelled with the trade name of a compound of barbituric.

'What's it say?' Bowes jerked his head towards the letter.

'Here's hoping 150 capsules will be enough. Sorry to cause extra trouble. Can't go on without Banjo. I didn't kill that bitch, Viv. Neither did he, I loved them both. Goodbye all,' said Robinson.

'Nature of a dying declaration,' said Bowes. 'Kind of pathetic. I think anyone'd accept that as evidence.'

'So do I,' said Robinson. 'I think his first letter was a suicide letter, too. But then I think he didn't commit on account of Trouper's Urge. You know, "Show must go on" stuff. I expect he did it tonight all right. Wasn't anyone in the theatre at the time he took those capsules, *and* his door was bolted on the inside.'

Bowes looked at the smashed panelling, and the scratches on the Sergeant's evening shoes, and smiled.

'Unless, of course, Peters knew something,' said Robinson, ruminating. 'There was no danger of your picking up anything about the positions of my six suspects,' he said, with a sudden change of tone. 'And now there are five.'

Bowes exploded.

'Mean to say you didn't *expect* anything? Rotten job to give a chap ... ' Bowes was becoming rapidly insubordinate, when they heard a hard double knock on the outside stage door. Truscott's cheerful young voice announced that he had brought this young lady along.

'And she says,' he ended cheerfully, disbelieving, 'that there are hundreds of clothing coupons hidden in the folds of Banjo's female clothes ... '

2

Sary O'Driscoll went into the hotel slightly ahead of Hampton Court. She stood on one side as he registered and cracked 'hail fellow, well met' jokes with the booking-clerk. She gave the impression that she thought herself of considerably more importance than anyone else in the hotel. Her fat paws were in front of her, grasping Hampton's bag to her waist. Her eyes glittered as Hampton turned away and disappeared with a page-boy in the lift. She then spent a firm ten minutes persuading the booking-clerk to move her room down from the servants' bedrooms to an ordinary single room on floor two.

II

Sary tapped on the door of Hampton's suite. He called out for her to come in. He was irritable, lying on his bed in his shirt-sleeves. He had taken his shoes off. His sour monkey's face was furrowed with anxious frowns. The room was depressingly luxurious. The curtain pelmet was a rich, dark purple. It was trimmed with heavy fawn braid. The bed was of gilt, known to auctioneers as 'French-style'. The management had put six ill-arranged dark red carnations in a glass vase, 'With their compliments to a great comedian'. The carnations lolled helplessly sideways. Their back view was reflected in a looking-glass framed in dark stained oak. There were 'Cries of London', equally framed in dark stained oak, on the beige walls.

'I was thinking you might of needed me,' began Sary. 'I was expecting you to be quite wore out, now. I'm partic'lar'ly sympathetic to people who are easy wore out. Mr Thomas now, when he was tired, he was downright pathatic.'

Outside, in the rain, a tram turned at the terminus. It seemed directly under Hampton's window. It ground and screamed, and Hampton cursed it bitterly.

'Shut the window, can't you, and ring floor service for a bottle of gin,' said Hampton in his usual manner. 'And look out my sleeping tablets. I'll need two tonight. And unpack me at the same time. And shut up about Mr Blasted Thomas of Dublin, I'm sick to death of him ...'

Sary was unperturbed.

'Trams are a desperate nuisance,' she said easily. She pulled the big curtains to get at the window-cords. The window-cords had china knobs, lined with gilt. The windows showed a good deal of coffee-coloured lace, stretched tightly sideways. 'They'd never be letting you sleep at all, the trams,' said Sary.

She unstrapped the big suit-cases and began to unpack methodically. Hampton was restless, tossing about on the bed.

'I'm too sensitive,' he said fretfully. 'That's my trouble. I *told* you to ring for gin.'

The trams were muffled now, by the glass and two thicknesses of curtain. But there were still hundreds of other noises in the hotel to rasp at Hampton's nerves. There was the sound of water splashing, somewhere near.

'The tablets don't seem to be here, Mr Court,' said Sary. She folded 'pantsies' and vests and rattled the stained oak drawers as she drew them in and out of the dressing-table. The carnations trembled as she did so.

'Not here?' snapped Hampton. 'Where are they, then? What the hell d'you mean, not here?'

'Well, Mr Court, they should be in this little leather stud box, now,' said Sary. 'Along with your studs. All, that is, but them pearl studs that woman had off you that time.'

Hampton was very angry. He rolled over and sat up. The ugly, luxurious bed bounced lightly up and down as he sat on it, and dangled his legs. He wore thin plum-coloured socks, and his sock-suspenders were ridiculous.

'No sleeping tablets,' he repeated. 'Not *there?*'

'Well now, did you ever have them anywhere else, Mr Court?' said Sary. She was seldom rattled by Hampton's anger. Pity and terror and her own physical danger could move her to tears. But she knew Mr Court and his 'little ways'.

'Weren't you bringing the bottle into Newchester one day this week, and having them made up again, child?' said Sary. 'Wasn't that it?'

Sary stood with her arms akimbo and looked down at Hampton. To do his unpacking she wore a white tie-over overall. She still had her brown velvet work-basket.

'Yes,' Hampton agreed with her, nodding his head up and down. 'I took them to Brydon and Atkins on Tuesday to have the prescription repeated. Had them made up . . .' He was speaking half to himself. 'Collected them on Tuesday afternoon . . .'

Reassurance crossed his face and wiped the frown from it. 'I left them in my dressing-room,' he said triumphantly. 'I left them under my looking-glass on my dressing-table.'

Sary sniffed.

'Brydon and Atkins,' she said. 'Would that be Mr Atkins' little concern as well, now?'

'Of course it is,' snapped Hampton. 'Don't be so silly. Go and get me my tablets. I'll never sleep through the noise of the trams ...'

He began to whimper. His chin trembled.

III

In the end it was agreed that Sary O'Driscoll would fetch Mr Court's sleeping tablets. He gave her his pass-key to the stage door. He told her once again where he had left the tablets. Sary, who had given in with a very bad grace, announced that it would be well past midnight before she got to bed. She also murmured something about no one getting overtime on *this* job. Hampton, now lying on his bed with his eyes closed, opened one eye like a vicious ferret.

'What's the matter?' he said. 'Want me to leave you all my money, I suppose. You're all alike. All the *lot* of you.'

And he closed his eye again.

Sary was furious. His accusation was perfectly true. She was quite fascinated at the thought that Mr Court might 'remember her in the Will'. Her broad white face, that was so like a flat bun, went slowly purple.

'Not at all,' she snapped. 'I've never taken a tack o' notice o' wills, and so forth, neither good n' bad. It's not legacies I'm after. I just want to see you right, Mr Court. I'd never let you down.'

Hampton mumbled indistinctly that he wished she wouldn't talk so much.

'I'm not your enemy,' he said suddenly, opening his eyes.

A particularly noisy tram turned under the window, screeching and jarring the hotel.

'No, Mr Court,' said Sary. There was a pause. 'There is something,' she said, 'that you could do for me if you've a mind, child.'

Hampton's eyes remained open.

'You know that little two-piece? The one I was telling you of? Believe me, 'tis topping. But I'm needing fourteen, fifteen coupons to get it.'

'*Clothing coupons?*' said Hampton. 'Is that all? You run along and get my tablets. You know I can always manage *coupons*.'

'Thank you, Mr Court,' said Sary.

And she ran along.

IV

Sary had difficulty in getting a taxi. The hall porter telephoned Tametaxi over and over again, and had no reply. Sary, as she looked down the flight of shallow stairs that led to the revolving doors, felt anger and gloom creep over her. The rain was falling monotonously, washing away the piles of dirty snow that lay in the gutters. The last tram had ground away. She turned to the hall porter.

'Is it far, the theatre, then?' she asked.

The porter was voluble. Well, now, no. It wasn't a step, really.

Sary had only to turn to the right when she went through the doors, and go straight along and the third on the left was Atkins Street. Did Sary know Atkins Street? Well, she must turn up it, and then, sure enough, she would come to the theatre ...

Sary thanked the hall porter and blessed him. But he did not enjoy it. He felt, obscurely, that he was being treated as an inferior. He went muttering back to his little glass cage and the switchboard. He said, under his breath, that Sary didn't half hate herself.

V

The city now glistened like a black oilskin. The lights went out one by one. The middle lights, that hung from the overhead cables, were all that remained burning in the main streets.

By day no trams run in Atkins Street, and so by night its pleasant proportions were lit by ordinary street lamps. As Sary marched along, her fat calves wobbling slightly at each step, a mis-shapen shadow chased her on the wall beside her. It ran ahead of her, stopped, disintegrated. Then it stealthily caught her up and began all over again. It was a long time before Sary realized it was her own shadow. It frightened her.

Also, the walls reflected the sound of her own bumptious footsteps. They echoed around her, multiplying themselves in endless pursuit. Sary's mind ran fearfully round the subject of 'Men', who lurked, she knew, in alleyways for the particular purpose of springing on her. By the time that she had arrived at the dark alley that led to the stage door of the theatre, she had worked herself up into an unwholesome panic. At the theatre worse awaited her. The stage door was open. She hesitated. Slow footsteps approached up stairs inside. From the dark theatre came two men carrying a corpse ...

Sary flattened herself against the whitewashed wall, rigid with disgust and terror. She screamed steadily for about a minute and a half.

VI

The noise brought Robinson running from the depths. Doris Peters echoed Sary's full-throated bellow with a little shriek. Truscott and Bowes moved to follow Robinson, but checked each other.

'Someone's to stay with miss, 'ere,' said Bowes.

'Well, who d'you suppose it was screamed?' said Truscott, who had gone rather white. He was the more nervously unstable of the two. His heart had stopped beating and was now going on with a fearful thump and rattle. 'Who do you think it *was*?'

VII

'Mr Court's personal maid,' gasped Sary. She was in a bad state. Sweat stood on her fat face and her eyes were fixed and staring.

'Well,' said Sergeant Robinson, reassuring. 'I am Sergeant Robinson. You'd better come downstairs. It's cosier there. What exactly do you want here at this time of night?'

And so, with soothing phrases and reassuring gestures that Sary afterwards described as 'downright fatherly', Sergeant Robinson propelled her gently towards Banjo's dressing-room.

''Twas Mr Court sent me out for his pills,' said Sary jerkily, descending the stairs. 'He'd left them in his dressing-room, he said. God preserve me, what was that I just saw now?'

And Sary, suddenly rooted to the spot, crossed herself, and glanced fearfully over her shoulder. Robinson, unmoved, asked for her name.

'Sary O'Driscoll,' he repeated. 'Well, well. Your Mr Court has had another blow. He's lost his other Ugly Sister. She's committed suicide.'

VIII

Sary returned to Hampton's suite with an hysterical account of her adventures in the Theatre Royal. She crashed into the room without ceremony, her velvet toque a little over one eye, her stumpy umbrella grasped like a weapon. Hampton remained on the bed.

'God help me, Mr Court,' began Sary. She poured her information at him in a flood of words and incoherent blessings. 'The streets and theatre all dark and dripping, and me outside in the rain and no one to ask. And then, as God's my witness, here's the stage door open and two fellers trampin' up with a great stretcher and a body on it . . . '

Sary paused to cross herself and Hampton coldly held out his hand.

'Where the hell are my pills?' he said.

'There you are, child,' said Sary, quite beside herself.

She flung them on the eiderdown. She sank in an arm-chair at the foot of the bed and began to weep noisily. She made vague gestures as though she thought she were wearing an apron, which she might cast over her head.

'And I broke out a-bawling, oh Jesus, Mary, Joseph, and the Sergeant took me downstairs. And there in th' dressin'-room there's two policemen *and* a fast clip of a piece, Doris Peters they called her (and she's no better than she ought to be). And there would be piles of clothing coupons, I never saw so many. And one of them crinolines of Mr Banjo's all slit up, believe me, 'twas a wicked waste. And oh, dear Mr Harry's dead now, too, and whatever will become of us?'

And here Sary O'Driscoll quite broke down and wept and wept, shaking all over like a jelly as she did so. Hampton Court slid from the bed to the floor and paced towards her. He was suddenly very angry indeed.

'Stop it, you silly Irish fool!' he said.

He carried a tooth glass of water in his hand, and he suddenly dashed it in her face.

'Shut up,' he said. 'Who d'you say is dead now? Harry DeFreeze?'

The room seemed unreal around them. Sary had the feeling that they were ghosts. She stared up at Hampton, afraid of him.

'He took his own life,' she said, and sniffed. She knocked her toque straight again as she tried to wipe the water from it. 'Oh, Gold help us, child, what ever will happen next? Mr Banjo, Mr Harry and Miss Vivienne all dead in a week. God rest their souls.'

Tears streamed down her fat, sodden cheeks.

'Never mind *them*,' said Hampton. 'Look what they've done to my pantomime.'

IX

He approached the telephone. He looked a very angry figure. He was, perhaps, a little mad and white foam crusted on his thin lips.

'Did you happen to notice,' he said, with cold, suety sarcasm to Sary, as he picked up the receiver, 'whether there was anyone on the switchboard?'

The receiver remained silent in his hand.

'Only the night porter, Mr Court,' said Sary. 'But, 'tis the will of God. Now, wouldn't ye ever relax and go to bed and leave it all 'til first thing tomorrow morning? 'Tis the best thing now, so.'

A faint squeaking in the receiver showed that the night porter had come back. Hampton paid no attention to him.

'Listen, you damned great fat fool,' shouted Hampton. He spun like a wood top, whipped by a street child, and the telephone flex wound round him as he spun. 'I have fifteen thousand pounds at stake in that pantomime. Cost of costumes, et cetera. Life is just addition and subtraction. The rest is conversation. If I can keep that show playing to capacity for *one* week, even, receipts'll pay me. Hand over fist. A week and we're safe. All of us. *I must get two more Ugly Sisters by the morning.* Do you understand, damn you? Who do you think'll pay your wages if I go under?'

Sary was completely seduced by this vehemence. Hampton poured himself another gin and drank it at a gulp, swaying by the telephone. Sary said, in an undertone, that she had always thought Miss *Birdseye* more of an Ugly Sister, really.

'And where will I get a Prince Charming from? Use your

head if you've got one,' cried Hampton. And he began to shout various trunk numbers into the telephone, reading them out from a little pigskin notebook which he held against his knee.

'Miss Birdseye certainly has lovely legs, God bless them,' said Sary helpfully.

X

Inevitably the hotel was turned upside down to give Hampton his own way. He lay on his bed and ruthlessly put through call after call to his dear, dear friends, the theatrical agents. They all seemed to be spending Christmas at Bournemouth, Brighton, Bexhill-on-Sea, Hastings and Margate, and whenever he got on to any of their private homes he had to be reconnected. When, around 3 a.m., the night porter began to show signs of wear and tear, and answered some of Hampton's favourite blasphemies with equally embarrassing language of his own, Sary was sent down to attack him at ground level, so to speak. Hampton chewed cigars into rags and jumped with nerves. Meanwhile the switchboard hummed, the telephone exchange made startled comments on the calls that came and went. Crackling conversation whizzed backwards and forwards between Hampton and various people called Saul, Maurice, Jock, Hermann and Abraham. Eventually Maurice, quacking like a duck from Bournemouth, suggested two Irish comedians. They were 'resting.' Back home in the 'ould country' for Christmas.

'Where, where, where? And shut up!' screamed Hampton, writing busily.

'Drimolaig,' cried Maurice faintly, and gave a telephone number.

The line, only faintly attached to Bournemouth, promptly went dead.

Of the rest of that nightmare dawn: of the hall porter red-eyed and gibbering with fatigue; of Sary, her eyes baggy and shadowed, her hat hopelessly awry, collapsed in Hampton's arm-chair, or (galvanized) leaping to the telephone to deal with Irish voices in Dublin, Cork and (eventually) Drimolaig, it is best not to speak. At 4 a.m. Hampton was foaming at two voices: Liam and Padraig O'Doherty, making them promise to start immediately for Dublin by hired motor-car. Liam and Padraig, blind drunk, sang him a snatch of 'M' Slattery's mounted foot' and agreed to do it. Padraig, indeed, howled enthusiastically that he had been an Ugly Sister for some years now.

'I've booked you seats on the afternoon 'plane to Manchester,' snapped Hampton, using grade one hypnotism. 'Call for your bookings at Aer Lingus. A car will pick you up at Manchester Airfield and bring you straight up here. Expected in the theatre at six for performance at seven. Salaries fixed where you arrive. Check?'

And, faintly enthusiastic, from the heart of the Irish bog, a voice answered 'Check!'

XI

'Now, Sary!' snapped Hampton, and turned to her again. She sat in the arm-chair with her mouth slightly open. Every now and then she fell asleep or nodded upright. Every time she did this her ridiculously smart hat fell over her eye a little further.

'Now, Sary!' said Hampton again. 'There's still plenty at

stake. The car and the Aer Lingus tickets have to be booked directly. The theatre must pay. Tony Gresham must do it. Wait. I'll write a note ...'

Hampton swayed towards the ornate writing-table and flipped out a piece of writing paper and some envelopes. He began to write. He had difficulty in writing at all times, but when he was slightly fuddled, and also in the middle of a brain-storm, his writing was hopelessly illegible.

Get on 'phone to Dublin Aer Lingus [he wrote] *and get
2 seats for 2 Irish comics (Ugly Sisters arriving tomorrow
evening) on afternoon 'plane for Manchester. Also
ring Tametaxi to meet them and drive them here from
M'Chester airfield for evening perform . . .*

The pen here trailed away into a meaningless squiggle that Tony might possibly recognize as the word 'performance' mixed up with the signature 'H. B. Court'. Hampton blotted it and put it in an envelope.

For some reason best known to himself he had taken off his trousers. He now appeared very unattractively dressed in a shirt, socks, and sock-suspenders.

'Put your hat on straight,' he said, viciously, to poor Sary and lurched across the room for his address-book.

Sary levered herself upright on throbbing legs and held out a hand for the envelope. She pointed out the time and again invoked the Deity and the Holy Saints. Did Hampton know it was 5 a.m.?

'That letter has *got* to be delivered,' cried Hampton. 'Take a taxi. I'll pay you back later.' He looked furiously at her. 'I'll deliver it myself,' he cried, and made to snatch it back; 'and you can collect your money and go in the morning.'

'I only want to see you right, Mr Court,' said Sary.

Her attempt at hauteur was mildly ridiculous.

Five minutes later she left the hotel on foot for Leazes Gardens. There were still no taxis. As she went she muttered under her breath an involved sentence that contained the phrase 'No consideration', and also (irrelevantly), 'Been scrup'lous all my life'.

3

At 5 a.m. old Mrs Hitch's house was nearly as silent as the grave.

In the three dark hours before the dawn the streets outside were deserted and echoing. Every sharp footstep was magnified by terror. Marylyn Franklyn had gone to bed about midnight, her hair tortured in a Ladye Jayne slumber helmet, her face plastered with cold cream. She lay uneasily in Mrs Hitch's 'combined double front'.

She could not see the room. She could hardly remember the dim Victorian pieces of furniture. The great double bed with its lace overlay, of which Ma Hitch had always been so innocently proud, never warmed up except for one little patch where Marylyn now lay. There was a round cupboard by the bed, and a middle light in a dark red fluted shade. There was a looking-glass hanging from a chain and a bamboo table with a green glazed china pot. But Marylyn would only have remembered they were there if she had got out of bed, gone to the door, pressed the old brass switch, and flooded them with light. She felt herself overwhelmed by darkness, alone and frightened. It was a terrible feeling.

Sometimes when Marylyn was in a mood like this she

imagined that she had screamed already. She could see herself split the darkness with a great cry of horror.

She was almost certain her rubber hot-water bottle had leaked . . .

II

Curled in his hard, narrow bed, Tony Gresham slept innocently in Ma Hitch's 'second-floor back'. His hair hardly showed. He did not snore. No phantom breathed on him. No tiny crash, or tinkle of cinder falling in the kitchen stove below, disturbed him, transforming itself to guilt. Tony did not even dream.

III

In the kitchen Mrs Furbinger put the tarot cards into their red leatherette box and stretched her short, fat arms above her head. The invalid Mrs Hitch, whose caprice in the last four hours had wavered uncertainly between 'a nice piece of fat bacon' and 'a strong cup o' tea' had finally fallen asleep. She had been delighted with her fortune, as interpreted by Mrs Furbinger.

The alarm clock on the mantelpiece showed five past five when Mrs Furbinger decided there was no point in going to bed. She was very comfortable where she was, thank you, dozing upright by the fire. At this moment Sary O'Driscoll (whose mental outlook could well be described as 'kicked over the traces and bolting down the road with the carriage in matchwood behind her') thundered with the knocker on the front door. She then rang the bell six or seven times. And as Mrs Furbinger, startled, stumbled along the passage to answer it, she knocked again.

IV

The effect of this sudden noise on the already apprehensive Marylyn was immediate. She sat up quivering and groped for her pink quilted dressing-gown with the maribou trimming. She kicked her cold feet into her mules. She made her way, through various pieces of bric-à-brac, to the window. She tore aside the heavy curtain.

Outside the rain had stopped. There was a white frost. It was dark, and Marylyn's breath steamed the window. She could see nothing. Below she could hear a murmur of voices. There was a tiny crash as the front door shut. It shut behind two people. There was a light confusion of overlapping footsteps that returned to the kitchen.

Marylyn was quite convinced it was Sergeant Robinson, returned to see *her*. And someone, some jealous beast, had intervened themselves. They were already entertaining him in the kitchen. The Sergeant was *her* property. Marylyn switched on the light, found the matches and lit the gas-fire. With rapid, angry gestures she took off her slumber helmet, wrenched out her pins and began to make up her face.

V

'Oh, believe me, Mrs F., I'm jaded simply,' remarked Sary O'Driscoll and collapsed into the arm-chair, where, five minutes ago, Mrs Furbinger had decided to spend the night. Sary drew her legs under her and spread them wide. She lolled back.

Mrs Furbinger said nothing about being quite jaded herself, thank you. Instead she reached for the kettle and began to make a new pot of tea.

'Yes, indeed. A cup of tea, 'twould be great so,' said Sary. 'My legs will hardly bear me. Oh, Mr Court's so inconsiderate, child. 'Tis never a wink of sleep I've had this night, 'tis Mr Harry dead now, God rest his soul, committed suicide they say, and two new Irish Ugly Sisters arriving from County Cork. 'Tis Mr Gresham I've been sent for.'

Sary stared all round her with her flat black eyes. Mrs Furbinger thought them very like boot buttons.

'So Harry DeFreeze is dead, too?' said Mrs Furbinger, undisturbed. 'That will be the other death in the tarot.' She nodded her head gravely. 'The nine of swords I noticed, together with the Last Judgement and the Lamb of God. I knew they could never signify Mrs Hitch. It was Harry they denoted, all along.'

'Pardon?' said Sary.

At that moment Marylyn Franklyn clip-clopped along the passage in her mules and stood staring down from the doorway. Her make-up was a little too fierce for the time of day. Her blonde hair was fluffed roguishly to her shoulders. Her pale pink satin dressing-gown was grasped firmly round her hips. She seemed the personification of disappointment.

'It was Mr Gresham I was wanting,' said Sary rudely.

Marylyn flushed. She advanced gaily enough and held out her hot-water bottle as proof of her innocent errand.

'Little Maggie heard voices,' she said brightly, as though

offering herself for canonization. She lapsed suddenly into rather irritating baby talk. 'I fought my botsy wotsy was leaking. Anything else gone wrong?'

She looked from Mrs Furbinger to Sary, who began her hysterical chant all over again.

'Mr Gresham must be wakened directly,' she intoned. 'He must get on the 'phone to Aer Lingus for the Irish comics. I have it all wrote down for me, by Mr Court. The panto's ruined else,' she ended. 'Oh, it's a lovely cup of tea, thank God, and very welcome, I'm sure.'

Mrs Furbinger had laid cups and saucers and poured out three cups of tea, while Sary chattered and Marylyn swung herself gaily on to the kitchen table. She drank most genteelly, curling her little finger like a pug's tail.

'Why, whatever's happened to the jolly old panto now?' she said. 'Wasn't Harry good enough for *your* Mr Court? Why does he have to get two Irishmen? I hate Irish comedians ...' she ended inconsequently.

'Because Harry DeFreeze is *dead*,' said Mrs Furbinger sombrely. 'He has killed himself.'

Marylyn's reaction was extraordinary.

'Oh, my God!' she cried involuntarily. 'But whatever could *he* have had to do with the clothing coupons?'

Everyone in the room stared at her as though she were a little mad. Marylyn Franklyn coughed and bit her lip. She put down her cup and saucer with a nervous clatter. She suggested lightly that she should go and wake Tony Gresham. But her face had gone a dull and angry red, and her eyes showed fear and misery and (said Sary O'Driscoll as she left the room) guilt.

VI

Tony Gresham emerged from his room blinking and rumpled in a brown Jaeger dressing-gown and brown Jaeger shoes. Apparently at night he was not at all the young exquisite. His pyjamas were flannel and a bold blue and white stripe into the bargain. He was inclined to sulk. He grumbled all the way downstairs to the kitchen, flopping from step to step.

'It isn't my fault that Harry's committed suicide,' he said, over and over again. 'I only hope he hasn't left *me* any money or taken out a *Life Insurance Policy* in my name. I shall be hanged, I expect, if he has.'

'What a thoroughly self-centred outlook,' said Marylyn Franklyn in her bitchiest voice.

'Don't be an ass, dear,' said Tony, in his most plaintive tone. 'How can you have a centred outlook?' He screwed up Hampton's message into a tiny ball and put it in his dressing-gown pocket. 'Oh,' he went on idly. 'By using a *telescope*, I suppose. But even *then* I'd have to focus it on myself, so it wouldn't really be an outlook.'

He was triumphant and very irritating. Marylyn clicked her tongue.

'No wonder this panto's gone on the rocks with *you* as stage manager,' she said.

'Brilliant, dear, brilliant,' said Tony. 'But it's not on the rocks yet.'

They came into the kitchen. After a little everyone expanded and relaxed round cups of tea. Sary (who alone understood the mysteries of the cross-Channel trunk lines to Eire) booked a time call for 8.30 a.m. to Aer Lingus. Between more cups of

318

tea and calls to Manchester airfield and Tametaxi, everyone put in an hour or two profitably enough. Marylyn Franklyn, saying such unanswerable things as 'Well, I know where I'm not wanted,' went back to bed.

'What would ever be the matter with her?' said Sary, before the door had closed behind her.

Conjecture ran high about 'the murder, the accident, the tragedy and that', as Sary called the events of the preceding day. It was agreed that Marylyn's remark about the clothing coupons had been most suspicious. Sary told the full story of 'all she had seen in Harry's dressing-room', which, as Tony rightly said, reminded him of a title on a mutoscope on Brighton pier. At mention of Banjo's tartan crinoline ('slit down the seams and a wicked old waste, if ever I see it') Mrs Furbinger leant forward, creaking.

'Did you say that *all* those cewpons 'ad been taken out of these female clothes of 'is?' she said.

Sary said at some length that she hadn't actually said so, but thought she had implied it.

'Didn't you think Banjo was rather going around with Franklyn, dear?' said Tony, putting one sharp elbow on the kitchen table. 'I think I'm rather hungry. I know I had that *idea*, because I didn't fancy her as my natural step mum at *all* . . . '

Sary said that there were few people that she (personally) disliked more than Marylyn Franklyn.

''Tis for God to judge, but she's a bad one, if there ever was one. Come to a bad end, I shouldn't wonder . . . '

'Na, na,' said Mrs Furbinger suddenly. 'No call for ill-wishing. We had enough bad ends this Christmas to last us over. Don't let's wish no more of them.'

At this point the wild shrilling of the Dublin call silenced them. But, if anyone in that kitchen had had the power a warrant would have been made out for the arrest of Marylyn Franklyn then and there. And Marylyn herself, rushing up the stairs on clattering mules, had only just time to escape before someone told her that listeners never heard good of themselves.

VII

The sparrows were saluting the dawn with their twittering before Natasha, Miriam and Timothy came to Bayleyside.

They were very late because Natasha had discovered a piano at 'Chez Josef'. She had wanted to examine the detail of the room more clearly, and had found the piano in a corner, as she wandered about, a six-branched silver candelabra held high above her head. The candles guttered wildly in the draught from the tall window as Natasha moved through the room. As usual she looked like an exotic figure from some unwritten ballet. A haunted ballroom, thought Timothy, watching her.

'I have been so happy here,' murmured Natasha. 'This evening has been beautiful. I would like to see more of this place.' It was at this moment that she found the piano and set her candelabra on top of it. Miriam leapt with a little cry of pleasure. Miriam was a fine executive musician. Her taste wavered between 'Sheep shall safely graze', 'Brigg Fair' and 'Kansas Kitty'. She played the first two now, rapt and excited, and Natasha and Timothy asked her to play something more sentimental.

'More sentimental and more of this moment,' said Timothy,

looking at Natasha's delicate profile, milky white in the candlelight.

So Miriam played various musical comedy tunes that belonged to the Edwardian era ('Up in a Balloon, Boys' and 'Tony from America') until, her intellect quite defeated, she broke into 'The Only Girl in the World'. She groaned as she played and Natasha laughed at her.

'Big romantic stuff, darling,' said Timothy, and grinned.

'You sound like a typewriter,' said Miriam. The tune that she played was 'Some day I'll find you'.

'Strange,' said Natasha. 'How potent cheap music is.'

'Don't,' said Timothy. 'You're making me cry so terribly.'

'Your eyes are clear and cool and your skin is shining,' said Miriam doubtfully. 'I don't know that I've got that quite right. I was in Ibsen that year, on tour.'

'Whose yacht's that?' said Timothy.

'The Duke of Westminster's, it always is,' said Natasha, like an automaton.

The dialogue developed insanely. Everyone was delighted with themselves. Miriam had even acquired a faint and attractive Cockney accent. Timothy continued to speak in a weird staccato fashion, like a teleprinter.

'You're looking terribly like a biscuit box.'

'Your voice takes on an acid quality every time you mention it.'

'Oi swear oi'll never mention it agoin.'

'I'm going round the world, you know, after . . . after . . . '

'After my honeymoon.'

'How was it?'

'My honeymoon? Very flat.'

'And the Taj Mahal?'

'Lint white, I believe, and very, very sweet.'

'Unbelievable, a kind of dream,' said Natasha.

There was a pause while Miriam began to play a selection from *Showboat*, as if she were trying to avert the evil eye.

'I think it is desperately depressing,' said Timothy, still in his typewriter voice. 'The hold that gramophone records have upon our generation.'

'Notoriously facile of emotion,' said Miriam.

'Are you two knowing how late it is getting?'

'Yes, we are,' said Miriam. 'But neither of us want to go to Bayleyside.'

'How many miles to Bayleyside, three score and ten, can I get there by candlelight, yes and back again,' said Timothy.

'I shall be *dying* if I am appearing as the fée dragée one moment longer in this dreadful pantomime,' said Natasha.

'Well then, don't appear,' said Timothy, briskly.

Miriam was horrified.

'Oh, but she couldn't walk out like *that*,' said Miriam. 'The show—'

'That is something I refuse to admit,' said Timothy. He gently took Miriam's hands from the keyboard and shut the piano lid. 'There isn't the faintest necessity for any show to go on *ever*. The members of your profession ran up that slogan to bolster their self-esteem. Natasha's esteem doesn't need any bolstering. If it does, I'll do it for her.'

'I think you're *awful*,' said Miriam, almost in tears. 'Of course the show must go on. Besides, they always do ...'

'That is quite a different matter,' said Timothy coldly.

'But darling Miriam is so public spirited,' said Natasha.

'Are you remembering how you became a house-mistress at Radcliff Hall School for Girls because the show must go on?'*

And Miriam hung her head.

VIII

Our friends drove back to Bayleyside a long way above their usual form. They had drunk several bottles of excellent claret 'Chez Josef', and had spent some time cleaning the grease they had spilt on the top of the piano. As they swirled along, determined to collect their baggage and never to set foot in Bayleyside thereafter, they recollected many songs of a beautiful and romantic nature that had not occurred to them before. They sang them very well, considering everything. Natasha possessed a small, true, breathy *mezzo-soprano*; Miriam was well aware of the moments when she went out of tune. Timothy had a very pretty baritone. He sang 'I did but see her passing by' so well that unshed tears stood in Natasha's eyes and clutched at Miriam's throat as they entered the Bayleyside gates.

The car rocked to a standstill in front of the house. Miriam announced that she had remembered something.

'A song called "Transatlantic Lullaby",' she said. 'Do you remember?'

All round them was country silence. An ominous light burnt in a window above them. They did not notice it.

'*Pom* pi pom, pi *pom*, pi pompey, pompey, *pom* pi pom?'

---

*Poison for Teacher.

suggested Timothy obediently, slewing round in the driving-seat. Miriam was sitting in the back.

'No! No!' she cried. 'Not like that. Like *this*. *Da* di da di da di *da* . . . '

'There is being a piano in the drawing-room,' said Natasha, wearily. 'Under all those hirrit photograph frames. It must be five o'clock and soon the milk will come . . .

Natasha did not need to translate the curious word 'hirrit' which she had that moment made up. Miriam and Timothy clambered out of the car and rushed, delighted, into the house, towards the drawing-room and the piano. If they had not been filled with such excellent claret, and if two of them had not been suffering all the disturbing pangs of undeclared love, I do not suppose that they could have behaved like this in someone else's house. They were all agreeably demented.

The dark drawing-room sprang hideously to life in the faltering electric light (the Atkinses made their own) and spurred them to further indiscretions. Miriam flung herself at the piano and began 'Transatlantic Lullaby' without further preamble. Natasha and Timothy leant on the lid and sang inaccurately, but with great feeling and tenderness. They all hummed and swayed and sang such words as they could remember. They made surprisingly little noise.

> 'The sky is smoky dark,
> The trees in Central Park,
> The trolley cars go whizzing past,'

sang Timothy.

'No, no,' said Miriam crossly.

'The lights fade one by one,
The sleepy day is done
And Broadway goes to bed at last . . .'

'Pardon me,' said a voice from the doorway.

IX

It was Tom Atkins. He was still wearing his grey homespun. He was smoking a cigarette that hung damply in his mouth. Quite obviously he had not been to bed at all.

'Kidder,' he said slowly. 'I'd rather you didn't wake her.' He advanced into the room as they stared at him, horrified. 'Not very well,' he added. 'Doesn't get much sleep at the best of times.'

His cigarette went out and he failed to relight it with the little object which he took from his pocket. He cursed under his breath. He took a match from a matchbox holder on a small table. It was a horrible matchbox holder of carved wood, in the shape of a monstrous bird.

'I'm terribly sorry, sir, I didn't think,' said Timothy. He shut the piano lid. It slipped and made a small crash and Tom Atkins winced.

'I'll say goodbye now, sir,' said Timothy bravely. 'Because I shan't be here in the morning.'

'Quite so,' said Tom Atkins, and stared at him with hard, bloodshot eyes.

But Natasha, who had been silent while this was going on, found her tongue.

'Good night,' she said, in her grandest manner. 'It has been

325

most *kind* of you to have been having us in this way. Miss
Birdseye and myself have at *last* been managing to get hotel
accommodation in the city ... '

'Grateful,' said Miriam.

'And comforting,' said Timothy.

'Sh ... ' said Natasha, nudging him.

'No need to go, delighted to have you, welcome at Bayleyside.
Kidder's nerves,' said Tom Atkins rapidly, with a certain desperate intonation in his voice.

But Natasha was too quick for him. She went by him, as
fleeting as a dream. She gave no offence, but she brooked no
interference. Tom Atkins remained at the foot of the stairs.
Timothy and Miriam fled to their bedrooms.

X

Outside the sparrows in the ivy seemed to be shouting a hymn
of freedom as Miriam appeared in Natasha's doorway.

'I say,' she said. 'That was odd, wasn't it? I should have
thought he would have joined in. After all, he's usually as tight
as a tick ... '

'That is just what is being so odd,' said Natasha.

She stared dreamily out at the Quaritch Hills, which became
plainer every minute in the grey morning light.

'What?' said Miriam.

'He should have been being fast asleep in bed snoring like
twenty pigs after yesterday night,' said Natasha. 'He must not
have been drunk at oll when he was backstage. He must have
been sober.'

4

Eventually Sary O'Driscoll decided to go back to the hotel. Hampton Court rang up and said there must be a call for rehearsal at twelve noon prompt, sacked Tony Gresham and re-engaged him, in a brisk three-minute conversation. He then spoke to Sary and said she must return immediately. He had plenty for her to do. Sary said, 'Yes, Mr Court', but she made no attempt to leave until she had squeezed every ounce of drama out of her situation. Yes, Mr Court, the air tickets were booked. Yes, Mr Court, the hired car for the Irish Ugly Sisters was laid on. But in the kitchen this was not the chief subject of conversation. Everyone agreed there would be an arrest that day.

Marylyn Franklyn was a firm favourite for the honour. Mrs Furbinger said that was wishful thinking. Sary O'Driscoll thought the wish was father to the thought. Tony Gresham yawned and said he was fed up with everything, and going back to bed.

The front door slammed behind Sary's fat, stretched bottom and her beer-bottle legs. The morning air smelt chill. Mrs

Furbinger said she thought Tony would be sensible to get what sleep he could, if he had that rehearsal at noon.

'Tell you what, ma, dear,' said Tony, pausing half-way upstairs. 'I'll never wake in time. Would you call me and come and have coffee in Atkins and Marshall on the way to the theatre? Perk me up a bit? The Terrace Tea Room? It's really quite nice.'

'I'd like that,' said Mrs Furbinger.

'It's a date, then,' said Tony.

He went upstairs. He kicked over Marylyn's shoes (left uselessly outside her bedroom door) and sent them rattling against the wainscot. Inside the room, Marylyn, replacing her slumber helmet, jumped nervously and tore it in half.

'Blast it,' said Marylyn.

And then she considered that she would have time to buy a new one at Atkins and Marshall's haberdashery counter before the rehearsal.

II

Timothy was already sitting at the breakfast-table in Bayleyside when Natasha came into the room. The sun shone most brilliantly on the window. It warmed the glass and began to warm Timothy's shoulders, where he sat with his back to the light. It also showed up the dust that waltzed and re-arranged itself in the sunlight as Natasha walked through it towards the coffee-pots.

'Miriam was here,' said Timothy. He stood up and pushed his plate away. 'But she has gone to the telephone.'

'The telephone?' said Natasha vaguely, and poured out some

tea. Timothy hovered uncertainly at her elbow and tried to help her. He got in her way and apologized.

'I'm so tired I can hardly think,' he said. He grabbed his hair and twisted it into a tuft. He grinned apologetically. 'I'm frightfully sorry. It seems that the *last* of the DeFreezes is dead. And Court has two Ugly Sisters coming from Ireland this evening, so he must rehearse them this morning . . .'

Every blade of grass could be seen, rough with dew or rain, outside the window. The sun had brought the Quaritch Hills to light, and the whole world blazed like a diamond.

'What is the point of that?' said Natasha, and took the silver covers off the breakfast dishes. She appeared to take it for granted that Harry DeFreeze was dead. 'Oh,' she said sadly. 'Dried egg. What a pity.' She put the covers back again. 'I mean, Miriam won't be able to rehearse *without* Ugly Sisters, and so there is being no point in rehearsing . . .'

'*Exactly* what I told that baboon,' cried Miriam, rushing into the room in a frightful rage. 'My tea's cold. Look at it. That beast Hampton is adamant. "Rehearsal at twelve sharp, Miss Birdseye", if you please, *and* a lecture on "The show must go on". To *me* of all people—'

'That is rather hard,' said Timothy, amused. He turned to Natasha. 'You don't seem surprised. About Harry being dead, I mean.'

'That one?' said Natasha, stretching towards the butter as gracefully as a Siamese cat. '*That* one had suicide written all over him.'

'How very disagreeable,' said Miriam.

'I hope I have nothing like that written on me,' said Timothy anxiously.

Natasha looked at him for quite a long time.

'I think,' she said finally, 'you have the makings of a very fine wastrel.'

III

A little later, when most people had managed to eat a little toast, Natasha asked where their host and hostess were.

'I am feeling,' she said, 'not quite *right* about leaving without saying proper goodbyes and thank yous. I shall write, of course,' she said. 'But that is not at oll the same thing.'

Miriam looked at her.

'I expect they'd be very surprised if you did any such thing,' she said. 'I don't suppose anyone has ever done anything civil like that for them in their lives. No reason why we shouldn't begin, though, I suppose.'

'Tom is not here,' said Timothy. 'Tom is gone.'

And he began to hum an old snatch under his breath called 'Great Tom is cast'. Natasha looked at him indulgently. Miriam was maddened.

'What d'you mean, "He's gone"?' she snapped.

'*And Christchurch bells ring one, two, three, four, five, six,*' sang Timothy. '*And Tom comes last.* He left in the Rover. Dressed for shooting. At least he was carrying a shot-gun. *And* he put a bandolier of cartridges in the back with it. I expect he's going to have a go in Quaritch Woods by himself,' he concluded blithely. 'Not a very good shot, old Tom.'

Timothy filled his cup again. The silence round him was suddenly uncomfortable. He looked up, startled, and caught Miriam's eye.

330

'Look here,' said Miriam. 'Do you really mean the man's gone, and he's armed?'

'I do,' said Timothy. 'If by "gone" you mean "driven down the drive", and by "armed" you mean "carrying a shot-gun". Why, what's the matter?'

And he put down his teaspoon and stared at Miriam, who shrugged her shoulders.

'Tell him, Natasha,' she said.

IV

Bowes sat over breakfast with Sergeant Robinson in the police canteen. It was a large room in the bowels of the police-station, tiled like a public lavatory and furnished with long, narrow tables and uncomfortable round-backed chairs. Sunlight did not reach it. It was, however, warm. Conversation could be carried on in the half-dark undisturbed.

As usual Sergeant Robinson sat very still and ate enormously. His left hand occasionally poked forkfuls of Welsh Rarebit under his neat, straw strip of moustache into his mouth. His jaw champed rhythmically. These were the only parts of Sergeant Robinson that moved. Bowes said nothing. He smoked and stared at the ceiling.

By and by Robinson finished his Welsh Rarebit and seemed disposed to talk. Bowes stubbed out his cigarette and gave the Sergeant his whole attention.

'Banjo DeFreeze,' said Robinson, 'expected to be murdered.'

'So you say,' said Bowes.

'He made two telephone calls on the afternoon of his death. He rang up the murderer?'

'Might have,' said Bowes.

'One call we know was a business appointment, making a date. What would you say *that* was to do with? Theatrical business? Not very likely. With his shady partner in crime who supplied him with clothing coupons?'

'I'd say,' said Bowes.

'So should I,' said Robinson, faintly irritated. 'With the murderer, too, I shouldn't wonder. Now. Banjo's entry in the theatre telephone book gives the two calls as tolls. Fivepennies—'

'Doesn't necessarily mean they weren't trunks,' said Bowes suddenly. 'Shillings or even more.'

'Let's assume he told the truth, just once, shall we?' said Robinson. 'The man was working his own switchboard, remember. Is it likely he had two trunks within such a short time of each other. He'd be most likely to put through numbers he knew well.'

'That's right,' said Bowes, although for the life of him he could not see why. 'Where'd you think the call was put through to, Sar'n't?'

'I have looked,' said Robinson pompously, 'at the circle the telephone directory draws around fivepenny calls. You'll find it in the front of the book of the county of Northshire. And the only place in the area known to one and all of our suspects is Bayleyside. So, it's all Lombard Street to a china orange those calls went to Bayleyside.'

'That's smart,' said Bowes. 'But who was the call for? Timothy Shelly?'

'I don't know,' said Robinson, and pushed back his chair. 'But I'm going to make out a warrant, Bowes, and I'm going to take it and get it signed.'

'But what name shall we make it out in, Sar'n't?' said Bowes plaintively.

'Make it out,' said Robinson impressively, 'in the name of Hampton Court.'

V

They made their way through the deserted room, past narrow tables crowned with crusted sugar basins and salt cellars containing dirty salt. As they paid for their breakfasts, Constable Truscott appeared, running lightly down the stairs, considerably out of breath.

'There's a lady,' he said. 'A lady in your office to see you. About the DeFreeze-Gresham business.'

'A lady?' said Sergeant Robinson doubtfully, taking his change. 'A lady, did you say? Or is it Miss Franklyn again? Remember, Truscott . . . ' and his voice dropped several keys. 'Remember, I have had no sleep.'

They climbed the stairs together. Truscott was voluble, excited, reassuring.

'Oh no, Sar'n't. 'S a lady, all right, I promise. 'S that Russian dancer from the panto. Miss' – he looked covertly at a piece of paper he held in his hand – '"Miss Nevkorina",' he said proudly. 'Says she has some evidence for you.'

VI

Darling Natasha was standing by the window with her back to the door when they came in. She looked down on Northshire Street with an expression like a bewildered angel, drawn by

Botticelli. The hum of the traffic grew every minute. Soon it would be eleven o'clock, the peak shopping hour for the city, and the streets would be jammed full from the Central Railway Station to the War Memorial.

'Miss Nevkorina?' said Sergeant Robinson. 'Please sit down. I hear you have something interesting to show me?'

Natasha did not sit down. She opened her bag and drew out an envelope. It was rather battered, shakily addressed to 'Mrs DuVivien, care of Miss Birdseye, Baker Street'. From it she shook a revolver bullet, of the type that is usually fired from an Army Service revolver. Robinson stared at it.

'The missing cartridge,' he said slowly. 'Where did you get that?'

Natasha burst at once into her story. She spoke with enormous violence. When she reached a bit of it that she particularly enjoyed she crouched, or grimaced, or acted it out. Robinson and Bowes watched her, fascinated.

'I am observing Mr Tom Atkins, trying to light his cigarette with it last night,' she began. 'Or rather, at about four o'clock this morning. And I am olso realizing that he is *pretending* to be drunk oll the evening. And when, before breakfast he go to have his bath.' Her story gathered pace and excitement ' . . . This morning I creep into the bedroom which he share, with twin beds, with Mrs Atkins, his wife, Kidder. You know her? *She* is still asleep, because she *has* been drunk last evening. Oh, it is so terrible the way these northcountry ladies are drinking . . . '

'I know, I know,' said the Sergeant. 'Go on. Go on. I saw her, too.'

'In bed?' said Natasha, startled.

'No, no, earlier in the evening, drinking. Go on about the cartridge.'

'Well. Mr Atkins has been emptying his pockets oll over his dressing-table top. Just as I am knowing he would.' Natasha paused, maddeningly, to give a demonstration of the way men empty their pockets. 'My ex-husband, Johnny, he, too, olways empty his pockets on the dressing-table top—'

'Never mind him!' cried Sergeant Robinson.

'And there,' said Natasha serenely, shutting her eyes, 'amid oll the loose change and the ten-shilling note crumpled, and the fountain-pen and the watch ... and oll, I *see* (as I know I shall) the revolver bullet. So I take it. And here I am.'

The Sergeant stared at her, amazed.

'Where was Mrs Atkins in all this?' he said.

'In the twin bed,' said Natasha. 'As I say.'

VII

It took Sergeant Robinson some little time to recover from Natasha's graphic description of the Atkinses in bed. When he did so he was still unconvinced. His life in the Newchester Police Force had hitherto been spent in awe of the power and glory of the Atkins family. Robinson would not part lightly from his preconceived idea about Tom and Kidder. He observed, dispassionately, that this beautiful Russian, with her strange eyes like pools where sunshine blazed, seemed to be in the grip of a passion very like righteous indignation. It was possible that it sprang from some inner knowledge of the truth. But there was all the more reason (he told himself) to be careful. *Because* Natasha was Russian and goodlooking and righteously indignant, she probably had an axe to grind. Russians (or so Robinson thought) are not ethical. And this one was probably interested in the young man T. Shelly.

So he looked at Natasha sceptically, and told her that it would take more than *that* sort of circumstantial evidence to hang Tom Atkins in his own city. Natasha promptly flew into a rage. She said that she had *seen* Tom. She had seen him distinctly shooting Banjo. Robinson needed more precious time to understand that Natasha had merely felt a psychic presentiment about the Lord Mayor, and had seen him, in her mind's eye. But oddly enough, out of all the things Natasha had said that morning, this came nearest to convincing Robinson. He had a great regard for womanly intuition, he said. His mother (he added) had been a woman and his wife was also one.

At this moment there came a sharp rat-tat-tat on the door, and Truscott's voice announced that 'Miss Franklyn was waiting to see him.'

'Hell ... ' said Robinson. He stood up uneasily and apologized. 'Look here, Miss Nevkorina,' he said. 'Stay here. I won't keep you a minute. I'll find what Miss Franklyn wants and get rid of her. Then we can continue.' He walked to the door, hesitated, and turned back, holding the handle. 'I've a little spicy story I'd like to tell you, in any case,' he added. 'About a case of indecent exposure.'

Natasha wrinkled her beautiful nose, and walked over to the window. Timothy Shelly had said he would meet her at Atkins and Marshall's men's shop at eleven o'clock. It was nearly twenty minutes to. There was no reason why Natasha could not spend another quarter of an hour, furthering the cause of justice, if she wished.

'I do not know,' she said out loud, 'that I shall have time to hear about that.'

But Robinson had already gone, at top speed, slamming the door behind him. All the papers on his desk were ruffled by the draught from the window.

Natasha looked down at the cold, windy street. People ran like ants, clutching their winter overcoats around them. There was a bitterly cold north wind. Clouds chased across the brittle sunshine. Every now and then Northshire Street was plunged in darkness, and then the sun blazed out again and the plate-glass windows of the shops glittered and winked.

Atkins and Marshall seemed particularly brave today. Two scarlet house flags, marked respectively 'A' and 'M', fluttered above it. Natasha could see shop assistants moving in the window, kneeling down, rearranging the dummy figures in stiff, helpless attitudes. Sticker labels announced *Gigantic & Genuine Reductions – New Year Sale*. Beyond them Natasha could see the sinister wax figures standing, like diplomats (male) with one hand extended in greeting; or elegantly, like society hostesses (female) with hand on hip.

During the next ten minutes Natasha was completely lost in a dream. Sergeant Robinson disturbed her, springing back into the room like a catapult.

'Miss Nevkorina!' he cried. 'I give you best, I really do.'

He sat behind his desk. To Natasha's consternation he offered her his hand to shake.

VIII

When Natasha had gravely shaken Sergeant Robinson's hand she asked why he would give her best, as he had suggested.

'I do not really know what you are meaning,' she said, very slowly. 'Nor what you are talking about.'

Outside the wind was rising. Some tin object fell with a crash and a rattle to the pavement and evidently went bowling along the gutter. Robinson leant back in his wooden swivel chair.

'This,' he said, and put a letter on his desk. It was written on familiar cheap red-lined paper. It was headed:

> My dressing-room,
> Theatre Royal

Good old Maryella,

When you get this, old lady, I may be pushing daisies. So if it's so I want you to do what I say. (I may be wrong about the feelings I have, but I never did use to be wrong over a feeling like danger.)

I don't trust Tom Atkins.

As you know, Maryella, I have been in biz for long with him, pushing the coops over the country at two bob a coop. He has them made up here by someone. No names no pack drill. Viv didn't trust him either, you know, old lady, and though you didn't like poor Viv (for reasons I won't give, good old Banjo!) her death was no accident. Atkins was standing by that lever sure as my name is Banjo.

Viv must have found out about Tom's coop running and given him a hot time. Viv was always short for dough. I think he knows I know. I made a date to see him this

afternoon. Well, old girl, he turned very nasty on the phone
just now when I called him up. So if anything happens
(mind it may not, I'm just being foolish) take this along to
the police and blow the gaff about the coops and oblige.

yr. loving Banjo

P.S. If nothing happens of course mum's the word. But if
the worst turns up ask Tony for my gold watch. It used to
pop for £50. Better than nothing. Well, we had some good
times, hadn't we?

B.

Natasha raised her lovely eyes and stared at the Sergeant.

'Who brought you this?' she said. 'Who, in heaven's name, is Maryella?'

'Marylyn Franklyn,' said Robinson, searching his drawers for something, rustling papers and generally making a fuss. 'Obviously we must arrest him this morning.'

'Why?' said Natasha.

Sergeant Robinson stared at her.

'There have been three deaths,' he said. 'Do you want any more?'

Natasha said she did not.

'But if you are not wanting more deaths I must be telling you that Tom Atkins is armed,' she said. 'He left Bayleyside this morning with a shot-gun.'

5

Tom Atkins sat behind his desk in his neat, beaver-boarded little office. He did not see the hideous things that surrounded him. The turmoil in his mind was hideous enough.

Ever since he had picked up that revolver by the telephone switchboard at the Theatre Royal, and had realized, with a start of pleasure, that it belonged to Timothy Shelly, he had been perfectly aware that he was going to make the usual murderer's mistake. Too good to be true that the revolver was *Shelly's*! No wonder he had been rattled trying to pin it on the fellow!

Kidder and Shelly. Shelly and Kidder. *He* had seen how gone Kidder was on Shelly when they were introduced by Viv at Bexhill-on-Sea. Viv's 'intended', indeed. He doubted whether they had even been married in the end. Damn Shelly.

But where the hell was the mistake? *That* was what he couldn't think. He could hardly think at all.

He had been losing grip since he over-bought so badly for the ironmongery and turnery department last January. He was hopelessly over-stocked, and no profits to show for it. The turnover wasn't quick enough. Any fool who walked through ironmongery could see those zinc buckets on his hands for keeps. He had always had a habit of putting lots of irons in the fire. He had always done things on a large scale. *That* didn't matter when he thought of nothing else. And in the old days the Government had been with him, not against him.

He couldn't *think* clearly any longer. Since that interview with that damned Banjo, since he had wiped the silly grin off his face for ever (there was some satisfaction in that, anyway); whenever he had been alone, or tried to work out a sum; then through all that welter of cost and wholesale price and forms and figures and staff troubles, came Banjo's blue-jawed face. First, grinning. Then with a look of bewilderment. Then a neat blue hole sprang in his forehead as he twisted to the floor and pulled the drawer with him. *Banjo* had mucked about with Kidder, too. He was sure of it. He could imagine it, anyway. Tom Atkins groaned and put his mouse-coloured head in his hands.

He had been a fool to shoot Banjo. A fool to take him into confidence over those coupons. *That* was where he had made his mistake. That afternoon Banjo had only been mildly unpleasant about the danger. And he only *suspected* he had pulled that lever. No one knew he had killed Vivienne, but himself, really. And *he* wasn't too sure, anyway. But anyone who killed Viv would be right. Sisters always split? Who had said that? Well, anyway, dead sisters always keep their mouths shut ... tell no tales.

If he and Kidder took a holiday *now* immediately and got away from it all, everything would be different when they came back. Quite, quite different. Perhaps they both needed more vitamins? Perhaps when he got sunburnt he would be less repulsive? All this horror really began with Kidder, all those years ago ...

If he hadn't married his handsome young wife, and failed to have children by her, and tried to impress her by his business acumen and cunning, and riches and social security, he would never have over-bought zinc buckets like that. And (worse than buckets) got on the wrong side of the law, recouping in the gowns department. It was easy, if one really knew the law, to get outside it. Or stay just inside it. But Tom Atkins, the cautious, clever feller, had grown into Thomas Atkins of Bayleyside, Lord Mayor of the city *too quickly*. He had got out of control. Would he ever be contented, or simple again? He would know better than to get married next time, anyway.

Tom sat up straight, in a strange state of triumph. It was probably at this moment that his rocking brain divided itself completely in two. A competent psychiatrist might have diagnosed the contributory factors as jealousy, sense of inferiority, overwork, nerve strain, and finally alcoholic poisoning.

'The whole thing is Kidder's fault,' he said out loud.

The walls swung round him like a horrible kaleidoscope. He had to grip hard on the desk to remember who he was.

Thomas Atkins of Bayleyside, in his own private sanctuary. He was all right. He was at the heart of things.

'Tom Atkins,' he said to himself slowly.

At that moment the telephone rang loudly. His nerves broke. They seemed to spiral away, screaming, into the corners of his office. What a curious fancy. First time he had ever thought of seeing something like nerves. They had felt like wires. Electric red-hot wires. He spoke coldly into the receiver.

'Tom Atkins here.' His voice sounded all right. He was rather pleased with it. He tried a different tone. 'Who is it?'

'Tom, Tom.' The voice the other end was breathless. 'Tom,

what's the matter? You know it's Kidder. Look, Tom. The police have been on. Sergeant Robinson said he was going to call and see you at the shop. I'm frightened, Tom. Tom!' She was urgent, terrified. 'Say something! Please.'

Her voice trailed away while he cleared his throat.

'What d'you want me to say?' he said, coldly sanctimonious.

'Oh, Tom, please don't be like that. Not now, Tom. Please, darling, what do the police want? Are you going to be declared bankrupt after all? What *is* it? I can face anything if only I *know*. Tell me, Tom, please, darling. Darling Tom, I'll do anything you like if only you tell me. We'll leave here, go to America, start again like you said last week, only tell me what's *wrong*? What is going to happen?'

Tom cleared his throat again.

'It's not very pleasant,' he said, in weird, detached tones. His tongue beat out the words like a hammer on a brass gong. 'I've killed two people and it's all your fault . . .'

He gently put back the receiver.

II

Marylyn Franklyn tit-tupped anxiously up Northshire Street. On her way she glanced at the massive clocks that dominated the various shops and stores. They were all slightly different, all mildly inaccurate. Still, she had just time to get to rehearsal.

It seemed pretty awful, really, but Atkins and Marshall were the only haberdashers near the theatre. The doors swung behind her. She went through the pressing, milling crowds towards 'slumber helmets, false fronts, collar and cuff sets'. It was exactly ten minutes past eleven.

III

Tony Gresham and Mrs Furbinger set down their cups in the Terrace Tea Room. The cups were white, inscribed with a facsimile reproduction of Tom Atkins' signature in scarlet. They moved towards the lift. Under Mrs Furbinger's saucer was fourpence for the waitress.

'I feel so much *better*, ma, dear,' said Tony, and pressed the buzzer. 'Extraordinary how coffee livens me up.'

Mrs Furbinger grunted in reply. It was an animal noise of small contentment.

'Better make 'aste,' she added, 'if we're to get to the theatre and please Court. Look. Nearly quarter past.'

IV

Precisely at this moment Hampton Court swore bitterly as he parked the Rolls-Bentley outside Atkins and Marshall. As he swung the steering-wheel he champed his jaws up and down on a cigar. There was a crash. His bumper had caught under that of an elderly Morris 8. Hampton blasphemed. He seemed to take it quite for granted. Sary, also, continued to take an interest in her shopping.

'And there's the new socks for you now, Mr Court,' she said, in a wheedling tone. 'You know you're needing them, since all of your others have holes in, God bless them.'

'They only have holes because you're too damned lazy to darn them,' said Hampton angrily. 'And I'm stopping right here in the car while you get them. It was the other man's fault, anyway,' he ended suddenly.

And Sary plunged into the whirlpool of Atkins and Marshall. Hampton sat back behind his wheel. He did not bother to clamber out to assess the damage behind him. For his own peace of mind, this was just as well. It was his own bumper that had been torn off.

V

'What happened?'

'Why have you been so long?'

'What did he say to you?'

Miriam and Timothy Shelly anxiously leant forward in Timothy's Ford V8. They gave an eager impression of anxiety and excitement. Natasha climbed in beside them before she replied.

'You are both looking like foxhounds at a meet,' she said inconsequently.

'Bellman and True are my middle names, if you like,' said Timothy rapidly. 'But for Heaven's sake tell us what goes on?'

Natasha traced a little pattern on the windscreen with her long, beautiful finger.

'It is going to be so terrible,' she said. '*Everyone* is going to be shot, I think. Sergeant Robinson and all of them are going in a wagon with tommy-guns. It is the greatest fun,' she added, with a bright, wild smile.

The high wind still blew insanely in Northshire Street. Here and there torn paper blew famously, tossing higher and higher in the air, above the roofs of the shops.

'Darling Natasha, please make sense,' said Timothy. 'Remember us? We are your friends. Your *friends*, Miriam and

345

Timothy. Who never did you a stroke of harm. Now. Please try and tell us. Why the tommy-guns?'

Natasha opened her lovely eyes very wide.

'But of *course*,' she said. 'To arrest Tom Atkins. He will shoot his way out. You will see. You said he had a shot-gun.'

The explosion of unbelief that followed this sweeping statement made Natasha shrug her lovely shoulders.

'Very well, then,' she said. 'If you are not believing *me*, drive to Atkins and Marshall. You will then be seeing for yourselves.'

VI

There was room for the car in a side street. They approached at the very moment that Hampton Court crashed his bumper. They stopped, to discuss among themselves what to do. Miriam was all for going away quickly, to be in time for the rehearsal. Timothy said not to be an ass, to wait outside and see what happened. Natasha alone was determined to penetrate the heart of the drama. Natasha won. They went into the store by a side door. They asked a young gentleman (in black coat and striped trousers) where was Mr Atkins, Mr Tom Atkins? He said 'Pleasure, sir', and Mr Atkins was in his office so far as he knew. He dazzled them with a gleaming smile.

'However, I think that he's engaged, modom,' he added, with much elegant gesturing of his backbone and neck. 'There were other gentlemen enquiring for him just now ...'

All round them milled the Newchester peak hour shoppers. They struck Miriam on the legs with their shopping-bags. They bumped into Timothy. They called to one another that they had last seen *Dor-*een in the soft furnishings.

'Come on!' cried Miriam, highly excited. 'It may be too late!'

'*Il est haut, il est haut*,' whispered Timothy.

And they ran on, pushing, while the shop-walker looked after them a little astonished.

VII

Natasha afterwards said that the first shot rang out as they were passing a notice that asked them to 'Come to Toytown Castle and get their New Year Gift from Santa in person'. Timothy did not know. Miriam was convinced that they were somewhere between 'This way to the Terrace Tea Rooms' and 'Carpets, Cork Carpetings, Cortesines and Linos', when panic first hit the shopping crowd.

Marylyn Franklyn's high-heeled shoes twinkled as she went to ground behind a glass counter filled with darning wool, wooden mushrooms and padded silk coat-hangers. Sary O'Driscoll was caught half-way, lilting through a sentence that reeked (as usual) of false charm, 'Wouldn't ye ever be directin' me to the gentlemen's socks at all?' Tony Gresham and Ma Furbinger came out of the lift very near Tom Atkins' office. They heard the shot. They saw the door fly open. And Tom Atkins came out, with a smoking shot-gun in his hands, howling like a wolf.

'And any more of you,' he cried, 'can get the same treatment!'

The store emptied as if by magic. In a second the pavements outside, in Northshire Street, were jammed with a terrified yelling mob, who pushed and shoved and cried that *Dor*-een was still in the soft furnishings.

Natasha and Miriam, concealed behind a roll of grey Wilton carpet, looked fearfully at each other.

'What happened?' said Timothy, picking himself up. He had fallen among a pile of Persian rugs.

'I am thinking he has shot the Sergeant,' said Natasha.

VIII

It was Bowes, the dependable, who first had the idea of advancing on Tom Atkins like Burnam Wood on Dunsinane concealed behind the wax models from the window. The whisper ran through the store that Robinson was bleeding to death in the maniac's office.

Bowes did not hesitate. The crash as his boot went through the plate-glass window could be heard at the War Memorial. He plunged in and swept up a young wax diplomat in his arms. The diplomat was wearing a navy-blue Melton cloth overcoat.

'We'll get the — yet, boys!' he cried.

The brief-case fell from the wax diplomat's hand. His Anthony Eden hat tilted a little foolishly over one eye. But he made a magnificent shield for Bowes, who advanced firmly down the shop floor, calling out to Atkins to do his damnedest.

His lead was followed quickly enough. Soon the shop was filled with determined figures, who advanced nervously at the crouch, with an out-sized matron at the carry, or a golf girl in a tweed skirt at the slope. And here came a stout, charging policeman, imperfectly hidden behind a pair of crossed seated legs, that ended at the hip and were labelled 'The Gwladys Knick-Set – Locknet, reinforced gusset 12/11¾'.

But Tom Atkins was no longer in his office.

Face downwards on the floor, 'Swiss' Robinson groaned out that Atkins had gone. He would climb, he thought, upwards.

'Surround the store,' he gasped. 'The man's a killer. He'll stop at nothing.'

Bowes looked fearfully around. But he did not falter.

'Here, Sergeant,' he said, handing over his diplomat. 'Take it. I can get another.'

It was at this moment that Atkins kicked in the glass roof above them, and fired down from the cash desk. It had been built above it in a conveniently strategic position.

IX

And now it seemed Tom Atkins had really gone raving mad.

He threw the wooden balls from the cash desk at the police-men. He set moving the whole vast rumbling mechanism of the overhead trolley railway for presenting change to cash customers. It clanked and snatched and shuddered, adding its strange noise to the general lunacy. Atkins fired several times at Truscott, who continued to advance relentlessly behind a wax sports gentle-man in creased beige plus-fours. Atkins must have realized that he was cornered, and that he had also put four ounces of lead shot into a squirrel lock coat carried by another constable. For he sprang up from the cash desk at the wires of the trolley rail-way. Swinging like a monkey he came screeching down towards Marylyn Franklyn, who was now cowering in the children's underclothing next door to the haberdashery amongst some pilch breechettes. The railway collapsed. The wires, twanging like harps, uncoiled in all directions. Here and there a bale of cloth was snatched up, or flung broadside into a glass case. The sound of Mr Atkins falling in a display of liberty bodices could be heard all over the store. Miss Burston, flat on her face in the fallen cards of collar and cuff sets, remarked to Sary O'Driscoll that she didn't know what the store was coming to, she was sure.

X

Local gossips, who afterwards tried to describe the extraordinary shambles on the ground floor of Atkins and Marshall, could understand everyone's reactions except those of Kidder Atkins. They had always disliked Kidder, they said, but even so she had gone a little far on this occasion.

Even the behaviour of Miriam Birdseye (she had peeped out of a roll of battered oilcloth, giggling helplessly) was treated with charitable contempt. 'Poor dear,' said local opinion. 'I expect she was nervous. And fancy having to play Prince Charming after all that.' They could even forgive Tom Atkins himself. He had run berserk down the store, dressed unbecomingly in his underwear, apparently in satyr-like pursuit of Sary O'Driscoll. Sary, of course, had 'burst out a-bawling'. Newchester could understand all this. It was at a loss, however, over Kidder.

Kidder had arrived, flushed and dishevelled, having driven furiously from Bayleyside, hatless. She had appeared in the shop at the exact moment when Truscott and Bowes relinquished their wax figures and formally charged Atkins with 'the unlawful killing of Benjamin (Banjo) Pilkington DeFreeze, and with hindering a police officer in the execution of his duty, and with wounding a police officer with intent to cause grievous bodily harm'. Tom Atkins, pathetic in his flapping shirt and clanking handcuffs, cautioned, had replied: 'I am not guilty of any criminal offence. I must see my solicitor at once. Send for Beverly Marshall.'

Kidder, however, poised in the street door, the sunshine making a nimbus of her handsome head, stole all the scene.

'Tom!' she cried, and brought all eyes upon her. 'There he is, the darling!'

6

Eventually, of course, the scandal in Newchester died down. The face of the old grey city was luminous and serene again, a shining peace, where no tongues wagged. But while the law delayed, while Atkins was arrested and the inquest dragged on interminably ... and the London papers got wind of it all ... and Baron Reuter flashed the news to the USA, while Atkins went into consultation with his lawyer and partner, Beverly Marshall, the trickiest man in Newchester; and it was decided that Tom Atkins should plead 'guilty', while 'Rex' subpoenaed its witnesses and took statements from them, while all *this* was going on, Newchester buzzed with excitement. There had never been such a scandal.

The disintegration of the establishment at Bayleyside was (as might be expected) complete. Tom Atkins' creditors foreclosed the day he was arrested. He was declared bankrupt. Kidder Atkins stayed in bed, sobbing, until the day of the realization sale, while Miss Burns vainly attempted to comfort her and (eventually) gave notice. Tom Atkins, who had been examined by various medical practitioners, consistently refused to see her. The fact that he was almost certain to be pronounced insane hardly relieved the state of her mind. Much of Kidder's day was spent in an advanced state of intoxication, drinking the remnants of the ex-Lord Mayor's spirit cellar. Most of her nights were passed under the influence of various drugs. She refused to go for a holiday, although repeatedly urged to by her mother, Mrs Franks, who would have paid. She persisted until the end of the trial that Atkins would shortly pull himself together and ask to see her. All this, too, was in the face of the evidence (passed on in a friendly fashion by Beverly Marshall) that Tom said the whole thing was Kidder's fault, from start to finish.

II

The other actors in the drama did not suffer quite as much.

Hampton Court, with his usual sublime lack of public spirit, refused to have anything to do with the case at all. He spent his time knocking hell out of the unfortunate Irish Ugly Sisters, who (he said) were amateurs. Sary, angrily forbidden by Hampton to have anything to do with the police or the papers, sat morosely in the stalls of the theatre, under Hampton's eye, sewing buttons on his pantsies. Once, she even went so far as to darn a pair of his socks.

Even so stories leaked out to the Press about the 'Double Panto Killing'. Even the frightening smudged photographs of Kidder and Tom (with the caption 'Mayor Alleges all Wife's Fault') did nothing to take the glare of unwholesome limelight from the *Cinderella* Company.

Darling Natasha, for a long time, was star witness for the Crown. She expected to have to stand up to a heavy cross examination by counsel on ballistics (of which she knew nothing) and revolver bullets. She rather looked forward to this, and often planned her witness-box dress in bed at night. She would wear demure grey, she thought, with touches of white at the throat and wrist. Eventually, when Thomas Atkins decided to plead 'guilty' with strong recommendation of mercy as the balance of his mind was disturbed at the time, Natasha was released from her subpoena.

Timothy was delighted. He had gone through every sort of mental hell on her behalf. Now he sat in Miriam's dressing-room, urging her to help him make Natasha leave Newchester.

'She really must give up this awful show,' he said.

'Yes,' drawled Miriam. 'For God's sake do, Natasha, dear, if you want to. Some Tots can perfectly easily do the powder-puff dance, or they can leave it out all together. I'm so sick of the whole thing I could *scream* ... I wish *I'd* an excuse to leave.'

'It is being the *drama* I am sick of,' said Natasha.

'It's only a nine-day wonder,' said Tony, on the floor by their feet, as usual.

'"There's no wonder so old as a nine-day-old wonder",' sang Timothy, under his breath, to the tune of 'No business like Show Business'.

'No, dear, but *seriously*,' Tony Gresham went on earnestly. 'It *is* all over now the defence have brought this plea in. I wouldn't blame anyone who went and left this panto down. It isn't as though you have a contract, dear. It really is hell ... '

'Tony and I,' said Miriam proudly, 'are going to rent a theatre together with his insurance money, and we're going to put on all the plays we've always wanted to ...' The insurance company, after fighting the claim tooth and nail, had eventually given in and agreed to settle in full.

'Ibsen,' said Tony, enrapt. 'And Tchekov. And Mum will play the "Cherry Orchard".'

'Thanks very much,' snapped Miriam. 'I shall do no such thing. I shall play *La Dame aux Camellias*. After a few more weeks of Prince Charming mum's tum will be fit for *anything . . .*'

III

And so it was that Timothy Shelly drove round from the County Hotel to the Saracen's Head one wet morning at breakfast-time to pick up Natasha.

His appearance had improved in the weeks of his interest in Natasha. He was now desperately well groomed and a little inclined to cut his hair too short. His jackets were the same faded tweed, but they were well pressed and carefully mended. He had bought some white silk shirts.

Natasha saw him leap happily up the steps and pick up her three suit-cases in his embrace. Behind him the dark Newchester streets were like a back-cloth. He was so brilliantly coloured. He was so very sweet. The arrangements for their journey were vague. They were supposed to be going to London. Natasha was delighted at this inconsequence. She came down the hotel steps like a princess. She saluted the weeping skies as though they were mid-summer blue.

Timothy stuffed the bags in the back, tucked a rug tenderly round her feet and slid behind the steering-wheel. The engine had been ticking over gracefully enough. Now Timothy swung away from the ugly glass portico and the matting marked 'Saracen's Head'.

IV

'Oh dear,' said Natasha suddenly. 'My little zipper bag with all my make-up. I have been leaving it by the reception desk.'

'Is it important?' said Timothy.

They were wrestling with the traffic on the north side of the River Tame. It consisted of the usual trams and lorries.

'Oh dear. If you only are *knowing* how important,' said Natasha.

Timothy did not hesitate. He stopped the car and turned back. Natasha purred with pleasure.

'It would have been taking Johnny *half an hour* to agree to go back,' she said happily. 'And then he would have been giving me a lecture on carelessness.'

'And who's Johnny?' said Timothy. He did not speak very sweetly.

Natasha looked at him wide-eyed.

'You are not knowing about Johnny, my ex-husband, the all-in wrestler who is olways trying so hard to re-marry me? *Everyone* is knowing about Johnny, I thought . . . '

Timothy swung the car to a determined halt a little short of the Saracen's Head car park. The space opposite the entrance was completely blocked by a flashy American car with cream-coloured and red fixings.

'All-in wrestler?' said Timothy vaguely. 'How nice that must have been, my dear.'

But he was inclined to change colour.

V

Inside the hotel he found the zipper bag easily enough. It had been left on the floor when Natasha paid her bill. As he caught it up and paced towards the revolving doors an enormously burly man blocked the way.

'Turribly sorry,' he said. 'But my name's DuVivien.'

'Oh yes?' said Timothy Shelly politely.

'I saw you pickin' up that zipper bag, that's all ... It's vurry like one m'wife Natasha used to have, and I'm anxious to have a word with her, if'n it's possible?'

'Oh well, sir,' said Timothy Shelly lightly. 'I expect there are hundreds of bags like this one, don't you?'

Johnny swayed on his toes and eyed this loose-limbed young man. A lock of fawn-coloured hair had fallen forward over his eyes. Natasha would have thought him irresistible. Johnny was not so sure.

'Yeah,' said Johnny, still looking at him. 'Yeah. I guess there *are.*'

He fingered the label, blatantly marked 'Natasha Nevkorina' where it lay, snug in his pocket. He raised his eyebrows at Timothy Shelly, who suddenly blushed.

'Look here, Mr DuVivien,' he said, 'if that's your name. Hundreds of women keep make-up in bags like these. You know that, don't you?' He paused and ran his hand through his lock of hair. 'But this one happens to belong to *my* wife. Lady Shelly ... '

Johnny blinked. He showed no other sign of emotion.

'Your ... ?' he began.

'Wife,' said Timothy Shelly firmly. 'And now, if you'll forgive me, I must honestly be going. We've rather a long journey ahead of us. Will you excuse me?'

And he brushed by him with elegance, going towards the entrance with light, unhurried steps.

Johnny stared after him. He assured the hotel foyer in round terms that he was god-damned if'n he had come all this way and done all that belly-aching detective work with the telephone books to be brushed off without speakin' to Natasha.

VI

Timothy and Natasha passed the Theatre Royal. They did not even think of Miriam, asleep in bed. Timothy was preoccupied, but Natasha's conscience had even allowed her to leave Hampton Court to do the powder-puff dance himself, if he liked.

'If the little man was olways being so agile as to be getting Miriam and me to be starting with,' she would explain to anyone who cared to listen, 'and those Irish young gentlemen to be ending with, I am now expecting Riabouchinska to be falling on his lap. Or Markova,' she added, after a thought.

The terrible silent premises of Atkins and Marshall ('closed for alterations') fell further and further behind them, as they swirled down towards the River Tame. They went through old-fashioned streets, along the quays, past Pudding Chare where Josef lived. Soon they were again driving south under the great, dripping arch of the famous Tame Bridge, flirting with the rest of the traffic, outwitting the ponderous trams.

Timothy said nothing until they were well in the country. The fields stretched away on either side of them in slabs of dull green and brown, sections of grass and plough, like an old-fashioned cake. Here and there a very small, very dirty island of snow, tucked under a clump of black pine trees, lost under the lee of a stone dyke, reminded them of Christmas. Their memories were only dim. They leapt forward into the future.

'Look,' said Timothy. 'We shall hit the Great North Road just below Boroughbridge. We could be in London by tea-time.'

'Hitting the Great North Road,' said Natasha dreamily. She sank down further into her beaver coat. 'How rough and rude this is sounding.'

Timothy laid his hand suddenly on hers.

'Darling,' he said. 'I do love you so very much.'

'That will be suiting me very well indeed,' said Natasha.

Timothy laughed.

'But one thing had rather struck me . . . ' he said. Every now and then he twisted his face to see her, to see how she was taking him. 'If we *do* go up to London you will get tied up with *your* friends, and I shall get tied up with my friends, and—'

'If I go to London,' said Natasha gently, 'I shall have to be getting a job.'

Timothy was aghast. The future was suddenly a dismal place where Natasha climbed agency stairs, and he waited for her outside in the car for ever.

'But you have a job!' he cried.

Natasha made a small noise of interest and interrogation. She sank lower and lower in her seat all the time.

'You are going to be the mother of my children,' said Timothy.

Natasha was vague.

'In County Cork?' she said. She spoke as mildly and as slowly as though she had never considered it before.

'Of *course* in County Cork,' said Timothy. 'You *know* they're in County Cork.'

The sun seemed about to break through the rain. There was a wide golden patch in the sky above them.

'Well then,' said Natasha. 'I do not want to be suggesting anything which might be boring, but I am certainly thinking in that case it would be better if we went to County Cork.' There was a pause. 'I do not really care for London,' she said.

At the next crossroads they turned west, for Fishguard.

VII

In Gloucestershire, Timothy complimented Natasha on her courage.

'My mother,' he said, 'will be delighted to have a daughter-in-law again who can ride straight.'

'What can you mean?' cried Natasha in alarm. 'I have never been to the huntings in my life except in Yorkshire on foot.' There was a pause. 'And I did not like it very much,' she whispered under her breath.

'I only meant that you were brave. It's an expression. Like playing with a straight bat. Oh hell! I mean, this beastly murder case we got involved in. It was *your* bravery over going into the Atkinses' bedroom when Tom was in the bath, and taking that bullet – that was what cleared me. It was frightfully courageous.'

He stuttered hopelessly, trying to explain himself.

'Not, thank God,' went on Timothy, 'that you had to give that evidence. But, my word, what courage. It was *marvellous.*

Such straightness. That awful bedroom. Darling, how could you do it?'

The admiration in his voice was overwhelming.

'But I did *not*,' said Natasha, in a sad, small voice.

'What can you mean, my own?'

'I was not going into the bedroom. It was not finding the revolver shell. I was making it oll up. But the Sergeant believed me.'

Timothy skewed round towards her. He was very excited.

'But that cartridge – that you put in the envelope – and gave to the Sergeant that morning? It wasn't Tom's? Whose was it, then? Where did you get it? *Natasha* ...'

'It was one of yours, darling,' said Natasha, and smiled her angel's smile.

But at the back of her mind lurked a troublesome thought. Riding straight, indeed. It did not really *sound* like Natasha's cup of tea.

Behind them, at a discreet and unobtrusive distance, followed Johnny DuVivien's vulgar roadster. Natasha might have been still more troubled if she had observed it.

DEATH GOES ON SKIS
Nancy Spain

'Her detective novels are hilarious – less about
detecting than delighting, with absurd farce and a
wonderful turn of phrase ... Nancy Spain was bold,
she was brave, she was funny, she was feisty'

SANDI TOKSVIG

Miriam Birdseye is daring, brilliant – and a long way from
The Ivy. Our dashing heroine, a famous revue artist, takes to
the slopes with her coterie of admirers. Champagne flows and
wherever Miriam goes she leaves a trail of gossip in her wake.

Fellow ski-resort guests include the celebrated Russian
ex-ballerina, Natasha Nevkorina, whose beauty is matched
only by her languor, Natasha's burly husband, nightclub owner
Johnny DuVivien, and the wealthy Flahertés, a family who
have made their money importing scents: handsome playboy
Barney, his wife Regan, their two obnoxious children and
the governess, Rosalie. Unbeknownst to Regan, Barney's
mistress, a film star, is also there with her husband.

When secrets start to unravel, tensions rise, and soon
amateur sleuths Miriam and Natasha have not one but two
murders to solve. In the hands of Nancy Spain, for whom
farce and humour are a lot more fun than a conventional
detective novel, the result is a deliciously wild ride.

POISON FOR TEACHER

Nancy Spain

'An either intense or sombre approach to crime is to Miss Spain foreign: in her world an inspired craziness rules ... Her wit, her zest, her outrageousness, and the colloquial stylishness of her writing are quite her own'

ELIZABETH BOWEN

Miriam Birdseye, ex-revue star and now professional sleuth, is intrigued when the headmistress of Radcliff Hall arrives at her Baker Street detective agency. A series of bizarre pranks have taken a sinister turn, and since Miss Lipscoomb found her gym rope half sawn through, she fears not only for her school's reputation, but for her life.

This is how Miriam and her friend, Russian ballerina Natasha Nevkorina, find themselves on board the train to a Sussex girls' school, in the unlikely guise of teachers. Before long the detective duo uncovers a blackmail plot, infidelity and a dizzying array of school schisms. Then a teacher is poisoned during the school play. Can they discover the culprit before the body count rises?

VIRAGO MODERN CLASSICS

The first Virago Modern Classic, *Frost in May* by Antonia White, was published in 1978. It launched a list dedicated to the celebration of women writers and to the rediscovery and reprinting of their works. Its aim was, and is, to demonstrate the existence of a female tradition in literature, and to broaden the sometimes narrow definition of a 'classic'. Published with new introductions by some of today's best writers, the books are chosen for many reasons: they may be great works of literature; they may be wonderful period pieces; they may reveal particular aspects of women's lives; they may be classics of comedy, storytelling, letter-writing or autobiography.

'The Virago Modern Classics list contains some of the greatest fiction and non-fiction of the modern age, by authors whose lives were frequently as significant as their writing. Still captivating, still memorable, still utterly essential reading' **SARAH WATERS**

'The Virago Modern Classics list is wonderful. It's quite simply one of the best and most essential things that has happened in publishing in our time. I hate to think where we'd be without it' **ALI SMITH**

'The Virago Modern Classics have reshaped literary history and enriched the reading of us all. No library is complete without them' **MARGARET DRABBLE**

'The writers are formidable, the production handsome. The whole enterprise is thoroughly grand' **LOUISE ERDRICH**

'Good news for everyone writing and reading today'
HILARY MANTEL

VIRAGO MODERN CLASSICS

AUTHORS INCLUDE:

Elizabeth von Arnim, Beryl Bainbridge,
Pat Barker, Nina Bawden, Vera Brittain, Angela Carter,
Willa Cather, Barbara Comyns, E. M. Delafield, Polly Devlin,
Monica Dickens, Elaine Dundy, Nell Dunn, Nora Ephron,
Janet Flanner, Janet Frame, Miles Franklin, Marilyn French,
Stella Gibbons, Charlotte Perkins Gilman, Rumer Godden,
Radclyffe Hall, Helene Hanff, Josephine Hart, Shirley Hazzard,
Bessie Head, Patricia Highsmith, Winifred Holtby, Attia Hosain,
Zora Neale Hurston, Elizabeth Jenkins, Molly Keane, Rosamond
Lehmann, Anne Lister, Rose Macaulay, Shena Mackay, Beryl
Markham, Daphne du Maurier, Mary McCarthy, Kate O'Brien,
Grace Paley, Ann Petry, Barbara Pym, Mary Renault, Stevie
Smith, Muriel Spark, Elizabeth Taylor, Angela Thirkell,
Mary Webb, Eudora Welty, Rebecca West,
Edith Wharton, Antonia White

CHILDREN'S CLASSICS INCLUDE:

Joan Aiken, Nina Bawden, Frances Hodgson Burnett,
Susan Coolidge, Rumer Godden, L. M. Montgomery,
Edith Nesbit, Noel Streatfeild, P. L. Travers

To buy any of our books and to find out more
about Virago Press and Virago Modern Classics,
our authors and titles, visit our websites

www.virago.co.uk
www.littlebrown.co.uk

and follow us on Twitter

@ViragoBooks